TWO CLASSIC *PROTECTORS* NOVELS
IN ONE EXCITING VOLUME!

THIS SIDE OF HEAVEN

A dangerous passion…
Though stalked by a madman bent on revenge,
Nate Hodges succumbed to the pull of a passion
older than time. Cyn Porter, the brown-eyed beauty
of his dreams—his impossible love—brought him
peace. She was his very soul. But he knew with
heart-shattering certainty that *he* could be her death.…

THE OUTCAST

She had been waiting…
For months clairvoyant Elizabeth Mallory
had been tormented by visions of a desperate stranger.
Now that man was here, on her isolated
Georgia mountain. Wounded and on the run,
he needed refuge. Could Reece Landry
be the answer to Elizabeth's lonely prayers?

**MORE *PROTECTORS* NOVELS
FROM SILHOUETTE AND HQN**

WORTH DYING FOR

GRACE UNDER FIRE

ON HER GUARD

SWEET CAROLINE'S KEEPER

ISBN 0-373-77078-2

THE PROTECTORS—THE BEGINNING

Printed in U.S.A.

BEVERLY
BARTON
THE PROTECTORS—
The Beginning

HQN™

CONTENTS

THIS SIDE OF HEAVEN

PROLOGUE

They walked together along the isolated beach, the small Timucuan maiden and her big Spanish conquistador. Each knew the other's thoughts and could feel the other's pain, but they could not touch in a physical way, for their mortal bodies had long since returned to the earth's soil.

They knew the time was near. The fulfillment of the ancient legend's prophecy was at hand. Soon a troubled warrior and the woman who could give him sanctuary within her heart and body would come to their beach, would abide within the walls of the old mission, and discover a passion known only by a precious few.

The maiden and her conquistador had known such passion, but had lost their lives in the hatred and destruction wrought by mankind's greed for wealth and power. For centuries the two lovers had roamed this Florida beach waiting for the heirs of their love to arrive and set them free.

"Soon," she whispered. "Soon, they will come."

"Yes," he said. "They will share the same eternal love that we do."

"And when their lives are united as ours could never be, we will be allowed to go."

"Yes, *querida*."

And they continued their nightly stroll along the surf-kissed sand, waiting here, this side of heaven—waiting for the day they could enter paradise.

CHAPTER 1

He heard the blood-curdling scream. Tremors racked his body. He knew he couldn't save her. With a moan of anguished pain and animalistic rage, he cursed the powers of heaven and earth.

Nate Hodges opened his eyes. His harsh, erratic breathing gradually slowed as he lay on his sweat-dampened bed. He looked around the dark bedroom, seeking reassurances in the familiar, reassurance that the agony he had just endured had, indeed, been a dream. No, not a dream—a nightmare. The same gut-wrenching nightmare that had tormented his sleep for the past few weeks.

Even though he knew why the dreams had begun again after all these years, he didn't understand why this dream was so different from the old nightmares, those cursed souvenirs of the war. Until two months ago when he had moved into the ancient coquina house by the ocean, he'd never experienced this particular dream. Unlike the ones that had plagued him after Vietnam, this one didn't involve the war.

He had not been overcome by the sickening smell of rotting flesh. He hadn't felt the splattering of a friend's blood on his face, or heard the moans of a teenager dying in his arms. He hadn't seen piles of pulverized bodies lying on the deck of an incoming boat. Those had been the old dreams, the substance of long-ago nightmares.

Only two things had been the same. Ryker had been there, his one icy blue eye staring triumphantly at Nate, his thin lips curved into a smile of psychotic pleasure. And *she* had been there. In the past, the woman had been his salvation—the calm voice, the soothing hand, his sanctuary from the madness from which he could not escape.

But in these recent dreams, she had cried out for him, and he had not been able to save her. His only hope for peace—destroyed by an old enemy.

Nate eased out of bed, the feel of the cold stone against his feet chilling his feverish body. He rubbed the back of his neck, stretching as he took several deep breaths. Reaching down to the cane-seated chair beside the bed, he picked up his jeans and pulled them on over his naked body. He retrieved the K-Bar knife that lay beneath his pillow, slid it into its sheath and attached it to his belt that hung loosely through the loopholes in his jeans. It had been almost five years since he'd worn a knife—since he'd felt the need for constant protection.

But for the last five years he'd thought Ryker was dead.

Nate slipped into a pair of leather sandals, then, as an afterthought, he grabbed his shirt and threw it over his shoulder.

Opening the heavy wooden door, he walked out into the long narrow hallway and, moving slowly, made his way to his den. The room lay in darkness, except for the shadowy glow of moonlight.

Looking through the wide, open-shuttered windows, Nate noticed the nearly full moon, its silvery yellow light illuminating the patio, the unkept gardens, the rock walkway leading from the back of the house to the gravel road. He opened the huge, arched wooden door and stepped outside. The salty, airy smell of the ocean filled his nostrils, mingling with the thick, heavy aroma of verdant Florida vegetation.

The cool night breeze caressed his bare chest, shoulders and arms. He slipped into his shirt, leaving it unbuttoned. Slowly, cautiously, he walked along the patio, through the high arched openings that ran the length of the L-shaped porch that extended from the back to the side of the house.

He'd done little to improve the shabby conditions of his new home since he'd moved in the last of January. But he hadn't purchased this place for its beauty or with any desire to redecorate or restore. This sturdy, solid fortress of a house had been purchased because of its isolated location. Except for the lone cottage across the road right on the beach, the nearest neighbors were a mile away at the state park. The realtor had assured him that the owners of the cottage seldom used the place except in summer. And that was good. Nate didn't want anyone else around when he had to confront Ryker. That was why he'd left St. Augustine, left his business—to protect his friend and partner John Mason, and John's family. Even with his departure, Nate wasn't sure the Masons were safe from a man as diabolically bent on revenge as Ryker, who would use anyone and anything to settle an old score.

Nate knew the final battle would be over long before summer. Ryker had been spotted in South America three months ago. It was only a matter of time until that mad dog would make his way to the States, find out where Nate was, and come after him.

Nate walked across the road, leaned against a massive cypress tree dripping with thick Spanish moss, and looked out at the ocean. So peaceful. So serene. Comforting—like the woman in his dreams. If there was one thing on earth Nate wanted, it was peace, blessed sanctuary from the scars of a war long ended, the savage memories of a lifetime spent as a navy SEAL, the bitter regrets of a childhood he could never change.

He had given up any hope of love or happiness so many years ago he could barely remember thinking such emotions existed. In childhood, he'd learned that he could count on no one except himself. As a protective mechanism, he'd closed his heart to love, and over the years, he'd found no woman capable of teaching him to entrust his life to another.

His years in the special services had only reinforced his negative attitudes. He had seen the ugly side of life more times than he cared to remember. He'd thought he could find the peace his soul craved when he left the navy nearly five years ago. But that had been when he'd thought Ryker was dead.

Nate rested his head against the tree, closed his eyes and remembered tonight's dream. He hadn't known where he was. He'd been lost in a dark, gloomy room filled with dirt and cobwebs, the smell of rotting wood and damp mustiness everywhere. He had realized he was in terrible danger. Ryker was there. Close. Yet out of reach. And *she* was there. What the hell was she doing with Ryker?

Nate opened his eyes suddenly, not wanting to see. But with his eyes wide open, he saw her lifeless body in Ryker's arms. The pain ripped through him hotter and more deadly than any blade could have. No. No. She couldn't be dead. She was his lifeline. She was his sanctuary. And Ryker had killed her for revenge. To get even with him.

Restless with a need he could not explain, Nate started walking toward the beach. He felt like a fool. The woman in his dreams had no name, no face. All he ever remembered afterward were her eyes—rich, warm brown—and her body. When she'd given herself to him in his dreams, he'd found a sanctuary for his heart and his soul in her arms.

The first time he'd dreamed of her, he'd been eighteen and a newly trained SEAL in Nam. He hadn't dreamed about her in at least a dozen years, not until—until he'd moved to Sweet Haven, to the secluded house where he waited for a man who was as ruthless and dangerous as he was himself.

Suddenly, Nate stopped dead still. His trained instincts told him he wasn't alone. Then he saw her. In a long, flowing dress—white and shimmering in the moonlight—she walked along the beach, at the very edge of the ocean. For one split second he felt as if his heart had stopped beating. Was it *her,* the woman from his dreams? He shook his head, then looked again. She was still there. She was real. No dream. No fantasy.

He knew she wasn't aware of him, of a stranger so close. She seemed to be lost in her private thoughts, and somehow, Nate could feel her loneliness. It was as if her frustration and pain and anger had invaded his mind.

"Damn idiot," he mumbled under his breath. "You've been by yourself for too long." That's what's wrong, he thought. Whoever she is, she isn't *her.* The woman in his dreams didn't exist.

Nate made his way back to the tree, stopping briefly before

starting across the road. He slowed his steps, cursing himself for the need to see her again. He turned around and watched while she walked farther up the beach, then stopped, slumping down, cuddling her body up against her knees.

Who was she? he wondered. What was she doing here? And what was wrong with her? He resisted the temptation to go to her.

For what seemed like hours, Nate stood in the shadows of the ancient tree and watched her. Once, he thought he heard her crying and had to fight his desire to comfort her. He wasn't the kind of man who comforted women, and yet...

She stood up, her long blond hair blowing in the mild spring breeze, her dress billowing around her small body. He watched, fascinated by the way she moved, the way her waist-length hair created a shawl around her shoulders. When she came nearer, he saw that her dress wasn't white. It was pale yellow—a pale yellow lace robe that hung open all the way down the front, with a matching nightgown beneath.

Nate's body hardened with arousal. He groaned inwardly. So what? he told himself as she headed toward the two-story stucco-and-wood cottage. *She's a beautiful woman and you haven't had sex in a long time.*

He didn't turn and go back to his house until she disappeared inside the cottage. He had no idea who she was, but obviously she was now his nearest neighbor. She was too close. He'd have to see what he could do to get rid of her.

Cynthia Porter poured herself a cup of hot coffee, laced it with low-calorie creamer and a sugar substitute, then walked outside onto the patio. The morning was crisp and clear, the sky baby-blue and filled with thin, wispy clouds. The early morning sun warred with the sharp April wind for dominance, one issuing Florida warmth, the other a reminder that winter had just ended in the Sunshine State.

She set down her cup on the glass-and-concrete table before pulling her royal blue sweater together, closing the top button. Seating herself in an enormous wooden rocker, Cyn picked up her coffee, sipping it leisurely as she tilted her head backward and closed her eyes.

It was her first night back here at her family's beachfront cottage in nearly six months, and she hadn't been able to get more than a few hours' sleep. Late in the night, she'd been so restless that she'd gotten up and taken a long walk on the beach, then she'd slept for a while. But she'd had that dream again—the familiar vision that she'd first had at fifteen, a week after her mother's tragic death in a plane crash.

But the familiar dream had been different this time—different from when she'd been fifteen; different from when she'd been twenty-one and the dream had come to her after her father's stroke; and different from when, four years ago, Evan had been brutally murdered. Always, at times of grief and great stress, the dreams would come, and somehow they comforted her. They gave her strength. *He* gave her strength.

The man in her dreams had no name, no face, no real identity, and yet she knew him as she had never known another man. Her heart knew him. Her soul recognized him as its mate. When she awoke, the only things she could remember were his eyes—the most incredible, moss-green eyes she'd ever seen—and his body, big and strong and protecting. This phantom of her dreams came to her to give her strength and protection and...love.

Cyn opened her eyes quickly and ran trembling fingers down the side of her face. Dear God, she had to stop this! She had to stop fantasizing about a man who didn't exist. Taking another sip of her sweet, creamy coffee, she began to rock.

The shrill ring of the portable phone brought her back to reality. She knew before she answered that the caller was Mimi. Dear, good-hearted Mimi. Her title could best be described as chief cook and bottle washer, but what would Tomorrow House do without Mimi Burnside's grandmotherly wisdom and love? How many runaways had been saved because of her generous nature?

"Hello," Cyn said.

"So, was I right?" Mimi asked. "Wasn't getting away to Sweet Haven just what you needed?"

"You were right, as usual. All I need is a few days to recover from the trial—"

"I'd say a few weeks." Mimi's tone was gentle, yet commanding. "Everybody, including me, expected you to be able to handle Darren's death." When Cyn made no reply, Mimi grunted. "If only we could have gotten through to that boy when Evan first brought him to Tomorrow House."

"It was already too late…even then." Cyn's hand quivered. The warm liquid sloshed in the cup. Standing abruptly, she threw the last drops of her coffee into the yard, then set the cup down. Clutching the phone tightly with both hands, Cyn choked back the tears, trying not to remember her husband's death, trying to forget the sight of his bloody body.

"Evan didn't think so," Mimi said.

Cyn remembered how Evan, in his gentle and caring way, had been so sure they could help Darren. Evan had been wrong. "Darren's drug addiction had taken over his life and turned him into a monster capable of killing."

"You'll come to terms with this the same way you did with Evan's death," Mimi assured her. "You have to continue Evan's work at Tomorrow House. There are so many hopeless kids out there who need our shelter, and need someone like you who really cares."

"I thought that I had put the past behind me when I went to see Darren in jail and accepted his pleas for forgiveness."

"None of us expected another inmate to kill Darren. It was a shock to all of us."

"I shouldn't have gone to pieces the way I did. People are counting on me, depending on—"

"Well, honey child, we all know you're a tower of strength. You've held your family together more than once, and you kept Tomorrow House running when the entire staff fell apart after Evan was murdered. But you're human. You're a woman who takes care of everyone around you. What you need is someone to take care of you for a change."

"Oh, Mimi, you're always trying to take care of me." No one un-

derstood, least of all Cyn, why she'd fallen apart, why the murder
of her husband's young killer had affected her so strongly.

"Well, somebody's got to," Mimi said. "What you need is time
away from us here in Jacksonville. You need to forget the problems
at Tomorrow House and stay away from the real world for a while."

"I can do that here at Sweet Haven."

"Stay for as long as you need to. I'll try to keep the natives from
getting too restless."

"Thanks." Cyn knew she could count on Mimi. They were kin-
dred souls, both dependable and nurturing women.

"I'll call you in a few days. Take care, honey child."

"Bye, Mimi." She laid the phone on the table, then focused her
attention on the beach, the sound of the lapping water soothing to
her nerves.

Cyn knew that Mimi was right. What she needed now was to
escape from the real world. And she'd done just that for a few hours
last night, but the dream world she had entered hadn't given her
any comfort. *He* had been there. Big and strong. But he had been
in danger. She had felt his fear, and knew that it was an alien emotion, one he'd long ago forgotten. He had not been afraid for himself, but for her.

Suddenly, without warning, Cyn saw him running along the
beach. Her breath caught in her throat, her chest aching, her heart
beating loudly. He was big and powerfully built, yet his tall, muscular body was trim. He ran with the speed and ease of a wild stal-
lion, his shoulder-length black hair flying around his face like a
silky mane.

Cyn blinked her eyes several times, uncertain whether or not
the man was real. She looked again. He was still there. His powerful body, clad only in cutoff jeans, raced into the wind, moving
farther and farther up the beach.

She realized how foolish she'd been, even for one moment, to
have thought that the runner on the beach was *him,* the phantom
protector from her dreams.

No matter how hard she tried, Cyn couldn't turn around and
walk away. She watched, fascinated by the stranger, by his incred-

ible physical condition, the absolute perfection of his darkly tanned body and by the length of his inky black hair. Even at this distance she could tell he wasn't some long-haired youth. He was obviously a man in his prime. The shoulder-length hair gave him a roguish quality, as if he were a buccaneer. No, she thought, as if he were an ancient warrior.

The conquistador? Cyn couldn't stop the image from flashing through her mind. Since childhood, when she'd first heard the legend, she had visualized the ancient warrior and his maiden. And now this man, this stranger on her beach, brought to life the haunting story of tragic love and a prophecy that the present would one day heal the wounds of the past.

Cyn gazed out across the horizon, noting that the morning sun was just beginning to ascend into the sky. She glanced back and saw the stranger run into the ocean, the surging tide covering his bronzed body in an aqueous caress as his powerful arms and legs glided through the water.

Who was this man, she wondered? And what was he doing on her beach? The nearest neighbor was over a mile away. All the land past her family's cottage and the old building across the road were part of a state park. Perhaps that was it. Maybe this man had run along the beach for miles and somehow ended up taking a morning swim near her home.

Time seemed to stand still for Cyn as she watched the stranger swimming, coming out of the ocean, walking along the beach. Then time began again when he suddenly turned and looked at her. He stood yards away, the sun bright behind him, but she could tell that he was staring at her. She had the oddest feeling that he wanted her to come to him. She stared at him for endless moments, until he turned and ran back up the beach. It took every ounce of her willpower not to follow him, not to run after him, not to call out.

Her whole body trembled, inside and out. When she went back into the cottage, she began to wonder if she'd imagined the stranger, if all the mental stress she had endured recently was causing her to have delusions.

Well, whoever he was, real or imaginary, it didn't matter. She'd never see him again. The last thing on earth she needed at this particular time in her life was a man.

Nate sat on the huge tan leather sofa in his den, the only room in his new residence he'd bothered to fix up. Once things were settled with Ryker, he'd get rid of this musty old house and return to his place in St. Augustine. With his feet propped up on an old trunk and a beer in his hand, Nate felt relaxed for the first time that day. A second run on the beach after lunch and another rigorous swim in the ocean had helped ease the constant tension with which he lived these days.

She hadn't been outside on her patio or on the beach when he'd gone out the second time. He'd noticed that a white minivan was parked around on the north side of the cottage and assumed it was hers. That meant she was still here, still too close for comfort, still in danger if Ryker showed up sooner than expected.

Whoever she was, she was beautiful, Nate thought. He couldn't erase the memory of her standing on the patio, the early morning breeze whipping her blond hair around her face, molding her thin cotton slacks to her rounded hips and legs. Although he'd sensed her presence when he'd been running, he hadn't allowed himself to acknowledge her until he'd come out of the ocean and faced her. He had stood there staring at her like some lovesick teenager, as if he'd been struck deaf and dumb by the very sight of her. Hell, he'd seen gorgeous women before, he'd even had his share of lovely ladies, but there was something about this particular woman. Something that sent a surge of both fear and longing through him. The longing he understood. The fear puzzled him.

He had wanted to speak to her, to ask who she was and how long she'd be staying at the cottage. But he'd just stood there staring at her while she stared back at him. After what had seemed like an eternity, he'd turned and run away. If he'd stayed another minute, he'd have been on her patio, taking her in his arms. His body had been hard with need.

Nate laughed, a mirthless grunt. If he'd gone toward her, she probably would have run into the house screaming her head off. If he'd gotten near her, he would have frightened her to death. After all, he was a stranger, a big, Hispanic-looking man with hair nearly to his shoulders. Hell, he was surprised she hadn't already called the police.

The insistent ring of the telephone jarred Nate from his thoughts. Before answering, he knew the caller had to be one of two people. John Mason or Nick Romero. They were the only two people on earth who knew where Nathan Rafael Hodges was.

"Yeah?" Nate asked when he set his beer down and picked up the phone sitting on the enormous Jacobean table behind the sofa.

"I need to see you," Nick Romero said.

"Maybe you should come here. See if anyone follows you. Let Ryker know where I am and get this thing over with."

"Meet me in Jacksonville. Tonight," Romero said. "We know where Ryker is, where he's been and who he's working for."

"You boys have been busy."

"The CIA kept track of him before he entered the country. Our man Ryker has made some powerful friends in Colombia."

"You could give me the information over the phone," Nate said as he ran one big hand up and down the moist beer can he'd placed beside the phone.

"Probably, but I think we should talk, face to face."

"When and where?"

"Let's make it an early night," Romero said. "How about nine o'clock at a bar called the Brazen Hussy?"

"I know the place." Nate recalled the sleazy bar where scantily clad ladies of the night and streetwise punk drug pushers mixed and mingled with the clientele. "Wise choice. Nobody's going to notice two more shady characters in a place like that."

Romero laughed. "Yeah, that's us, a couple of shady characters."

"Hey, Romero."

"Huh?"

"Have you done something about protection for John and his family?" Nate knew that Nick Romero would have to call in a few favors to get any type of protection for John and Laurel Mason and their son, Johnny. But there was no way to be sure that once Ryker found out about Nate's business association and friendship with the Masons that they would be safe. Nate had distanced himself from the Masons, hoping to protect them, but there was always the chance that Ryker would harm Nate's friends regardless of the circumstances. Ryker would do anything to see Nate sweat, to prolong the torture.

"I'm working on it. It's just a matter of time."

Nate could hear the hesitation in his old friend's voice, and instinctively knew that there was more. Something Romero didn't want to talk about. "What is it?"

"I've got to ask you something," Romero said. "But I don't want an answer right now. Think about it and tell me tonight."

"What?"

"Do you know a man named Ramon Carranza?"

"Carranza?"

"Think about it, Nate. This Carranza has been showing a definite interest in you."

"Who is he?" Nate asked, certain he'd heard the name before. Where or when, he wasn't sure.

"We'll discuss it tonight. The Brazen Hussy. Nine," Romero said and hung up.

Nate replaced the receiver, picked up his beer and walked across the room. The whole den was filled with knives. Elaborate display cases covered the walls, the desk and the tables. Nate reached down on the wide pine table by the windows, picked up a small wood-and-glass case and opened it. He lifted a sinew-sewn hide sheath into his big hand, then removed the Apache scalping knife with its sinew-wrapped handle.

What does this guy Carranza have to do with Ryker? Nate asked himself. *What ungodly secret has Nick Romero unearthed?*

Cyn pushed the bits of lettuce and tomato around in the salad bowl. She had tried to convince herself that she didn't really want any of the chocolate-marshmallow ice cream she'd picked up at the store less than an hour ago. After all, she'd made it through the entire trial without reverting back to her old habit of using food as a crutch. But, with each bite she took, the nutritious veggies with which she'd concocted her enormous salad tasted more and more like cardboard.

Shoving the bowl aside, Cyn stood up and turned toward the refrigerator. *Don't do it,* she told herself. *Stay away from that ice cream and your hips will thank you for it.*

With her hand on the freezer, Cyn closed her eyes, cursing under her breath. *It's that man,* she thought. *He's got me acting irrationally.*

She had survived Evan's death, four years of loneliness, the yearlong trial to convict her husband's killer. She had sought refuge here at the beach so she could come to terms with Darren Kilbrew's senseless murder. Somehow she could make sense of it all. She had to. But what she didn't need was the intrusion of some stranger, a man she identified, foolishly, with her phantom dream lover.

She wished she hadn't been sitting at the desk beside the back windows when he'd taken his swim in the ocean this afternoon. If only she hadn't seen him again, she never would have made that hasty trip into town. There was something about the stranger that unnerved her. Somehow she knew he was no ordinary man. Her instincts told her that he was dangerous.

Cyn let her hand drop from the freezer door. Maybe what she needed was a swim, a vigorous swim in the cool springtime ocean. Anything was better than this nervous hunger inside her, a hunger she had hoped chocolate-marshmallow ice cream could appease.

Leaving the kitchen, she headed for her bedroom to put on a bathing suit. Just as she walked down the hallway, the telephone rang. Who on earth? she wondered. Even though her father and her brother David knew she was here, she doubted either of them would have reason to call her. And Mimi certainly wouldn't be calling again. That left only one person.

Cyn opened the door and walked across the bedroom to where the portable phone lay at the foot of the twin bed by the window.

"Hello?"

"Cyn, how are you?" the man asked. "Everyone here at Tomorrow House is very concerned about you."

"I'm all right, Bruce," Cyn lied. She wasn't all right. She probably would have been if some savage-looking stranger hadn't appeared on her beach and stirred her imagination into overdrive. But, of course, she couldn't tell Reverend Bruce Tomlinson such a thing. "Is there something wrong? I know you wouldn't have disturbed my vacation otherwise."

"Well...I hated to call, and Mimi practically threatened me, but—"

Cyn thought Bruce sounded whiny. Scratch that. She thought he sounded more whiny than usual. The current director of Tomorrow House had little in common with Reverend Evan Porter, who, although he'd been the gentlest of gentlemen, had been quite capable. "What's the problem?"

"It's that Casey kid who came here about a week ago. I told you he would be a problem."

Cyn wanted to scream. For the past four years, Bruce had come to her with every situation too nasty, too dirty, or too much trouble for him to handle. "What has he done?"

"It's not what he's done," Bruce said. "It's what he's going to do tonight. Mary Alice overheard Casey on the pay phone. I thought maybe I should call the police, but Mimi is totally opposed."

"Bruce, you're not making any sense." For the eleven millionth time in four years, Cyn wanted to shake dear Reverend Bruce Tomlinson until his teeth rattled.

"Casey is meeting some guy tonight to buy drugs, and he's...he's taking Bobby with him."

"Bobby!" Cyn had suspected that Casey was a user, but Tomorrow House had made many a runaway addict welcome for brief periods of time, had even helped a few kick the habit. Evan's death had been the only tragic result of giving safe haven to a junkie.

"I thought I should just confront the boys, but Mimi said confronting them would do no good, that Casey will leave in a few days and Bobby might go with him if I push him too far. She suggested that I speak to Bobby alone."

"Did you?" Cyn asked, praying silently. Bobby was a good kid, only thirteen. He'd been at Tomorrow House for nearly a month, longer than most, and there was a chance he would eventually agree to try another foster home.

"I couldn't. He's gone."

"What?" Cyn cried, gripping the phone tightly.

"And Casey's gone, too. I imagine they left early for their night on the town."

"Did Mary Alice overhear where they were going to meet this dealer?" Cyn asked.

"Some place called the Brazen Hussy at around nine-thirty, to-night. I've never heard of it, but I can guess by its name what sort of establishment it is. What on earth am I to do?" Bruce's voice sounded as distraught as Cyn felt.

"Don't do anything Bruce. It isn't our place to play policemen with the kids who come to Tomorrow House." Cyn recited the words she'd been told over and over again. "If we start calling in the police, the word will get out and none of these boys and girls will come to us when they need help so desperately."

"But Bobby—"

"I'll take care of this."

"What are you going to do?" Bruce asked.

"I'm not sure, but I'll think of something." Cyn knew she should take her own advice, but she also knew that she wouldn't.

"I'm sorry I bothered you at a time like this. I realize how badly you needed to get away from all the problems here, but I didn't know who else to call. You're our tower of strength around here, Cyn. We just don't know how to deal with you being...well, out of commission, so to speak."

"Don't tell Mimi that you called me," Cyn advised the minister. "She'd never bake you another pineapple upsidedown cake as long as you live."

Bruce chuckled in his good-natured way. "Thanks, Cyn. You take care, and hurry on back to us. We miss you."

"Goodbye, Bruce. And don't worry about Bobby. Just leave him to me."

Cyn punched the off button and lowered the antenna, then tossed the telephone back onto the twin bed. She moved her overnight bag off the wicker settee, put it on the floor and sat down. Dear God, what was she going to do?

Bobby, abandoned at the age of five by his parents, had moved from one foster home to another. His last foster father had physically abused him and he'd run away. He'd been eleven at the time and had been on the streets ever since. Cyn could only imagine the nightmares the boy had lived through, but she knew one thing for certain. Bobby had never used drugs.

What would Evan have done in this situation? she asked herself, and immediately knew the answer. Evan would have gone after Bobby and Casey. He would have talked to the boys and, in his own loving yet professional way, would have talked Bobby into returning to the shelter. Cyn had become just enough of a realist in the past four years to know that Casey might be a lost cause.

Did she have the nerve to go to a place like the Brazen Hussy? She'd be a fool to go alone at night to one of the most notorious bars in town. But what choice did she have, other than calling the police?

She would just put her can of Mace and her whistle in her purse, dress appropriately and pray that her guardian angel would protect her.

CHAPTER 2

"**R**yker is in Miami," Nick Romero said, then took a leisurely sip of his Scotch and soda, eyeing Nate Hodges over the rim of his glass.

Instead of replying immediately, Nate let the information soak in as he glanced around the smoky bar. Tonight the Brazen Hussy was as loud and smelly and crowded as it had been the last time he had stopped by, over a year ago.

Noticing the small group of teens crowded around a table at the far side of the room, Nate took a deep breath before turning his attention back to Romero. "Some of them aren't dry behind the ears, but the scum that owns this place doesn't give a damn. He's been busted twice for allowing minors in this place, but somehow he manages to stay in business." Nate grunted with disgust. "Just look at them. They're smoking pot and waiting around for their dealer to show up."

"When did you start worrying about kids you don't even know?" Romero asked. "I'll bet if you bothered to check every boy would have an ID to prove he's of age."

"Yeah, fake ID."

"They really think they're tough, don't they? I was just like them once. I thought that growing up in a tough neighborhood had pre- pared me for anything. Until I went to Nam."

"They'd all flip out if they knew a big, badass DEA agent was sitting across the room from them."

"I'm not here tonight as an agent." Romero gave his old SEAL comrade a hard, intent look. "I'm here as your friend."

"Yeah, I know, and I'm grateful even if I don't act like I am."

"I've arranged for some protection for John's family. Unofficially, of course. By the way, how is he now that he's a happily married man?" Romero grinned, then took another sip of his drink.

"Happy," Nate said, not looking directly at Romero, but at some point over his shoulder where a tall, buxom brunette was giving him the eye. "He says he's in love, and damn if I don't believe him."

"Who would have thought it, huh? The three of us shared some good times together, didn't we?"

"Yeah." Nate gave his head a negative shake when he noticed that the brunette was coming straight toward him. He wanted her to know he wasn't interested. He'd lost his taste for her type years ago. "But you and I shared some bad times, too."

"Mm-mm, starting with when we first got to Nam and our entire platoon got the runs from drinking the Vietnamese water."

Nate chuckled, the memory distant and harmless enough to laugh about. "So, Ryker's made it to Miami. No big news. We knew it was just a matter of time." Nate lifted the glass of straight bourbon to his lips, savoring the taste when it hit his tongue.

"He's working for the Marquez family as a bodyguard."

"Big-time drug dealers." Nate wasn't surprised. Ian Ryker had been a mercenary, a soldier of fortune and a drug smuggler. He was the type who understood the system and used it to his advantage. No matter what, he always found a loophole, a back door out of trouble. "What else does Ryker do for them?"

"He's an enforcer," Romero said. "He's been with the family for over a year, first in South America, now here."

"Were they the ones who got him out of the prison where we thought he'd died?" Nate asked.

"Our information is sketchy, but it's possible. All we know is that Ryker was reported killed five years ago when he was serving a sentence for smuggling, then miraculously, he reappeared a few months ago, alive and well and back to business as usual."

"Who spotted him?" Nate knew that Ryker would have taken no

chances of being seen, of making himself visible, and, with his looks—a patch over one eye and his left hand missing—it would have been difficult for him to move around Miami incognito.

"Not one of our guys." Romero looked squarely at Nate. "Remember the man I asked you about earlier today?"

"Ramon Carranza?"

"It seems Señor Carranza's right-hand man made a discreet phone call to someone at the agency. He knew the connection between you and Ryker. He used your name. The man knew too much about you, Nate."

"Just what was the message, and why didn't Señor Carranza make the call himself?"

"Carranza never gets his own hands dirty. You know the type. But I'd say, for some reason, he wants you to know that he's involved," Romero said, shrugging. "As for the message, well, I'd call it a warning."

Nate grunted as he rubbed the side of his jaw. "A warning from Carranza?"

"Oh, yeah. From the big man himself. You've been advised to go into hiding if you're smart."

"Just who is this Ramon Carranza?" Nate asked.

"He's a retired businessman. A former Miami resident. He moved to St. Augustine a few years ago, about the same time you came back home." Romero picked up his glass, downing the last drops of his Scotch and soda.

"Are you saying there's a connection?" Nate narrowed his eyes, wrinkling his forehead.

"I was hoping you could tell me. Carranza is associated with all the right people and all the wrong people. The man knows everybody, and I mean everybody. He ran a ritzy casino in Havana back in the forties and fifties. When he moved to Miami before Castro took over in Cuba, he already had connections." Romero opened his dark eyes in a wide if-you-know-what-I-mean stare. "He's an old man, late seventies, but he's still powerful."

"Did you get the name of the guy who called the agency for Carranza?"

"Emilio Rivera. They've been together for years."

Nate shook his head. "Never heard of him."

"We've been doing some checking—"

"We?" Nate didn't like the sound of this. Something was damned queer about the whole thing.

"When a man like Ramon Carranza starts giving us information, it's only natural that we'd wonder why."

"What did you find out?"

Romero glanced around the room, motioned for the barmaid, then ran one dark, lean hand across his face. "This isn't the first time Carranza has shown an interest in you. It seems that, through both legal and illegal sources, he's been keeping track of your activities for years."

Nate felt a hard tightening in the pit of his stomach. Some man, some former godfather figure, had been keeping tabs on him. "How long?"

"Best we can figure out, ever since Nam."

"Ever since I first met Ryker. Is that what you're saying?" Nate asked.

"Carranza and Ryker have friends and associates in common. Presently the Marquez family. Who's to say that Ryker wasn't working for Carranza back in the seventies? The black market, drugs. Could be Carranza's been keeping tabs on you as a favor for an old buddy."

"Then why would Carranza have his man send me a warning?"

"To add a little extra pressure, maybe?"

"Ryker wants to see me sweat," Nate said.

The barmaid appeared, took the men's order, and left.

"The DEA is very interested in Ryker, and even more interested in his connection with the Marquez family, so we're in on this with you Nate, whether you want us or not."

"I don't have much choice, do I?" Nate finished off his bourbon just as the barmaid set his second drink down in front of him. "And what interest does the DEA have in Carranza?"

"None, other than his possible connection to Ryker."

Nate gripped the glass in his big hand, sloshing the contents around and around as he stared down sightlessly at the liquid. He had enough problems in his life right now without having a puzzle to solve. Was Carranza friend or foe? Was he really trying to warn Nate or was he trying to help Ryker?

"Well, well, take a look at that, would you?" Romero said, emitting a low, sensual growl as he stared across the room. "What is something like that doing in a place like this?"

Slowly, with total disinterest, Nate glanced across the room, looking at the woman who'd gained his friend's attention. He felt as if he'd been hit in the stomach with a sledgehammer. It was her. The woman from the beach. The woman who was staying at the cottage across the road from his house. And she looked sorely out of place walking into the Brazen Hussy, although she had obviously tried to dress for the occasion. Wearing a red silk jumpsuit, a pair of four-inch red heels and teacup-size gold hoops dangling from her ears, she should have looked like any of the other "working girls" casing the bar for an easy mark, but she didn't. Even with the added touch of red lipstick and red nail polish, she still emitted an aura of innocence. Her beautiful face was too fresh, her eyes too warm and bright, her movements too hesitant for her to be a pro.

"Maybe her car broke down," Nate said. "Or maybe she's slumming."

"I don't think so," Romero said, smiling as he watched the woman cross the room. "She looks too classy for a one-night stand. But, if I thought she was interested—"

"You always did have a weakness for blondes." Nate had seen his friend succumb to the charms of more than one blond beauty over the years. But this woman wasn't for Nick Romero.

Laughing, Romero slapped Nate on the back. "And you, my friend, never had a weakness for anything."

Until now, Nate almost said. Hell, what was the matter with him? The woman didn't mean a damn thing to him. He didn't even know her. So what if just looking at her aroused him? Half the guys in the bar were probably readjusting their pants right now.

"Weaknesses can get you killed," Nate said.

"Oh, but what a way to die!" Romero reared back in his chair, bringing the front legs up off the floor. "She's bound to get into trouble, alone in a place like this. Maybe I should offer my assistance."

When Romero lowered his chair back on the floor and started to get up, Nate threw out a restraining hand. "Don't."

Romero sat back down, glaring at Nate. "Hey, old pal, I saw her first. Remember the rules."

"The rules don't apply here." Nate looked past Romero, his gaze riveted to the woman who had approached the table of noisy, swaggering teens. "But if they did, then she'd be mine. *I* saw her first."

"You what?"

"Last night. On the beach." Nate watched as she placed her hand on a boy's shoulder. What the hell was she doing in a place like the Brazen Hussy? he wondered.

"Tell me more," Romero said.

The group of teenage boys stared up at her when she approached their table, Casey easing back his chair as if he intended to stand. When she put her hand on Bobby's shoulder, he slumped down in the chair and hung his head so low his chin rested on his chest.

Casey smiled at her, a cocky look on his youthful face. "What are you doing here, Ms. Porter, checking out the action?"

"Shut up," Bobby said in a whispered hiss.

"Hey, you two know this sexy freak?" A husky young blonde asked, turning in his chair, sticking out his muscular chest.

"Yeah, we know her," Casey said, standing up to face Cyn.

The blonde stood up and walked behind Bobby's chair to stand beside Cyn. "Introduce us."

"Lazarus my man, meet Cyn Porter." Casey's laughter chilled Cyn. Obviously, the boy was already high.

The husky youth reached out and ran the tips of his fingers across Cyn's cheek, watching her, obviously waiting for a reaction. "Cyn, huh?" He laughed, the sound menacingly unnerving. "I like it. Lazarus Jones, at your service, baby doll."

Cyn's earlier uncertainty when she'd made the decision to come to the Brazen Hussy turned into outright apprehension. Jutting out her chin, she tried to appear undisturbed by the boy's crude come-on.

When she slowly pulled back away from his sweaty touch, he snickered and flashed Cyn a lascivious smile that turned her stomach. "Tell me, is Cyn ready to sin tonight?"

She looked down at his hand, noticing the thick coiled snake tattoo that began at his knuckles and ran up past his wrist. "Are you the *man* Casey and Bobby came here to meet tonight?" Cyn asked, trying to keep the tone of her voice calm and steady.

"Ms. Porter, please…" Bobby knocked Cyn's hand from his shoulder in an effort to stand, but Casey shoved him back down into his chair. "How did you know where to find us?" Bobby began to tremble.

"You don't really want to be here, do you, Bobby?" Cyn asked. "Why don't you and I leave, go get a hamburger and talk?"

"Hey, baby doll, you can't leave yet," Lazarus Jones said, placing his arm around Cyn's waist. "Besides, you can't have any fun with a kid like him. Hell, he's probably still a virgin."

Bobby jumped up, his big blue eyes glaring at Lazarus. "Leave her alone! Come on, Ms. Porter, I'll go with you."

"Sit down, kid. You came here for a little blow, didn't you? The party hasn't even started yet." Lazarus pulled Cyn up against him. "I got enough for you, too, baby doll. Enough of everything."

When Lazarus rubbed himself against Cyn, fissions of panic exploded in her stomach. Her whistle and Mace were inside her purse, which was inconveniently trapped between her and the muscle-bound delinquent.

"I'm not interested in anything you have, Mr. Jones," Cyn said, staring him directly in the eye, hoping her false bravado would pay off.

Lazarus released her momentarily, long enough to shove another teen out of his chair and onto the floor. "Get up and give the lady your seat."

When Lazarus grabbed Cyn by the arm, she tried to pull away. He held fast. She began raising her leg, slowly, intending to knee her overly zealous admirer in the groin. Bobby knotted his hands into fists, thrusting one out in front of him.

Suddenly, Lazarus Jones released Cyn, then dropped to his knees. A very big man stood behind Lazarus, his hands on the boy's shoulders, the pressure from his hold keeping him subdued. Letting out a stream of colorful obscenities, Lazarus squirmed, trying to free himself, but to no avail.

Cyn looked up at her rescuer. Her head began to spin. Her knees bolted. She grabbed the back of a chair to steady herself. It was him. The man on the beach. He was even bigger, darker and more deadly close up.

He looked different fully clothed and with his long hair pulled back into a short, neat ponytail. Wearing faded jeans, a dark cotton shirt, tan sport coat and snakeskin boots, he looked a little bit like a cowboy, Cyn thought. No, not a cowboy—an Indian dressed in white man's garb.

While Lazarus, still on his knees, continued his tirade, the other boys at the table began to get up, one at a time, and move backward. No one else in the Brazen Hussy paid much attention, except another big, dark man a few tables over who was watching the situation with amusement. Cyn couldn't help but notice him when he nodded at her and smiled.

"What would you like for me to do with him?" Nate asked Cyn, tightening his hold on the boy.

"Hey, man, what's she to you?" Casey asked. "Lazarus didn't mean no harm. He just considers himself a ladies' man."

"Is that right…Lazarus? Are you a ladies' man?" Nate didn't smile, but the tone of his voice was teasing.

"Let me go," Lazarus said, snarling his features into a threatening look. "If you know what's good for you, you'll let me go and get the hell out of here before I kill you."

Nate did smile then. Cyn thought it was the coldest, most dangerous expression she'd ever seen on a man's face. Nate released his hold on the boy.

Lazarus jumped up, pulled a switchblade from his pocket and thrust it toward Nate in a show of manly triumph. Cyn sucked in her breath and stepped backward. Dear God, what was she doing here? Why had she been stupid enough to think that dressing like a hooker and carrying a can of Mace and a whistle in her purse would protect her? Hadn't Evan's senseless murder taught her anything? The very sight of the knife in Lazarus's hand intensified the terror that had been building inside her for the last few minutes. Since Evan's death, the sight of a knife in another person's hands created irrational fear in Cyn.

The other boys at the table backed up further, even the swaggering Casey. Bobby stood beside Cyn, grabbing her hand, trying to pull her away.

"I don't know what kind of hold you had on me, man," Lazarus said, swaying from side to side in a macho strut. "But you came up on me from behind. Things are even now. We're face-to-face, and I'm going to stick you, big man, and watch you fall to your knees."

Nate knew that he could take care of this cocky young hood quickly and efficiently in the way only a trained warrior could. After all, he knew more ways to kill a man than most people even knew existed. But he had no intention of physically harming this streetwise punk. Scaring a little sense into him, however, was a different matter.

"Please, don't do this." Cyn heard a pleading female voice say, then realized she had spoken the words. Dear God, this couldn't be happening. It just couldn't! One of these men was going to get hurt, maybe both of them, and it would be her fault. She had thought she could handle the situation, been so confident in her ability to do what Evan would have done. But Evan died like this, a tiny inner voice reminded her, stabbed to death when he'd tried to help a wayward teenager.

While Cyn and the group of boys watched, while the dark man several tables over simply glanced their way, while a couple of barmaids stopped to view the scene, Lazarus Jones lunged toward the older man. The switchblade in his hand gleamed like shiny sterling silver in the smoky, muted light of the barroom. Cyn cried out. Bobby held her hand so tightly she winced from the pain.

From out of nowhere it seemed to Cyn, her rescuer pulled a knife—longer, wider, larger than his opponent's. Within seconds he had knocked Lazarus's knife to the floor and turned him around to face Cyn, twisting his arm behind his back and holding the deadly blade to the boy's throat.

Cyn could see the fear plainly in Lazarus Jones's eyes. Obviously, he thought he was going to die. Cyn prayed he was wrong.

"I think you owe the lady an apology," Nate said, letting the sharp blade of his knife rest against the boy's flesh.

"I...I'm sorry. I—"

"Please, let him go," Cyn said.

"Should I let you go, Lazarus?" Nate asked, leaning down slightly so he was practically whispering in the boy's ear. "Should I set you free so you can keep on selling drugs to other kids? So you can rob again, maybe even kill?"

"Hey, man, how the hell did you know—" Lazarus trembled with the certain fear of a man facing death.

Cyn felt hot, salty bile rise in her throat when she realized what kind of human beings she was dealing with. The boy was so brutal and uncaring, and her rescuer was twice as deadly as the boy. Dear Lord in heaven, this wasn't the kind of world she wanted to live in. She had spent the last ten years of her life trying to help change things, trying to make a difference. She hated violence, and yet she seemed unable to escape it.

Nate shoved Lazarus toward his companions. "Get out of here, and pray to whatever God you believe in that our paths never cross again."

Lazarus and his entourage left in a big hurry, Casey following quickly. Bobby released Cyn's hand, but continued staring at the big man coming toward them.

"Bobby—" Cyn had no more than said his name when he ran. "No, Bobby. Wait," she cried out, but didn't try to follow him, knowing she would never catch him. Bobby was too adept at running and hiding.

Nate hadn't felt such rage in a long time. It had been years since he'd wanted to kill another man, but the moment that cocky boy had touched her, Nate had wanted to rip him apart. He hated to admit it, but the brutality within him, the way he so often used violence as a means to settle problems, made him, in a strange way, no better than the smart-mouthed young hood he'd just subdued. Violence breeds violence. It was a fact he couldn't deny.

"Are you all right?" he asked, as he folded his lock-blade knife, reached beneath his jacket and slipped it into a leather sheath attached to his belt.

"Yes." She stared up at him, her heart pounding so loud and wild she thought surely he could hear it.

"What the devil are you doing in a place like this? Don't you know you could have gotten yourself raped or killed?" He wanted to grab her and shake the living daylights out of her. Then he wanted to pick her up and carry her out of here to some isolated place where he could make love to her.

"Look, no one asked you to interfere," Cyn said, tilting her chin upward in a defiant manner. "What made you think I couldn't handle the situation?"

"What made me...?" Nate glared at her flushed face, noting the anger in her dark brown eyes. Rich, warm brown eyes. "That young stud had plans for the two of you."

"Do you realize that your interference could well have ruined a boy's life?" Even though she knew she should be thanking this man for coming to her rescue, she was lashing out at him, some deep-seated instinct warning her to protect herself from the emotions he had stirred to life within her.

Nate moved closer, but didn't touch her. "What are you talking about? Which boy?"

"Bobby, the boy that was clutching my hand." Cyn took several deep, calming breaths. "Bobby's a runaway who has been staying at Tomorrow House, and we had just about talked him into trying a new foster home."

"Tomorrow House?" Nate's stomach tightened. Hell and damnation, what was she, some sort of social worker? Might know, the first woman he'd truly wanted in years would turn out to be some bright-eyed, sanctimonious do-gooder. "Don't tell me, you're some sort of undercover nun, out to save the world."

Cyn stiffened her spine, gritted her teeth and glared up at Rambo-to-the-Rescue. "I'm Cynthia Porter, and I'm assistant director at Tomorrow House, a church home for runaway children. Two of our boys, Bobby and Casey, came here tonight to buy drugs. I came here to try to persuade them not to. To try to get Bobby to return to a place where he feels safe."

Nate could see the zealous determination in her eyes. Rich, warm brown eyes. "The kid will probably come back on his own."

"After what happened here tonight, I'm not so certain. You scared him half to death." Cyn noticed that the man who'd been watching from several tables over had just gotten up and was walking toward them. "Your friend?" she asked.

Nate felt Nick Romero's approach, slanted his eyes just enough to pick up the other man's shadow in his peripheral vision, and nodded affirmatively. He wondered if this woman realized that they'd met before. She'd made no reference to having seen him on the beach. "Romero, meet Cynthia Porter, assistant director at some shelter for runaways."

Romero reached out and took Cyn's hand, brought it to his lips and brushed a feather-light kiss across her knuckles. "I'm delighted, Ms. Porter. I was afraid Nate might forget to introduce us. I'm Nicholas Romero, and the man who just saved you from a rather unpleasant evening is Nathan Hodges. But you can call him Nate."

Nathan? Nathan Hodges. Nate. His name was Nate. Cyn noticed the stormy darkness in his eyes as he glared at his friend. Up until this very moment she'd thought his eyes were deep, dark brown because they appeared almost black. But they weren't brown. They were green—an incredibly dark green. Powerful eyes. Stunningly green, set in a hard, bronzed face with sharp cheekbones, a strong nose and a wide, full mouth. Recognition shot through her like a surge of electricity. Those were *his* eyes. Her phantom protector. Her dream lover.

She stared at him, unable to stop herself. Her breathing quickened, her pulse accelerated, her flesh tingled with some unknown excitement.

It isn't *him,* she told herself. It can't be.

Nate studied her closely as she stared at him. He didn't think he'd ever seen such a beautiful woman—every feature perfect, combining to create an unforgettable face. Large brown eyes framed by thick dark lashes. Small, tip-tilted nose, luscious, full-lipped mouth. And golden blond hair hanging in long silken waves down to her tiny waist.

He looked at her, lost in the warmth of her rich brown eyes. He knew those eyes. They had haunted his dreams for twenty-five years.

The blood in his veins ran hot and wild, some primitive longing surging through him. He couldn't, wouldn't, give a name to what he was feeling.

It isn't *her,* he told himself. It couldn't be.

"Could we give you a ride home, Ms. Porter?" Nick Romero smiled as he looked back and forth from Nate to Cyn.

"What?" she asked, aware of nothing and no one except the big, dark man whose green eyes held her under their spell.

"I asked if you came here in a cab and need a ride home. I'd be glad to take you." Romero grasped Cyn's hand.

"I'll take her." Placing his arm around Cyn's shoulder, Nate gave his old friend a warning glare.

Romero released her and stepped backward, grinning.

"That...that won't be necessary, thank you," she said. "I drove here. I'm parked out front."

"Then let us escort you," Romero said.

"I will." Nate pulled Cyn close to his side, completely ignoring Romero.

Before Cyn knew what had happened, Nate had escorted her outside. She felt overwhelmed. Nate Hodges was quite a commanding person.

"Where's your car?" he asked.

"It's the white van over there." She pointed down the street. "I'll be all right now. Thanks."

Nate didn't release her. Cyn sighed, and allowed him to walk her to her van. Opening her purse, she fumbled with the keys, almost dropping them. Nate took the gold initial key ring from her trembling fingers.

"Don't ever do something this stupid again," he said as he inserted the key and unlocked the van.

"What did you say?" How dare he issue her orders.

"Coming into this part of town alone was a stupid thing to do. You were asking for trouble. You were damned lucky that I was here tonight."

"I've lived thirty-five years without your help, and I think I'll make it another thirty-five. Just who do you think you are, my guardian angel?"

He took her chin in his big hand, tilting it upward so that she was forced to look into his eyes. "Tonight, that's exactly what I was."

His words sent a tremor racing through her. This man was a dominant, protective male, and for some reason she felt as if he'd staked his claim on her. "Then thank you, Mr. Hodges and...and goodbye."

Cyn stepped up into the van, inserted the key into the ignition and started the motor.

"Don't come back to this part of town even if Bobby and Casey don't show up at the shelter." Nate leaned down into the van, his face so close to hers she could feel his breath.

"Has anyone ever told you that you're—"

"I'm used to giving orders and having them obeyed," he said.

"That's obvious."

"Go straight home."

"Yes, sir!" Cyn slammed the door, then maneuvered the mini-van out of the parking space.

Nate watched until the van's taillights disappeared into the traffic. He turned, walking in the opposite direction where his Jeep Cherokee was parked. When he passed the front entrance of the Brazen Hussy, he noticed Nick Romero coming out the door.

"She's quite a woman, isn't she?" Romero slapped his old friend on the back.

"Stay away from her," Nate warned.

"Well, well. I've never seen you so proprietary when it came to a woman. What is it with you and her?"

"Nothing, absolutely nothing." Nate began walking away, moving toward his car.

Nate neither wanted nor needed Cynthia Porter in his life, especially not now when just being his friend was potentially dangerous. All he wanted was peace. Blessed peace. He had longed to put the past behind him. He wanted to forget the memories of a war that still haunted him, and to come to terms with the man he had been, the man who had served his country for twenty years.

Romero followed. "You said you'd met her before?"

Nate slowed his quick strides and turned to face his old SEAL comrade. "There's a cottage across the road from the house I bought. It's the only other house within a mile. She's staying there. She was there last night and again this morning, and I've got to find a way to make her leave. She's in danger."

"Hey, pal, Ryker's coming after you, not after Cynthia Porter."

Nate tried to erase the scene forming in his mind, the vision of *his* woman's lifeless body in Ryker's arms. "Anyone near me when Ryker shows up will be in danger."

"Whatever your feelings are for Ms. Porter, they're mutual. I saw the way she looked at you." Romero put his hand on Nate's shoulder.

"I have no feelings for her, and if you think she has any for me, then you're mistaken." Nate unlocked his car. "She isn't going to be in my life long enough for Ryker to know of her existence."

Cynthia Porter wasn't the woman in his dreams. She couldn't be. Ryker was going to kill that woman—and destroy Nate's soul.

CHAPTER 3

The drive from Jacksonville to Sweet Haven seemed endless to Cyn. Her mind was racked with utter confusion, and her heart rioted with a mixture of far too many emotions. She had never experienced a night quite like this one, and she'd certainly never met a man like Nate Hodges.

Gripping the steering wheel tightly, Cyn turned east off Interstate 1. She glanced in her rearview mirror to see if he was still following her. He was. Damn him. She tried to tell herself that if he was staying somewhere in the state park he was on his way home, too, and not actually following her. But her feminine instincts told her that his Jeep would still be behind her van when she left the highway in Sweet Haven and drove down the narrow road to the beach.

While keeping her eyes glued to the road, she rummaged around in the cassette holder between the bucket seats, counted the tapes until she reached the fourth one, then pulled it out and slipped it into the player. Within seconds, fifties sound filled the inside of the very nineties van.

Cyn loved the music from the period just before and after her birth, the romantic, sentimental songs that promised love and happiness no matter how many times your heart had been broken. The song playing on the tape was "True Love," and Cyn found herself humming, then mouthing the lyrics along with the singer.

No one seeing her now would believe that the trim, attractive, mature Cynthia Porter had once been a plump, naive teenager who had lived in a world of romantic fantasies, listening to dreamy songs like the ones Johnny Mathis sang and watching movies like *Love Story* and *Dr. Zhivago*.

The songs on the tape changed again and again as Cyn raced through the dark night, her speed ten miles over the limit, as if she thought she could outrun the feelings that the man driving so close behind her had created. Nate Hodges's eyes might remind her of the man in her dreams, but he wasn't *him*. Nate was too big, too mysterious...too dangerous to be the gentle, protective guardian who had always come to her to offer her comfort and hope in times of greatest loss and deepest sorrow. But why, then, did she sense that she knew Nate, that it was inevitable that their lives would be joined, that sometime, somewhere, she had belonged to him?

The bright headlights of an oncoming car nearly blinded Cyn. She slowed the van to several miles below the speed limit just in time to see the turnoff to the beach. Taking a right, she glanced in her rearview mirror and saw that Nate had turned directly behind her.

She was tempted to pull off on the side of the road, wait until he stopped, then get out and demand that he quit following her. She wanted to tell him that he didn't have to see her safely home, that there was no danger for her in Sweet Haven. But she didn't stop until she pulled into the driveway at her cottage.

Jerking the keys from the ignition, she opened the door and hopped down onto the stone walkway. Expecting Nate to drive his Jeep in beside her van, Cyn turned around to greet him, the words "thank you and goodbye" on the tip of her tongue. Her eyes widened in surprise when she watched him pass her cottage. Where is he going? she wondered. Didn't he realize she lived on a dead-end road, and even though he probably lived nearby, there was no way out except the way he'd come in?

He turned into the overgrown drive across the road. She sighed with relief, assuming he was going to turn around. When his Jeep disappeared behind the old shell-rock and wooden house that had stood deserted since its last owner had died nearly two years ago,

Cyn planted her hands on her hips, shaking her head in bewilderment. What did he think he was doing?

She waited for a few minutes, thinking his Jeep would reappear. It didn't. Well, whatever kind of game he was playing, she wasn't going to cooperate. With an exasperated groan, Cyn went into her cottage.

Stumbling over a footstool in the living room, she cursed herself for not leaving on a light when she'd left. She kicked off her heels, then reached out to turn on a nearby table lamp. Hopping around on one foot, she massaged the throbbing toes that had collided with the footstool. She headed toward the kitchen, flipping on light switches as she went. She opened the freezer, pulled out a half-gallon container of chocolate-marshmallow ice cream and set it on the table.

"Where is he?" she said aloud. Was it possible that he planned to stay the night in the abandoned house across the road so he could watch over her? "You're fantasizing again, Cynthia Ellen. Nate Hodges is not your protector. He's a ruthless, deadly man. Tonight, you saw what he's capable of doing."

Cyn retrieved a long-handled spoon from a nearby drawer, sat down at the table and opened the ice cream carton. Sticking the spoon into the frozen dessert, she lifted a huge bite to her mouth.

Think about something besides him, she told herself. *You've got enough problems without borrowing trouble. You took a dangerous chance tonight hoping to help Bobby, and maybe even Casey, and where did it get you? Into trouble—trouble spelled N-A-T-E. Stop that now! Concentrate on finding a way to help Bobby.* There was no telling where the boy was right now. She only prayed that he wasn't with Casey.

Cyn slipped the smooth, creamy chocolate concoction into her mouth, savoring the rich, sweet taste. She dipped the spoon in again and again as she devoured her edible nerve-soother. That's what Mimi called Cyn's addiction to sweets, especially ice cream.

Mimi. That's it. She needed to talk to Mimi. Checking her watch, she saw that it was after midnight. She couldn't call the elderly woman at this hour, no matter how badly she needed a motherly shoulder to cry on. The heart-to-heart talk she so badly needed would have to wait.

While Cyn finished almost a third of a carton of ice cream, she tried to figure out just what she would do if Nate should appear at her door tonight. She'd tell him to get lost. No. She'd thank him again for coming to her rescue, then she'd say a polite goodbye. Or maybe she would invite him in for coffee.

Without even thinking about what she was doing, Cyn got up and prepared her coffeemaker. Just as she flipped on the switch, she realized what she'd done. What was wrong with her? Did she actually want Nate Hodges to come by for coffee? A man like that? A man who carried a deadly knife. A man who had subdued a muscular young man half his age with the ease of a wolf overpowering a rabbit.

She took a deep breath, groaning at the pungent odors her own body and clothes emitted. God, she smelled like a sweaty, smoky, whiskey-perfumed streetwalker. Running her fingers over her face, she realized she probably didn't look much better. She'd overdone the makeup just a bit tonight in the hopes of fitting in at the Brazen Hussy.

Forget about Nate Hodges, about phoning Mimi, about where Bobby and Casey are, she told herself. What she needed was a long soak in the bathtub and a good night's sleep.

Maybe she wouldn't dream about a man with incredible green eyes.

Nate prowled around the den, feeling like a caged animal. If he let himself, his feelings for Cynthia Porter could close in, corner and trap him. He didn't know why, now of all times, she had come into his life. He'd been alone most of his forty-two years. He didn't want or need the complications of a permanent relationship—now or ever. He'd never been in love, had never believed the crap about that undying, forever-after emotion.

Love was only a word. His mother had loved his father, but that love had given her nothing but grief. The man for whom she'd borne a child hadn't cared enough about her to marry her. For all

Nate knew, his mother had been one of countless women his father had *loved* and left behind.

And when his mother had died, he'd been handed over to his uncle, a man who'd taught Nate, early on, that love was for weaklings and only the strong survived. Nate was strong. He'd lived through years of physical and verbal abuse from the man who'd taught him to trust and depend on nothing and no one except himself. Hate was a powerful teacher. And Nate hated Collum Hodges—almost as much as his uncle had hated him.

He didn't want or need a woman in his life, depending on him, caring for him, demanding more of him than he could give. Oh, he'd had his share of women over the years, but he'd never allowed one to mean more to him than a temporary pleasure. No woman had ever pierced through the painful scars that protected his heart—except *her*. The woman from his dreams, the woman with the warm, rich brown eyes, the woman who gave his heart and soul sanctuary within her loving arms.

And for some stupid reason he had allowed himself to think, for a few crazy minutes, that Cynthia Porter might be that dream woman come to life. What had given him such delusions? Even if his beautiful neighbor did have the same hypnotic brown eyes, it didn't mean that she was— *Stop it!* He cursed himself for being a fool. He had more important things to worry about than a woman—any woman.

Ryker was in Miami working for one of the most notorious drug families in the country. Nate knew his days were numbered. Soon, maybe sooner than he'd planned, Ian Ryker would go hunting, searching for a man he blamed for the death of his lover and the loss of his eye and hand.

Nate had relived that day a hundred, no, a thousand times, and he knew there was nothing that he or any of the other SEAL team could or would have done differently. They had all regretted that the woman had been killed, accidentally, in the crossfire when she'd tried to protect Ryker. Momentarily paralyzed by the sight of his Vietnamese lover's lifeless body, Ryker's reaction to Nate's attack had been a second off, costing him his eye, his hand and perhaps, over a period of time, his sanity.

Nate longed for a drink, a stiff belt of strong whiskey, not the watered-down bourbon he'd been served at the Brazen Hussy earlier tonight. He didn't want to remember Nam or any of the death-defying assignments he'd taken part in during the years he'd been a SEAL. He wanted no more violence in his life. All he wanted was peace.

Running his fingers through his hair, he loosed the band that held the thick black mass into a subdued ponytail, releasing it to fall freely down his neck and against his face. He walked over to the three-legged pine cabinet sitting in the corner of the den, opened a drawer and pulled out an almost-full bottle of Jack Daniel's. Undoing the cap, he tipped the bottle to his mouth and took a short, quick swig. The straight whiskey burned like fire as it coated his mouth, anesthetizing his tongue, burning a trail down his gut when he swallowed.

Hell, he shouldn't need this. He'd never been a man to use liquor to solve his problems. He recapped the bottle and shoved it into the drawer.

Cyn. He'd heard the boy named Casey call her Cyn. What a name for a church shelter worker. She looked like sin—pure, damn-a-man's-immortal-soul type of sin. All soft, female flesh, with round hips, tiny waist and full breasts. And golden-blond hair. God, a man could go crazy thinking about that mane of sunshine covering his naked body. .

But the one thing he couldn't forget about her, no matter how hard he tried, were her eyes. Those rich, warm brown eyes.

Nate took in a hefty gulp of air, then released it slowly. The heady aroma of sweat and smoke and liquor clung to his body, hair and clothes. Damn, he needed a shower—a cold shower—and about eight hours of dreamless sleep.

Within minutes, Nate had stripped and stood beneath the cleansing chill of the antiquated shower in the house's one bathroom, located just off the kitchen. For a while he simply stood and let the water pour over his hot, sticky body. A body heavy with desire.

He had to focus on something besides Cyn Porter, or he'd be up half the night if he didn't settle for a less-than-satisfactory, temporary solution. Think of something pleasant, he told himself. He tried to recall the carefree shore leaves he'd shared with Nick and occasionally with John, days they'd sowed their wild oats in countries all over the world.

But his most pleasant memories were hidden deep in his heart, tucked away in a private section he had marked with No Trespassing signs. The happiest moments of his life had been spent with his mother when he'd been a small boy. Although she'd died when he was six, he could still remember what she looked like, what she smelled like, how she'd felt when she'd held him close.

Grace Hodges had been a beautiful woman. Tall, slender, elegant. She had been the only person who'd ever loved him, and in the years since her death, he'd often wondered why she hadn't hated him. After all, he'd been a child born to her from a brief affair with a man who had deserted her, and soon afterward had gotten himself killed. Nate's father had been no good. And he was just like his father. His uncle had told him that—often.

"Your old man was some mixed-breed sonofabitch who ruined my sister's life," Collum Hodges had delighted in telling Nate. "If I'd had my way, she would've had an abortion. Our family had the money—we could have found a doctor. But no, she had to have you, and keep you, a constant reminder of her dead lover. She disgraced herself and the whole family. And now, I'm stuck with you, you dirty little bastard."

Nate told himself that his uncle's taunts no longer hurt him, that he was immune to the racial slurs his dark, Hispanic looks had garnered him over the years, especially as a boy growing up in an affluent north Florida Anglo neighborhood. The only anguish he endured now was knowing how badly his mother had suffered because she had refused to give away her lover's child.

And what about that lover? Nate had wondered about his father. Who had he been? Had he known, before his death, that Nate existed? And if he had, had he cared?

What difference did any of that make now? Nate asked himself as he stepped out of the shower and reached for a huge white towel. He had enough immediate problems without dredging up any from his childhood.

Drying off quickly, he walked down the hall, his body still damp and totally naked. His bare feet made a slight slapping noise as he moved over the slick stone floor. As soon as he entered his bedroom, he reached down, checking under his pillow for his K-Bar knife, then fell into bed. The night air felt chilly, but he didn't pull up a blanket or even a sheet. He lay there in the dark room, listening to the quiet, blessing the solitude. He closed his eyes. Restless and frustrated, Nate tossed and turned, longing for peace, for the pure dark moments of sleep when all his problems vanished.

If only he could sleep without dreaming—without seeing *her* lifeless body and Ryker's one gloating blue eye staring at him.

Cyn slipped the cassette into the tape deck sitting on the first shelf of the bookcase near the back door. The living room in the cottage ran from front to back, the entire length of the house, so that both front and back doors exited from the same room.

Listening to songs from the fifties always reminded Cyn of her mother. Her father had often said she had inherited her romantic nature from Marjorie Wellington, who had lived an ideal life with a loving husband and two children—until it all ended tragically when the small airplane on which she'd been traveling crashed. Denton Wellington had been devastated, and had blamed himself because Marjorie had been touring the state on behalf of his congressional election.

Cyn would never forget how amazed family and friends had been that the plump, shy, fifteen-year-old Cynthia had shown a strength and courage that quite literally held both her father and younger brother together in the weeks and months following Marjorie's death. Cyn suspected that it was then that her fate had been sealed. Soon, everyone who knew her grew to depend upon her strength—in any crisis and under any circumstances.

Perhaps it was because others quickly forgot that Cyn, too, needed occasional support and comfort that the dreams started.

For months after Marjorie's death, she dreamed of the strong, protective man with the incredible green eyes.

Cyn heard the small antique clock in her bedroom strike twice. Two o'clock. Pre-dawn hours when the world slept, when most people were lost in comforting renewal. But she couldn't rest.

After taking a long, soothing bubble bath, she'd slipped on her aqua silk gown and crawled into bed. After over an hour of endless tossing, she'd gotten up, put on her robe and rambled around the cottage, finally making her way into the kitchen to pour herself a cup of the coffee she'd prepared earlier. She knew sleep would be impossible. She couldn't stop thinking about what had happened tonight.

She had met the stranger, the handsome and magnetic man she'd seen on the beach. The man with the green eyes that so reminded her of her dream lover. She found it difficult to imagine Nate Hodges as a comforting protector, someone capable of unselfish care and ultimate gentleness. Cyn felt certain that he was as hard and cold and dangerous as the knife he had put to Lazarus Jones's throat tonight. And yet...she couldn't dismiss the feeling that she knew this man, that she'd known him all her life. Perhaps in another life?

Cyn shook her head, crossing her arms over her chest and gripping her elbows in a fierce hug. What made her think something so outrageous? She was tired. Exhausted. The stress that had been building in her life for the last year had taken its toll on her emotions. The always-strong, always-reliable and in-control Cynthia Ellen Wellington Porter had finally reached the limits of her control. She had begun imagining things, things like seeing a resemblance between that brute Nate Hodges and the man from her dreams.

Opening the door leading to the patio, Cyn watched the sky, dark and mysterious, filled with countless stars and one big, bright moon. She breathed in the sharp, poignant smell of the ocean, felt the crisp, cool wind coming off the Atlantic. Leaning backward, she rested her head against the door-frame.

Sooner or later, she'd have to sleep. But not tonight. What if *he* came to her to comfort her? What if, after all these years, she would awaken to remember more than his eyes? What if, as he held her within the strength of his arms, she looked at his face and saw Nate Hodges?

The softly rhythmical cadence of the surf as it swept over the shore lulled Cyn's ravaged nerves like the sweetest lullaby. Looking out at the ocean, she watched as wave after gentle wave covered the beach, then retreated, only to repeat the process, again and again.

Drawn by the night, the hypnotic lure of the ocean, the smell of the water and beach, the big, yellow moon and the romantic music coming from inside the house, Cyn stepped outside. The wind chilled her for a moment, then her body adjusted as she walked to the edge of the patio and took a step down. Just as she reached the final step, her bare feet encountering the sand, she saw him.

He was at least twenty feet away, standing alone on the beach. Noticing that he'd changed into cutoff jeans and a clean shirt, and the end of his short ponytail appeared damp, Cyn assumed he had returned home to bathe. Where was home for him? Surely, somewhere close by.

Had he, too, tried unsuccessfully to sleep? Somehow she knew why he had come back, why he was on the beach taking a late-night stroll. He was seeking sanctuary from the demons that plagued him, and he was coming to her for the peace that could be found only in love. At the thought, she shuddered, wondering how on earth she knew that Nate Hodges was haunted by the past, that he was lonely and hurting, and in desperate need of her comforting arms. How could she possibly know such things about a total stranger?

He walked toward her, each step slow and deliberately measured, as if he were wary of her. She could feel his uncertainty, so strong was his apprehension. This big, dark and dangerous man was afraid of her. For some reason, he didn't want to be here right now, lured into coming to her as surely as some force beyond her understanding had guided her outside to wait for him.

Mesmerized, Cyn watched him approach. So tall. So big. So overwhelmingly male. Her mind told her to run, to escape the predatory look in his eyes, but her heart told her to open her arms to him, to take him into her comforting embrace and give him sanctuary. Cyn shivered with anxiety and with a need she didn't want to admit was sweeping her away, near the point of no return.

Nate moved closer, his gaze taking in every inch of her with undisguised hunger. So small and soft and alluring, she couldn't be real, he told himself. But she was. She was as real as the star-laden sky, the ancient ocean and the granules of sand beneath his feet. And she was his woman. The woman he'd dreamed about since he'd been eighteen. No matter how badly he wanted to deny it, he couldn't. A man whose life often depended on gut-level instincts, he knew, deep in his soul, that Cynthia Porter was the brown-eyed lover from his dreams, the woman destined to be his, the woman Ian Ryker would seek out and destroy.

And he knew he had no right to be here, on her beach, his soul reaching out for hers. Getting close to this woman would mean trouble for both of them.

Her waist-length blond hair hung in disarrayed waves, the ends slightly moist as if she'd recently bathed. Her femininely round body was encased in aqua silk, the material as blue-green as the ocean and just as fluid where it clung to her curves.

He took a step forward, then waited. He could see the rapid rise and fall of her breasts, as if her breathing had become labored. He took another step. She stood, unmoving. Her lips parted, but she didn't speak. His next step put his body within inches of hers.

He looked into her eyes. The sight that met his gaze was like a welcome home, so familiar was the rich brown warmth.

Cyn couldn't move. She stood, transfixed, her gaze mating with his, the experience unbelievably erotic, as if they had often exchanged this visual love play many times while their bodies joined in life's most primeval dance.

Finally, he broke eye contact as he glanced downward at her breasts, her waist, her hips and legs. Cyn felt his gaze as it moved over her, making her nipples harden with desire, her knees weaken with longing and her femininity moisten with passion.

She had never known such raw, primitive feelings. This man, this big, savage beast of a man, made her long for things she had never experienced—except in her dreams.

Nate reached out, running the back of his fingers across Cyn's cheek. When she moaned, softly, sweetly, he felt his whole body tighten with arousal. God, he had never wanted anything so badly.

She leaned her face into his caressing hand. Suddenly, he shot his fingers into her hair, grasping a thick handful. She moaned again, tilting her head backward, arching her neck.

"You shouldn't be out here," he told her. "You shouldn't have been waiting for me."

"What…what makes you think I…I was waiting for you?" she asked as she felt him loosen his tenacious grip on her hair, allowing his fingers to cup her scalp. "After what happened tonight, I couldn't sleep. That's why I'm out here."

"You knew I'd be back." His moss-green eyes, eyes so dark a green they appeared black, held her with their mesmerizing power.

"Where…where did you go, after you followed me here?"

"I went home. Like you, I've been trying to sleep and couldn't."

"Home? Where's home?"

"Didn't you know that I'm your neighbor? I bought the old house across the road." Using his gentle hold on her head, he brought her closer to him. Their bodies touched. Nate groaned when her soft breasts grazed his chest. Even through their clothes, he could feel her, his body reacting in a natural masculine fashion.

Cyn sucked in a deep breath, her head feeling light and slightly swimmy. "You bought Miss Carstairs's old place?" Dear God in heaven, Nate Hodges, the living, breathing embodiment of a ruthless warrior, was living in the old coquina house, built on the grounds where the Spanish mission had stood. Miss Carstairs had sworn that the storage rooms had been part of that original mission. And she had told Cyn the legend, time and again, of the ancient warrior and his Indian maiden whose spirits were doomed to wander this earth until a new warrior and his mate fulfilled the prophecy.

"The realtor told me that the owners didn't use this cottage in the winter months." Nate let his other hand roam downward, from Cyn's shoulder, over her arm, inward to her waist.

"It's spring," she whispered.

"You shouldn't be here," he said. "No one should be here. I need to be left alone."

"You've been alone for far too long." She wasn't sure how she knew that Nate Hodges was the loneliest man she'd ever met, that he'd spent a lifetime without the warmth of sharing. She just knew. Instinctively, she felt his loneliness, his pain. When he grabbed her hip and shoved her body into his, she didn't resist.

"Why now, Brown Eyes? Why now?" He took her mouth with the greed of a man starving, his lips feasting on the sweet surrender he found. It was just as he knew it would be, the feelings erupting from within him somehow familiar and yet more devastating than any he'd ever known.

She accepted the hard, relentless thrust of his tongue, the bruising force of his lips. No one had ever kissed her like this, no man had ever aroused such unrestrained longings within her. She couldn't understand why, but the very savagery of his lips on hers, his big hands raking her body, brought back memories of their wild matings. Memories from her dreams of him? she wondered, and then ceased to think at all.

She knew he'd opened her robe when the cool night air hit her chest a second before he covered her breast with his hand.

He wanted to lie her down, here in the sand, and take her. More than anything, he wanted to bury himself deep inside her, feel the shudders of her release, hear her cries of satisfaction. He touched her lips with his in a quick, light kiss before moving to her ear and nipping the lobe with his teeth. "I'm a dangerous man."

"I know." He didn't have to tell her how dangerous he was, didn't have to warn her that she should stay away from him. Her mind had already issued its own warnings, but her heart was incapable of heeding them.

He captured her in his arms, burying his face in her neck, groaning so low the sound was barely audible. Cyn threw her arms around him, letting her hands slide down his back, savoring the feel of his corded strength. He was so big, so powerful. Just touching him was ecstasy.

Her hands continued their downward trail until she reached his waist, then she felt it—the leather sheath attached to his belt. She ran her fingers over the warm, supple leather.

He's wearing a knife, she thought. The knife he had held at Lazarus Jones's neck? She stiffened, her whole body going rigid against him.

He knew her hand was on his knife sheath and realized she was afraid. He wasn't sure why she was reacting so strongly, but perhaps it was for the best. Neither of them seemed capable of resisting the other. Sexual attraction could be powerful. But no matter how much he wanted this woman or she him, now was the wrong time.

Ryker is coming for you, Nate reminded himself. If she's with you, anywhere near you, he'll use her. Get away from this woman and stay away or your recent dreams are likely to come true.

"I've killed men with that knife." For twenty years, from Nam to every cesspool in the world, he'd used his special skills to subdue the enemy, to achieve the goals of his superiors. At first, the killing had been difficult, but it had been a release for all the pent-up rage he'd felt as a kid. But eventually, the killing became easier. Until one day it became too easy, and Nate knew he had to get out—or lose what was left of his soul.

She dropped her hand from the sheath as if it were a burning coal. Trembling, she closed her eyes and gulped down a tortured sob.

Nate took her by the shoulders and gently shoved her back, an arm's length away from him. Gripping her soft flesh, he met her questioning gaze.

"I know every conceivable way there is to kill a man, and I've used my knowledge to teach others." He could feel her withdrawing. He wanted to beg her not to leave him, to understand, to accept the beast within him, to give his savage heart peace.

"You were a soldier?" She stepped backward.

He let his hands drop from her shoulders. "I'm proficient at using everything from a machine gun to a flamethrower. I've learned how to rig claymores, how to construct homemade booby traps and how to turn rope or piano wire into a deadly weapon."

He waited for her to run. She didn't. She stood there staring at him, tears misting her eyes.

"I was a navy SEAL for over twenty years," he said. "I make no apologies for who I am. Not even to you."

She didn't know what to say, how to respond. How could she ever explain to him that she had been having dreams about him for twenty years, that she had thought her dream lover was a gentle man, comforting and caring? How could she accept the fact that, after all this time, her green-eyed protector was actually a brutal warrior?

He saw the doubt and confusion in her eyes, and wished that she had never stepped out of his dreams into reality. When she had come to him in his dreams, she hadn't judged him, hadn't been appalled by the blood on his hands, hadn't cringed at the sight of the battle scars marring his body.

"I won't bother you again," he said, turning away from her.

She wanted to reach out, to call him back, but she couldn't. She was afraid. She stayed on the beach, watching him until he disappeared from sight. Hesitantly, she raised her fingers to her mouth, running them across her kiss-swollen lips. On a strangled cry of fear and remorse and unfulfilled longing, Cyn ran toward her cottage.

Nate Hodges needs you.

The ocean's gentle roar seemed to moan a premonitory message. She tried not to listen.

CHAPTER 4

Cyn placed the small wicker basket on the kitchen table as she debated with herself about the decision she'd made. Common sense told her to stay away from Nate Hodges. He was, by his own admission, a dangerous man. She didn't need a man, any man, least of all a troubled one. And she knew that Nate was a very troubled man.

If she'd learned anything from the tragedies she'd endured in recent years, it was the senseless waste that violence brought into the lives of both the perpetrators and the innocent alike.

Nate Hodges was no innocent. "I was a navy SEAL for over twenty years," he'd told her. "I make no apologies for who I am. Not even to you."

She kept reminding herself that a man like that didn't need anyone caring about him, worrying about him, wanting to be his friend. And, even if he did, she was hardly the right woman for him. He was a violent, dangerous man who carried a knife and was quite capable of using it. She abhorred violence of any kind, and the very thought of a knife brought back all the vivid memories of Evan's brutal murder.

The oven timer sounded. Cyn slipped her hand into the mitt, lifted the muffin tin from the stove and placed it on a wire rack to cool.

"Don't do this," she said aloud. "Be sensible, Cynthia Ellen. You can't take care of the whole world. You can't fix whatever's wrong in this man's life."

The whole time she was giving herself rational advice, she was searching the cabinets for a jar of Mimi's homemade orange marmalade. The delectable preserves would taste great spread atop the bran muffins.

She lined the basket with a soft, clean towel, then removed the muffins from the tin and placed them in the linen nest. Covering the muffins, she slid the small marmalade jar and a container of her favorite gourmet coffee inside the basket.

Taking a deep, confidence-boosting breath, Cyn picked up the basket and headed out the back door. She didn't want a sexual relationship with Nate Hodges, she told herself, despite the fact that no man had ever made her feel the way he'd made her feel last night. She had simply allowed her imagination to run rampant, she'd given herself over to the magic of moonlight, the power of an old legend and the potency of a virile man. In broad daylight, it would be different. He was a troubled human being; she was a woman long used to giving comfort to the troubled. Indeed, Cyn couldn't remember a time in her life when someone hadn't needed her, depended on her, expected her to take care of them.

Perhaps she was being foolish. Perhaps Nate would throw her offer of friendship back in her face. But, mother-to-the-world that she was, Cynthia Porter couldn't turn her back on the loneliness and pain she'd felt in Nate Hodges. She knew, on some instinctive level, that if ever anyone had needed her, he did.

Nate gulped down the last drops of strong, black coffee, then reached for the glass pot and poured his third cup for the morning. After less than three hours' sleep, he needed the caffeine boost.

His informative meeting with Nick Romero, the one-sided combat with Lazarus Jones and the ever-present knowledge that Ryker was alive and bent on revenge pumped adrenaline through Nate's body, preparing him for what lay ahead. A man long used to sleepless nights, Nate was surprised that he felt so lousy this morning. Hell, it was all her fault. That brown-eyed witch. He wasn't used to thinking about one specific woman, worrying about her, wanting her until he ached with frustration.

He had wanted her last night, more than he'd ever wanted anything in his life—and he could have taken her. Even though she'd been repulsed by the idea of his past, she had still wanted him. He knew she had felt exactly what he had. Life wasn't fair, he thought. It offered you the fulfillment of a dream, then changed that dream into a nightmare. He couldn't have Cyn Porter. Making her his woman would put her life in jeopardy.

Through the dense fog of his thoughts, Nate heard a loud rapping on his front door. Who the hell? No one knew where he was, except Romero and John Mason.

Within minutes he opened the heavy wooden door and glared at his unexpected visitor who, holding a small wicker basket in her hands, flashed him a brilliant, cheerful smile. Looking like springtime sunshine in her pale yellow slacks and matching cotton sweater, Cyn was beautiful—neat, clean and flowery-sweet. Her hair was knotted in a large loose bun at the nape of her neck, and a pair of tiny diamond studs glimmered at her ears.

"Good morning," Cyn said, reaching deep down inside herself to find the courage not to run from his scowling expression. *He needs you,* she reminded herself. *Just like the kids at Tomorrow House. He's a wounded soul.* "It's a glorious day, isn't it?"

Nate stared at her, wondering why she was here and puzzled by her warm, friendly attitude. After last night, he had been fairly sure she'd never want to see him again. After all, he'd hardly gone out of his way to be charming.

When he didn't reply, she laughed, the sound a forced show of bravado. "Aren't you going to invite me in?" she asked. "I've brought breakfast."

He gave her a quizzical look, then glanced down at the basket she held out in front of her. "You've brought—"

"Breakfast. I baked fresh bran muffins, and I've got some homemade orange marmalade." She took a tentative step forward, and when he didn't speak or make any attempt to allow her entrance into his home, she shoved the basket at his midsection. "Here, take this and show me to the kitchen. Have you made coffee yet? I've brought some vanilla nut coffee. It's a new blend I tried, and it's delicious."

Without thinking, Nate reached out and took the wicker basket, stepped backward, just enough for her to move past him, then turned to watch her prance into his home. Dammit, she was like a steamroller—a velvet steamroller, but a steamroller none the less. It was quite obvious that Cyn Porter was a woman used to taking charge, accustomed to issuing orders and expecting them to be obeyed. A hint of a smile curved the corner of his mouth as he thought that it was one thing they had in common.

"You haven't done much in here, have you?" Cyn wasn't sure what she had expected, but it certainly wasn't this dreary expanse of hallway. She glanced around at the open double doors on each side of the entrance. One room was empty, void of any furniture, and the windows were covered with dusty shutters that blocked out the vibrant morning sunshine.

"I've only been here a couple of months." He closed the front door. "The kitchen is straight back."

He wasn't sure what sort of game she was playing, but he'd indulge her for the time being. Maybe she was as hungry for him as he was for her. If she was looking for a quick tumble, he would, under ordinary circumstances, be more than interested. But his life was hardly his own at the present, and the last thing he needed was a woman in his life, a woman Ryker could use against him.

Cyn headed down the long, dark corridor, her sandaled feet making loud clip-clap noises as she walked along the stone floor. "You need to open this place up and air it out. It's awfully musty."

He followed her into the kitchen, set the basket down on the small wooden table in the center of the room, and pointed toward the drip coffee maker. "I've already made coffee. I'm afraid it's nothing special, just plain old high-octane java."

"Oh, that's all right. One cup won't hurt me. Pour us both a cup and I'll fix the muffins." Cyn glanced around the room, trying not to let her disgust show. The plastered walls probably had once been a soft yellow; now they were a putrid shade of tan. A small compact refrigerator sat in the corner, like a square white dwarf in the huge room. A long, wooden table placed against the back wall held a shiny new microwave, a rusty-looking hot plate, and a coffee machine. Two rickety wall shelves hung between the only window, an antiquated sink sat directly below. Sunshine sparkled off the metal faucets.

Nate wanted to ask her what she was doing here. Last night they had come close to making love. Then she'd discovered his knife sheath and had been unable to disguise her fear and disgust. "I'm pretty much baching it here. All I've got are some paper plates."

He looked over at her then, and his heart stopped for a split second. Her back was to the window and the radiant sunshine turned her hair to pale gold. She smiled at him, her brown eyes warm and inviting. Whether she knew it or not, she was offering him something he badly needed. She brought light into his darkness, giving solace to his pain, happiness to his sorrow, and matching his hard strength with a gentle strength equally as powerful.

"That's fine," she said, taking a step toward him. She had caught a glimmer of emotion in his dark green eyes, a glitch in his armor. "Get the paper plates and napkins. You do have some napkins, don't you?"

Nate shook his head. Damn, he hadn't planned on entertaining while he was here. "I've got some paper towels."

"Okay." Glancing around, she saw no chairs. "Where do you sit to eat?"

"In the den," he told her, handing her a couple of paper plates and a roll of towels. "It's the only other room in the house with furniture except for my bedroom."

While Nate poured coffee into two clean cups, ignoring his already filled mug, Cyn placed muffins on the paper plates and set the marmalade jar on the table. "I'll need a spoon or knife or something if you want some orange marmalade."

"I'll take my muffins plain," he said, handing her a cup of coffee, then picking up a plate. "Let's go in the den and sit down."

Cyn watched him carefully as he turned around and headed out of the kitchen. Wearing cutoff jeans and an unbuttoned shirt, he was every bit as big and savage-looking in broad daylight as he had been in moonlight. Maybe more so, with his long hair hanging loose, almost touching his massive shoulders.

She followed him back down the dark hallway, through a set of double doors and into a huge room. Well, he isn't a total barbarian, she thought as she surveyed Nate Hodges's den. The floors were wooden, the walls a faded white plaster, the arched, open-shuttered windows long and unadorned. Bright light filled every nook and cranny. Although sparsely decorated, the room held a leather sofa, three unmatched chairs, a desk, a small corner cabinet and several tables.

Her footsteps faltered, then stopped abruptly. She stood, frozen in the center of the room, her gaze riveted to the wall.

Nate realized immediately what was wrong. She was staring, transfixed, at part of his extensive knife collection hanging on the walls. Even though he'd known he would be living here only until his confrontation with Ryker, he hadn't been able to leave behind his highly prized knife collection at his house in St. Augustine. That was why the den had been the only room he'd bothered to fix up.

She trembled, sloshing the hot coffee around inside her mug. Acting quickly on instinct, Nate set his cup and plate on the desk, rushed over to her and grabbed her mug out of her hand. "Are you all right?" he asked.

"Yes. No. I..." Cyn felt numb. All her life she'd had an aversion to violence, to guns and knives, weapons of any kind. But since Evan's brutal murder, the very sight of a knife sent shivers of fear spiraling through her.

"May...may I sit down?" she asked, her voice quivering.

Nate put her plate and her mug down on the wood-and-metal trunk in front of the sofa, then placed his arm around her, guiding her down and into the cool softness of the leather cushions. "Take it easy. Okay? Maybe I should have warned you."

"I...it was seeing all these knives...the swords." Cyn sat rigid, crossing her legs at the ankles, arching her back away from the sofa.

Nate ran a soothing hand across her shoulders. "Hey, Brown Eyes, I'm sorry. I knew you didn't like the feel of my knife last night, but... I'm sorry. I just wasn't thinking when I suggested we come in here."

She turned to face him, her cheeks flushed, her eyes overly

bright. "My husband was stabbed to death." She took in a deep breath, then let out a long sigh, willing herself not to cry.

So, Nate thought, she hates my knives because some bastard used one to kill her husband. He was finding out just how different he and Cynthia Porter really were—opposites in every way. The more she found out about him, the more she was bound to dislike him. "I'm sorry about your husband."

"I apologize for overreacting." She forced herself to glance around the room. Knives, swords, sabers and daggers filled her line of vision.

"I've been collecting knives all my life. I'll bet you collect something. Most people do." He wanted to make her understand that his knife collection wasn't some deadly monster any more than he was. He wanted her to see past the superficial, past the obvious, for her to take a chance and reach his soul. He didn't know why it was so important that this woman accept him. He just knew that it was.

"I collect records from the fifties. I've got an extensive collection, and I've put most on cassette tapes." Her body's outward trembling subsided, but tremors still churned in her stomach. She knew he was trying to help her relax and adjust to the unfamiliarity of her surroundings. Somewhere beneath all that burly macho hardness, a touch of compassion existed in him.

He studied her intently, memorizing every line of her smooth, flawless face, every golden glimmer in her rich brown eyes.

He turned from her, uncertain what to say or do. How could he make a gentle woman understand the brutal life he'd led? How could he ask her to give his bitter existence her sweetness, to turn his anger into joy, to accept the man he was? He couldn't, even if he wanted to. If she was a part of his life, Ryker would find out and use her against him. Nate Hodges had no weaknesses. And God only knew he didn't need any now.

Seeing such an anguished look of desperation cross his face broke Cyn's heart. She didn't want to hurt him, for on some instinctive level, she knew he had already been hurt enough. What he needed, what he wanted, what his heart craved, was solace, compassion and...love. She had never turned from a fellow human being in need. But was it her motherly instinct that longed to comfort Nate Hodges, or her womanly instinct that longed to know him and care for him? She wasn't certain. All she knew was that, despite her better judgment, she couldn't desert this man.

Cyn reached out and placed her hand on his arm. He flinched. She squeezed his hard, smooth flesh. "I want to thank you for last night...for stepping in and...and subduing Lazarus Jones."

"I thought you were angry because I scared off your runaway boys." Nate looked down to where her small hand gripped his arm. He liked her touch—strong, yet gentle.

"I never should have gone to the Brazen Hussy. I acted irresponsibly." She squeezed his arm again, then released it. Reaching out, she retrieved her coffee mug from the trunk. "I wanted to help Bobby...and Casey, too. I did what I thought Evan would have done."

"Evan?"

"My husband." She held the mug in both hands, entwining her fingers.

"What happened to him?" Nate felt a twinge of something alien, an emotion he'd never known. It was foolish, but he couldn't help but think of Cyn's dead husband as a rival.

Cyn took several quick sips of coffee, thankful that it was still relatively hot. "Evan was a minister. After our marriage, he asked the church to assign him to Tomorrow House. The place had just opened, and we both knew we could make a contribution."

"Your husband was a minister?" Nate hadn't even realized he'd spoken the words aloud until he saw her nod her head. Nate wondered how he, a man waiting to kill or be killed, could compete with the memory of a saint?

"Evan was devoted to the kids, to trying to help them. It was his whole life, and it became mine, too." She didn't want to admit to Nate that there had been times when she had, selfishly, envied those kids to whom her husband had given all his time and most of his love. "Four years ago, a young boy named Darren Kilbrew came to us. He was a drug addict."

Nate saw the torment in her eyes, could hear her quickened breathing. "If this is too painful——"

"I thought I had come to terms with what happened. I...I thought..."

"You don't have to tell me."

"Perhaps if I tell you, you'll understand why I feel the way I do."

Nate nodded his head, his gaze attentive, never once leaving her face.

"Darren stabbed Evan to death, then robbed him." Cyn bit her bottom lip, tightened her hold on her mug and turned to face Nate. "The last thing Evan said to me before he died was that he wanted me to continue his work at Tomorrow House."

Taking her mug from her, Nate placed it back on top of the trunk. He put his arms around her and pulled her into his embrace, the action as natural to him as breathing. As if he'd done it countless times.

She went to him, allowed him to enfold her within the strength of his big body. It felt so right, as if the place was familiar, as if he'd held and comforted her often.

Cyn could never remember feeling so safe, so protected. Relaxing against him, she absorbed his strength, somehow knowing that he understood how desperately she needed him. She waited for the tears, but they didn't come. Had she given all there was to give to Evan's memory? she wondered. Had the pain finally subsided enough where she could truly accept his death and the death of his killer?

"Darren, the boy who killed Evan, eluded the police and wasn't captured until last year," she told Nate, still safe within his arms. "He...he was killed in jail. By...by another inmate. Stabbed to death." The last words escaped her lips on a tortured sigh.

Nate hugged her to him, feeling fiercely protective, primitively possessive. He stroked her hair, letting his fingers lace through the long blond strands as he loosened the bun. "Scream if you want to, rant and rave and cry at the injustice. You don't have to be strong right now. Nothing's going to hurt you. I'm here. I'll take care of you."

The sobs that clogged her throat, almost choking her, erupted then, and tears filled her eyes. And for the first time since she'd been a small child, Cyn accepted comfort and strength from another, instead of giving it. They sat there on the tan leather sofa in Nate's brutally male den while Cyn cleansed her heart of a pain she'd been unable to wash away with four years of crying. Gradually, her breathing returned to normal, her ragged little cries silenced. She eased out of his arms, not allowing herself to look at him. If she saw his eyes, she would be lost—forever.

Wiping the remnants of moisture from her eyes and cheeks with the tips of her fingers, Cyn tried to smile. "You must think I'm a real crybaby. I'm usually in much better control."

"Maybe you keep too tight a control over your emotions," he said, reaching out to take her chin in his big hand.

"Normally, I'm a tower of strength." Even when he tilted her face upward, she refused to look at him, cutting her eyes sideways, glancing over to the windows.

"Cyn?" He wanted her to look at him so that he could see what she was thinking. Her brown eyes were like windows to her soul, so expressive, so transparent.

She jerked away from him, stood up and began pacing around the room. "I haven't been down here to the cottage since last summer. I just came for a minivacation. I'll probably be returning to my apartment in Jacksonville in another week or so."

"Were you running away? Is that why you came to Sweet Haven?" he asked, then cursed himself.

Why was he taunting her about running away when that was the very thing he wanted her to do? He wanted her to run back to Jacksonville. And the sooner, the better. He didn't need the complications she could create in his life. If he had to worry about her safety, he wouldn't be as alert to protecting himself, and Ryker would use any advantage he could to win the upcoming battle.

Stopping by the table situated directly behind the sofa, Cyn ran her fingers over the array of cases that held an assortment of knives, and made a decision. "Yes, I suppose I was trying to run away. But now, I'm running back to the safety of what I know, of what I want to do with my life. Tomorrow, I'm going back to work. Half days."

"Are you sure it's what you want to do, or what you feel obligated to do for your late husband?" He stood up and moved around the sofa toward her.

She stared at him, puzzlement in her eyes. "What would make you ask such a question?"

"You said you had promised your husband."

"Tomorrow House was *our* dream, not just Evan's. You can't begin to imagine how many kids there are who need someone to care."

"Yeah, you're probably right. I haven't exactly spent my life helping the needy." He realized that she had no way of knowing that he had once been one of those kids who desperately needed someone, anyone, to care. He'd spent his whole life trying to escape from the past, not once confronting it or ever thinking about helping other kids with problems similar to his own.

"You said you were a navy SEAL, so you were helping others by serving your country." She had heard the self-condemnation in his words, the hidden pain masked behind his reply, and she couldn't bear to know he was hurting.

He was surprised to hear her defend him. He couldn't believe it. This woman who abhorred violence, who was scared of his knives, who condemned his brutality, was actually defending him. Damn, did she have any idea how that made him feel?

Nate came up behind her, gripped her by the shoulders and lowered his head so his lips were against her ear. "You're the most beautiful, desirable woman I've ever known." When he felt her trying to pull away, he tightened his hold. "Don't balk, Brown Eyes. I have no intention of ravishing you no matter how much I'd like to."

"I...I really should leave," she gasped, listening to the sound of her heartbeat roaring in her ears. When she tried to pull free, he let her go. She backed up several steps, then turned to face him.

He needs you, she reminded herself. *It's obvious he's never been friends with a woman.* The thought of exactly what he had been with other women unsettled Cyn. This man wasn't her type. He was nothing like Evan. So why was she so attracted to him? What was there about him that made her want to be with him? "I'll take care of you," he'd said, and in that moment, she had wanted his strength, had felt such relief in being allowed to lean on someone else.

"I don't want to be ravished...but if...if you need a friend..."

He looked at her, his eyes devoid of any emotion, his face a mask. She waited, wondering why he didn't say something, thinking perhaps she hadn't spoken the words aloud.

"We can never be just friends," he said.

"But Nate, I—"

"Go back to your cottage, Cynthia Porter, and stay away from me." He didn't want to send her away. He wanted to pick her up, carry her to his bed and spend the rest of the day and night making love to her. "I'm a dangerous man whose past is finally catching up with him."

"I don't understand."

"You don't have to understand. Just leave." Nate's voice was harsh. He'd meant it to be. He didn't dare let this woman become a part of his life. Not now. Not ever.

Cyn couldn't speak. She merely nodded in acquiescence, turned and ran out of the den. Stopping in the hallway, she leaned against the wall, gasping for air as she struggled to maintain control of her emotions. He didn't want her friendship. He'd made that abundantly clear.

"I...I won't bother you again," she said, not looking back as she moved hurriedly toward the front door.

It took all his willpower not to run after her, to ask her to stay, to demand that she take him into her loving arms and give his heart and soul the sanctuary he so desperately needed.

But he didn't. He let her go. For her sake, he had no other choice.

Nate aimed the Arkansas toothpick, the long, sharp blade gleaming like quicksilver in the afternoon sunlight. With expert ease, he threw the weapon toward its target, knowing, without looking, that the knife had hit its mark. In the past two months of daily practice, he had regained his once-renowned skill. But how much good would it do him in a fight with Ryker?

Ryker might demand a face-to-face confrontation, but he wouldn't fight fair. It wasn't his style. Nate had to be prepared, as battle-ready as he'd ever been in Nam or afterward on the numerous assignments he'd undertaken during his days as a SEAL. Ryker was as skilled, as ruthless, as prepared to die as Nate. They were equal opponents, except that Nate had been able to hang on to his sanity. Ryker hadn't.

Retrieving the knife, he returned to his designated spot by the cypress tree in the backyard, took deadly aim and sailed the dagger through the air. Once again it pierced the makeshift wooden dummy's heart.

What would Cynthia Porter think if she knew that many times he had killed victims by covering their mouth with his hand, jerking their head up, exposing their neck and then, with a quick diagonal slice, severing their carotid artery? A bloody, messy kill. But very effective.

She would be appalled, utterly disgusted. Even if the threat of Ryker's imminent arrival didn't stand between them, his Special Forces past would.

The faint, distant ring of the telephone drifted through the open windows. Nate pulled the knife out of the dummy, slipped it back into its sheath and walked quickly inside the house.

"Yeah?" He took several deep breaths.

"Are you busy?" Nick Romero asked.

"Sort of," Nate said.

"Not in the middle of entertaining your blond neighbor, are you?"

In no uncertain terms Nate told his friend what he could do to himself.

"Keep talking like that and I'll hang up without telling you why I called." Romero's chuckle vibrated over the phone lines.

"What's up?" Nate ran his hand through his loose hair.

"Just got off the phone with John."

"What happened?" Nate didn't want John involved, didn't want anyone else getting in the way, maybe getting themselves killed.

"Seems some strange guy approached John's wife Laurel at the local supermarket. Said a friend of his wanted to send a message to Nate Hodges."

"Damn! Where was her protection? I thought you said you had her and John covered."

"We do now. Our man was late getting in position," Romero said. "Mrs. Mason wasn't hurt. The guy didn't touch her. She told John that he was very courteous."

"Did she give John a description?" Nate wondered if Ryker had sent a colleague or had come himself.

"It wasn't Ryker."

Nate heard the hesitation in the other man's voice. "But?"

"This guy told Mrs. Mason to tell you that your old buddy Ian Ryker was on his way to St. Augustine and he'd be looking you up soon."

"Make sure nothing happens to Laurel and John," Nate said, then slammed down the phone.

Not all the horrors from his past had prepared him for his present torment. He'd seen buddies die——in Nam and other godforsaken countries around the world. But not once had a friend been in jeopardy because of him. Now anyone who was a friend or acquaintance was in danger. He had to keep Cyn Porter out of his life!

CHAPTER 5

What the hell is she doing? Nate slammed on the brakes, bringing his Jeep to a screeching halt a few feet away from Cyn Porter, who stood in the middle of the road.

He stuck his head out the open window. "Are you trying to get yourself killed, woman? I nearly ran over you."

Cyn cursed the fates that had thrown her together with Nate Hodges again. After their ill-fated breakfast ended yesterday, she'd sworn she'd never go near him again. By his less-than-friendly attitude, she could tell that he felt the same way.

Walking around to the driver's side of the Jeep, Cyn counted slowly to ten before replying. "I can assure you that I'm not suicidal. If you'd been driving at a normal speed on this dead-end dirt road, you would have had no problem stopping."

"What were you doing in the middle of the road?" he asked, trying not to notice how good Cynthia Porter looked in her jeans and sweater.

"Wasn't it obvious? I was trying to get your attention."

"There are other ways, you know."

"Don't get smart with me," she said, her voice growing steadily louder and more agitated. "The deliveryman left a package at my house for you."

Nate tensed, every nerve in his body going deadly still. He hadn't been expecting a delivery. "Where's the package?"

"I just told you that it was at my house."

"Why didn't you just bring it out here?"

"Look, your swords are lying in the middle of my living room floor where they fell out of the package. I'd appreciate it if you'd come and get them." She flashed him a quick, phony smile, then turned on her heels and walked back toward her cottage.

Swords! Who the hell had sent him swords? And how had they wound up in the middle of Cynthia Porter's living room floor? Nate turned his Jeep into her drive. By the time he'd parked and gotten out, she was on her doorstep.

"Wait up," he called out, taking giant strides to reach her before she entered the house.

Turning on him just as he stepped up behind her, Cynthia blocked the doorway. "Just go in, get them and leave."

"What else did you think I'd do?" he asked.

"I didn't want you to think that I was inviting you to stay or any-thing after you made it perfectly clear yesterday that you neither want or need my friendship." *Stay angry,* she told herself. *If you stay angry, he can't get to you. And whatever you do, don't look into his eyes. You'll be offering him more than friendship if you see that passionate need he can't disguise.*

"Will you move out of the way, please?" he asked.

She moved inside. He followed. "There they are," she said, point-ing toward the floor where a long box lay, one end open. Part of a heavy metal sword lay half in and half out of the box, and beside it was a matching sword, only a few inches of the tip still inside the box. Nate recognized the pieces immediately. They were excellent reproductions of Norman swords.

Who the hell had sent them? And why? Everyone who knew Nate knew about his collection. Even Ryker.

"I didn't open them," Cyn said. "When I walked in here with the box, the bottom just came open and the swords fell out. I was so startled, I dropped them."

"Have you touched them?" Maybe Romero could get some prints if the sender had been careless enough to leave any. If it had been Ryker, the swords would be clean.

"Most certainly not. The very sight of those things repulses me." What was wrong with him? Cyn wondered. For heaven's sake, the man collected knives, why was he so surprised that an order had arrived? "And I didn't touch the card, either."

She nodded toward the floor, then tapped her foot beside the small envelope that had floated out of the box when it sprung open.

Nate hesitated no more than a second, but long enough for Cyn to notice. He acted almost afraid to touch the card. She shook her head to dislodge such a ridiculous notion. Nate Hodges afraid? Don't be ridiculous.

He glanced around the room. "I need to use your phone."

"Is something wrong?"

"I want you to stay out of this." He made the mistake of grabbing her by the shoulders. The moment he touched her, he wanted to pull her closer, to tell her everything, to confess the danger he was in and the danger that would threaten her, too, if she became a part of his life.

"Nate, if something's wrong—"

"Why don't you go for a walk on the beach…or take a ride. Go somewhere until I can get this mess cleared up." Hell, he knew she wasn't about to leave. He hadn't given her an explanation, he'd just issued her an order.

"You forget, this is my house." She had sense enough to realize that Nate Hodges was in trouble whether or not he thought she was clever enough to figure it out. "You may not want me involved in this, whatever it is, but don't you think it's a little too late, now?"

"If you're smart, you'll pack your bags and go back to Jacksonville. Right now."

Cyn walked around him and the weapons lying so deadly in their stillness on her living room floor. Sitting down on the couch, she crossed her arms over her chest. "Do whatever you need to do. I'm not leaving."

Nate uttered a few choice words under his breath. He wished he could order Cynthia Porter to leave, but he couldn't. For whatever reason, she was determined to stay. Hell, it was as if she honestly thought she could help him, and there was no way he could persuade her otherwise without telling her the truth. And he wasn't about to do that.

"Fine, sit there and behave," he told her. "But stay out of the way and don't ask any questions."

"The portable phone is right there on the coffee table."

Nate picked up the phone, punched out the numbers and waited. The moment he heard Romero's voice, he said, "I'm at Cynthia Porter's cottage. While I was out, a guy delivered a package containing two Norman swords. He left them here. They're lying in the middle of Ms. Porter's floor. There was a card enclosed."

"Has she touched anything?" Romero asked.

"Just the outside of the box."

"You think they're a gift from our friend Ryker?"

"That's my guess." Nate watched Cyn. She sat quietly on the sofa, her hands crossed in her lap, her chin tilted upward as she gazed at the ceiling.

"Probably no point in checking for prints, but I'll bring a guy with me. Just stay put."

Nate laid down the phone, then sat beside Cyn. "You remember my friend, Nick Romero, from the Brazen Hussy?"

She nodded, but didn't look at him.

"Well, he's coming over and bringing someone with him. Romero will probably ask you a few questions about the deliveryman—"

"Just who are you, Nate Hodges? And what sort of trouble are you mixed up in?" She uncrossed her arms, reached out and touched him, her hand covering his where it lay on his leg.

He pulled away from the warmth of her touch. It wouldn't be easy to open up, to tell her the truth, to share his past with her, but God in heaven, he wanted to. By choice, he'd been alone all his adult life. But he was tired of being alone, tired of being afraid to care.

"Nothing that needs to concern you, Cyn."

She felt as if he'd slammed a door in her face, the door to his life that was clearly marked Private. Why was he so afraid to let her help him? Didn't he know she was very good at taking care of others? "It'll be…interesting to see Mr. Romero again," she said, smiling, but still not looking directly at Nate. "He's very charming, isn't he?"

Nate gave her a harsh look. "You aren't interested in Romero, so don't bother pretending you are."

"What makes you think I'm not interested in Nick Romero?"

Reaching out, Nate cupped her chin in his hand, his grasp infinitely tender, his thumb and fingers biting gently into her flesh. "Because you're interested in me."

She looked at him then, unable to stop herself. What she saw in his eyes both frightened and excited her. "You need me," she said, her voice no more than a faint whisper.

More than you'll ever know, he said silently as he released her chin. "Don't try to use Romero to make me jealous. It won't work."

Nate hated to admit that he was jealous of his best friend, but he was. After Romero had sent the swords and note to the lab with another agent, Nate had done everything he could to persuade his old buddy to leave, but Romero had stayed. And, although Cyn hadn't deliberately flirted with Romero, she had been friendly and cooperative, answering his questions without asking him any in return. Nate would have already left, but Cyn had invited them to stay for lunch, and after Romero had accepted, what else could he have done but stay?

Now the three of them were sharing afternoon coffee on Cyn's patio. Romero was his usual charming, flattering Casanova self—as smooth as silk. His friend's way with the ladies had never bothered Nate before. Usually, he watched Romero's magic skills with amusement. But not today. Nate had never felt such gut-wrenching jealousy. Cyn Porter, whether he wanted her to be or not, had become important to him. She was more than just another woman, and she most certainly was not a woman he wanted to share.

When the phone rang, they all jumped. Cyn answered, then handed the phone to Romero. Nate glanced over at her just in time to catch her staring at him.

"Swords were clean. The note, too," Romero said. "Your guess about the gift-giver is probably right."

Nate merely nodded. The note had been typed. *For your collection*...the words as meaningful or as meaningless as anyone's personal interpretation.

"Fine," Nate said, having been reasonably certain that the gift had
been from Ryker. Just his little way of letting Nate know that his
whereabouts were no longer a secret. But it didn't mean Ryker was
in town. On the contrary, the little gift was more than likely just
another method of making Nate sweat. Maybe Ryker's business associate, Ramon Carranza, had arranged to have the swords delivered. After all, this guy Carranza lived close by, just a few miles
away in St. Augustine.

"Would you care for some more coffee, Nick?" Cyn asked, trying
to concentrate all her energies toward playing the perfect hostess
while avoiding any eye contact with Nate. She had never deliberately
tried to make one man jealous of another, and having done so today
made her feel uncomfortable. But Nate had a way of making her act
out of character. She had seldom met anyone, man, woman or child,
who didn't respond to her loving and caring attitude. Nate had made
it perfectly clear that he wasn't interested in being friends.

"I'd love to take you out for dinner tonight," Romero said. "I
know this great seafood place down—"

"She can't go," Nate said.

"Sorry," Romero said, turning toward his friend. "I didn't realize you and Cyn had plans for tonight."

"We don't," Cyn said.

"Well, we do," Nate said at the same time Cyn spoke.

"Which is it?" Romero asked, grinning. "You do or you don't?"

Once again Cyn and Nate answered simultaneously.

"We don't."

"We do."

"Hey, I'm out of here," Romero said, standing. Taking Cyn's hand
in his, he bestowed a gentlemanly kiss. "Looks like my friend has
staked his claim."

Cyn decided the best course of action was to say and do nothing until Nick Romero left. After all, her problem wasn't with him.
It was with Nate Hodges.

The moment she heard Romero's car start, she turned to Nate. "Do you want to tell me what's going on?"

"There's a guy who's been giving me some trouble. He probably sent the swords as some sort of joke. He's got a sick sense of humor." Nate noted that she didn't seem overly impressed with his explanation. The way she was staring at him made him wonder if she was getting ready to douse him with the contents of her cup. "Romero works for the government, and I knew he could get everything checked out."

"I'd ask more questions, but I doubt you'd answer them." Cyn stood, placed her cup on the concrete-and-glass table, then turned to Nate. "I don't know what sort of trouble you're in, and it's obvious you don't want me to know. So be it. But I wasn't referring to the swords or whatever mess you've gotten yourself into. I want to know why you told Nick that we have a date for dinner when we don't."

"I don't want you getting mixed up with Romero."

"Why not? He's a friend of yours, isn't he?"

"Hell, woman, he's got a thing for blondes." Nate jumped to his feet, his eyes dark with warning.

Cyn took several steps backward. "I like Nick."

"And he likes you. Romero likes all pretty blondes, and most of them like him." Didn't she understand that he cared about her, that he didn't want to see her harmed in any way. After all, if her safety wasn't uppermost on his mind, he'd have her in his bed right now, making slow, sweet love to her. "Stay away from Romero if you don't want to wind up just another number in his little black book."

"Are we going out for dinner?" she asked.

"What?"

"Are we going—"

"No."

"Then leave."

"What?" he asked.

"I said leave."

"Fine." He crashed his coffee cup against the top of the glass table, cracking the ceramic mug. "Go back to Jacksonville and get out of my life." He stalked away.

Maybe he was right, she thought as she watched him disappear around the side of the house. She had come to Sweet Haven to rest, to get away from all her problems, from the memories. But being Nate Hodges's neighbor had simply created new problems—problems she had hoped she could handle by offering the man her friendship. She'd been a fool. There was something far stronger than friendship between them. Nate wanted to be her lover, but for reasons only he knew, he was determined to send her away. And for reasons only God knew, she was just as determined not to leave him.

Nate stood at a distance, watching her for a long time before pushing himself away from the tree and heading out onto the beach. He hadn't intended seeing her again, but he knew he had to get her to leave the cottage, return to Jacksonville, to the safety of her apartment. If Ryker came to Sweet Haven, Nate wanted Cynthia Porter long gone.

Cyn saw him approaching. She had noticed him a good while ago standing by the cypress, staring out at the ocean, occasionally glancing at her as she strolled along the beach. He looked remarkably handsome in his leisure attire. His cutoff jeans, his wrinkled shirt, his leather sandals. He'd combed his hair back and tied it with what looked like a shoe string.

"Hi," he said as he came up beside her, falling into step with her as she continued walking up the beach.

"Hi." She looked away quickly, not even momentarily slowing her stride.

"I'm sorry about the way I acted earlier. I've got a lot of problems in my life right now, and I took some of my frustration out on you." He had decided that somehow, some way, he had to get Cynthia out of his life, out of Sweet Haven and back to the safety of her Jacksonville apartment. But how was he ever going to get around to the subject of her leaving? He'd tried the hardball approach and it hadn't worked.

"I don't understand you, Nate. You're such a complex man. You can be so gentle, so understanding...and then you turn into a monster." What was he doing here, following her? She wanted an explanation. His apology just wasn't enough.

"I'm not used to women like you any more than you're accustomed to men like me. It's only natural that we'd have a difficult time understanding each other."

"You send out mixed signals," she said, slowing her pace so that she could look at him. "It's as if you're pulling me toward you with one hand and pushing me away with the other." She didn't miss the slight tightening of his jaw, the strained quiver.

"Like I told you, I've got some major problems in my life right now, problems I don't want to involve anyone else in." Could he make her understand without telling her about Ryker? If only he hadn't met her now when a relationship with her would mean putting her life on the line.

"You have problems. I want to help you." She stopped walking and turned to him, placing her hand on his arm. "I'm a good listener."

Damn, the last thing he needed was a caring woman. The touch of her small hand on his arm sent off alarm bells through his entire system. Cyn was a sweet temptation, one he was finding harder and harder to resist. "Look, Brown Eyes, I'm trouble with a capital T." He pulled away from her tender touch. "I'm a cynical, uncaring bastard with nothing to offer a woman like you except a scarred body, an unfeeling heart and a past that's filled with blood and violence."

"Another man, a lot like you, came to this beach once. Centuries ago. He even stayed in your house." She saw the bewilderment in Nate's eyes, and knew he'd never heard the legend. "I'd love to see inside the old mission again."

"The old mission?" He racked his brain trying to remember what the realtor had said about a mission. Something about a part of his house being hundreds of years old, dating back to the late sixteenth century. "Who was the man?"

"Obviously, you haven't heard the ancient legend. I can't believe the realtor didn't use it as a selling point," Cyn said, starting to walk again, moving toward the dirt road that separated their homes.

"She said something about part of the house dating back several centuries. The old storerooms, I think." Nate followed Cyn across the road. "I don't remember her saying anything about a legend." But then, he hadn't heard much of what the realtor had said about the house's history. All that had interested him had been the isolated location.

"I haven't been inside since Miss Carstairs died." Cyn stopped just short of Nate's porch. "Let me show you inside the storage rooms and I'll tell you the legend."

Nate followed her along the arched porch until they reached the area in question. What was he doing? he wondered. All he'd intended was to talk to her and try to persuade her to leave Sweet Haven. Now, here she was at his home, telling him some farfetched tale of an ancient warrior she said was a lot like him. And he was following along behind her like some doting puppy.

"Do you have a key?" Cyn held out her hand as she stepped up to the outside metal door of the vine-covered room.

"It isn't locked," he said. "Nothing in there but a bunch of old junk. I think the former owner used it as a storage shed."

Cyn took hold of the heavy metal door handle. The hinges creaked loudly when she gave the door a gentle nudge. As she opened the door fully, sunlight poured into the darkness, and minuscule motes of glittering dust danced in the air.

"I haven't been in here since I was a teenager and used to come over and visit Miss Carstairs. She always kept this door locked." Cyn laughed, remembering the old woman who'd filled her head with stories of Florida's past, of numerous battles, countries fighting to claim this gloriously beautiful land as their own, of dark-skinned natives, of Spanish invaders—of a Timucuan maiden and a conquistador.

"Was she afraid someone would tote off some of this treasure?" Nate asked as he stepped inside the large coquina room and looked around in the dreary gloom at moldy, cobweb-covered chairs, chests, crates, rotting boxes and a wooden bed.

"I don't think there was this much stuff in here back then, but Miss Carstairs wasn't worried about thieves. She was worried about ghosts. I never could understand how she thought a locked door would prevent spirits from entering if they wanted to."

Nate spied what looked like the remains of a meal, an aluminum drink can, a wrapper from a candy bar and the butt of a cigarette. "Looks like I've had company." Had Ryker sent a scout out ahead? One of Carranza's men? The thought that someone had been this close to him without his knowledge bothered Nate. Were his instincts that rusty? If they were, he was in big trouble.

Cyn spied the objects on the floor. "Probably just some vagrant taking shelter from the night. Or maybe even a runaway. I've found a couple of kids right over there on the beach."

Nate doubted that any of Ian Ryker's associates would have invaded this room and sat around eating candy and drinking a cola. More than likely Cyn's assessment was correct, and the vagrant or runaway was probably long gone by now. But there was always the possibility... "Who knows, maybe Miss Carstairs's ghosts like Hershey bars."

Cyn smiled at him, thinking what a marvelous sense of humor he had. "Did Spanish conquistadors eat Hershey bars?"

At the word conquistador, Nate flinched. Cyn noticed his reaction. "What's wrong?" she asked.

"Nothing." It had been years since anyone had called him that, not since he'd left the SEALs. Conquistador had been a nickname given in fun that had eventually become a hated symbol of everything from which Nate wanted to escape. "And no, I doubt the Spanish conquerors brought along any candy. Why did you ask? Was one of Miss Carstairs's ghosts a Spaniard?"

Cyn reached down, pulling a dusty box out from underneath a dilapidated chair. "Mm-mm. There are two ghosts," Cyn told him. "A man and a woman. He's a Spanish conquistador and she's a Timucuan Indian maiden."

"And how did Miss Carstairs know who her ghosts were?" Nate watched as Cyn rummaged around in the box, pulling out musty, moldy books. Already, he didn't like the sound of this old tale. Although the comparisons between himself and the ancient warrior were minuscule, the word conquistador was an undeniable bond. But he knew better than to tell Cyn about it.

Cyn stacked the books on the floor. "There's a legend about the ghosts who roam Sweet Haven's beach. Miss Carstairs told me she heard the legend when she was a child."

"Exactly what is the legend?" Nate asked, surprised that he was truly interested. It was this damned room, he thought. It piqued his curiosity.

"The maiden's and the conquistador's spirits are doomed to—" Suddenly and without warning, Cyn knew she had to escape. The feelings overwhelmed her. There was danger here in these rooms, danger and passion and death. The legend that had been so much a part of her life since childhood had now taken on a sinister aspect that frightened her.

She stood up, reached out and took Nate's hand. "Let's go back outside. You're right about this room. Nothing but junk here."

The warmth of her hand where it touched his spread through him like wildfire. He clasped her hand tightly and followed her outside into the daylight, away from the shadows, away from the panic that had claimed her. He knew fear when he saw it. It had been a part of his life for too many years for him not to recognize the signs. Cyn was scared, but he couldn't understand why. Was there something about the legend that seemed more real to her when she'd been in the storage rooms?

Pulling on his hand, Cyn began to run. He ran beside her. For some reason, she'd felt oddly chilled when she'd begun to tell him about the legend. It was as if an icy breeze had caressed her body. If those coquina walls could speak, she knew they would tell a story of great love and heartbreaking tragedy.

It was as if something or someone had been warning her. The fear she'd felt inside those cold ancient rooms had not been for the two long-dead lovers, but for Nate—and for herself. Nate was in danger, from something or someone who had the power to destroy him. She couldn't explain how she knew. She just did.

She slowed down near the cypress in the yard. Resting her back against the tree, she took a refreshing breath of ocean air, then smiled at him. How could she tell him about her fears without sounding like a complete idiot? Maybe she was. Maybe she'd let her imagination run amok. After all, she had convinced herself that there was a similarity between Nate and the conquistador who had died on this beach, his lover beside him.

Nate gripped her shoulder, his strength gentle yet commanding. "What's wrong? What happened in there?"

She covered his hand with hers, slowly pulling it away from her body to hold it to her cheek. "I'm not sure. I've always been fascinated by the legend, but I've never...never really believed it. Not the prophecy part, anyway."

"The prophecy?"

"I guess it's the fact that you're a warrior—"

"A former warrior."

"I suppose I associate the violence in the legend with the violence in your life."

"Tell me the legend," he said, taking her face in his hands, framing her cheekbones with his thumbs.

"The legend tells of a beautiful Timucuan maiden, with hair to her knees and a smile that enticed many a man. But she loved only one. A big Spanish conquistador. They came here to the mission to be married. You see, she had deserted her family's heathen ways and had converted to Catholicism. The priest married them." Cyn stopped talking. She didn't want to start crying. The legend, as beautifully romantic as it was, did not arouse all the feelings of magic and hope and love that it once had. Reality changed things. For the first time, she began to truly wonder what it had been like for those ancient lovers. What fear had they known? By whose violent hand had they died? And why?

"I take it that they didn't live happily ever after." Nate stepped toward her, his body leaning forward, almost touching hers.

"No. They were found dead, murdered, the morning after their marriage. Their bodies lay, naked and entwined, on the beach. The beach in front of my cottage." Tears escaped her eyes, trickling down her face, moistening the strands of her hair that curled around her ears. She wasn't crying for the lost lovers, but for herself and for Nate. There was a special bond forming between them, a physical attraction that drew them to each other. But they were such different people, with such opposing views on life. How could she ever love a man who'd made his living killing others? Could she ever reconcile herself to wanting a man to whom violence came as naturally as breathing?

Nate moved his body against hers, lowering his head until his lips hovered over her open mouth. "Why do the ghosts haunt the beach?"

"The legend says that until another warrior and his maiden find eternal love on this beach and are united in a way the ancient lovers could never be, then the conquistador and his Timucuan maiden can never enter paradise." Cyn could feel his breath, hot and moist against her lips.

"The legend doesn't make any sense." he nipped at her bottom lip, then soothed it with the tip of his tongue. "Surely the Spaniard and his bride had a wedding night. If they made love, then they were united."

"Who knows," Cyn whispered, longing for his kiss.

"And who cares," Nate said. "It's just a legend, isn't it?"

He took her mouth then, thrusting his tongue inside, tasting her sweetness. He ran his hands up and down her back, then crushed her to him, wanting to devour her, seeking out every inch of her flesh, needing to be a part of her.

She whimpered, then flung her arms around his shoulders. He moved his lips along her neck, into the hollow of her throat. She cried out his name. She wanted this man, wanted him here and now.

He jerked away from her, stepping backward, looking at her flushed cheeks and swollen lips? God, what was he doing? What was he thinking? He'd let some stupid tale of ancient lovers spin crazy dreams in his mind. He'd gone to find Cyn in the hopes of persuading her to leave Sweet Haven, and instead he'd lost his head and tried to make love to her.

"Nate?" She looked at him with those rich brown eyes, her gaze questioning him.

"Dammit, Cyn, I'm sorry." He took a tentative step toward her, then stopped. "I want you…I want you badly."

"I…I want you, too," she said, finally admitting the truth to him and to herself.

"Look, I don't have anything to offer you but a brief affair—"

"What if I said, all right?" The words escaped her mouth before thoughts of agreement had even reached her brain. She couldn't allow her heart to answer for her. If she did, she would be lost.

"No, it's not all right. If we'd met a year ago, then maybe. But not now."

"Why not now?"

He grabbed her by the shoulders. "Anyone close to me is in danger. I can't explain. The less you know, the better."

"But, Nate—"

"I can't risk it."

She reached out, touching his cheek with the palm of her hand. "Some things are worth the risk." Dropping her hand, she turned and walked away.

Nate let her go.

CHAPTER 6

Cyn stood outside Tomorrow House inspecting the faded metal sign, thinking how the weathered condition of the sign epitomized the shelter's money problems. Oh, the sign could be easily redone, probably the cheapest repair job needed. The building was another matter. The church paid the rent on the one-story brick structure and provided the services of Bruce Tomlinson, but everything else was paid for by donations, and all the workers were strictly volunteers. Except Mimi. The sixty-year old woman, widowed eight years ago, had no other source of income.

No one, not even Mimi, knew that Cyn paid her salary, but all the volunteers did know that Cynthia Wellington Porter lived quite comfortably off a sizable trust fund set up by her paternal grandfather the day she'd been born.

Opening the front door, Cyn walked inside and was immediately bathed in bright sunlight. A few feet away, a small crowd of teens stood staring up at the ceiling. Cyn's eyes followed their line of vision. She gasped when she saw the large ragged hole in the plaster ceiling, the rafters exposed like the weathered gray skeletons of a decayed carcass. Circular water stains dotted the ceiling in several places all around the open gap.

"What happened?" Cyn asked as she neared the group of gawking kids.

"I think a bomb exploded in the attic," one freckle-faced boy said.

"Naw," a black girl said, laughing, "I think Reverend Tomlinson cut that hole so his prayers could get past the ceiling."

Cyn clamped her teeth together in an effort not to laugh. Bruce Tomlinson was a very nice man, and quite dedicated to his work, but his overly pious attitude did little to endear him to the kids he encountered at Tomorrow House.

A tall, robust woman with graying red hair stepped out of a room at the end of the hall. Wiping her hands on her large purple apron, she grinned when she saw Cyn.

"Welcome back," Mimi Burnside said, giving Cyn a bear hug. "I see you've noticed our skylight. Lets in the sunshine, the moonlight, the cool breeze, and if it rains, it'll let that in, too. Of course a real bonus is that it's created an extra entrance for insects."

"When did this happen?" Cyn asked as she started toward her office, Mimi following.

"Yesterday. Luckily, nobody was standing directly in the line of fire, but we had one heck of a mess to clean up." Mimi closed Cyn's office door behind them.

Cyn picked up a stack of mail from the edge of her green metal desk, an army surplus purchase. "That roof has needed repairs for the past three years, but we simply haven't had the money. Has Bruce called someone to come out and give us an estimate?"

"What do you think?" Mimi settled her hefty frame onto one of the three metal folding chairs lined up across the back wall in the office.

"Let me guess." Cyn grabbed the back of her swivel chair, pulling it away from the desk. "He expects me to take care of it this morning. And he also expects me to come up with the money."

"Right on both counts." Mimi cocked her head to one side and gave Cyn a long speculative look. "You seem to be back to your normal self, but I sense something's wrong, Cynthia Ellen Porter. Are you sure you're ready to come back to work?"

"I'm fine."

Mimi puckered her lips, squinted her hazel eyes and shook her head. "No, you're not."

"I haven't been sleeping much."

"If you've been worrying about Bobby, then I can set your mind to rest. He came back last night."

"Thank goodness."

"He told me about what happened at the Brazen Hussy. He was worried about you." Mimi crossed her arms over her ample bosom. "I assured him that you were fine."

Cyn felt her cheeks sting with the beginnings of a blush. No doubt Bobby had told Mimi about Nate Hodges. "I never should have gone to the Brazen Hussy."

"Who was he, this one-man army that rescued you?"

"Nathan Hodges, a former navy SEAL, and...and my new neighbor." Cyn knew she might as well be honest with Mimi, because sooner or later the woman would worm every detail out of her.

"New neighbor?"

"He bought Miss Carstairs's old house."

"Well, well." Mimi got up, rubbed her chin and walked to the door. "So a warrior has finally come to the old mission, to the haunted beach."

Cyn snapped her head around, her brown eyes focusing directly on Mimi's Cheshire cat grin. "I should never have told you about that legend."

"What's the matter? Something change your mind about how romantic that old legend is?"

"It was a beautiful story, tragically romantic...as long as it remained just an ancient legend. But now..."

"Now what?" Mimi asked, laughing. "Are you afraid you and your warrior are destined to fulfill the prophecy?"

"Sounds crazy, doesn't it?" Cyn had tried not to think about the parallel between the ancient lovers and Nate and herself. "Who's to say that Nate's the first warrior to come to the Sweet Haven beach? And I'm certainly no maiden."

"Nate, huh? Already on a first-name basis?" Mimi opened the door, hesitated momentarily, then turned around.

"We're so completely wrong for each other. His whole life is the total opposite of mine. For heaven's sake, Mimi, the man collects knives."

"If it's meant to be, there's nothing you or this Nate can do to stop it."

"We're never going to see each other again." Cyn raised her voice, wanting to make sure Mimi heard her, hoping her adamant tone would convince the other woman of her sincerity.

Mimi didn't turn around or acknowledge Cyn's remark in any way. *Dammit,* Cyn thought. *That's all I need, Mimi Burnside trying to pair me off with a man determined to keep me out of his life, a man who, by his own admission, isn't even interested in a brief affair.*

Nate heard the noise again. There was something in the storeroom, something making a whimpering sound. Could it be an injured animal that had taken shelter? Even though the door was closed, it was possible that a stray cat or dog could have crawled in through one of the partially boarded windows.

Nate opened the door and stepped inside, moving cautiously, just in case the animal might attack. It took a few minutes for his eyes to focus in the semidarkness. Glancing around, he noticed nothing changed from the day before, but then he heard the sound again. God, whatever it was, it sounded almost human.

Suddenly, a small dark shadow in the far corner moved. Nate took several tentative steps toward the movement. Without warning, a skinny kid hurled herself from behind a tall chest and, running past Nate, made a mad dash for the door.

"What the—" Turning quickly, Nate reached out, grabbing the little hooligan by the neck.

The child let out a frightened scream and began struggling. Thrashing arms and legs pelted Nate as he dragged the scrappy kid outside.

"I'm not going to hurt you," he said. "Stop your squirming!"

"Please…" Gradually, the child ceased struggling.

Nate took a good look at the intruder. Damn, it was a brown-eyed little girl with dirty, stringy black hair. Had this child been hiding in his storage rooms, eating candy and drinking cola? Probably. But that would hardly explain the cigarette butt.

"Hey, honey, it's all right." The child broke into tears. Nate released her, but kept a restraining hand on her back.

"I...I didn't do nothing wrong." She gulped and looked up at him, fear in her eyes.

That's when Nate noticed the fresh purple bruises on the side of her pretty face. His gaze traveled the length of the child's scrawny body, noting that her shorts and blouse were faded and dirty and that a line of fading bruises covered her left arm and the backs of both legs. Nausea rose in Nate's throat. If he could get his hands on the person who'd beaten this child, he would make sure that animal never touched her again.

"What's your name?" he asked.

She looked at him, her eyes wide and wild with fright. "Just let me go, okay? I didn't know somebody lived here."

"Did your mother or father do this to you?" Nate asked, pointing to her battered face.

"I won't go back. You can't make me," she screamed and started to balk.

Nate placed a restraining hand at her waist, then cursed himself when she cried out in pain. Dear God, he needed to get this child to the hospital. "Look, honey, I think we need to get you to a doctor."

"No!"

"You're hurt."

"It ain't so bad. I don't want no doctor, no police. They'll make me go back, and I'd rather die than go back." She curled up, dropping to her knees, her whole body trembling.

"No doctor. No police," Nate assured her. "I know a lady who helps kids like you. She works at a place called Tomorrow House in Jacksonville."

"She'll call the police."

"No. She'll help you. Give you a place to stay, some food and a doctor who won't report you to the police." Nate picked the child up in his arms. She trembled as if she were in the throes of a seizure.

This abused little girl needed help, and he intended to see that she got it. He also intended to make sure he got her away from Sweet Haven, away from him, as quickly as possible. She couldn't come back. If she did, she, too, would be in danger from Ryker. If the cigarette butt had been left by one of Ryker's cronies, then it was a miracle the child hadn't already been faced with the unspeakable. Dear God, what if she had? What if the bruises...? No, Ryker's type didn't just abuse, they killed. The Marquez family and Ramon Carranza were people who left behind no witnesses.

Nate headed toward Cyn's cottage, got halfway across the road, then remembered that she'd told him she was returning to work today. Making a hasty turn, he carried the little girl into his house. He eased her fragile body down on the sofa in his den.

"I promise that no one will hurt you. My friend is a nice lady. She'll take care of you."

Damn, this was one more complication he didn't need in his life. He was fast reaching the breaking point. And that's exactly what Ryker wanted. No doubt his old enemy was delaying the inevitable because he was enjoying the game, savoring each new torment, loving the idea of making Nate wait and watch and agonize.

Nate dug a ragged phone book from the desk drawer and searched through the tattered pages until he found the listing for Tomorrow House. Dialing the number, he watched the child, who had curled into a fetal position, her arms crossed over her chest.

"I need to speak to Cynthia Porter," he said. "And hurry, it's an emergency."

Nate had tried talking to the child on the drive from Sweet Haven to Jacksonville, but he'd finally given up when he realized she wasn't going to reply. She sat, huddled on the front seat of his Jeep, her eyes red and puffy, the bruises on her face vividly apparent in the bright Florida sun.

She couldn't possibly know how well he related to her, how completely he understood her withdrawal. How many times had he run from his abusive Uncle Collum? How many times had the police returned him to that vicious man's clutches?

God, how he wished there had been a Tomorrow House in his past, and a caring, giving woman like Cyn Porter. But there had been neither. No one had given a damn about a wild and rebellious boy. No one had wanted him, least of all his mother's older half brother. No one, except Uncle Sam. The U.S. Navy had wanted him, and they'd had him, body and soul, for twenty years. He'd given the SEALs the dedication and loyalty many men gave their families. The navy had been his salvation as surely as it had been his damnation.

The only decent thing Collum Hodges ever did for his nephew was sign the enlistment papers allowing him to join the navy at seventeen. He'd never forget his uncle's parting words.

"Maybe they'll ship your worthless butt off to Nam and let those gooks use you for target practice. God knows, you're no good for anything else."

Nate had never fully understood his uncle or the man's unrelenting hatred. Collum Hodges had been a bigoted, embittered man, and an ambitious one. His sister's illegitimate child had been a social embarrassment to him, and the fact that the boy quite obviously had Hispanic blood in him outraged Collum, whose conservative Anglo friends were less than accepting of Grace's mix-breed child.

Gripping the steering wheel tightly, Nate pulled his Jeep into the only empty parking space available, a half block down from Tomorrow House. He got out, walked around the car, opened the door and lifted his passenger up and into his arms.

Cyn stood in the open doorway, watching Nate walk up the sidewalk. He carried a small, unmoving child. When he'd told her that the little girl needed to see a doctor, Cyn had placed a call to her friend, Callie Reynolds, who did a great deal of volunteer work for the shelter. Callie, a successful St. Augustine pediatrician, promised to drive up on her lunch break.

Nate took the steps up to Tomorrow House's entrance two at a time. "Have you gotten in touch with a doctor?" he asked.

"One will be here around twelve-thirty." Cyn winced when she noticed the purple bruises on the child's face. Even though she'd seen this sort of thing more times than she cared to remember, she hadn't hardened herself to the reality that there were people in this world capable of brutalizing children. "Bring her on inside. Mimi has fixed her something to eat."

Nate followed Cyn down the hallway and into the kitchen. A big redheaded woman, busy stirring some delicious-smelling concoction in an enormous kettle atop an old stove, turned and smiled at him. He nodded an acknowledgment, then set the little girl down at the table.

The child stared at the bowl of cereal and the glasses of milk and orange juice, then looked up at Cyn with questioning eyes. "He said you wouldn't make me go back. You won't, will you?"

Cyn clutched the top of the chair opposite the one in which the child sat. "No one is going to make you do anything. All we want to do here at Tomorrow House is help you. Would you tell me your name?"

The little girl shook her head. "Can I still have the food, even if I don't tell you my name?"

With tears trapped in her throat, Cyn couldn't respond immediately. She glanced over at Mimi.

"You eat up, honey child," Mimi said. "And if you're still hungry, it won't be long until lunch. I'm working on some good old chicken stew."

The child picked up her spoon, dug into the cereal and ate as if she were starving. After finishing the last bite, she gulped down the orange juice.

"Mimi, would you let our young visitor keep you company here in the kitchen while I give Nate a tour of Tomorrow House?" Cyn asked.

"You ain't calling the police, are you?" The little girl jumped up, her eyes wide with fear.

"No," Nate told her. "Stay here and help Miss Mimi with lunch and I'll come say goodbye before I leave."

"I'll see if Bobby wants to come give me a hand, too," Mimi said. "That boy's good at helping."

"Who's Bobby?" the little girl asked.

Cyn and Nate left the kitchen. He followed her into the hallway. Children of various ages, sexes and races moved freely around the building, some passing Cyn and Nate in the hall, others busy watching television, playing Nintendo and shooting pool, as well as sweeping, mopping and dusting.

"You said on the phone that you found her in the old mission." Cyn nodded to several smiling youngsters.

"The storage room," Nate said. "And yeah, she's probably the one who left the cola can and candy bar that we found yesterday."

"How about the cigarette butt?"

"Possibly. But I doubt it." He knew the chances were good that the cigarette butt had been left by one of Ryker's friends, but there was no point in trying to explain that to Cyn. "What can you do for the kid? She doesn't look a day over eight or nine." Nate glanced around at the boy who stood in an open doorway across the hall. Recognizing him, Nate nodded. Bobby slipped back into the game room, silently disappearing.

"He came back last night." Cyn nodded toward where the boy had been standing. "More than likely, he's afraid of you after seeing your macho demonstration at the Brazen Hussy." She reached out, placing her hand on Nate's arm. "Why don't we go into my office and I'll tell you what our options are as far as your little waif is concerned."

The moment she touched him, he wanted to drag her out of this place and back to the beach. He wanted to be alone with her, to explore where that one simple touch could lead.

He followed her the few yards to her office, but just as they started in, a short, stocky man, wearing a suit and tie, approached them.

"Hello, Cyn. I'm sorry I wasn't here to greet you on your return this morning, but I had a breakfast appointment with the Reverend Lockwood," Bruce Tomlinson said, placing his hand on Cyn's shoulder.

The moment the other man touched her, Nate wanted to knock his pale, immaculately clean hand off her. He wanted to issue a warning. But he didn't. Instead, he glared at the man.

"Bruce, I'd like you to meet Nate Hodges. He found a badly beaten little girl this morning and brought her to us." Cyn squeezed Nate's arm, smiling at him.

"Unfortunate. Unfortunate." Bruce made a tsk-tsk sound with his tongue against his teeth and shook his head.

"Nate, this is Tomorrow House's director, Reverend Bruce Tomlinson." Cyn wasn't surprised at the tension she felt as she introduced the two men. It was only natural that two such opposite extremes of the male species would be wary of each other. The gentle, weak, condescending Bruce and the fierce, strong, proud Nate.

Bruce, ever the gentleman, held out his hand. Nate merely nodded, completely ignoring the other man's cordial gesture. "Mr. Hodges, I wonder if you'd mind giving me a few minutes alone with Mrs. Porter. I have an urgent business matter to discuss with her."

Beneath her hand, she felt Nate's arm tense. She couldn't take a chance on what response he might make. "Bruce, if you want to ask me if I've done anything about the ceiling, then I can tell you that a roofer will be here tomorrow." Cyn pointed toward the hole in the ceiling near the front entrance.

Nate's gaze wandered over the gaping hollow. "What happened?"

"An old roof, rotting wood and too much rain this past winter," Cyn said. "We've needed a new roof for years, but just couldn't afford one."

"Then how are we going to pay a roofer now?" Bruce asked. "We don't even have enough money to pay this month's bills. Reverend Lockwood is very concerned. He says that it's a real possibility that the church will have to close us down."

"They've been saying that for the last six months," Cyn reminded him. "Look, Bruce, I'll find a way to cover the cost of roof repair, even if I have to pay for it myself."

"Oh, my dear girl, we couldn't allow it. You do too much already. Working here without a salary, donating everything for the game room—"

"Hush, Bruce! Go...go do some paperwork, and quit worrying so much. Everything will work out. Remember, the Lord helps those who help themselves. And I have every intention of finding a way to help us."

"Very well." Bruce gave Nate a cold, silent look. "Goodbye, Mr. Hodges." Then he walked away.

"Prissy little guy," Nate said, laughing. "I don't think he likes me."

"Probably not. Did you like him?" Cyn pulled on Nate's arm. "Let's go in my office so none of the kids will overhear more than they already have."

Nate followed her into the surprisingly pleasant room. All the furniture was old, the metal desk, file cabinets and chairs were an army green. The walls had been painted a lighter shade of green, a very soothing hue. Open blinds covered the long narrow windows facing the street.

"Have a seat." Cyn pointed to one of the metal chairs.

Nate sat down, never once taking his eyes off Cyn. "How can you afford to work here without pay and to donate equipment for a game room?"

Cyn seated herself behind her desk. Not knowing how he'd take the news that she was independently wealthy, she hesitated. "Well, I—"

"Your husband leave you a bundle?" Nate asked. "What were you two doing with this place, playing social workers?"

Cyn straightened in her chair, took a calming breath and placed her clasped hands on top of her desk. "My husband wasn't wealthy. He was a dedicated man of God, a man who gave all his time and love to Tomorrow House."

"That must have been difficult for you, being the wife of a man who put you second in his life." Nate watched as her face paled, and knew he had struck a nerve.

Damn him! Cyn thought. But as much as she wanted to lash out at him and deny his accusations, she couldn't deny the truth. She decided it was best to make no comment on her marriage to Evan. "I was born into a wealthy family. My father is Senator Denton Wellington of Georgia. My mother was a St. Augustine Phillips. My grandfather provided me with a substantial trust fund."

"La-di-da." He should have known. A woman didn't have the poise and strength and self-assurance Cyn Porter possessed without having had it bred into her. She had the kind of classy looks and dominating personality that only comes from having been raised with money. "Did your rich parents give you your nickname?"

"I beg your pardon?" Cyn glared at him.

"Oh, it's a cute nickname, but I just wondered if your family thought it suitable for someone so…so pure and sweet and virtuous. I mean, how many ministers' wives do you think are called Cyn? And how many work at a church shelter?"

"For your information, my younger brother gave me the nickname when he was only three and couldn't pronounce Cynthia. My rich parents thought the name was adorable. And my minister husband found it a constant source of amusement. Evan had a wonderful sense of humor."

"I imagine Evan was just about perfect in every way."

"I think we should confine our discussion to the little girl you brought here. Otherwise we're liable to exchange blows…verbal blows." Cyn leaned back in her chair, praying that her voice sounded more composed than she felt. She had no intention of discussing Evan with this man. She would not allow him to force her to admit that her marriage had been less than perfect, that often she had longed for a husband as dedicated to her as he'd been to his work— that she had needed a man with whom she could share life's burdens and not try to shoulder them all by herself.

"I'm listening." Nate decided right then and there that the sooner he could get the hell away from Cyn and her blasted shelter full of emotionally starved kids, the better off he'd be. He didn't need to care about this woman or her damned bunch of hooligans. So what if his body craved her the way an alcoholic craves liquor. So what if he felt the deepest empathy for these kids because he'd once been one of them.

"A friend of mine, Dr. Reynolds, will check the child and see if she needs medical treatment. I can offer her a place to stay, get our volunteer psychologist to talk to her, try to persuade her to let us locate her parents."

"No police, remember," Nate said. "She'll run like hell if you push her too hard."

"I know. Believe me, we'll do all that we can to help her, but in the end, we can only do so much."

"Yeah." He stood up, walked to the door, then turned and faced her. "How much longer are you going to be staying at your family's cottage?"

"Eager to get rid of your only neighbor?" she asked.

"Look, Cyn, this thing between us can't go any further." He grasped the doorknob in his big hand.

"Exactly what is between us?" She stood up, meeting his stare head-on.

"Cut the act, lady. We want each other. Badly." He noted that her cheeks were turning pink. "Now isn't the right time for me. I've never had anyone special, never wanted or needed anyone, and I sure as hell don't want to get involved with you, especially not now."

"Why not now?" she asked, then averted her gaze from his perusal, glancing down at the wooden floor.

"Like I've told you, I'm a dangerous man," he said, wishing that he didn't have to frighten her away. "And I have dangerous friends."

"You're not a criminal, are you?" she blurted out before thinking how the question would sound.

"No, Brown Eyes, believe it or not, I've always considered myself one of the good guys."

Cyn walked around the desk, moving quickly toward Nate. Just as he opened the door, she placed her hand on his arm. His muscles hardened under her touch. "Nate?"

"Look, honey, if you're so hungry to get laid, why don't you ask Bruce? I'm sure he'd be delighted. Me, I don't have time to play house." He saw the startled expression on her face change to one of hurt, and he hated himself for having to say something so totally demeaning to her. But he had to make her stay away from him.

She dropped her hand from his arm and stood staring at him, willing herself not to cry as he turned and walked away. Suddenly tears gathered in her eyes. With the tips of her fingers, she swatted at them as if they were pesky flies.

While Cyn was trying to curb her tears and make some sense out of Nate's brutally insulting statement, she heard footsteps. Turning, she saw Nate's little ragamuffin coming toward her.

"Did he hurt you?" the child asked.

"Who, honey? What are you talking about?"

"That man. Nate. Did he hurt you? You're crying." The child walked over to Cyn, looking up at her with sympathy in her eyes.

"Oh, no, honey, he didn't hurt me." Cyn dropped to her knees, longing to reach out, take the child in her arms and offer her comfort.

"But you're crying." She reached out and wiped away a tear from Cyn's eye.

"We had a little disagreement, and he said something that hurt my feelings. That's all." That wasn't all, Cyn thought. Nate Hodges had been deliberately cruel. He'd wanted to make sure she left him alone. His ploy had been so obvious, she'd have to be an utter fool to think he'd meant what he'd said. Something bad was going on in Nate's life, something so horrible that he didn't want Cyn involved. Didn't he realize that she was already involved, whether she wanted to be or not? Didn't he have sense enough to know that neither of them had any control over the way they felt?

The little girl stroked Cyn's cheek. "My name is Aleta."

Cyn smiled, reached out and gave Aleta a gentle hug. The child hugged her back. "Well, Aleta, how about lunch? I think I smell Mimi's apple cobbler."

She took Aleta's hand, led her toward the dining hall, then sat down beside her. Within a few minutes the room filled with children from the smallest eight-year-old to the biggest eighteen-year-old. Bruce joined them, said a prayer, then retreated to his office to eat lunch alone. Cyn knew that if Nate had stayed, he would have shared lunch with the kids.

Oh, Nathan Hodges, if you think you've seen the last of me, then you'd better think again. On some instinctive level, Cyn realized that no matter how hard she and Nate might fight the attraction they felt for each other, neither of them could control it.

CHAPTER 7

Cyn sat at her desk, absentmindedly rubbing a pencil back and forth between her hands. Three days after returning to work half days, here she was still at Tomorrow House at three-thirty in the afternoon. Although there was more work to do than time to accomplish it all, she should have been out of here by noon, but she hadn't been able to concentrate all morning. Indeed, she'd had difficulty keeping her mind on her job since her last unpleasant confrontation with Nate.

Mimi had offered a motherly shoulder to cry on, but even talking to Mimi hadn't solved her problem. She'd gone and fallen in love with a man totally unsuitable for her, a man who epitomized the one element she despised most in this world—violence. If she knew what was good for her, she would listen to Nate's warnings to stay away from him.

How had she allowed something like this to happen? She wasn't the type to do stupid, irresponsible things like falling in love with a man she barely knew. Of course, she had to admit that she had always been susceptible to romantic fantasies—a real sucker for legends and myths and fairy tales. But, dear Lord in heaven, Nate Hodges was hardly a romantic hero. Far from it. He was no Sir Lancelot. No Romeo. And certainly no Cary Grant, Robert Redford or Kevin Costner. He was more the Genghis Khan-Jesse James type. A man like the bad-guy heroes so often portrayed by Humphrey Bogart, Clint Eastwood and Charles Bronson.

Damn! Stop thinking about him. Cyn threw the pencil down on her desk, scooted back her chair and stood up. Gazing outside, she watched as people scurried along the sidewalks and the beginnings of afternoon work traffic clogged the street. Momentarily closing her eyes, she listened to the soft, constant drizzle that dampened the cool April day.

Soon the view outside blurred as Cyn's mind focused on her memories of Nate Hodges, of the sight of him running along the beach. Every day for the past three days, she'd stood on her patio and watched him, waiting and hoping he would stop and talk to her. Once, on the first day, she had run out to him, calling his name. He'd stopped briefly, given her a hard look, and left her standing on the beach, feeling like an utter fool.

If he didn't want her, then why was she so certain that he did? She knew that Nate needed her, more than anyone had ever needed her. Why wouldn't he let her love him?

Don't do this to yourself. Concentrate on Tomorrow House, on the kids who so desperately need you. Think about Bobby and Aleta and the dozens of others who depend on you.

She wasn't sure what would become of Bobby. Since his return to Tomorrow House, he'd spent only one night, the other two he'd spent on the streets, doing God only knew what with boys like Casey. She'd tried everything she knew. Nothing worked. He was a good kid in a bad situation.

Aleta. Poor little Aleta. She was twelve years old, but didn't look it. She was a small, frail child, a little girl afraid of everything and everyone. After Callie had examined Aleta and assured Cyn that there was no permanent damage and her outward wounds would heal in a few days, Cyn's relief was short-lived. What on earth was she going to do with Aleta? If she called the police, Aleta would only run away again, so great was her fear of being returned to her abusive mother, a woman, Aleta had confided in Cyn, who stayed drunk almost all the time.

Tomorrow House was only a temporary solution to the ever-growing problem of runaway children. The institution had been founded to provide temporary food, shelter and assistance to the boys and girls who had no other place to go, no other safe haven, no other sanctuary from the horrid existence found on the streets.

A slight knock sounded on her door seconds before Bruce Tomlinson entered, a forlorn expression on his round face.

"I need to speak to you," he said. "I'm afraid the news isn't good."

"Then sit down, Bruce, and tell me what's wrong." Cyn motioned toward one of the folding chairs.

"No, no. Sit down if you'd like, but I'd rather stand." He moved nervously around the room, wringing his hands together as his round head bobbed up and down. "Cyn, I just got off the phone with Reverend Lockwood. The council met this morning and...and, well, things don't look good for Tomorrow House."

She knew what he was going to say, had known it was inevitable and had been dreading this day. "How bad is it?"

"Church funds are limited. They can't give us an increase of any kind this year. If...if we can't raise enough to cover the deficit, then the church will close Tomorrow House." Beads of perspiration dotted his pink forehead.

"How long?"

"If we can't raise enough to cover expenses for the next six months, the church will officially close Tomorrow House at the end of May." Bruce shook his head. "It's a terrible shame, Cyn. I know how much this place means to you, how much work and love you and Evan put into it."

Cyn leaned back against her desk, resting her hip on the edge. "Evan and I came here as newlyweds. Tomorrow House had just opened. Evan was the very first director."

Bruce came over and put a comforting arm around Cyn's shoulders. "Do you want to tell Mimi and the volunteers, or do you want me to? And what about the kids?"

She straightened her shoulders, tilted up her chin and gave Bruce a defiant look. "I'll explain the situation to Mimi and the others, but I don't want one word of this getting back to the kids. I'm not going to let the church close us down. I've invested ten years of my life in this shelter."

"But how on earth do you think you can raise that kind of

money in a little over a month?" Bruce gave her a quick hug, then released her.

Cyn moved around her desk, sat down and began rummaging through the bottom drawer. "More donations. We've got some millionaires who've contributed big money to this place. I'll just make a few phone calls and see if they don't want to be even more generous."

"Cyn, I think you're kidding yourself."

"Why don't you go on and do whatever it is you do this time of day," Cyn said. "And leave this problem to me. I promise you that Tomorrow House is not going to close its doors at the end of May or the end of this year or any other year."

"Very well." Bruce walked to the door. "If there's anything I can do to help, you'll let me know?"

"Of course." Wimp! Cyn thought, then chastised herself for expecting more from Bruce than he was capable of giving. How often in the past four years had she wished that Bruce Tomlinson was half the man Evan Porter had been? If Evan was here, he'd be fighting the church's callous decision. Evan would have found a way to keep Tomorrow House open. But Evan wasn't here, so it was up to her to keep his dream alive.

"What's the matter with Brucie?" Mimi Burnside asked as she walked into the office carrying a tray, which she placed on Cyn's desk. "Expecting you to come up with the solutions to all our problems here at Tomorrow House?"

Cyn retrieved a thin manila folder from the bottom drawer, slammed the drawer shut and sat up in her chair, clutching the folder in her right hand. "Close the door, will you, Mimi?"

The big redhead walked over, closed the door, then pulled a folding chair up to the desk. "This is serious, isn't it? Mary Alice told me Bruce had been on the phone with Reverend Lockwood. Money problems again, huh?"

"Unless we can come up with enough money to cover the next six months' expenses, the church plans to close Tomorrow House at the end of May." Cyn laid the folder down on her desk. "I've got to come up with some pretty hefty donations. And soon."

"I've seen this coming." Mimi handed Cyn a cup from the tray. "Here, drink some tea and we'll talk. And eat that sandwich. You didn't even take time out to have lunch today, and that's not like you. You usually have a healthy appetite."

"Too healthy." Cyn accepted the cup of tea. "I've had a lot on my mind today. Besides, I've been raiding the refrigerator too much at night lately."

"Well, it must be bad, whatever it is, to make you turn to food. Dare I tell you what I think you should do?"

"What are you babbling about?" Cyn sipped the tea, enjoying the warm sweet taste.

"That man, that Nate Hodges, he's got you running around in circles, honey child. And I say, if you want him, then go get him."

"Oh, for heaven's sake, Mimi, that man is a total barbarian. He's…he's in some kind of terrible trouble. All he wants is for me to stay away from him, and, believe me, that's just what I intend to do." Cyn knew she had lied to Mimi, but she couldn't lie to herself. If Nate Hodges called her this very minute, she would go to him.

"Easier said than done. 'Cause I think this thing is bigger than the both of you. I think it's completely out of your hands." Mimi picked up her cup of tea and took a healthy swallow.

"You're being ridiculous."

"Am I? Look, honey child, I've lived a lot of years and known my share of men. Lust and love are two things folks just don't have no control over."

Cyn crinkled up her nose as if she'd suddenly smelled something unpleasant. "He isn't the sort of man I could build a future with. He's too…too—"

"Too much of a man?" Mimi asked. "Not the sweet, gentle, turn-the-other-cheek type you're so used to. But my guess is that when a man like Nate Hodges loves a woman, she's the most important thing in his life."

Groaning, Cyn cast her gaze heavenward. "Why did I ever trust you with so many of my deepest, darkest secrets? I should have known you'd use them against me when I was at my weakest.

You're the only person I ever told about my jealousy of Evan's dedication to Tomorrow House."

Mimi took another hearty sip of tea, then set her cup down on the tray. "Because, like you, I'm the mother-to-the-world type. Even strangers tell us their problems. Besides, we're friends who can trust each other. There's nothing wrong with a woman wanting to come first in her man's life. We all need to be loved."

"Even Nate?" Cyn asked, clutching her cup in both hands.

"That man definitely needs you, honey child."

"He thinks he doesn't need anyone. He's so strong, so capable of taking care of himself. Maybe he doesn't need me. Besides, it doesn't matter. We're all wrong for each other. He's nothing like Evan."

"I like him," Mimi said. "He's more man than Evan ever was. Just the kind of man a strong, caring woman like you needs. I'd say you two are perfect for each other."

"Mimi—"

"He's gone wanting for a long time. It shows in his eyes. He's like the kids that come here. Ain't nobody ever loved him the way he needs to be loved. And you, Cynthia Ellen Porter, have got the kind of heart that could heal that man's soul."

Cyn didn't like the thoughts that Mimi's words created in her mind. The legend said that someday a warrior in need of peace would come to the beach, to the old mission, and would find solace in the arms of a woman, the only woman on earth capable of giving his heart and soul sanctuary.

"I want to change the subject. I don't have time to try to figure out why Nate and I met now, when he's involved in something he won't talk about and I've got Evan's dream to save."

Puckering her lips into a frown, Mimi grunted. "What can I do to help?"

"Just keep being my friend. Keep putting up with me." Cyn tapped her slender fingers on the manila folder.

"What have you got there?" Mimi asked.

"A list of all our contributors." Cyn opened the file folder. "I plan to see each one of our major contributors and ask for...no...beg them for another donation."

"I suppose you plan to hit your father up first thing?"

"I know I can count on Daddy." Cyn lifted the list from the folder and scanned the pages quickly, reading out the names of the people who'd donated over a thousand dollars.

Cyn's eyes focused on one name. She didn't remember ever meeting the man, but she knew that for the past five years he had been Tomorrow House's largest contributor. "This is who I'll contact first. He's donated ten thousand dollars every year for the past five years."

"Who in the world has that kind of money to give away?"

"Ramon Carranza. I'm going to call and try to set up an appointment with him."

"I've heard of that guy," Mimi said, thumping her cheek with her index finger. "My friend Georgia, who lives in my apartment building, has a nephew who works for this Carranza. Waylon is the gardener, and he told Georgia that his boss was a very wealthy man. Got money invested in just about everything, and he's involved in a casino out in Vegas and another in Atlantic City. And the dog tracks."

"He's probably a millionaire and needs the tax write-off large donations can provide for him."

"Rumors are that he was once a very big man in Miami, back when the Cubans ran things, before the Colombians took over."

"My goodness, Mimi, you sound like an expert on Florida crime," Cyn said.

"Naw, I'm just an old woman who likes to gossip. People like this Carranza guy make for interesting conversation."

"Well, at this point I'm willing to give Ramon Carranza the benefit of the doubt. No one knows for sure how he made his money. We don't really know that he's a crime boss, do we? And in a way it's only fitting that bad money should do some good."

"My guess is the old man is trying to soothe his conscience before he dies. Probably thinks he can buy his way into heaven."

"He's an old man?" Cyn asked. "How old?"

"Nearly eighty. Waylon told Georgia that he ain't got nobody. No children, and his wife died years ago."

"He lives alone?"

"Except for the servants and his bodyguard," Mimi said.

"Bodyguard?"

"Well, he is very rich."

"I suppose you're right. I just hope I can persuade him to share those riches with us."

When she exited Interstate 1 directly behind the big black limousine, Cyn wondered who would be visiting Sweet Haven in such opulent style. Her curiosity peaked when she noted that the limo turned off onto the beachfront road. As she followed the huge, slow-moving Caddy, Cyn's puzzlement increased when the vehicle passed her cottage and pulled up in front of Nate's house.

Cyn parked in her drive and got out, balancing the paper grocery bag on one hip and her briefcase and purse on the other. She couldn't help but stare across the road at the enormous man getting out of the driver's side of the limo. She didn't think she'd seen such a mountain of a man except on TV wrestling. The stranger wasn't wearing a chauffeur uniform however, but a tailored, dove-gray, three-piece suit. Even at this distance, she could make out the man's strong Hispanic features.

Stepping up on the front porch, she readjusted the grocery bag, then inserted her door key in the lock. As soon as she heard the opening click, she glanced again across the road. The gargantuan man stood at Nate's front door. Who on earth was he? And why had he come to see Nate? Could this man possibly be the dangerous enemy of whom Nate had spoken?

Giving the door a push with her hip, Cyn stepped inside, dropping her purse, key ring and briefcase on the nearest chair. Clutching the paper bag in her hand, she started toward the kitchen, stopped dead still, turned around and walked back to the open door. Peering outside, she took one more look across the street.

Nate stood on his porch talking to the big stranger. She was too far away to hear even the sound of their voices, and she couldn't make out the expression on either man's face. Suddenly, Nate shoved his front door open and waited until his guest entered before returning inside.

Cyn slammed the door and made her way to the kitchen. She placed the paper bag on the table and rummaged through it, removing the perishable items first. All the while she put away her groceries, Cyn kept thinking about Nate's visitor.

Enough already! she told herself. *You've got better things to do than worry about your unfriendly neighbor.* And unfriendly was exactly what Nate had been the last three days.

After a light supper of tuna salad, Cyn poured herself another glass of iced tea, put on a Patti Page tape and settled down on the over-stuffed chintz sofa in the living room. Picking up the manila folder, she pulled out the contributors list, her gaze immediately focusing on the name she'd circled in red. Memorizing the number, Cyn dialed her portable phone.

A female voice answered. "Ramon Carranza's residence. May I help you?"

"Yes, this is Cynthia Porter. I'd like to speak to Mr. Carranza about Tomorrow House in Jacksonville."

"Very well, Ms. Porter. Please hold."

Cyn gave a silent prayer of thanks that she'd had no trouble getting through to Ramon Carranza. She waited and waited and waited. Finally she began tapping her fingers on the sofa's armrest, patting her foot to the gentle rhythm of the music and even humming along with the tune.

"Hello, Señora Porter. This is Ramon Carranza. How may I help you?" The voice was strong and deep and only slightly accented.

"Mr. Carranza," Cyn said, her own voice breathless. "I'm the assistant director at Tomorrow House in Jacksonville."

"I'm very familiar with Tomorrow House. I wholly support your efforts to help young runaways."

"That's wonderful, Mr. Carranza, and we're extremely grateful for your generous yearly donations." Take it slow and easy, she cautioned herself. Just use your feminine charm and don't push so hard.

"But surely you are calling for more than to thank me." The tone of his voice had grown lighter, less formal.

"As a matter of fact, I am. You see, if we can't raise a substantial amount of money before the end of May, the church plans to close us down, and I simply can't let that happen. I know it's presumptuous of me to be pleading with someone who's already been more than generous—"

"Señora Porter, I would like to invite you to have brunch with me tomorrow, here at my home. I would be delighted if you can find the time to accept my offer."

"Delighted...lunch...tomorrow...at your home?" God, she knew she was babbling, but his invitation had been so unexpected, so totally out of the blue.

"May I take that as a yes?" he asked, amusement clearly in his voice.

"You most certainly may," Cyn said. "What time?"

"Shall we say around ten-thirty?"

"Ten-thirty would be fine."

"Will you need the services of my chauffeur?"

"No, thank you." For a split second her mind wandered to the limo parked across the road. Did Ramon Carranza's chauffeur drive a big, black Caddy, too? "I'll drive myself. And...thank you for agreeing to see me."

"It would be no problem for my chauffeur to come for you. Just give me your address."

"I'm staying at my family's beach house in Sweet Haven right now, Señor Carranza. It's on the other side of nowhere. The only two cottages out here are mine and Nate Hodges's across the road."

"Living in such isolation, I hope your neighbor...this Señor Hodges...is a man you can count on for assistance?"

Clearly his comment was a question, and Cyn found his fatherly concern endearing. "Oh, believe me, Nate is definitely a man I could turn to if I were in trouble."

"Nate? Then he is a friend of long acquaintance, yes?"

"Actually, no. We only met recently. He just moved into the house across the road a few months ago."

"It is always good to make new friends."

"Yes," Cyn said with a sigh, thinking how she would hardly describe her relationship with Nate as friendship. "It was kind of you to offer to send your chauffeur for me, but it will be easier all around for me to just drive myself."

"Very well, then. I'll be looking forward to meeting you, Señora Porter."

"Yes. Thank you, thank you so much." Cyn punched the off button on the telephone, held it up against her cheek and smiled. She had a lunch date with a man who could solve all of the shelter's problems. Somehow, some way, she was going to make a good impression on Ramon Carranza and sweet-talk him into becoming Tomorrow House's savior.

Now, if she could only figure out a way to solve her other problem, she thought as the tossed the phone onto the sofa and got up to walk over to the front windows. The limo was still parked at Nate's house. Dammit, why had that infuriating man come into her life? Even if he were willing for them to explore their feelings for each other, he'd made it perfectly clear that he wasn't interested in a permanent relationship with a woman. Well, if she could charm thousands of dollars from a man rumored to be a former Miami crime boss, then who was to say she couldn't teach a hardened warrior how to love?

Nate stood in the middle of his den eyeing the man standing directly across from him. Hell, he hadn't seen a man that big since Sonny Rorie, a survival instructor from his days at Coronado, that do-or-die time when he'd been a SEAL recruit.

"You said you had news of Ryker?" Nate asked, wondering just who the hell this guy was, one of Ryker's front men or some agent he didn't know. From the looks of him, Nate's first guess would have been a sumo wrestler.

"I do," the man said, his voice laced with a slight Spanish accent.

"Who are you?"

"Emilio Rivera."

Nate widened his almond-shaped eyes, a questioning frown wrinkling his smooth forehead. So, he thought, this is Ramon Carranza's bodyguard. "Where did you get your information?"

"My employer has his sources," Emilio said.

"And just who is your boss?" Nate asked.

"I am sure that your friend, Señor Romero, has already informed you of my employer's identity."

"Maybe you should inform me."

"Very well. Ramon Carranza has sent me to tell you that your enemy, Ian Ryker, has left Miami and is en route to St. Augustine."

"I've been expecting him, so this really isn't such urgent news." Nate noticed the big man flinch, his jaw tighten.

"Ryker already knows your exact location. We estimate that in approximately three days, he will make his move on you."

"Just what is Carranza's stake in all this? And why the hell should I believe anything you tell me?" Nate didn't like puzzles, especially not ones that involved his life.

"Señor Carranza is a very wealthy and powerful man. He has instructed me to tell you that everything he has is at your disposal if you wish to simply *disappear*. Ryker has signed your death warrant, Nathan Hodges. If you stay here, one of you will die."

Why would Ramon Carranza offer him the means by which to escape Ryker? Nate wondered. The man obviously had something to gain. Or perhaps it was all some elaborate trap. Maybe Carranza liked to play games as much as Ryker did. "What is your boss's interest in me and Ryker? What possible reason would he have to want to help me?"

"If you wish to start a new life in another country, with a new identity, of course, we can arrange for the woman to join you," Emilio said.

"What did you say?" The tension in Nate's stomach wound tighter and tighter until it spread through his whole body.

"Señora Porter. If you wish for her to join you—"

Moving with the speed of an attacking leopard, Nate pulled his knife to the other man's throat.

Emilio, seemingly undisturbed by Nate's aggressive response, stood perfectly still. "You can put your knife away, Señor Hodges, I mean you no harm. But you must know that if we found out about Señora Porter, Ryker will find out about her, too."

"There is nothing to find out about. She's my neighbor. I hardly know her." Hell, how had this happened? Nate asked himself. The one thing he hadn't wanted was to involve Cyn in his sordid battle with Ryker. "Tell your boss that I don't run from a fight, that I'm ready for Ryker."

"And Ryker is ready for you," Rivera said. "A smart man would accept my employer's offer."

"Tell Señor Carranza, thanks, but no thanks. I'll take care of my problems, my way." Nate had no idea what Carranza's stake in all this was, but there was no way he would trust any acquaintance of the Marquez family. Carranza was his enemy as surely as Ryker was. Nate had no doubts about that.

"Very well. We thought as much." Emilio stared down at the knife Nate still held at his throat. "Would you mind?"

Slowly, cautiously, Nate lowered the knife. "You still haven't told me why your boss is so interested in me."

"I'm afraid I can't answer that."

"Can't or won't?" Nate asked.

"There is no need for either you or Ryker to die," Rivera said.

"Is that what this is all about?" Nate asked. "Carranza is so afraid that I'll kill Ryker, he's willing to send me on a little all-expenses-paid vacation? Ryker must be very important to your boss, or perhaps to some of your boss's friends."

"If you change your mind, feel free to contact me." Emilio Rivera smiled, the expression softening his tough, lived-in face. He handed Nate a business card. "I'll tell Señor Carranza of your decision."

"You do that." Nate watched his uninvited guest leave, not bothering to follow him to the front door.

Just what the hell was that all about? Nate wondered. Something was damned screwy here. Something just didn't add up. What connection did a retired Cuban *businessman* have with the new Colombian regime? Birds of a feather? Or did Carranza's connection to Ryker supercede his old enemy's association with the Marquez family? And why had Emilio's powerful employer kept tabs on Nate since his days in Nam? As a favor to Ryker?

Nate walked over to the desk, picked up the phone and dialed. While he listened to the ringing, Nate looked at the card in his hand. The name and address of a local restaurant was printed on the front. He flipped the card over. Scrawled in heavy black ink was a St. Augustine phone number.

"Yeah?" Nick Romero answered, his voice loud and clearly agitated.

"I've got a news bulletin for you," Nate said.

"What?"

"Guess who just paid me a visit."

CHAPTER 8

Nate sat in the cool stillness of his den, with only the sound of his own breathing to keep him company. He caressed the smooth blade of the straight razor he held. It was old, he knew, but exactly how old, he wasn't sure. Old enough to have belonged to his grandfather.

Closing the blade, he cradled the razor in his palm, then clutched it tightly. Had his knife collection started the day his mother had given this to him? he wondered. She'd placed it in his hand the last time he'd seen her, pale and weak in her hospital bed.

"This was my father's," she'd told him. "It belonged to his father, and he would have wanted you, his only grandson, to have it."

Nate tossed the razor down on the metal trunk in front of the sofa as he stood up. He didn't think about his mother often, nor did he let his mind dwell on his tortured childhood, his abusive uncle. But when he did, the hatred festered inside him, feeding the loneliness and bitterness from which he couldn't escape.

In the thirty-six years since his mother died, Nate had been alone and unloved. A boy always on the outside looking in. A man whose untamed life had taught him brutal lessons about the dark side of humanity. But there was light in this world, something pure and good shining through all the dark horror. He had seen a glimpse of that light in his mother, and he saw it in Cynthia Porter. She was truly light to his darkness, joy to his pain, sweetness to his bitterness. She held the key that could unchain the heavy bonds holding him prisoner in a cold, bleak and lonely existence.

After a lifetime of waiting for her, and not even realizing he was waiting, she had finally materialized. From out of his dreams, Cyn had entered his world, igniting the fires of a passion he had known only in the shadows of his fantasies. She was real, not some imaginary lover who had haunted him for so long. She was flesh and blood, and he wanted her as he had never wanted anything in his life.

But she could never be his. He didn't dare risk letting her into his heart. As long as Ryker lived, anyone close to Nate would be in danger.

Restless, anxiety and longing frazzling his nerves, Nate paced the floor, finally throwing open the door and walking around the yard. In the distance, the ocean's steady heartbeat and the cries of an occasional gull echoed in his ears, creating a tune that blended perfectly with the vivid portrait of an isolated Florida beach, warm and damp after spring rain.

He knew he had to find a way to get Cyn to move out of her cottage, to leave Sweet Haven and return to Jacksonville. After what Emilio Rivera had told him, he knew that Cyn's life was already in danger if she stayed here. If Carranza knew about Cyn, then no doubt Ryker would soon learn of her existence. He had to make sure that Ryker understood the woman meant nothing to him. He couldn't allow Cyn to be caught in the terror from his past.

He had to talk to Cyn, maybe even tell her just enough to persuade her to cooperate. She was proving to be a very stubborn woman. It had taken every ounce of his willpower the last three days to stay away from her. And the day she'd run to him on the beach, he had wanted nothing more than to lie her down in the sand and take her. Instead, he had given her a stern, disapproving look, then run away.

God, what it took for a man to reject a woman like Cyn! Maybe she didn't want to want him, but she did. He saw it in her eyes, those warm, rich brown eyes. Every time she looked at him, she told him she wanted him.

Would it be so wrong, he asked himself, to spend one day with her? It might be all they ever had, the only chance for him to find, even momentarily, an escape from the pain that ruled his heart. He could go to her now, ask her to be with him, and later, when he had absorbed some of her light into his dark soul, he would make her understand that, for her own sake, she would have to leave Sweet Haven.

Cyn tapped her bottom teeth with the tip of her long fingernail as she scanned the pages of the paperback novel. Although she was having difficulty concentrating on the story, she was determined to finish the book. Reading was great escapism, and it had usually worked in the past to take her mind off her problems, but it wasn't working this evening.

She couldn't stop thinking about Nate Hodges, about the black limousine and the mysterious danger surrounding the man she longed to help. Slapping the book closed and tossing it down beside her on the couch, Cyn clinched her teeth, released a loud huffing breath and balled her hands into fists.

"Damn. Stop doing this to yourself." Jumping up from the couch, she headed toward the kitchen. If a good book didn't work, then maybe food would.

"Why won't he let me help him?" Cyn asked herself aloud. "He's so alone and in so much pain, and yet he keeps shutting me out."

She placed her hand on the refrigerator handle, but before she could open it, she heard several loud knocks coming from her front door. With her heart racing and her stomach swirling, Cyn rushed to the door, knowing before she saw him that Nate Hodges had come to her.

She swung open the door. His gaze met hers, his moss-green eyes pleading silently. She smiled. He looked so good, so very, very good. His jeans were old and faded but clean, and they fit his lean, muscular hips and legs like a snug, well-worn glove. His khaki-green cotton shirt encased his broad shoulders and chest tightly, then billowed out around his flat stomach and narrow waist. He had tied his hair back into the familiar ponytail. He looked big, rugged and dangerous. But in his eyes, she saw his soul, a dark, hungry soul in desperate need of light and nourishment.

"Nate."

He thought he'd never heard anything as beautiful as his name on her lips, and he knew he'd never seen anything as lovely as Cynthia Porter. Wearing a sheer yellow cotton blouse and skirt, with her golden-blond hair spilling freely to her waist and her flesh tanned to a tawny cream, she looked like a sunbeam—strong and bright and life-giving.

He wanted to bask in the warmth of her brown eyes, to reach out and draw her shimmering sweetness into his bitter heart.

"I need to talk to you," he said, thankful that she hadn't slammed the door in his face. Of course, he'd known she wouldn't. His heart had assured him that she would welcome him.

"Come in." She stepped aside to allow him the space to enter her living room.

He hesitated. "Look, we both know that there's something pretty strong going on between us, and…and I realize we can't just keep ignoring it."

"You're the one who's been trying to ignore it."

"Brown Eyes, I'd like nothing more than to make love to you, to explore the way I feel about you." He leaned toward her, placing one big hand on the doorframe. "But my life is complicated, too complicated to involve a woman like you."

"Then why are you here?" she asked, trying to disguise the catch in her voice, the disappointment in her heart.

"We can have this evening. That's all I can give you." He reached out and ran the back of his hand across her cheek, down her neck and chest to where her blouse covered her breasts. He wanted to say let me love you, let me drink my fill from your cup of life, let me find sanctuary in your arms.

"I don't understand." Her breath caught in her throat when his hand moved lower, down the front of her blouse, his knuckles raking across the small pearl buttons. "You keep…keep contradicting yourself. You say one thing, then do the opposite. You keep changing your mind."

He stopped his hand just below her left breast, spread open his palm and clutched her waist, pulling her toward him very slowly. "Come home with me. Give us this evening, and I'll try to explain."

She would never understand it in any logical fashion afterward, but her reaction to his request had nothing to do with rational thought. She swayed toward him, allowing him to enfold her in his embrace. She slipped her arms up and around his neck, standing on tiptoe to reach the band around his hair. With trembling fingers, she snapped the band, allowing his hair to fall freely down his neck and around his face.

He saw the hunger he felt reflected in her warm brown eyes, and he longed to take her mouth, to ravish her lips. But he didn't. He had to muster all his self-control. If he kissed her now, he'd be lost.

Rubbing her cheek with his, he held her to him, savoring the feel of her soft, womanly body. "Do you like steak?" he asked.

She cocked her head to one side, looked up at him and smiled. "See what I mean about saying and doing totally opposite things?"

"No contradictions," he said, loosening his hold on her. "My actions have been telling you that I want you, and what I'm trying to do with words is ask you for a date."

Cyn laughed, the sound deep and real and sweet. Her laughter filled his heart, warming the coldness, softening the hardness. "Are you inviting me to your house for a steak dinner?"

"Sort of." He released her completely, except for one slender hand that he held tightly. "I'm not much of a cook, but I can grill a steak, if you'll help with the potatoes and salad—"

"Do you like ice cream?" she asked, her whole body swimming with giddiness. She felt like shouting and singing and dancing around and around. She was going to spend the evening with Nate Hodges. They were going to have a date—a real, honest-to-goodness date. Maybe there was hope for them, after all.

"Love it," he said. "Why?"

Tugging on his hand, she pulled him inside her house and led him to the kitchen. "I'll pack a basket of goodies to take over to your house. We'll fix ourselves a banquet."

He wanted to tell her that she was the banquet, a true feast for his lonely heart and tortured soul. And he *would* tell her—tonight.

Nate sat on one end of the tan leather sofa, and Cyn sat on the other end. She had curled her feet up underneath her skirt; he had stretched his long legs out on top of the metal trunk. One of her Patti Page cassettes played on his stereo, the music and lyrics of "What'll I Do?" filled the ultra-masculine room.

They had shared a delicious meal, after-dinner drinks and discussions on subjects ranging from the weather to politics. They'd even broached the subject of his boating business in St. Augustine, from which he'd said he was taking a leave of absence.

More than once she'd tried to steer the conversation around to his past, and every time he'd artfully dodged her questions. Finally she gave up and began entertaining him with stories of how her father had disapproved of practically every boy she'd ever dated.

"Once I realized that no matter how perfect a boy was, my father was going to find something wrong with him, I figured out a way to make him appreciate the fine young man I'd been bringing home."

"And just how did you do that?"

"I started dating the absolutely worst boys in school."

"Who were the worst boys in school?"

"Oh, you know, the ones who rode motorcycles, wore an earring and had hair down to their shoulders." Playfully she reached out and flipped the end of his ponytail.

"Did your strategy work?"

"Of course. And it only took two perfectly awful dates before Daddy was asking about 'that nice young man' I'd dated a few weeks earlier."

"Such a manipulative female." He laughed, a genuine chuckle from deep inside. She made him feel good. Damned good!

"Not manipulative, just smart."

"And did you enjoy being a bad girl?"

"I've never been bad. I've always been a good girl. Ask anyone who's ever known me." She sat up straight, easing her legs out from beneath her skirt, inching them slowly toward Nate's where they lay stretched out on the trunk. "Cynthia Ellen Wellington Porter has always been a strong, sensible, levelheaded girl who could shoulder any burden, overcome any tragedy, and take care of anyone and everyone who needs her."

"And who takes care of Cynthia Ellen?" The moment he felt her leg touch his, he wanted to pull her close, entwining their legs in a sensual braid while their bodies joined in a passion neither could hide.

Cyn rested one of her legs atop his, the other cuddling beside it. "I take care of myself and everyone else. I have ever since my mother was killed in a plane crash when I was fifteen. I'm a take-charge person. I've been that way for so long, I can't be any other way."

"Didn't your husband take care of you?" Nate asked, wondering how a man could possess such a woman and not protect her as fiercely as he would the world's greatest treasure.

"Evan was a good man, but he was too busy taking care of all the kids at Tomorrow House to take care of me." Her eyes glazed over momentarily with a faraway pain, then brightened to their normal rich warmth. She felt as if she were betraying Evan's memory to criticize him in any way. It hadn't been his fault that he had never been able to give her the kind of possessive passion she had so desperately wanted.

Noticing Nate staring at her with a mixture of suspicion and understanding in his eyes, she tried to smile at him. "Besides, I didn't need taking care of. Haven't you guessed by now that I'm a mother-to-the-world type of person?"

"Mothers, even mothers-to-the-world, need husbands to take care of them." His own mother had desperately needed his father. She had been strong, strong enough to have and keep an illegitimate child in the morally judgmental fifties. But Grace Hodges had been so alone, so in need of—

"Nate, what's wrong?" Cyn asked, reaching out to take his hand, squeezing it tenderly.

"What?" He looked at her, his moss-green eyes slightly dazed.

"You looked so sad."

"I was thinking about my mother." He brought Cyn's hand to his lips, kissing it softly once, twice, three times. "She was a strong woman like you, but she needed someone to take care of her sometimes and there was no one there for her."

"Your father?" Cyn felt his pain. It filled his eyes.

It marred his handsome face. He made a sound somewhere between a groan and a snort. "I never had a father. I don't even know who he was. Anyway, it doesn't much matter. He's dead. He died before I was born."

"Oh, Nate, I'm so sorry." She held his hand even tighter, longing to take him in her arms and give him comfort. But she wasn't sure he would accept it, not right now when the pain was so great.

"All he ever gave her was me." Nate pulled away from Cyn's hold and stood up, his back to her. "A bastard child of uncertain heritage who never fit into her blue-blooded Anglo family."

Nate began to walk around the room as if movement alone would ease the tension from his big body. "His name was Rafael. She told me that much. I guess she had to, since she named me after him."

"Nathan Rafael." Cyn thought how well the name suited him, how perfectly it blended his mixed heritage.

"She said I looked like him, and I guess I must. I sure don't resemble anyone in her family, except for my green Anglo eyes."

"Your eyes?" Cyn asked as she stood up and went to him. "You have green eyes like your mother?" She touched his face with tenderness.

"Don't feel sorry for me." He stepped back, away from her touch. "I don't want your pity."

"What *do* you want from me?" she asked, her voice quietly pleading.

"Nothing. Everything. Too much. More than any woman could ever give." He couldn't stand seeing the look in her eyes, the pure, undisguised love. He turned away, moving toward the windows. Didn't she know that if he took what she was offering, he would destroy her? Even if Ryker didn't pose an immediate threat, Nate knew he would still be the wrong man for Cyn. She was so gentle and caring, so filled with love for the whole world. And he was a man filled with bitterness, a man who had spent a lifetime fighting the realities of a brutal world far removed from Cynthia Porter's awareness.

Following him, she placed her hand on his shoulder. She wanted to tell him that she was willing to give him everything, all that was her, every beat of her heart, every fiber of her being, the very essence of her soul. Didn't he know she already belonged to him?

"Take a walk with me," she said. "Show me the old mission again before it gets too dark to see inside." She wasn't quite sure why she'd made the suggestion, but somehow she knew it was the right thing to do.

Without turning around, he nodded. "No one knows for sure those old storage rooms were once part of a mission." Then he turned around, his face a mask of calm, hiding the emotions he was fighting to conquer. "Inside the sensible, levelheaded Cyn Porter is the soul of a romantic."

"Who, me?" She breathed a sigh of relief, knowing she could handle a cordial Nate much easier than a brooding man in pain. "Just because I love fairy tales and myths and want to believe in legends, you call me a romantic."

"Come on, Persephone. Go with me into the darkness." He held out his hand.

Cyn felt the instant chill, the shuddering anxiety that claimed her. His words held a meaning he had not intended. She reached out and took his hand, knowing that she would follow this man anywhere, even into the jaws of death—and beyond, to the depths of Hades or through the gates of heaven.

Twilight shadows fell across the earth while the fading colors of dusk painted the sky with muted tones of pink and lavender. A gentle evening breeze murmured through the trees and bushes, its cool breath caressing Cyn and Nate the moment they stepped outside.

"Is there no entrance to the mission inside the house?" Cyn asked when they stood in front of the arched doorway.

"I think there used to be, but someone plastered over it years ago. Probably long before your Miss Carstairs lived here."

Nate shoved the heavy door open, standing aside to allow Cyn to enter first. Even though he didn't believe in ancient legends and certainly not in ghosts, Nate felt the same curiosity here that he'd felt the first time he'd come to these rooms with Cyn. He couldn't quite pinpoint the source of his uncertainty, but he knew there was something here waiting for him, something he wasn't yet ready to accept.

Cyn stepped inside and stopped abruptly, hesitating until her eyesight adjusted to the darkness. Faint evening light seeped through the boarded windows and crept in from the open doorway. Slowly, cautious in her movements, Cyn walked inside, glancing around, searching for something, for anything, that could explain why this place drew her like a magnet. She'd felt it the time before when she'd come here with Nate.

She wasn't sure how she knew, she simply knew that once, long ago, something wonderful had happened here and something horrible. She trembled.

"Are you cold?" Nate asked.

"Don't you feel it?" she asked. "The joy. The pain."

Damn this place to hell and damn his crazy imagination. She'd asked if he felt it. Yes, hell, yes, he could feel it, but he didn't want to. "This is a damp, dark, musty old building. You're letting that stupid legend make you imagine things."

She moved around the room, quickly, almost frantically, her breath coming in quick, ragged spurts. "They were married here, you know. The priest married them."

What was wrong with her? Nate wondered. She was staring at the back wall as if she saw more than moss-coated shell rock partially obscured by a stack of battered furniture and decaying cardboard boxes. He reached out, grabbing her by the wrist. "Come on, Cyn, let's get out of here. Let's go for a walk along the beach."

"They died here," she cried. "He killed them both in this very room and dragged their bodies out onto the beach." Cyn fell against the wall, her hot, flushed face seeking comfort on the cool stone surface.

Just as her knees buckled and she began to sway, Nate caught her up in his arms and rushed outside. Deeply inhaling the clean evening air, he felt his chest rising and falling with the heaviness of his breathing. The moment she'd said *they died here,* he'd known the ancient lovers had been killed in the mission—the Timucuan maiden and her Spanish conquistador. But the images that had flashed through his mind had not been of long-dead lovers, but of Cyn and himself. And Ryker.

"Oh, Nate, you felt it, too, didn't you?" She clung to him, her slender arms draped around his neck, her fingers threaded through his hair.

"Cyn, don't do this to yourself." He carried her across the road and onto the beach.

"Are you saying you didn't feel them, feel their joy, share their pain?" she asked as he lowered her to her feet, allowing her body to slide down his slowly, sensuously.

"I'm saying that we both can't let our imaginations run wild." He wanted her. Now. His body was hard, pulsating, throbbing with desire. How could he answer her, how could he admit that even now, the passion flowing through his veins like an untamed river was more than one man's passion? How could he tell her, without sounding insane, that he wanted to make love to her again, to find the fulfillment he had found only in her body, to come home to her arms and find the sanctuary his soul had sought for so long?

"It's as if we've been together before," she whispered, clinging to him, her lips pressed against his chest where she was unbuttoning his shirt. "Oh, Nate, I'm scared."

"It's all right, Cyn. I'll never let anything or anyone hurt you." *Tonight is all you'll have with her,* he told himself. *Take her, only if you're sure you can let her go afterward.*

"It's not just the legend. There's more." She breathed in the deeply masculine smell of the big man holding her so protectively in his arms. "I'm not afraid for them. They died hundreds of years ago."

"Don't think about it, Brown Eyes." He lowered his mouth, brushing the top of her head with tender kisses.

"It's us. You and me and the mission. And this beach. Oh, Nate, tell me what kind of trouble you're in. You need me. I can help you."

He took her mouth with the savagery of a man pushed beyond the limits of his control. Holding her close, Nate conquered her lips with unrelenting pressure, impaling her soft moistness with his tongue. Without really knowing anything, she already knew too much. She had sensed the truth as surely as he had. If he couldn't find a way to prevent it, Ryker would kill them both inside the old mission and drag their bodies onto the beach...the way the ancient conquistador's enemy had done.

Was that how the ancient legend's prophecy would be fulfilled? he wondered, his heart aching with some unknown emotion, his body suffering the tortures of the damned. His need for this woman went beyond any normal desire he'd ever felt, and he seemed powerless to stop himself from devouring her whole.

She moaned as her body quivered with response, pushing, clawing, straining for closer contact. How could she endure much more? she asked herself. Never had such overwhelming desire consumed her. If she didn't mate with this man soon, she would die from the insatiable hunger.

They drank the sweetness of each other's lips, their tongues dipping, licking, thrusting in a parody of a more intimate act. He moved his hands over her in a frenzied exploration, savoring each new curve, and yet remembering the feel of her as if he'd touched her a hundred times. She clung to him, her fingers in his hair, her nails scratching at his neck, his back, his shoulders.

Together they sank to the ground, their knees cradled in the gritty sand. He yanked open her blouse, popping the buttons in his haste. Lowering his head, he took one tight nipple into his mouth, sucking her through the sheer yellow lace of her bra. She arched her back and moaned from the sweet ecstasy that was building between her thighs.

Still kissing her, Nate shoved her onto the ground, straddling her, looking down at her, dying with the need to be inside her.

Cyn felt lost in a world of dreams, so often had she seen those moss-green eyes staring down at her, felt the throbbing pressure of this special man needing to mate with her and her alone. But this was no dream, this was reality and he had promised her tonight, only tonight. No matter how precious this one night could be, would it be enough? Could she give herself to him and walk away as if nothing had happened? Could he?

"Nate," she whispered, her hands braced against his chest. She could feel the strong, powerful thud of his heart under her fingers.

"I want you," he said, his voice ragged with desire.

"Only for tonight?" she asked, unsure where she'd gained the strength to question their future.

Stunned by her inquiry in the midst of their lovemaking, Nate hesitated. Still straddling her, he gazed down into her warm brown eyes. "I'll want you forever," he told her truthfully. "But all we'll ever have is tonight. There's no future for us."

How could he tell her that soon, very soon, he would fight the last battle of his life with an opponent as skilled and deadly as he himself was? If he allowed her to stay with him, to become a part of him, then she would die as surely as she had in his dreams.

"I want you, Nate. I...I love you." She saw the fires ignite and burn in his eyes when she told him that she loved him. "But I want more. I want you to trust me enough to share your problems with me. I want you to let me help you."

Nate jumped up, grabbed her hands and jerked her up beside him. He reached out, taking her by the back of the neck, bringing her close. Bending over, he kissed her forehead. "Go away, Brown Eyes. You want more than I can give you."

She stared at him, not knowing what to say or do. More than anything she wanted to tell him to make love with her, that tomorrow didn't matter, that nothing but the two of them and this moment mattered. But she couldn't.

He released her. "You'll find someone else, someone like your Evan. A man who owns his own soul." He turned and walked away.

"Nate..."

He didn't slow his stride, even though she kept calling his name over and over again.

Cyn stood in her open front door looking across the road at the coquina-and-wooden house. The late-night rain had washed the earth, leaving the world outside coated with fresh moisture. Overhead, streaks of gold-kissed pink hinted at the dawn sunlight still hidden on the other side of the universe.

She hadn't slept even though she'd gone to bed. After hours of thinking and crying and praying, she'd gotten up. For the past thirty minutes she'd been staring across the road at Nate's house, wondering where he was and what he was doing. Was he sleeping? She doubted it. If he was hurting as badly as she, he was probably wide-awake and cursing the day he'd met her.

Her fearless warrior had reached out to her last night, and she, in her weak need for permanence and fear of the unknown, had turned him away. She'd been a fool. She should have accepted what he offered, no questions asked, and had one perfect night to remember for the rest of her life.

Was it too late? she asked herself. If she went to him now, would he reject her?

Cyn tied the belt around her aqua silk robe, walked outside and closed the door behind her. With her heart in her throat, the rapid beat roaring in her ears, she crossed the road.

Lifting the heavy metal door knocker, she announced her presence. No answer. Again and again she beat the knocker against the wooden door. Finally, she turned away, but couldn't bring herself to leave. With slow, purposeful strides, she moved along the arched portico to the back of the house. The first tentative rays of dawn light fell across the earth, kissing awake the lush, unkempt vegetation in Nate's garden.

She saw him, and sucked in her breath. He stood on the rock walkway in the garden, only a few feet from the house. The early morning breeze caressed his hair like a lover's hand, the long black threads whipping his cheeks. He was naked, only the wind and the morning sun touching his flesh as she longed to touch it.

His body held the scars of a warrior many times wounded in battle, but she knew that the deepest, most painful scars lay buried in his heart, and that unhealed wounds marred his soul.

Shivers of fear and longing swirled inside her, growing, moving, increasing in strength, as she stood silently in the dawn of a new day and brought the sight of Nathan Hodges, standing boldly, arrogantly naked, into her heart and into her soul. His body was big and bronzed, corded with thick, tight muscles, and it gleamed like polished metal, damp from the rain, slick and sleek. The only hair on his body was nestled around his powerful maleness, and its color matched the midnight black of the long tresses that touched his shoulders.

Never had she seen anything as beautiful as the man who stood before her, his very maleness beckoning to her, his masculinity calling to her to come to him, to give herself as a sacrifice to his desires, to match him thrust for thrust, hard strength to soft strength, man to woman, in a mating ritual that would join their souls forever.

Moving almost as if in a trance, Cyn went to him. Nate knew she was there moments before he actually saw her. He had felt her. Already, she had become a part of him. He waited while she moved forward, stopping an arm's length away. Never letting her gaze falter, she stared up at him.

After hours of restless tossing, he had gotten out of bed and come outside. He'd been waiting for her, knowing in his soul that she would come to him. The sensible, levelheaded Cynthia Porter wouldn't want to come, but romantic Cyn, who believed in fairy tales and myths, would be unable to resist the unearthly magnetism that had claimed them. They were doomed. Whether caught in the spell of some ancient legend or simply overwhelmed by their own sexual needs, Nate didn't know. But he did know that Cyn was his, she had always been his and she would be his forever. As surely as he needed air to breathe, he needed her.

He watched, transfixed by her beauty, while she untied her belt and slipped out of her robe, letting it fall to the rock walkway beneath her feet. The breeze tousled her hair around her face and shoulders and molded her thin, aqua gown to her round curves. Without saying a word, she reached up and lowered the straps of her gown, one at a time. They dropped down onto her shoulders. Her breasts swelled above the silky material, her nipples pressing against the softness.

When she reached up to tug on the bodice of her fitted gown,

Nate stepped forward, pushing her hand away, replacing it with his own. With a slow, gentle tug, he pulled the gown down to her waist, baring her full, rounded breasts. He ran the tips of his fingers down the length of her body, from neck to waist, letting his hand still momentarily when he touched her breast.

She moaned when he flicked her tight nipple with his fingernail. He jerked her to him, crushing her swollen, throbbing breasts against his chest. She felt him, all of him, hard and hot and pulsating.

He was so big, so primitively male, that she shuddered with a maiden's fear of conquest, knowing that soon her body would accept the wild thrusts of his huge body.

He ran one hand down her hip, over her buttocks, kneading softly, clutching her soft flesh in his callused hand, bunching the silky fabric of her gown. With his other hand, he grasped her head, spearing his fingers through her golden hair, letting it ripple over his hand, his bare shoulder and arm.

Easing his hand lower and lower, he edged her gown higher and higher, until he was able to slip his hand beneath and touch her naked skin.

She ached with emptiness, her femininity pulsing painfully with a need only this man could appease. "Please," she whispered, her lips parting on a sigh as his hand moved between her legs to caress her inner thigh.

"Tell me what you want." He maneuvered his fingers between her closed thighs, dipping inside her damp, sweet body. Her thighs parted, her knees melting.

"Make love to me." She struggled for breath, then lost it completely when he circled her throbbing need with his thumb and forefinger.

With one agile move, he jerked her gown down her hips, letting it puddle around her feet like a pale aqua pool. He could smell her heat, thick, heavy, female moistness waiting for him to lay claim to it. It was all he could do not to take her where they stood, not to plunge into her with all the violent need commanding his male body.

He kissed her then, his lips tenderly loving at first as he tried to control the desire raging inside him. She was everything he'd ever longed for—and more. Deepening the kiss, his tongue boldly lunged and was met by the equally powerful drive of her tongue. Challenged by her forceful response, the seeds of a long dormant passion blossoming with an untamed fury, he lowered her down, down, down onto the soft, wet grass. With his knees straddling her hips, he gazed at her naked beauty, devouring her, drinking in the sight of her womanliness. Then he looked into her eyes—warm, rich, brown eyes that had haunted his dreams for twenty-five years.

He shook with desire, wanting her, needing her as he had never needed anything. He wanted to take her with all the savage wildness he barely controlled, but knew he mustn't allow himself that pleasure. No matter how strong a woman Cyn Porter was, she was also small and fragile and hadn't known a man's possession in a long time.

Nate prayed for the strength to take her gently, but the moment she touched him and called out his name, he knew he was lost.

She let her hand rest on his stomach, longing to lower it and take him within her grasp. "Nate...Nate..."

In one swift, perfectly coordinated move, he entered her, his thrust hard and demanding, calling forth all the unleashed passion in her soul. She cried out, so great was the pleasure of their joining, such pure, unforgettable rapture. She arched her body, lifting her hips to meet each vigorous lunge, a shattering crescendo of sensation taking over her body, spiraling out from her core, spreading into every nerve ending, every cell.

He lowered his head, his black hair caressing one breast while his mouth suckled the other. Tiny fissions of undiluted ecstasy exploded within her. She writhed beneath him, arching higher and higher, seeking a closer joining.

Taking her hips into his hands, he lifted her against him and increased the tempo of their lovemaking. "You want more?" he asked, his voice thick with desire.

"Yes...more." She clung to his back, her nails scoring his bronzed flesh with love trails.

"Deeper. Faster." His thrusts grew wilder, hotter, more intense.

"Yes!" she screamed. "Harder...harder..."

And he obeyed her command, giving her the depth of his hardness. Suddenly she cried out, tears of joy cascading down her cheeks. He listened to her moans of fulfillment, taking them into his mouth, savoring their sweet, undisguised surrender. She was his once again, as she had been in his dreams, only the reality far excelled the dreams. He felt her shuddering release, her body tightening, clenching him like a tight fist. With one final, brutal stab, he fell headlong into climatic fulfillment. His groans echoed in the stillness of the early morning, their guttural eruption the sounds of a healthy male animal who had claimed his mate.

Cyn had never known such total wonder, such complete and utter satisfaction. Nothing in her life had prepared her for Nate Hodges's possession.

His big body lay over her, damp and hot and heavy. He raised himself onto his elbows, looking down into her dazed brown eyes. "Did I hurt you?" He knew he'd taken her with savage force, seeking his own pleasure while trying to give the same to her.

"No," she said, reaching up to touch his face, a face so dear to her. "But I am lying here in the wet grass and I'm getting cold."

He smiled. Standing, he pulled her to her feet and picked her up. She shivered, partly from the cool morning breeze on her damp flesh and partly as an aftershock from such unequaled fulfillment.

"Stay with me a few more hours." Holding her naked body against his, he stepped inside the house.

"Will you send me away then?" she asked, knowing the answer before he replied.

"I'll have to," he said.

"Let me help you. Let me stand by you through whatever trouble you're in." She kissed his neck as her fingers laced themselves through his long hair.

"I don't want to talk about it. Not now. I want to make love to you again while I still can." He carried her down the long, dark corridor, kicked open his bedroom door and placed her on his rumpled sheets.

She opened her arms, taking him into her body, giving her lover, her fierce and lonely warrior, the safety he could find only within her embrace.

Nate took all she had to give, knowing he would never get enough. But for now, he was satisfied. For now he had found a sanctuary for his heart and soul.

Later, he would have to send her away. Even if these precious moments were all they would ever have, he could survive as long as he knew she was alive and safe. But if anything ever happened to her, if Ryker harmed her, then Nate knew he would be eternally lost. Cynthia Ellen Porter was his very soul.

CHAPTER 9

Cyn sat on the edge of the bed in Nate's sparsely decorated bedroom. She pulled the lapels of her aqua robe across her breasts, then tightened the belt. When she had awakened, she'd found her gown and robe on the wooden chair beside the bed. Nate, dressed in nothing but his cutoff jeans, had been standing by the window looking outside.

They hadn't spoken as their gazes met, and the hot passion that had existed between them in the previous hours ignited once again. She'd been shocked by her own primitive need to have him touch her.

When he had approached her, she'd held up the sheet that barely covered her naked body.

"We need to talk before you leave," he had said. "I brought in your gown and robe from the garden. Put them on while I fix coffee."

He'd left her alone then, giving her time to think about what she had done and what she was going to do now. She loved Nate Hodges. That and that alone was the only clear fact in her mind. She had come to him last night, throwing caution to the wind, forgetting everything except the passionate need to become his woman.

And now, he was going to send her away.

Common sense told her that she should go, leave him and find a way to overcome the overwhelming desire she felt for him. After all, he was hardly the kind of man she would have chosen for herself. He had spent almost all of his adult life as a navy SEAL, a professional warrior, a trained and highly skillful killer. By his very nature, Nate was a violent man. How could she ever reconcile herself to loving a man capable of destroying another human being with his bare hands?

And yet, how could she keep from loving him when every feminine instinct she possessed told her that Nate Hodges needed her, more than he had ever needed anyone or anything in his life?

Nate entered the bedroom. He handed her a mug filled with freshly brewed coffee. "Sugar and milk," he said.

Accepting the mug, she smiled. "Thanks."

He sat down in the wooden chair beside the bed. Their knees almost touched. Cyn readjusted her sitting position, moving her legs away from Nate's.

"Should I apologize for what happened?" he asked, looking at her, trying to gauge her reaction.

She stared down into the creamy brown coffee. "What happened between us was a mutual decision. I...I came to you because I couldn't stay away. And...and you—"

"Took you because I couldn't stop myself."

Jerking her head up, she glared at him, wondering if he regretted making love to her. "You make me feel vulnerable, Nate, and I don't like feeling that way. For as long as I can remember, I've always been the one in charge, the strong one, the one others came to for help, depended on to solve their problems."

"You can't help me, Cyn."

"So you keep telling me." She took a sip of her coffee, then circled the warm mug with both hands. "But knowing you don't want my help doesn't stop me from wanting to give it to you."

"For once in your life, let someone else take care of you. Let me make sure you're safe." He bent over slightly in the chair, dropping his hands between his spread knees. "I can't allow you to become important to me. It would put you in danger."

"I don't understand."

"The less you know, the safer you'll be."

Cyn jumped up, the contents of her mug splashing onto her silk robe, staining the aqua material with wet tan splotches. She flung the mug, coffee and all, across the room. With a splintering crash, the ceramic cup broke into pieces and the muddy liquid splattered the wall, then spread down onto the floor.

"It's too late to shut me out of your life. Haven't you got sense enough to realize that?" She stood in front of him, her intent gaze fixed on his startled face. "I'm in love with you. Whether I want to be or not. Do you think I go around sleeping with men I don't love?"

Nate stood up. When he tried to touch her, she shoved against his chest. "Of course I don't think you—"

"Maybe what we shared didn't mean anything to you. Maybe you can just send me away and go on with your life." Cyn sucked in the soft inner flesh of her mouth, closing her teeth downward in an effort to keep herself from crying. "I hate your damned knife collection." She jabbed her index finger into his chest. "I despise the fact that you spent twenty years in the SEALs, doing God only knows what." She jabbed him again. "You're a man who uses violence to settle his disputes. I've seen you in action. You're a deadly weapon."

Her words wounded Nate more surely than any knife in his extensive collection could have. Her every accusation was right on target. How could he defend himself to a woman as loving as Cyn? Why should he even try?

He grabbed her by the shoulders so quickly that she didn't have time to evade his capture. She struggled momentarily, then stopped trying to pull away from him.

She met his fierce stare head-on. "Loving a man like you goes against everything I've ever believed in, and yet I can't change the way I feel. Something inside me tells me that you need me, and yet you keep trying to send me away. I think I have a right to know why."

Tightening his hold on her shoulders, he pulled her closer, so close her breasts brushed his naked chest. She trembled with desire from the intimate contact. Heat spread through his body. "I don't need you, Brown Eyes. Not the way you think." Hell, he knew he was lying to her, but he couldn't lie to himself. He needed Cyn Porter as surely as he needed air to breathe, but the last thing she needed was him—a man who could bring danger and death into her life.

Cyn took in quick, ragged breaths as she stared at Nate, love and longing in her eyes. "Am I making a fool of myself?" she asked, her voice trembly with tears.

"We're both fools," he told her, his own voice deliberately hard and controlled. He dropped his hands from her shoulders. "We've allowed our hormones to get us into a dangerous situation."

"There's more between us than overactive hormones." Stepping away from him, she tilted her head slightly, then stuck out her chin, a defiant, determined look on her face. "What we shared went beyond good sex."

Nate fought the urge to take her in his arms, the overwhelming desire to admit to Cyn that what he felt for her went beyond anything he'd ever experienced, even in his dreams. "The sex was good, wasn't it?"

"Don't do this, Nate. Don't try to alienate me by playing the chauvinist male."

"But that's exactly what I am. I'm no Prince Charming, no answer to a maiden's prayers. You said yourself that loving me goes against everything you've ever believed in."

"What kind of trouble are you in?" she asked, taking a tentative step toward him, knowing that he was deliberately trying to be insulting enough to make her run.

He held out a restraining hand, a visible reminder that he didn't want her to touch him. "There's a man I knew years ago. In Nam." Nate walked across the room, wanting to put physical space between him and the woman who was so determined to help him. Dear God, how much he wanted to accept what she was offering. But he couldn't.

"A part of your violent past?" Somehow she knew that whatever danger he faced, he intended to confront it by calling upon his skills as a warrior. *Live by the sword, die by the sword* flashed through Cyn's mind.

"Yeah," Nate said, hating the look of condemnation he saw in her eyes. "Something happened between me and this man, something you don't need to know about." How could he ever tell Cyn the whole story and expect her to understand? Without knowing any specific details of his past, she was already repulsed. If she knew the bloody facts, she would hate herself for loving him.

"You can tell me anything. I'll understand." She went up behind him, wanting to put her arms around him, longing to ease the pain she heard in his voice, saw in his slumped shoulders. If only she could help him put his violent past behind him, and teach him how to live in peace. Surely he could change. All he needed was for her to show him how. Violence didn't solve anything; it only destroyed life.

"The less you know, the better," he said.

"Then tell me what I need to know." She reached out, allowing her hand to hover in mid-air, almost touching his tense back.

"This man, Ryker, swore he'd kill me someday, swore revenge. For the past five years, I've thought he was dead, that I didn't have to be constantly looking over my shoulder, waiting for the day of reckoning." Nate turned, facing her. "He's alive. He's on his way to St. Augustine, and when he finds me, he's going to try to kill me."

She touched him then, unable to stop herself. He grabbed her hand where it caressed his cheek, and buried his mouth in her open palm.

"Oh, Nate. Nate…" Tears gathered in the corners of her eyes, spilling over onto her cheeks.

Suddenly he pulled her into his arms, nuzzling her neck, whispering her name. "If you were my woman, you'd be in danger. I can't let that happen." He wouldn't allow anything to happen to Cyn. He knew as surely as he knew the sun rose in the east that this woman was his soul. If she died because of him, he would be eternally lost.

"I think it's too late, Nathan Hodges. I'm already your woman, and we both know it." She held on to him with the fierce protectiveness of a mother lion safeguarding her cubs, of a strong female willing to go the limit to take care of her mate.

"But Ryker doesn't know it. He must never know. You have to get out of my life and stay out. For both our sakes." Nate remembered that Ramon Carranza had found out. How could he hope to keep her safe from Ryker when he had such powerful and ruthless friends? Nate released her, and when she refused to let him go, he pulled away.

"Can't the police help you? Surely they won't allow a man to just hunt another man down like an animal."

"Brown Eyes, you don't understand, you couldn't even begin to imagine. We're talking about jungle warfare here. We're talking about two trained killers who are evenly matched. This has nothing to do with any kind of civilized law you know."

The blood ran cold in her veins. No, she had never known anything about that kind of world, those kind of men, and yet, somewhere deep inside of her, she understood. "Two warriors who will fight to the death."

The look in her eyes ripped into his gut. He wanted to take her back into his arms, to reassure her that if he came out of this alive, he'd come for her. But he knew better than to promise anything. "What do I have to say or do to make you understand that if Ryker finds out about you, he'll use you to get to me?" A kaleidoscope of images flashed quickly through Nate's mind. Ryker's icy blue eye. His triumphant grin. Cyn's lifeless body in Ryker's arms.

"Nate..." She reached out for him.

"I'm sorry, Brown Eyes, sorrier than you'll ever know."

Although she longed to touch him, to reassure him with her embrace, she realized he wanted her to stay at arm's length, that he was fighting the desire to keep her with him.

"You're approaching this problem the wrong way," she said. "Violence can't be the only solution. This man, this Ryker, can't fight you if you're not willing. If what he's seeking is a confrontation, then don't give it to him."

"Dammit, woman, do you think all I've got to do is tell him I don't want to fight? When a man is intent on killing you, you have only one choice, and that's to defend yourself."

"Let the police take care of Ryker. That's their job. Protecting law-abiding citizens from criminals." She clenched her fists at her sides in an effort to keep from touching him.

"The way they protected your husband?" Nate asked, knowing

full well that his words would hurt her, but determined to make her realize the naiveté of her thinking. "And what about the boy who killed Evan? There are times when a man has to take care of himself."

A knot of unshed tears lodged in her throat. Her hands jerked. She balled her fingers tightly against her palms, her nails cutting into the soft flesh. "Damn you, Nate Hodges. You know Evan was nothing like you. His situation and yours have nothing in common. He didn't seek out violence, it was thrust upon him."

Didn't she realize, Nate wondered, that despite his brutal past, he wasn't seeking danger; it was seeking him. "Your husband chose to try to help a boy addicted to drugs. He put himself and you in danger by doing that."

"No." She placed her hands over her ears and turned from Nate as tears escaped her eyes, falling in thin, warm streams down her cheeks. As quickly as she had shunned the sight of him, Cyn spun around, her damp eyes glaring. "Evan was the most gentle man I've ever known, the most caring. He always put the needs of others before his own. He...he was as opposed to violence as I am. He didn't realize he was in danger, that he was putting me... Darren Kilbrew brought violence into our lives. His whole life had been filled with it, just like yours has been."

"I didn't spend twenty years as a criminal, killing innocent people. I was one of the good guys, dammit. I worked for the government, defending this country. Just like the police, my job was protecting others, the people of this country." He saw the look of disbelief in her eyes, the lack of understanding. Could he ever make her realize that countries, as well as individuals, often had little choice in choosing violence over peace. "When danger threatens, when violence is thrust upon you, then you have to fight in order to survive. Ian Ryker will give me no choice."

"I don't think you want one," Cyn told him.

"That's not true."

"Then let me help you." She watched him carefully, praying for some sign of agreement. "Together we can find a way. You don't have to meet him on a field of battle. You don't have to fight a duel to the death."

"You don't understand," Nate said. Cyn, in her innocence, had no knowledge of a man like Ryker. Despite the fact that her husband had been brutally murdered, she didn't know anything about professional killers. "Darren Kilbrew was a kid half out of his mind on drugs. The drug was as much Evan's murderer as that boy was. Ian Ryker is different. He kills for the sheer pleasure of it, and the longer he can make his victim suffer, the better he likes it."

"What about Nick Romero?" Cyn asked. "He's some sort of government agent, isn't he? Let him or whatever agency he works for take care of Ryker."

"Romero is already involved, but that's not going to solve my problem. Ryker wants me. I can't let someone else fight my battle."

"You don't want to."

"All right," he admitted, "I don't want someone to fight for me, to die for me. This is between Ryker and me. I don't want any innocent bystanders getting in the way."

"Is that what I am, an innocent bystander?"

Hell, how did he answer that question? he wondered. Of course she was more than a bystander. She was his woman, and more than anyone else, she was in danger. "Yeah, Brown Eyes, that's exactly what you are."

She tried to see beyond the words, past the cool, unemotional statement, but his expression gave away nothing. He seemed totally unmoved by her tears, her offer of help and her profession of love.

"I have a ten-thirty appointment this morning," she said as she walked past him, not giving in to the impulse to take one final look at him in the hopes that some emotion would show on his face.

By the time she reached the front door, she realized he wasn't following her. And she was glad, she told herself. She had fallen in love with a man incapable of loving her in return. Not once, not even when they had shared the most passionate intimacies, had Nate told her he loved her. She had allowed her own sexual desire and the fantasy spell of an ancient legend to overrule her common sense.

Nate was right. She should get out of his life and stay out. For both their sakes.

Cyn opened the front door. Just as she stepped outside, she heard him coming up behind her. Hesitating momentarily, she waited for him to touch her or to say something to her. He did neither. Turning her head, she caught a glimpse of him in the doorway. Their gazes met for one brief instant before he closed the door.

Cyn jumped out of her van, glanced down at her watch and groaned. She was fifteen minutes late for her brunch date with Ramon Carranza. She hoped the wealthy Cuban was lenient with tardy guests.

Standing on the stone walkway, she scrutinized the Spanish-style mansion. It was exactly what she had expected. A two-story cream stucco house with a red tile roof, arched windows and doors, and a lawn filled with palm trees.

Stepping up, she hesitated briefly as she studied the beautifully carved wooden door. She had to make a good impression. She had to convince this man to help Tomorrow House. Of course, he wasn't her last hope, but he was her best chance. A man with enough money to donate ten thousand dollars a year to a small shelter for runaway teens had enough money to solve her problems, at least temporarily.

Cyn rang the doorbell. Instantly, a young woman opened the door and smiled a friendly greeting.

"Señora Porter?"

"Yes." Cyn walked inside the enormous foyer. If she hadn't been raised in her father's ancestral home in Savannah, she would have been awestruck by the grandeur of Ramon Carranza's home. But Cyn was quite accustomed to fine antiques, impeccable decorating, homes with museum-style quality.

"Please follow me," the maid said in slightly accented English as she led Cyn down the hallway and out onto a back patio.

Spring flowers, in large concrete pots, surrounded the wide expanse of open courtyard just beyond the patio. A glass table had been set with pristine white linen, sparkling china and heavy crystal.

"Please be seated," the maid said. "Señor Carranza received an important telephone call only moments ago. He will join you shortly."

"Thank you." Cyn sat down when the maid went back into the house.

She was grateful to the person who had called Ramon Carranza. Perhaps he wouldn't even be aware that she had arrived late.

The day was beautiful, she decided, looking up at the clear blue sky. Everything was fresh and crisp and caressed with Florida sunshine. The day should be perfect, but it wasn't. Not for her. She was in love with a man who didn't love her, a man totally unsuitable for her.

She remembered the first time she had awakened this morning. Nate had been awake and lying beside her, propped on his elbow while he watched her. He had kissed her, held her, and made slow, sweet love to her. How could a man give of himself to a woman the way Nate had given to her and not love her?

"Señora Porter," a deep, throaty voice said. "I hope you don't mind eating outside. I know it is only the first day of May, but after last night's rain, the world is so clean and fresh and bathed in the sun's warmth."

Cyn glanced up at the tall, elegantly dressed man who had just stepped out onto the patio.

He took her hand, kissing it with Continental flair. "You are even more beautiful than I had imagined."

"Why, thank you, Señor Carranza. I'm flattered." Cyn felt awed at the sight of the elderly gentleman. She wasn't quite sure what she had expected, but it certainly hadn't been this handsome man, so tall, so broad-shouldered, so incredibly suave with his mane of white hair and his thick white mustache. His black eyes sparkled with intelligence and curiosity.

"You must call me Ramon, as all my friends do." He sat, taking the chair opposite her. "And you and I are going to be good friends, *si?*"

"Yes, I hope so." Cyn thought there was something familiar about this man. Perhaps she had seen his picture in the paper.

"I hope you like seafood, Señora Porter." Ramon waved his hand,

and as if on cue, a plump, dark-haired woman appeared carrying a huge serving tray.

"I love seafood." Cyn's mouth watered at the sight of the scrumptious shrimp cocktail the woman set before her. "And please call me Cyn."

When he widened his eyes in surprise, an amused look on his face, Cyn laughed, then said, "My name is Cynthia, but all *my* friends call me Cyn."

"What a perfectly delightful nickname."

All through brunch, they discussed a variety of things. Everything from music to wine, but somehow the discussion kept coming back around to the fact that Cyn was living alone in Sweet Haven with only one close neighbor. It seemed of great interest to Ramon Carranza that Nate Hodges was a man Cyn could count on for protection. She simply didn't understand Señor Carranza's interest in her personal life.

"I came here to ask you for money, and yet we seem to have discussed everything except Tomorrow House." Cyn had enjoyed her meal and the charming old man's company, but there was something in his persistent questions about Nate that bothered her. Something she couldn't quite put her finger on.

"Ah, but it is a foregone conclusion that I will give you the money you need. I will give you a check to cover the expenses of your shelter for the next six months." Ramon sipped his wine, eyeing Cyn over the rim of his crystal glass.

"You will?" Cyn gasped. "But...but how did you know that I needed enough money for six months' expenses?"

With a toss of his hand, indicating that it was nothing for him to know the closest, most-guarded secrets of others, he smiled at Cyn. "I am sure you are aware of the fact that not only am I a very rich man, I am a powerful man with many powerful friends. My friends know many things, and what I want to know, they find out for me."

A cold chill raced along Cyn's spine, reminding her that no matter how charming Ramon Carranza was now at nearly eighty, it was reputed that he had once been a part of the Cuban mafia.

"Why does my shelter interest you so much, Señor Car…
Ramon?"

He took another sip of his wine. "May I be perfectly honest with
you, Cyn?" His wide smile displayed his sparkling teeth against the
background of his white mustache and leathery brown skin.

Uncertain how to reply, she simply nodded as she returned his
smile. A tight knot formed in the pit of Cyn's stomach, as niggling
little doubts wafted through her mind.

"I could say that it is because I consider myself a philanthropist,
but I am not. I could say that I was once a boy without a home who
needed a place like Tomorrow House, but it would be a lie." His
smile widened. "You have heard rumors about me, have you not?"

How was she supposed to answer a question like that? she wondered. "People always like to gossip about the wealthy."

Ramon laughed hardily, the sound deep and husky. "Such a dip-
lomatic reply. But I would expect no less from a politician's
daughter."

"You know who my father is?"

"Senator Denton Wellington of Georgia."

"But how—"

"I give to charity, my dear little Cyn, for two reasons. As a tax
write-off, first and foremost. And, I am an old man, reared in the
Catholic faith. In case there is a hereafter, it would not hurt for me
to make some small recompense before I die." He looked down into
his almost empty wine-glass as if it were a pool reflecting his past.

"Do you know my father?" She couldn't shake the notion that
perhaps Ramon Carranza was generous to Tomorrow House in particular because he was one of her father's acquaintances. But surely
her father wasn't foolish enough to accept campaign contributions
from a reputed crime boss.

"Do not worry yourself." He tilted the glass to his lips and swallowed the last drops of wine, then set the goblet on the table. "Your
father and I have never met. He is not indebted to me in any way."

Cyn hoped the relief she felt wasn't visible on her face. As deb-
onairly charming as Ramon Carranza was, there was something
about the man that disturbed her. There had to be a reason why

he'd gathered so much information about her personal life, why he seemed so interested in the fact that she was living alone in Sweet Haven. "I enjoyed brunch very much, Señor Carranza——" When he widened his eyes as a reminder, she quickly corrected herself, "Ramon. I'm very grateful for your offer to help us. I simply can't let the church close down Tomorrow House. You are aware of how much money it will take?"

"The check is already written." He reached inside the breast pocket of his coat and pulled out a long white envelope, then handed it to Cyn. "Please make sure it is the correct amount."

With trembling fingers, Cyn opened the envelope and peeped inside. She sucked in her breath. The amount was thousands of dollars over the desperately needed amount. "Señor Car... Ramon, how can I ever thank you?"

When she looked across the table at the elderly Cuban gentleman, she saw that he was watching her intently, the fierceness of his scrutiny frightening. Then suddenly his expression softened, and he smiled again. "There is no need for thanks. My motives are selfish."

Cyn scooted back her chair, dropped her napkin on the table and stood. "Thank you again...for everything. I should be going. There's never enough hours in the day at Tomorrow House."

Ramon stood, regally commanding with the wide breadth of his shoulders and his towering height. He took her hand, kissed it, but did not immediately release it. "I ask a favor, my dear little Cyn. One that should be no problem for you."

Her heart accelerated. She knew she had nothing to fear from this man, and yet he frightened her. She tried to smile. The corners of her mouth turned up slightly. She tried again, opening her mouth for a more friendly appearance. "Certainly, Ramon."

"Your only neighbor...a Señor Hodges I believe you said. Please give him a message from me."

When she tried to pull her hand away, he tightened his hold briefly, then released her. "You want me to give...a message to Nate?" Cyn could feel the heat rising from her chest, covering her throat, suffusing her face.

"Tell this Señor Nate Hodges that he should keep close watch on such a beautiful neighbor. Anything could happen to a lovely woman living all alone. Perhaps I am just an old-fashioned man, but I believe a woman should have a protector."

Cyn laughed, the sound halfway between a cry and giggle. Why was he so interested in her safety? "It's so kind of you to be concerned about me, Ramon, but I can assure you that women today are quite capable of taking care of themselves."

"Ah, yes. The modern woman." Ramon made a circular motion with his hand, a gesture of acceptance. "But you will pass along my message to your neighbor all the same, will you not?"

"The next time I see him," Cyn said, knowing that she had no intention of seeing Nate Hodges anytime in the near future.

CHAPTER 10

Mimi met her at the door the minute Cyn entered Tomorrow House. The place was a riot of confusion, with kids lining up in the hallway for lunch, a crew of workmen banging away on the roof, while two dirty, bearded men worked inside to repair the ceiling. From the game room, the noise of a loud advertisement for a foreign car competed with the screeching of a hot new hard-rock group blaring from the radio.

Rushing out of his office, Reverend Bruce Tomlinson, his eyes wide, his forehead dotted with perspiration, came barreling toward Cyn.

"Things are pretty wild around here," Mimi said, placing a motherly arm around Cyn's shoulder, guiding her toward her office and away from Bruce's inevitable approach.

"Noisy, too, huh?" Cyn laughed, allowing Mimi to herd her into her office.

"I gotta talk fast because Brucie's going to be in here any minute. Look, you got a tall, dark, good-looking visitor and Brucie ain't liking it a bit."

"Nate's here?" What was he doing here at Tomorrow House? After the way they had parted this morning, she'd been certain that he wouldn't seek her out again. After all, he'd made it perfectly clear that he didn't want her in his life.

"Did you know he was coming?" Mimi asked, leaning against the door when she heard Bruce take hold of the doorknob. "Bobby has told Bruce all about the Brazen Hussy, and Bruce thinks our Nate is a bad influence on the kids. You know what a jerk Brucie can be. Besides, I think he's a mite jealous. He's been sweet on you for a long time."

"I set him straight about that over a year ago, Mimi."

"Well, I know you did, but the fact is he's being downright un-friendly to Nate. You won't let Bruce run our man off, will you?"

Cyn dropped her purse and briefcase on top of her desk, then straightened the pleats in her navy skirt. "Move out of the way and let Bruce in before he wears himself out shoving on the door."

Mimi stepped aside and Reverend Tomlinson came bounding into the room, practically falling over his own feet. "You need to see about that door, Cyn," he said. "It's sticking again. I thought I'd never get it open."

"Oh, I think Mimi can take care of the problem," Cyn said, try-ing not to smile. "Come on in, Bruce. Did you want to see me about something important?"

"That man is here." Bruce puffed out his basset hound jaws, took a monogrammed handkerchief from his coat pocket and wiped the perspiration from his upper lip.

"If you're referring to Mr. Hodges, then I think you should know that he's here as my guest. We have some business to discuss." Cyn removed her white cashmere sweater and hung it on the back of her chair. She had no idea why Nate had come to Tomorrow House, but whatever the reason, it was certainly none of Bruce's business.

"Bobby told me all about the Brazen Hussy, how Mr. Hodges car-ries a knife, how he single-handedly subdued that boy," Bruce said. "What sort of business could you possibly have to discuss with a man like that?"

"Personal business, you ninny." Mimi stood in the doorway. "I'll be in the lunchroom if you need me," she said to Cyn before leaving.

"That woman's behavior is outrageous!" Bruce stuffed his hand-kerchief back into his pocket.

"Mimi is the heart of Tomorrow House. The kids love her." It was on the tip of Cyn's tongue to tell him that Mimi's contributions to the shelter far outweighed his. "And my business with Mr. Hodges is none of your concern. Like Mimi said, it's personal."

"I see."

"Look, Bruce, we have something more important to discuss than your misgivings about Mimi and Na—Mr. Hodges." Picking up her purse, Cyn unsnapped the catch, pulled out a white envelope and waved it around in the air. "I have here a check that will more than cover the expense of running Tomorrow House for the next six months. Call Reverend Lockwood and tell him that we have a patron saint."

"My word, Cyn, is this true?" Bruce shuffled nervously like a child trying to postpone a trip to the bathroom.

"Quite true."

"Who?" he asked, then gave Cyn a puzzled look.

"Ramon Carranza." Cyn smiled as she remembered her unusual brunch with the elderly Cuban gentleman.

"The name sounds familiar."

"He's a retired businessman. No family. A charming and generous man." Cyn asked God to forgive her for the little white lie she'd just told Bruce. After all, it was for a good reason and for a good cause. Although she had some misgivings about taking money from a man with Ramon Carranza's reputation, she knew Bruce would absolutely refuse. Where she was able to see life in various shades of gray, Bruce saw it only in black and white. Considering the fact that Tomorrow House would close without Señor Carranza's generosity, Cyn figured that what Bruce didn't know wouldn't hurt any of them.

"I'll call Reverend Lockwood immediately." Bruce turned to go, then stopped short. "Cyn, I don't think Mr. Hodges is the kind of role model the boys need. Bobby seems in awe of the man."

"I thought Bobby might be a little bit afraid of—"

"Well, if he was, he no longer is," Bruce said. "The two of them have been playing pool for the last hour. I still don't wholly approve of you putting that pool table in the game room."

Cyn slumped down on the edge of her desk, crossing her arm over her waist and resting her chin on the knuckles of her other hand. Watching Bruce walk out of her office, she sighed and shook her head. How could two men as different as Evan Porter and Bruce Tomlinson both have been ordained by the same church and placed in the same position as director of Tomorrow House?

After locking Ramon Carranza's check in the small safety box in her desk, Cyn went in search of Nate Hodges. As much as she wanted to see him, she dreaded facing him. Somehow, she knew he hadn't come to profess his undying love for her.

She found him in the game room, standing back and watching Bobby as the boy studied the pool table, contemplating his next shot.

Nate saw her the minute she walked in. Sunshine. That's what he thought of every time he saw her. Pure, clean, bright light. No dark places, no hidden shadows. A woman as honest and good and loving as this old world could create.

He had talked to Romero after Cyn had left this morning, asking if there was any way to get protection for her. Romero had said it was doubtful, but he'd see what he could do. Nate knew that Cynthia Porter's best protection was staying away from him. But just in case it was already too late, just in case Carranza was Ryker's comrade, then Nate had to make sure she was kept safe. He'd placed a call to Sam Dundee right after his conversation with Romero. Dundee was the best bodyguard in the business, and as long as Romero couldn't come up with federal protection, then a hired gun would have to suffice. Of course, he wasn't sure how Cyn would feel about having a bodyguard. That's why he'd come to Tomorrow House—to tell her about his decision to hire Sam Dundee. He just hoped he could persuade her to agree.

"Lunchtime, guys," Cyn said as she walked into the game room.

Bobby laid his pool cue on the table. Smiling, he pointed to Nate. "He's winning, anyway. Man, Cyn, he's good at everything. You should see him playing Nintendo."

"Won't you join us for lunch?" she asked, her eyes filled with questions as she looked at Nate. "Bobby, you go ahead and save us a couple of seats."

"Thanks, I'd like to join you." Nate hung the cue sticks on the wall holder and restacked the fifteen balls.

The lunchroom was crowded and noisy, but the food was hot and delicious. Nate sat beside Cyn, aware that she was doing her level best to avoid any eye contact with him. She had every reason to be angry about this morning. After all, he'd spent hours making love to her and then had sent her packing. He had tried to explain, but she hadn't bought his explanation.

"Did you make your ten-thirty appointment?" Nate asked.

"Yes." Cyn picked up her glass of iced tea and sipped slowly.

"Mimi said you had a brunch date with some millionaire you were hoping would make a large donation to Tomorrow House." Nate cut into the slice of chocolate cake with his fork.

"That's right."

"Did you get the money?"

"As a matter of fact, Señor Carranza gave me a check to cover all the expenses for the next six months." Hearing Nate choke, then cough, she turned quickly to him. He glared at her. "Are you all right?" she asked.

Nate's stomach knotted tightly. He could hear the roar of his heartbeat in his ears. She had lunch with Ramon Carranza? Damnation! How the hell had Carranza gotten to Cyn so quickly?

"How did you meet Ramon Carranza?" Nate asked.

"Do you know Ramon?"

"I've heard of him." Just who the hell was this Carranza? Nate had been turning the question over in his mind for days now and had asked Romero to dig a little deeper into the mysterious Cuban's background. Regardless of what Romero found out, Nate knew one thing for certain. Ramon Carranza meant trouble for him.

"I suppose everyone in Florida knows about his reputation," Cyn admitted, trying not to allow her conscience to bother her about taking money from such a man. Possibly dirty money— even blood money.

"Then if you know about his criminal past, why did you agree to meet with him?"

"He's been contributing ten thousand dollars a year to Tomorrow House for the past several years. He was the logical person to contact when I needed more money." She didn't like the tone of Nate's voice or the accusation she heard in his words. How dare he, of all people, condemn her. "Besides, I found him to be a very charming man."

"Did you indeed?"

"Will you kindly lower your voice. Everyone is staring at us."

"Then let's finish this conversation in private." Dropping the paper napkin he held in his hand, Nate stood up abruptly, grabbing Cyn by the arm and jerking her up beside him.

"Good idea," she said. "I happen to have a few questions I want to ask you."

It took them fifteen minutes to finally get away from the kids, from Bruce's reappearance to tell her that he'd spoken to Reverend Lockwood, and to settle a squabble between the inside and outside repairmen.

The minute the door of Cyn's office closed behind them, Cyn placed her hands on her hips and swirled around to face Nate. "Why are you here?"

"Your questions will have to wait a few minutes. We're not through discussing Ramon Carranza and why the hell you took money from a damned crime boss."

"Reputed crime boss. Señor Carranza has never been convicted of a crime," Cyn said, her breath huffy. "I think we should give him the benefit of the doubt, don't you?"

"No, I don't. Reputed crime boss, my rear end. He was a top dog in Cuba back in the forties and fifties and moved his operations to Miami when Castro took over."

"You seem to know an awful lot about Señor Carranza. Why is that?"

Hell! He'd opened his big mouth and said more than he should have. "Word gets around." Nate reached out, grabbing her shoulders. When she tried to pull away, he tightened his hold. "The point is this—stay away from Carranza. He's bad news."

"I won't have you dictating whom I should and should not see. I don't need a protector despite what you and Ramon Carranza might think." Cyn struggled to free herself from Nate's tenacious grip.

"Be still." His words were low and deep and commanding. "What did you mean when you said that Carranza thinks you need a protector?"

"Will you let go of me?"

"What did Carranza say to you?"

"It was no big deal." Nate was frightening her, more than Ramon had. Was there some connection between the two men? No, please, Lord. No.

"Tell me, anyway."

"I just happened to mention to Señor Carranza that I was staying in Sweet Haven and you were my nearest neighbor."

Nate's curse word stung Cyn's ears.

"What's the matter with you?" Cyn tried to push some bothersome, half-formed doubts out of her mind. Now was not the time to let her imagination run wild. "It was no big deal. Señor Carranza simply asked if you were someone I could count on if I needed help."

Nate squeezed her shoulders so forcefully that she let out a yelp of pain. He released her immediately. "Is that all?"

"Well, he said I should give you a message."

Hot coals filled Nate's stomach, burning through his insides. Carranza had sent him a message—a warning? And he had used Cyn as his messenger. "What was the message?"

"Aren't you taking this a little too seriously?" Cyn asked, puzzled by Nate's attitude, and yet bothered by the shadowy suspicions she couldn't escape.

"He said to tell you to keep a close eye on me, because anything could happen to a woman living all alone."

Nate turned from her, afraid she would see the fear in his eyes and discern for herself the danger their relationship had put her in. Under his breath, he let out a string of rather crude curses. Carranza was sending him a warning, all right. There was no doubt in Nate's mind that the old Cuban knew Ryker and was working with him.

"You've got to move back to Jacksonville, to your apartment." He wasn't going to tell her that Nick Romero was working on getting her some government protection. It would be hard enough to explain why he wanted to hire a private bodyguard for her. That news alone would probably scare her to death. But what choice did he have, especially since Carranza had issued his warning?

"I don't want to leave Sweet Haven, not yet. Don't you think you're overreacting?"

"You're going back to Jacksonville," Nate said. "And I'm hiring someone to protect you."

"You're what?"

"Ryker could show up in a few days. Maybe even tomorrow. I don't want you anywhere around me when he does show."

"I...I'll go back to Jacksonville tomorrow if that's what you want, but I will not have some...some guy watching my every move."

"Not just some guy. A private bodyguard. Romero recommended him. He used to be a DEA agent."

"No."

"Yes. I've already put a call in. He can be in Sweet Haven today, and he'll help you move your things back to Jacksonville and keep you—"

"I can't leave yet," Cyn said.

"Yes, you can and you will."

"We're having a picnic at the beach this evening. Mimi is already making preparations for the food. Bruce has borrowed a bus from the church. The kids are expecting to spend May Day at my beach house."

Nate slammed his big fist into his open palm. Cyn jumped at the unexpected noise. "If you can't cancel the picnic, then you'll have to leave when it's over and not come back until you hear from me...or Romero."

"I'll go, but I refuse to have a bodyguard."

"We'll see."

"No bodyguard!"

"What do I have to say or do to make you understand that if Ryker finds out about you, he'll use you to get to me."

"Nate…" She reached out for him.

He turned and walked out of her office, not once looking back.

Sitting down in her swivel chair, Cyn huddled over her desk and buried her face in her hands. She cried then, for Nate, for herself and for two ancient lovers. Someone had murdered the Timucuan maiden and her conquistador. A man named Ryker wanted to kill Nate, and if he knew she was Nate's woman, he would kill her, too.

Nate spotted the black Cadillac limousine the minute he stepped out of Tomorrow House and onto the sidewalk. Emilio had parked across the street, almost a block away, but in this neighborhood, a limousine stuck out like a sore thumb. Undoubtedly, the man wasn't trying to hide.

Jaywalking, Nate crossed the street. When he reached the black Caddy, he leaned over and pecked on the side window. Emilio Rivera opened the door and stepped out, his six-foot-eight, three-hundred-pound body towering over a six-foot-two, two-hundred-pound Nate.

"Has your boss got you following me?" Nate asked, slipping on his aviator sunglasses.

"I'm keeping an eye on Señora Porter." Emilio glanced across the street, nodding toward the one-story building that housed Cyn's shelter.

"Tell your boss that I got his message."

"Ryker is in St. Augustine. Señora Porter will soon be in danger."

Nate felt the blood run hot in his veins, fear and anger heating it to the boiling point. "Tell Carranza that I will hold him personally responsible if anything happens to Cyn Porter."

"Such a fierce protector," Emilio said. "Señor Carranza said you would be."

"Carranza can go straight to hell for all I care."

Nate thought he saw the corners of Emilio's mouth turn up slightly as if he were about to smile and caught himself. "*Si,* I will tell him how you feel."

Nate stood on the street watching the black Cadillac until it was out of sight. As soon as he could get to a telephone, he was calling Sam Dundee. Like it or not, Cyn was going to have a bodyguard.

Cyn handed Bruce the plastic bag filled with damp bathing suits, then turned to pick up a basket of leftovers from the late-afternoon picnic.

"I think that's got it," Bruce said. "We'd better be on our way, it's past six now."

"You go on," Mimi Burnside told him. "I'll be there in a minute." The big redhead grabbed Cyn by the arm and pulled her away from the open bus door. "Why are you moving back to your apartment tonight? I didn't think you were a quitter."

Cyn looked away from Mimi, waving at some of the kids who were hanging out open bus windows. Deliberately avoiding direct eye contact, Cyn tried to explain her reasons without revealing too much. "Nate has some personal problems that he has to work out before we can even think about a future together."

"And just why can't you stay here and help him work out those problems?" Mimi scowled at Bruce, who stood on the first step of the bus entrance, motioning for her to hurry.

"Nate doesn't want me here," Cyn said.

"Hogwash."

"Thanks for caring so much." Cyn hugged Mimi, as a child might seek comfort from her mother. "I love you, but don't push me on this. Please take my word that I'm not giving up on Nate, I'm just doing what's best for both of us for the time being."

"Well, if you ask me—"

"Mimi." Cyn gave her friend a pleading look.

"You know where to find me, day and night, if you need to talk." Mimi gave Cyn a bear hug, turned around and walked toward the bus. "I'm coming, I'm coming," she said to Bruce, whose round face was lobster-red from the heat and his agitated state of mind.

Cyn stood at the edge of the road, watching the bus until the red taillights disappeared. She let her gaze stray across the road, knowing that Nate was home, waiting—waiting to send her away.

She couldn't bring herself to turn around and go inside. The desire to run to Nate overwhelmed her. Her legs ached with the pressure she exerted to keep them from moving toward his house.

Reminding herself that she still had to pack before her long drive back to her Jacksonville apartment tonight, Cyn began to turn, the effort taking all her willpower. And then she saw him. He stepped out onto his front walkway, stopping abruptly when he glanced in her direction. He threw up his hand and waved. Stunned, she simply gazed back at him, watching while he moved toward her, down the walkway, across the yard and then the road.

She thought he looked as breathtakingly male as a man could look, all six-foot-two inches of hard, lean muscles and bronze flesh. He moved quickly, with the swift, sure stride of a jungle animal. Quiet. Deadly.

When he was within a few feet of her, she could see him plainly in the bright outdoor lighting she'd turned on for the picnickers. His expensive clothes gave him an air of elegance, but the unbuttoned shirt, worn without a tie, and the short black ponytail proclaimed him a rebel, a man who lived by his own rules.

"Cyn, we need to talk." He took several slow, tentative steps, stopping within arm's reach of her. She seemed wary, almost afraid. The last thing on earth he wanted was for her to be afraid of him.

"You didn't have to come over to remind me to leave. I was just going in to pack. I'm returning to Jacksonville tonight, and I won't come back to the cottage until you tell me it's all right." She turned around, hoping he wouldn't see the tears forming in her eyes.

He reached out and took her by the shoulders, pulling her back up against his chest. Feeling the tremors that racked her body made him curse the fates that had decreed the two of them should meet now when all he could offer her was danger.

"Before you leave, we have to talk." God, she felt so good. Soft, warm and all woman. He wanted nothing more than to lift her into his arms, lower her to the ground and take her quickly, spilling himself into her while listening to her feminine cries.

"I thought we'd already said all there was to say this afternoon." Belligerently, Cyn tried to pull away, but he held fast, tightening his big hands on her shoulders.

"Let's go inside." How was he going to be alone with her long enough to explain everything she needed to know and not succumb to the desire raging within him? The last thing he wanted was to send this woman away.

"This afternoon you said it was dangerous for me to be with you. Has that changed?" Cyn gave in to the longing to lean back against him, to absorb the power and strength of his big, hard body.

Lowering his head, he nuzzled the side of her neck, his lips savoring the taste of her sunshine-fresh hair as he kissed the golden strands. Loosening his tenacious hold, he ran his hands up and down her arms. "No, that hasn't changed." He felt her stiffen, knew she was already withdrawing from him. "I've arranged for a bodyguard, and I don't want any arguments."

She whirled around, her brown eyes wide, her soft lips parted on her indrawn breath. "I don't want... Oh, Nate, is it really necessary?"

"Sam Dundee is waiting for you in Sweet Haven. He's going to follow you home tonight. He'll keep an eye on you until Nick Romero can arrange protection."

"Protection? More than a bodyguard?"

Taking her hands into his large ones, he pulled her toward him. "Government protection. Ryker works for the Marquez family, the leading drug dealers in Florida. Romero and the DEA are involved, at least, unofficially."

"Why must I...why...?"

"Because I can't protect you and keep you away from me at the same time."

"I could stay with you," she said hopefully, gazing up at him with such love in her eyes that he thought he'd die from the pleasure-pain that her fearless devotion gave him.

"No, Brown Eyes. I want you far away when I meet Ryker." He turned her hands palm up, and lavished hungry kisses across her tender flesh. "I want you to promise me to be careful. Allow Sam Dundee to do his job. I'll call when Nick has a man in place so you'll know the change has been made."

"When will I see you again?" she asked, breathless from his nearness. She ached to hold him, to take him into her arms and into her body and find again that hot, sweet, secret place where they had gone together in the moments of total fulfillment.

"Not until it's all over. One way or the other."

"Nate, I don't understand any of this, especially Ramon Carranza's involvement." Before Nate could reply, Cyn gave him a warning look. "Don't try to deny that there's something going on between you and Señor Carranza."

"I'm not sure about Carranza. That's something else I'll have to deal with once I've eliminated Ryker." When he felt her cringe at his choice of words, he regretted his bluntness.

When she tugged on her hands, he released her. "Do I *have* to leave you tonight?" she asked.

No, his heart screamed. *Stay. Stay with me forever,* his soul cried. "Yes," he said.

She slipped her arms beneath his jacket and around his waist, hugging him tightly. She ran her fingers over the smooth leather sheath that held his knife. She willed herself not to tremble, not to be repulsed by the deadly weapon strapped to his body. "I don't want to leave you."

He grabbed her, lifting her off her feet. "Do you think I want you to go?" He took her mouth with all the savage hunger within him, longing to devour her sweetness, desperate to know again the pure pleasure that her loving heart and body could provide.

She accepted his marauding lips, the conquering pillage of his thrusting tongue as she returned, full force, the power and passion with which he took her. The world around her seemed to fade into a haze of swirling darkness, a sea of brown, edged with pale light. This man, his virile energy, his intense masculinity, surrounded her. She could feel him drawing her into his body, consuming her femininity, taking strength from her womanly power.

Nate trembled. Dear God, he had to let her go! No matter how much he wanted her or how badly he needed her, he had to send her away. To keep her safe.

Slowly, reluctantly, he eased her down the hard, muscular length of his body, allowing her softness to slide over every inch of his pulsating manhood. She clung to him, her slender arms draping his neck, her lips parted on a sigh of pure pleasure as their bodies caressed each other's.

"You have to leave," he told her, but his big hands still lingered around her waist.

She didn't say a word, only looked at him, her eyes speaking for her heart, pleading with him. It might be the wrong time and the wrong place, but the feelings were right. Nate had never been so sure of anything in his life. He had never truly needed anyone. He'd made sure of that. He had spent a lifetime protecting himself from the weaknesses that dominated other men's lives. No one had ever broken through the protective shell Nathan Rafael Hodges had constructed around his heart, a barrier of solitude and indifference that kept him safely apart from the emotional attachments to which most men succumbed.

But Cynthia Porter had done what no other woman had ever done. She had put a crack in Nate's defensive armor. She meant more to him than she should. If he allowed his selfish need to overcome his common sense, he would be putting her life in danger. But her life was already in danger, he reminded himself.

He swooped her up into his arms, leaving her breathless and clinging to him with all her might as he carried her inside her cottage. Kicking open the slightly ajar front door, Nate entered the living room. Without hesitation, he lowered her onto the chintz sofa and covered her body with his own.

"I need you," he breathed into her ear, his mouth moist and hot against the side of her neck. "I need this." He ground his hips against hers, crushing her trembling body deeper into the sofa.

"Yes." She would have refused him nothing, so powerful was her desire, so overwhelming her love. Even knowing that he would send her away afterward, she still wanted to give herself to him.

He kissed her, his lips masterful in their seduction. Moving his fingers to the hem of her cotton pullover sweater, he jerked it up and under her arms, revealing her lace-covered breasts. Lowering his head, he took one nipple into his mouth, sucking greedily through the lacy barrier.

"I want you naked," he told her, lifting her up to remove her sweater. Quickly, he unsnapped her bra, removed it and tossed it to the floor.

He buried his face between her breasts, allowing his tongue to paint an erotic trail from one erect nipple to the other. She arched against him, thrusting upward against his throbbing arousal.

"Oh, Nate, I want you so much." Her voice sounded strange to her own ears, distant and haunting.

He grasped the elastic waistband of her slacks, tugging downward until he encountered her bikini briefs. Slipping his fingers inside the top of her panties, he lowered both underwear and slacks down and off.

When she fumbled with the buttons on his shirt, Nate lifted himself off her and removed his jacket, tossing it toward a nearby chair. In his haste to rid himself of his shirt, he popped several buttons.

"I want to feel you against me." Lowering his body back down onto her, he rubbed his broad, smooth chest over her breasts, the action tightening her nipples to diamond-hard points. "Woman… woman…you make me crazy."

"I want you so much, I'm hurting." She reached out, trying to undo his belt and was startled when he pushed her hands away. "Nate?"

"I want you aching even more." He ran his hand between her thighs, delving his fingers through the tight blond curls and between her moist folds. "I want you so wet and hot and throbbing that you'd do anything to have me inside you."

She moaned, squirming beneath the knowledgeable strokes of his fingers as he fondled and petted her sensitive flesh. Beginning at her breasts, Nate aroused her to a fever pitch with the repeated licking and sucking motions of his mouth and tongue as they created a fiery path downward. He eased her legs further apart, his kisses coating the inside of her thighs.

She writhed beneath him, her body responding to his every touch as if it had never known a man. And indeed, Cyn thought, her mind dazzled by torrid sensations, every time with Nate was like the first time. Powerful. Hungry. Lustful.

His mouth covered her intimately. She groaned.

He tortured her, bringing her close to the edge, then retreating, returning to bring her to the edge again.

She grabbed handfuls of his shiny black hair, trying to pull his marauding mouth away. "Please…please…"

Raising his head, he looked at her, satisfied by the wild look in her eyes, the passion-drugged expression on her face. Inch by inch, he edged his body upward until he covered her, then he raised himself on his elbows, lowered his head and took one peaked nipple between his teeth.

Cyn cried out from the pleasure. Her body was so sensitized that a mere touch shot through her with aching intensity. "Now!" she cried out, gripping his buttocks in her hands, clutching the soft fabric of his trousers.

Nate jerked his zipper open, shoved his slacks and briefs down below his hips and rammed into her with shocking force. He felt her buck beneath him, heard her loud moans, and smelled the strong, heady aroma of her womanly scent. He wanted to ask if he was being too rough, but he was too far gone to be capable of speech. The world condensed to include nothing except the two of them—her body, his body, the fast hard thrusts of his manhood, the answering undulating rhythm of her femininity.

Sweat-slick and passion-hot, they mated, with the hard, heavy needs within them ruling their every move until one final lunge propelled them through the timeless ecstasy of fulfillment. She shook with a release so strong she thought she might never recover from the forceful shudders that continued claiming her when his life force emptied into her. His groaning cries of fulfillment echoed in the stillness of the cottage as his body trembled.

Her man, stronger and more powerful than most, lay weak and drained in the arms of the woman who loved him. Loved him enough to die for him. Even enough to kill for him. The thought of loving someone so deeply and completely frightened her. She had known Nate Hodges for such a short period of time, and yet it seemed that she had known him always, that he had been a part of her from the day she'd been born.

With their bodies still joined, Cyn snuggled against him, caressing his back, whispering love words to him. He claimed her mouth for a leisurely kiss. She felt his sex hardening within her as his tongue slipped inside her mouth.

"One more time, Brown Eyes," he said, and began again the ancient dance that bound them together eternally.

CHAPTER 11

Nate lifted her suitcases into the van, slammed the door and stepped away. He couldn't touch her again. If he did, he'd be lost—he'd never be able to let her go.

"I'll follow you to the gas station," he said. "Sam Dundee is waiting there. He'll be as inconspicuous as possible so you can go on about your life as usual. No one should notice his presence if he's as good as Romero says he is."

The moonlight cast honeyed shadows across her face, and the night breeze stirred the loose tendrils of her long hair. He knew she was close to tears, and if he prolonged their goodbye, she would be crying soon.

"I'll let you know when Romero gets someone to replace Dundee." He took one last long look at Cyn before getting behind the wheel of his Jeep Cherokee, which he'd parked beside her van.

Feeling numb, Cyn started the engine and maneuvered the minivan out of the driveway, and onto the deserted road. Within five minutes, she slowed down in front of the closed gas station. A tall, broad-shouldered man stepped out of a compact car. Cyn pulled the van to a stop, but remembering Nate's instructions, didn't get out. She watched as Nate drove in beside her, jumped out of his Jeep and went over to speak to the man he'd hired to protect her.

She could hardly believe her life had come to this—that she had to live in fear that some madman would use her to get even with

Nate. Never once had she sought out violence, but it had come to her, ripping her life apart. Why, dear God, why? Was Nate right? Did you have to face violence when it was thrust upon you and fight for your own salvation? And for the safety of those you loved?

Cyn sat quietly but impatiently until Nate and the other man approached her. When the two neared, she got a close-up look at her bodyguard. He was big and blond, with a hard, weathered-looking face and a muscular body that seemed to be in prime condition.

"This is Dundee," Nate told her, then gave the other man a warning stare. "Make sure nothing happens to her." With that said, Nate got in his Jeep and drove away, not once looking back.

Cyn tried to open the van door, wanting to run after Nate, needing to cry out to him for one final word of goodbye, but Dundee's big body pressed against the door. "It's time to leave for Jacksonville, Ms. Porter."

Clinging to the last shreds of her composure, Cyn nodded her head, silently agreeing. Perhaps it was best not to be allowed a farewell look, a final touch.

As Cyn made the journey from Sweet Haven to her Jacksonville apartment, she remembered the last moments she had shared with Nate. They had made love twice, each time a passionate sharing, an eternal bonding that transcended the merely physical act that brought them both so much pleasure.

After they had showered together and redressed, he had set her down at the kitchen table and told her about Ian Ryker. She knew he hadn't told her everything, that he had spared her all but the necessary facts.

"I knew Ryker in Viet Nam. We hated each other," Nate had told her. "Ryker was a mercenary, and it was a known fact that he was supplying drugs to Uncle Sam's boys. Although American by birth, Ryker's loyalties were questionable, and his morals nonexistent."

Cyn had listened patiently while Nate explained the reasons Ryker held such a deadly grudge against him. "On an assignment deep into Vietcong-held territory to capture a hamlet chief that we hoped could give us specific information about enemy supplies and movements, Ryker and I met face-to-face.

"Ryker was involved with the village chief's daughter and had sold out to the NVA. During the Vietcong chief's capture, his daughter was accidently killed in the crossfire when she ran to Ryker for protection. I have no idea whose fire actually killed the girl, only that in the split second that it took Ryker to react to his lover's death, I opened fire on him. My SEAL team barely escaped with our lives and our prisoner."

Cyn realized how difficult it was for Nate to tell her about what had happened so long ago, in a country halfway around the world. In those moments while he shared a painful part of his past with her, Cyn began to understand what had made Nate Hodges the hard and lonely man he was today. And it made her love him all the more.

"For several years after the incident, I thought Ryker was dead, but then he showed up, out of the blue, missing a hand and an eye and warning me that, one day, he'd get even with me.

"I didn't live in fear, but I dreaded the day he'd make good on his threats," Nate had told her, while he sat tall and rigid at her kitchen table, his face solemn, his eyes haunted with tormented memories. "I stayed in the SEALs. Spent twenty years in the navy, and I always kept vigil, waiting for Ryker."

"Oh, Nate." When she had reached across the table and tried to take hold of Nate's hands, he'd pulled away.

"Five years ago, reports came in from South America that Ryker had been imprisoned for smuggling and had been killed in a prison fight. The reports were wrong. He reappeared a few months ago. I knew then that it was only a matter of time."

Cyn pulled into the parking area of her apartment complex. Leaving her suitcases inside, she locked the van and looked around, searching for Dundee. He parked and got out of his car. Dear God, how could her life have changed so drastically in so short a period of time? Although violence had marred her safe existence when Evan had been brutally murdered, Cyn lived her daily life on a fairly normal, safe routine. Violence had lain on the outskirts of her civilized life.

But Nate Hodges had changed all that. Loving a warrior had

thrown her into harm's way. Filled with all of mankind's imper-
fections, this earth fell far short of paradise, but Cyn wanted
this life and the love of the man her heart and soul had been
waiting to find. Eternity's perfection could wait. All she had
ever wanted was within her grasp. The man of her dreams was
here with her in this imperfect world—here, this side of
heaven.

Morning sunlight brightened Nate's den, shimmering on the
wall-mounted swords and reflecting off the numerous glass cases.
Nate snapped the lid on the suede-lined case and placed his prized
Gurkha hunting dagger alongside several other cases containing
many precious treasures. A loner by choice, Nate was attached to
few people and even fewer things. But his extensive knife collection meant a great deal to him.

He would never forget Cyn's reaction to this room filled with
the acquisitions of a lifetime. She hated knives as much as Nate
loved them. For he did, indeed, love knives. He loved the look and
feel of them. And he loved their capabilities. In the right hands, a
knife was a tool of endless diversity.

But Cyn's husband had been stabbed to death, and erroneously,
she blamed the weapon as well as its user. Damn, how had this happened to him? How had he allowed himself to become involved
with a woman as gentle and loving as Cynthia Porter? She offered
him her heart and her body, freely, but he knew loving her could
cost him dearly. He had found with Cyn something he'd only
dreamed about, something he didn't believe existed. She had given
his soul the sanctuary it craved. Her pure, sweet goodness had enveloped the cold darkness within him, bringing him warmth. She
filled his world with light. But he would have to keep his past from
destroying her before he could accept what she offered.

The loud pounding noise aroused Nate from his thoughts. When
he opened the front door, Nick Romero rushed inside.

"What the hell are you doing here?" Nate asked. "If you've got
a man to cover Cyn, you could have called."

"I'm still working on that." Nick ran his fingers through his curly black hair. "Dammit, man, why did you have to pick now to finally get seriously involved with a woman?"

"What the hell's the matter with you?" Nate knew something was bothering Romero, more than having to twist a few arms and call in some favors to get protection from the agency for Cyn.

"I could use a cup of coffee. I haven't had time for even a taste this morning." Romero didn't look directly at Nate.

"In the kitchen. Come on."

Nate led Romero into his makeshift kitchen, poured him a cup of hot coffee and led him outside to the patio. A sky filled with soft clouds and morning sunshine promised the warmth of an early spring day.

"So, what's up?" Nate asked.

Romero took several hefty swigs from the coffee, then, looking out at the overgrown garden, he said, "John is all right, but there was an explosion aboard one of your cruisers early this morning."

Cold fear chilled Nate's body and coated his mouth with a metallic flavor. "Where's John?"

"He's been with the police all morning, trying to answer questions without telling them the complete truth." Romero took another deep swallow of coffee. "There's nothing left of the boat, and one of your employees, a guy named Wickman, got hit with some of the debris. He was on the pier."

"How is he?"

"Emergency room's already released him."

"I need to see John," Nate said.

"No, you don't." Romero finished the last sips of his coffee, and, clutching the empty cup in one hand, he placed his other hand on Nate's shoulder. "John is taking his wife and son home to Alabama to stay with her family until this thing with Ryker is settled. He wanted me to tell you. He said you'd understand."

"Hell, yes, I understand." Nate shrugged off Romero's hand as he paced up and down the long archway that led from the patio to the wraparound porch. "His first priority is to protect the woman he loves and their child."

"Ryker is in St. Augustine," Romero said. "The bomb explosion was just his way of announcing his arrival. We both know that."

"Looks like my time has just about run out."

Cyn flipped through the television channels, hoping to find something interesting enough to grab her attention. Alone and restless after a full day's work at Tomorrow House, she longed to forget that a hired bodyguard stood watch outside her apartment, that miles away Nate might be engaged in battle with his enemy, that she was powerless to change the inevitable.

"National Geographic" was on the educational channel, and under normal circumstances, the program would have piqued her curiosity about the subject, but tonight she didn't care about the plight of any species. All she could think about was Nate, alone and in danger.

Rational thought told her that he was better off without her, that her presence would have harmed him far more than it would have helped him. But her irrational heart told her that he needed her, that a woman should stand by her man and face the enemy with him. She was beginning to understand that there were times in one's life when turning the other cheek meant certain death. *When violence is thrust upon you...*

She flipped off the television, dropping the remote control on the plaid colonial sofa. Well, what was she going to do? She had already eaten a late dinner, cleaned the kitchen, done a load of laundry and taken a bubble bath. She had tried reading, doing a crossword puzzle and watching TV. Nothing worked. Nothing had taken her mind off Nate. They had been apart less than twenty-four hours, and already she was miserable without him. If only he were safe. If only this nightmare would end. If only he would come to her and stay with her forever.

Cyn went into her compact kitchen and opened the refrigerator. Resisting the urge to devour a quart of chocolate ice cream, she reached for the diet cola and poured herself a tall glass.

Maybe she could play solitaire until she got sleepy. Where had she put that deck of playing cards? she wondered. Remembering that she and Mimi had played poker several months ago right here at the kitchen table, Cyn figured she had put the cards in one of the nearby cabinets. Before she had a chance to search for the missing deck, the telephone rang.

She removed the receiver from the wall phone. "Hello."

"Cynthia Porter." The voice on the other end was distinctly male, deeply baritone.

"Yes." She felt an irrational uncertainty creep through her like a slowly spreading plague.

"You have made a fatal mistake," he said, enunciating each word with precise deliberation.

"Who is this?" She knew, dammit, she knew. If he had found her, he had found Nate.

"You signed your own death warrant when you became the Conquistador's woman."

"What?" Cyn cried out. The dial tone sang in her ear.

She dropped the phone. It hit the floor with a resounding clatter. Stepping back, she stared at the dangling cord, her mind reeling with panic. Taking several deep breaths, Cyn hunched over and covered her face with her hands. Stay calm, she told herself. Think. Think.

Reaching down, she picked up the telephone and dialed Nate's number. The phone rang and rang and rang. Where are you? *Answer, please answer. I need you.*

"Hello," Nate said.

"Oh, thank God, Nate."

"Cyn, what's wrong?"

"Please, tell me that you're all right." She leaned against the wall, clutching the phone tightly in both hands.

"I'm fine. Do you hear me? I'm all right. Tell me what's wrong. What happened?"

"He…he called."

"Who called?"

"Ryker."

"Did he tell you who he was?" Nate asked.

Pressing her hand into her mouth, Cyn bit down on her fist trying to curb the flow of tears.

"Cyn!" Nate's voice was loud and insistent.

"He said...he said that I had signed my own death warrant...when...when I became the Conquistador's woman."

"Listen to me very carefully," Nate told her. "Go outside and get Dundee. Tell him that I said for him to stay inside with you until I get there."

"But Nate——"

"Do what I told you. I'll be there as quick as I can."

"Nate, why did he call me?"

"Because he's playing a game," Nate told her. "It's called 'Let's make Nate sweat.' He wants me to know that he's aware that you're important to me, that he knows where you live and how to get to you."

After she'd spoken to Nate, Cyn calmed down considerably and fixed a fresh pot of coffee for Dundee and her. They were both on their third cup when the doorbell rang.

Dundee pulled a Magnum from his shoulder holster and stood to the side of the door, his big hand hovering over the doorknob.

"Ask who it is," he instructed her in a whisper.

"Who is it?" she asked, her voice so tight and highly pitched she barely recognized it as her own.

"Nate. Open the damned door!"

Releasing the safety latch, she opened the door and flung herself into Nate's waiting arms. He lifted her off the floor in his protective embrace. God, he hated himself for allowing this woman to become so important to him. Until she had come into his life, he'd never had a weakness, and now he had a major one, just at a time when he needed to be strong and invulnerable.

Half walking her, half carrying her, Nate guided Cyn to the sofa. Dundee closed the door behind them.

Cyn ran her fingers over Nate's face, stroking his flesh, cherishing the sight of him, alive and safe in her arms. "I was so afraid that he'd found you...that——"

Nate covered her moving lips with his index finger, momentarily silencing her babbling. He looked over her head where it rested on his chest and saw that Dundee held a Magnum in his right hand.

"Go check around outside. Scout out the area," Nate said. "I'm going to take her to a friend's house, and I want to make sure we aren't followed."

"Sure thing," Dundee said. "I'm glad you're here. I couldn't convince her that you were all right."

The moment Dundee left, Nate took Cyn's face in his hands, stared at her tear-filled eyes, then released her. Why her? he asked himself, and why now? The last thing he needed was to have to worry about her safety when his own life was on the line. Ryker must be laughing his fool head off, Nate thought. The minute Carranza told Ryker about Cyn, he probably realized that using her to destroy Nate would be the sweetest form of revenge. After all, he blamed Nate for his lover's death.

"Call Mimi and tell her that you'll be spending the night," Nate said. "Then go pack a bag."

"Mimi's? You want me to stay with Mimi?" Cyn's gaze questioned him. "I don't understand. I don't understand any of this."

"Ryker knows where you live."

"But how—"

"How doesn't matter." If he told her about Carranza, she'd think it was her fault and start feeling guilty. But she wasn't guilty of anything except loving a man like him—a man who had no right to let his emotions overrule his common sense. "Dundee will stay with you at Mimi's until I talk to Romero and get a government man to protect you."

"No, please, Nate." She grabbed hold of his jacket lapels, tugging fiercely. "Don't leave me. Don't send me to Mimi's. Let me go home with you. You can protect me."

He held her face tightly, probing the depth of conviction that showed plainly in her rich brown eyes. He released her face and pulled away from her. "I can't protect you and fight Ryker at the same time. Try to understand that you're safer without me."

"Are you safer without me?" she asked.

He stood up, rammed his hands into his jeans pockets and strode across the room. "Yes."

She turned to face him, nodding her head in a gesture of understanding. "Why…why did he call you the Conquistador?"

Nate's face visibly paled. No one had used that damnable nickname in years. Hell, how had a label given to him by a friend turned into a curse? "It was my nickname. I acquired it in SEAL training at Coronado."

"Why—"

"Nick Romero dubbed me. Everybody called him Romeo because he was such a ladies' man. While we were in training I acquired a reputation. Because of my Hispanic looks and…undisputed abilities as a commando, Nick started calling me the Conquistador. The name stuck. In Nam, and for years after the war."

"I see."

"No, lady, you don't see." His voice was filled with all the pent-up rage he felt.

Nate cared for Cyn, more than he'd ever cared for another human being, but he hated himself for caring so damned much. He had allowed her to become far too important to him. He had put her life in danger by loving her. "You don't see a damned thing but some fairy tale legend about a couple of ancient lovers. Of all the men on earth, why did you pick me, huh? Why me?"

She gasped, new tears flooding her eyes as she huddled into a ball and hugged her legs up against her chest.

More than anything, Nate wanted to drop to his knees beside the sofa and put his arm around her trembling shoulders. But that sort of stupidity would solve nothing. This woman was one of his biggest problems. He had to get her out of his life—for both their sakes.

"You've made me weak." he stood with his back to her, fear and anger combining to strengthen the warrior within him. "I've never had a weakness before in my life, and it's the last thing I need right now. You are the last thing I need." When he heard her choked sobs, the anger inside him grew, building until he wanted to rage at the world, to appease that anger on Ryker. But Ryker wasn't here.

He turned on her then, facing her, afraid for her. "Ryker's going to try to use you against me. He's already using you. He knew when he called you that the first thing you'd do was get in touch with me, tell me what he said. It was his way of turning the screws, of prolonging my agony. He knows that, if you're with me, all I'll be able to think about is protecting you. I won't be thinking like a warrior, but like a lover. That kind of thinking could get us both killed."

"Are you saying that...that..."

"I don't want you with me. You're trouble, lady, more trouble than I can handle."

"Nate, please..." She reached out for him again, and felt as if he'd physically shoved her away when she saw the rejection in his eyes, the withdrawal in his stance. She was losing him, and she couldn't bear the loss. "If you loved me—"

"I don't!"

The pain was unbearable and yet she bore it. The tears that had only moments ago run so freely from her eyes lodged inside her, building the ache that threatened to choke the life from her. Nate had never told her that he loved her, but he had never said that he didn't. Until now. Did he honestly think that there was nothing more between them than the physical desire neither of them could deny?

"Call Mimi. I'll explain things once we get there." He could feel her pain, and it was almost his undoing. But he would not allow himself to comfort her. More than love and comfort, Cyn needed his strength. Only his strength could protect her.

"Should we...involve Mimi?" Cyn asked. "Won't my going there put her in danger?" An icy numbness had taken control of Cyn's emotions. She felt nothing, absolutely nothing. The pain of Nate's harsh rejection had spread through her so quickly that it had anesthetized her feelings.

"Dundee will make sure we aren't being followed. He'll stay with you and Mimi until an agent arrives." Hesitating for a brief moment, Nate looked at her. He hated himself for hurting her, but he hated himself even more for putting her life in danger. "Call Mimi. Change clothes. Pack a bag."

"Where will you go after you take me to Mimi's? Back to Sweet Haven?"

"No. I've already called Romero. I'll be meeting him."

Cyn walked on unsteady legs toward her bedroom. Pausing momentarily in the doorway, she turned slightly. "You're going after Ryker, aren't you? You're not going to wait for him to come to you."

"He's already come to me," Nate said, his voice deadly soft. "He knew exactly what he was doing when he called you. By threatening my woman, he issued me an invitation, one he knows I won't refuse."

The blessed numbness inside her began to dissolve, leaving her with the tiniest emotional sensation. He had called her his woman. "Is that what I am?" she asked. "Your woman?"

"The Conquistador's woman. That's what Ryker thinks you are," Nate said, and saw the spark of hope die in her eyes.

CHAPTER 12

Nate decided that Mimi Burnside was not only a sensible woman, but a human being with a heart of pure gold. He had liked the older woman the minute they met, but seeing her motherly concern for Cyn made him like her all the more.

"Don't worry about a thing," Mimi said as Nate laid Cyn's suitcase at the foot of her bed. "I'll call Brucie in the morning and tell him that I've come down with the flu or something and that Cyn is going to be playing nursemaid so neither one of us will be in to work."

Nate couldn't help but smile as he watched the big redhead, her graying hair rolled on soft pink curlers and her five-foot-ten-inch body wrapped in a blue chenille robe. Large-boned and buxom, Mimi Burnside looked more like an aging burlesque queen than a former factory worker turned housekeeper.

"You go ahead and put on your gown, honey child," Mimi told Cyn, then turned to Nate. "You come out in the living room with me while she changes."

Nate obeyed, following Mimi. Once outside the closed bedroom door, she leaned over and whispered, "I've got a gun. A .25 automatic. I don't usually keep it loaded, but I've got the bullets for it."

"Do you know how to use it?" he asked, not in the least surprised that she had a gun.

"Yeah. My first husband taught me how. Good thing, too, since I had to run off that no-good bum I married the second time. He tried to use me for a punching bag one time too many." Mimi pointed to the sofa covered with a bright flowered slip-cover. "Sit."

"Are you sure you were never in the service? You sound a lot like my old boot camp drill instructor." Nate sat down, relaxing just a bit, certain that he had brought Cyn to the right place.

Mimi laughed, the sound hearty and unrestrained. "That Dundee fellow a friend of yours?" She nodded toward the front door.

"He works for me."

"A hired gun?"

"Something like that."

"When should I expect that government man?" Mimi asked.

"Possibly by morning. When I leave here, I'm meeting Nick Romero."

"You two going a-huntin'?" Mimi widened her slanted cat eyes.

"You just take care of Cyn and don't worry about me."

"We'll both worry about you," Cyn said as she opened the bedroom door.

Nate looked up. His heartbeat accelerated. She looked so small and fragile standing there in her aqua satin robe, her hair hanging loosely to her waist.

When she neared the sofa, he stood. He wanted to reassure her that everything would be all right. But he couldn't lie to her, and if he took her in his arms, he might never be able to let her go.

"This will all be over soon," he said. "Whatever happens——"

Her tormented cry ripped at his heart like the talons of a mighty bird. "Don't say that."

"Cynthia Porter has always been a strong woman, someone people could depend on. Be strong now." Silently he added, *"Be strong for me, Brown Eyes. I need your strength."*

"Go and do what you have to do." Silently she added, *"I'll be waiting for you...forever."*

Hastily, before his courage deserted him, Nate left. Mimi came up beside Cyn and placed a comforting arm around her shoulder. As Nate walked out into the hallway, Cyn noticed Dundee step out of the shadows. He came inside and closed the door.

"You ladies go on to bed whenever you like. I'll just sack out here on the couch."

Mimi squeezed Cyn's shoulder. "Come on, honey child."

"I don't think I can sleep," Cyn said, leaning her head against her friend's arm. "How can I rest not knowing what's happening with Nate, wondering if he's killing or being killed?"

Mimi led Cyn into her small bedroom. The light from an imitation Tiffany lamp spread a colorful glow over the unmade bed. "If you can't sleep, then we'll just have us a slumber party. We'll sit up the rest of the night and talk."

"It's not fair to involve you in this." Cyn turned to Mimi and was reassured by the smile on her face. "Nate seems to think we'll be safe with Dundee keeping guard over us."

Mimi gave Cyn a persuasive nudge, suggesting she sit. Cyn slumped down on the side of the bed. Mimi went around to the other side, got in, and propped several pillows behind her as she sat up against the headboard. "Nate knew what he was doing bringing you here. The only way that Ryker fellow could get to you would be through me."

Burying her hands in her face, Cyn cried silent, painful sobs. Mimi reached out and touched Cyn's back. "Go ahead and cry it all out. Better do it here with me than to let Nate see you like this. He's already worried enough about you."

After cleansing her heart with a torrent of uncontrolled crying, Cyn wiped her eyes with her hands, scooted up in the bed to sit beside Mimi, and pulled a blanket up over her legs. "I thought that losing Evan was the worst thing that could ever happen to me, but I was wrong."

"You're not going to lose Nathan Hodges," Mimi said.

Cyn tried to smile at the firm conviction she heard in her friend's voice. She wanted to believe. "I never knew you could love someone the way I love Nate. It's…it's as if I've always loved him."

"Since you were fifteen and dreamed about him for the first time?" Mimi asked.

"It *was* Nate in my dreams. The same eyes. The same body. The same strength." Cyn fumbled with the frayed edge of the blanket with which she'd covered herself. "But the man in my dreams was more than just Nate. He was…oh, Mimi, you'll think I'm crazy if I tell you."

"So, tell me anyway. I'm probably crazy enough to believe you."

"Do you know what Nate's nickname in the service was?"

"Does this have something to do with your dreams?"

"Yes." Cyn cleared her throat. "They called him the Conquistador."

Mimi sucked in her breath. "Who…but that's just a coincidence, honey child."

"Maybe. Maybe not."

"You think the man in your dreams was the ancient warrior whose soul is supposed to roam the beach at Sweet Haven with his Indian bride?"

"Part the ancient warrior and part Nate, the modern warrior who will set the lovers free to enter paradise."

"Well, I'm not sure I actually believe it." Mimi's nervous smile could not disguise her doubts.

"I'm not sure I do, either, but…every time Nate touches me, it's as if he's touched me a hundred times before. I've known him for such a short time, and yet I feel as if I've known him forever."

"I think you're tired and stressed out. In the last few weeks, your whole world has been turned upside down. If your belief that you and Nate are the lovers in the prophecy who will set a couple of ancient souls free helps you get through this ordeal, then who am I to think you're crazy?"

"He told me he didn't love me," Cyn said.

"When?"

"Tonight."

"Did you believe him?"

"I did when he told me," Cyn admitted.

"And do you still believe him?"

"No."

Cyn laid her head down on a large, soft pillow. Closing her eyes, she prayed for a few hours of sleep. Dreamless sleep.

Nate didn't spot Nick Romero's car when he pulled into the all-night diner's parking lot. No doubt Romero had used a government vehicle. Something a lot less conspicuous than the sporty 1968 silver Jag he drove.

When Nate entered the diner, the big plastic clock above the counter reminded him that it was after midnight. The aroma of strong coffee mingled with the fading smells of numerous meals and the ever-present odor of grease. The place was spotlessly clean, but the equipment and furniture had seen better days.

Nate glanced around the partially deserted eatery. A couple of guys sat at the counter drinking coffee, a middle-aged couple sat cuddled lovingly in a back booth, and an elderly man sat alone up front, reading a newspaper. Nick Romero sat in the second booth from the front door, and he wasn't alone. He was talking to a very attractive brunette.

Damn Romero, Nate thought. What the hell was he doing flirting with some dame? Nate knew that Romero liked women, and had spent over forty years living up to his nickname, but now wasn't the time for him to make a new conquest.

Nate approached the table, determined to control the urge to jerk Romero up by his collar and to send the brunette packing.

Romero looked up at Nate and smiled. "Sit down, old buddy, and let me introduce you to the lady."

Nate sat down on the opposite side of the booth and gave Romero a deadly look. "I haven't got time to meet any of your *friends*. This is business. Remember?"

Romero's smile widened. "Don't get bent out of shape. This lady is an agent. Donna Webb is going to be keeping an eye on Cyn until you finish things with Ryker."

Nate took a closer look at the woman sitting beside Romero. She appeared to be in her early thirties. Dressed in jeans, turtleneck pullover and a baggy plaid jacket, she could have passed for the average woman on the street.

Nate offered his hand. Donna took it. "I left Cyn at Mimi Burnside's. Dundee is with them."

"What did you think of Dundee?" Romero asked.

"I think he's capable," Nate said.

"Yeah, he's capable." Shaking his head, Romero laughed. "Sam Dundee was one of the meanest, toughest agents I ever worked with. He always reminded me a little bit of you."

"Then I'm glad he was available on such short notice," Nate said, then turned his attention to Donna Webb. "Cyn will probably feel more comfortable with a female agent. She hates the idea of having a bodyguard. I haven't told her yet that we're planning on sending her to her father's home in Savannah."

"You realize we can't force her to leave Jacksonville if she isn't willing to go," Donna said.

"She'll be willing to go," Nate said. "I can promise you that."

Nate spent the next thirty minutes drinking coffee, discussing the situation and making plans with Romero and Agent Webb. By the time the three of them left the diner, Nate felt reassured that Donna was as capable of protecting Cyn as any male agent.

Outside, the cool night air swirled around them. Overhead storm clouds obscured the pale moon and blackened the normally starry sky. Streetlights illuminated the parking lot, as did the huge neon Open 24 Hours sign flashing with bright, colorful light.

"Do you want to go with me to drop Donna off at Mrs. Burnside's?" Romero asked.

Nate shook his head. "No. I've already said my goodbyes."

"Okay. I'll meet you at your place in a couple of hours and we'll start tracking Ryker. If he can find you, then we should be able to find him."

Donna put her hand on Nate's arm. "Don't worry about Ms. Porter. I promise to take good care of her."

"Yeah, I know you will." Nate forced a fake smile, feeling nothing but loneliness and dread.

Romero and Donna headed straight for the brown sedan parked on the left side of the diner. Nate walked in the opposite direction toward his Jeep.

A speeding car flew down the street in front of the diner. No other traffic stirred at such a late hour. At first Nate heard the roar of the motor, then, out of the corner of his eye, he saw the vehicle swerve off the road, as if the driver had lost control.

Adrenaline pumped through his body like floodwater through a broken dam. Turning quickly, he caught a glimpse of a metal object sticking out of the car window, something held by the man sitting on the passenger's side. The moment his mind registered the object as a gun, Nate yelled out a warning as he dropped to the sidewalk, seeking cover behind the Camaro parked beside his Jeep.

The earsplitting sound of an Uzi firing repeatedly echoed in Nate's ears. Hunched on his bent knees, Nate made his way down the front of the Camaro as the Uzi's lethal clatter rang out a deadly toll. He saw Donna go down, her slender body crumpling, her arms flying about in midair as the force of the Uzi's bullets ripped through her. Then the attacker turned his attention to Romero, who had just pulled his automatic from his shoulder holster. His hand was in mid-aim, his gun pointed, when he took his first hit.

Nate opened his mouth on a silent scream of protest. Then suddenly, he felt a sharp pain lance his side.

As quickly as the car appeared, it disappeared. The silence following the ungodly round of shots was morbid in its intensity.

Dammit all, he had never figured Ryker would try a sneak attack. He'd been so sure that he would want a face-to-face confrontation.

Running his fingers inside his jacket and alongside his rib cage, Nate felt the wet stickiness of his own blood. He knew he'd been hit.

As he struggled to stand, he noticed all the diner's customers coming to the door. But not one of them ventured outside. Nate saw that neither Donna nor Romero was moving. Blood covered both bodies. Nearby vehicles were dotted with splashes of red. Puddles of crimson formed on the sidewalk.

Nate checked Donna first. She was the closest to him. One of the bullets had taken off a chunk of her neck. She was dead.

Romero groaned when Nate leaned over him. "It's my leg," he said. "I'm bleeding like a stuck hog. I think he got the artery."

No matter how many times Nate had seen a comrade's body riddled with bullets or shattered by an explosion, the sight still sickened him. With trained instincts, Nate inspected the large hole in Romero's leg, then administered the correct amount of pressure to stop the flow of blood from the femoral artery which the Uzi's bullet had severed.

Turning his head toward the array of onlookers hiding inside the diner, Nate yelled, "Call an ambulance!"

The elderly man who had been quietly reading his newspaper stepped outside. "I done called 'em. Told 'em it was a shooting and to hurry." He hesitated in the open doorway. "Is she dead?"

"Yeah," Nate said. "She's dead."

"How about him?" the man asked, nodding toward Romero.

Nate looked down at his friend. "He's alive, and by God, he's going to stay that way."

By the time Dundee answered the insistent ringing of the door-bell, Mimi and Cyn were standing in the living room, belting their robes and yawning.

Cyn's heart beat overtime. She had never known such fear. Not knowing whether a killer or the bearer of bad news stood outside Mimi's apartment triggered a surge of adrenaline within Cyn's trembling body.

Holding his Magnum, Dundee motioned for Mimi and Cyn to step back inside the bedroom. With one quick move, he swung open the door and aimed his automatic.

"Put your gun away, *amigo*," Emilio Rivera said.

"Who the hell are you?" Dundee asked.

Peering out into the living room, Cyn gasped when she saw Ramon Carranza's huge bodyguard. Mimi gave her a shove and they both took several tentative steps, stopping abruptly when Emilio glanced their way.

"What's wrong?" Cyn asked.

"Señora Porter." Emilio's dark eyes rested on her briefly, then looked over at Mimi. "Señora Burnside, you will help her dress. Please. Señor Carranza is waiting outside in the limousine."

Cyn moved forward, hesitating several feet away from Emilio. "What's happened? Why does Señor Carranza want to see me?"

She grabbed the back of the sofa, clutching the flowery material in her hands.

"Señor Carranza will explain everything. But you must hurry, *señora,*" Emilio said.

"Now see here, one cotton-pickin' minute." Mimi put her hands on her ample hips, giving Emilio a warning glare. "You ain't taking this girl nowhere unless we get the word from Nate Hodges. Ain't that right, Dundee?"

"I'm afraid I must insist," Emilio said. "You can trust us, Señora Porter."

"Now that's where you're wrong, pal." Dundee, his automatic still pointed at Emilio, moved toward their uninvited visitor. "We know we can't trust you."

"*Señora,* surely after all Señor Carranza has done to help you, to finance your shelter, you can trust him." Emilio took a step toward Cyn.

Dundee moved quickly, placing his big body between Emilio and Cyn. "You go back downstairs and tell your boss that Ms. Porter isn't going anywhere with him."

"But he only wishes to take you to the hospital to see Nathan Hodges," Emilio said.

"What?" Cyn cried out. "What's happened to Nate?"

"Don't listen to him," Mimi said, grabbing Cyn by the arm. "It's some kind of trap."

Jerking out of Mimi's grasp, Cyn rushed toward the bedroom. Mimi caught her just as she swung open the door. "Don't be a fool, gal!"

Dundee edged closer to Emilio, who hadn't budged an inch. "What happened to Hodges?"

"He was shot in an ambush coming out of some seedy diner," Emilio said.

Cyn cried out. She clutched Mimi, feeling as if her own two legs weren't sturdy enough to hold her weight. If Nate was hurt, she had to go to him. Nothing and no one was going to keep her away from him. Not Ramon Carranza or Emilio Rivera. Not even Dundee. "I've got to go to the hospital."

"And so you will, honey child," Mimi assured her. "Mr. Dundee here will take you, won't you?"

Dundee never took his eyes off Emilio, but he nodded agreement as he stepped closer to his opponent. "You can go tell your boss that Ms. Porter doesn't need a ride to the hospital."

Emilio, as if reconciled to the fact that Cyn was not going to leave with him, turned toward the outside door. "I will relay your message."

"One more thing," Dundee said as Emilio opened the door. "Tell your boss that Ms. Porter won't be out of my sight for a minute. My job is to take care of her, and I always do my job, no matter what."

The minute the front door slammed shut, Cyn slumped into Mimi's arms. "What if…if Nate's dead."

"Honey child, we don't—"

"While you're getting dressed, I'll make a few phone calls," Sam Dundee said. "If I don't get some answers, we'll go straight to the hospital."

Pulling out of Mimi's comforting arms, Cyn rushed into the bedroom and began changing clothes. Mimi followed, closing the door behind her.

"Carranza was crazy if he thought you'd just go with him, and even crazier if he thought Dundee would let you go." Mimi flung open her closet, and, standing on tiptoe, reached up to the top shelf. Turning around, she held out a small handgun and a loaded clip. "I'll go with you if you insist on going, and I'll take along my little baby here."

Cyn stuffed her red blouse down into her navy slacks, pulled up the zipper and grabbed a sweater from out of her open suitcase lying on the bed. The minute Mimi laid the gun on the bed and began removing her housecoat, Cyn stared at the automatic. She had never held a gun. She hated them as much as she did knives. She despised any type of weapon.

"You aren't going with us, Mimi," Cyn said. "This isn't your problem."

When Mimi started to protest, Cyn held up a restraining hand.

"I will not put your life in any more danger, but it seems I can't escape. I'm beginning to understand what Nate meant about having violence thrust upon you."

Cyn stared down at the gun lying on Mimi's bed. What if the only way to protect her life was to use that gun? What if the time came when Nate's life depended on her being able to defend him? Cyn, her hands wet with perspiration and trembling with uncertainty, picked up the automatic, inserted the clip and reached for her purse.

"I'll borrow this," Cyn said, placing the gun inside her leather bag.

"Be careful," Mimi said. "Let Dundee do his job. And call me when you find out something about Nate."

Several loud raps on the bedroom door interrupted any further conversation. "Are you ready, Ms. Porter?" Dundee asked. "I haven't been able to find out much over the phone. Hodges and Romero have both been admitted to the hospital."

Giving Mimi a quick hug and kiss, Cyn opened the door. She left the apartment with Dundee, pausing briefly in the hallway to wave a final farewell to Mimi.

As they walked down a flight of steps, Cyn asked her bodyguard. "Was Nate shot?"

"Gunned down."

"Oh, my God!"

"He and Romero and a female agent were riddled by an Uzi when they came out of a local diner about one-thirty this morning."

Cyn forced herself not to cry, not to faint. Walking briskly to keep up with Dundee, who held her securely by one arm, she followed him outside and into his car.

Cyn's worst fears had come true. Nate had been so sure that Ryker would confront him man-to-man. "Are they alive?"

"The woman is dead. My sources couldn't tell me anything about Romero or Hodges except that they were both still alive when the ambulance brought them in to the hospital."

Cyn leaned her head back against the seat. The thought of Nate hurt, maybe even dying, was almost more than she could bear.

The trip to the hospital seemed endless as the streets began to blur. The lights and the darkness merged. Cyn prayed. She couldn't lose Nate. If he died, they would be as doomed to an eternity without fulfillment as the ancient lovers were. If Nate died, she didn't want to live.

CHAPTER 13

Nate leaned against the wall just inside the first emergency room cubicle. He felt like hell. His side hurt despite the painkiller the nurse had shot into his hip, over his stringent protests. And he had a headache the size of Texas. He picked up his jacket, belt and sheath off the nearby chair, placing the belt and sheath over his arm and covering them with his jacket. He ran his fingers over his bandaged side, grimacing from the pain that bending his arm caused. Looking down at his opened shirt, he thought about trying to button it, then decided it wouldn't be worth the effort.

J. P. Higdon, Nick Romero's boss, had just left. He had assured Nate that everything possible was being done to save Romero's life and that the agency was handling the situation with the local authorities.

For the last two hours, on the ride to the hospital and while the emergency room staff treated his gunshot wound, Nate had relived those few fatal moments outside the all-night diner. Had they been careless? How had Ryker known where they were meeting? Had Carranza had him under surveillance? Or maybe one of Ryker's associates in the Marquez syndicate? Nate felt guilty. He shouldn't have been so certain that Ryker wouldn't resort to an ambush. What hurt the most was knowing that he himself hadn't really been the gunman's target. Romero and Webb had been the intended victims. Webb was dead and Romero was hanging on by sheer willpower.

Ryker had issued a warning. Nate knew that, one by one, Ryker was going to attack the people closest to Nate. First John Mason. Now Nick Romero. There was only one person left... the most important person. And Ryker would try to kill her. Nate knew that as surely as he knew her death would destroy him.

Nate's big body shook, not from shock or pain, but from fear. Closing his eyes tightly, he sought to block out the fear, but instead the visions that flashed through his mind only heightened the terror. Dreams. The dreams of his brown-eyed lover that had once given him so much comfort. Dreams of Cyn lying dead in Ryker's arms.

Nate's eyes flashed open. He saw her. Her long golden hair hung in disarray over her shoulders, across her breasts, a vivid contrast to her bright red blouse. Her gaze moved in every direction, and he knew she was searching for him. God, it was good to see her. Not until this very minute had he realized how much he needed her.

She looked down the hallway. She stared at him, their eyes speaking a language only their hearts could understand.

She cried out and ran toward him. Dundee followed, rushing to keep up with her.

All the pain and fear and love that she felt came to the surface, full force, the moment she saw him. He was alive. Willing herself not to fling her arms around him proved to be the most difficult thing she'd ever done. She stopped, only inches separating them. With trembling fingers, she reached out and touched his face.

"Nate. Oh, Nate." Her voice was a fragile whimper.

She glanced down at his bandaged left side, wondering how serious his wound was and why he wasn't lying in bed instead of standing, partially dressed, just inside an empty cubicle. When he spread his right arm in a come-to-me gesture, Cyn lunged into his uninjured side. He pulled her up close against him, encompassing her within his strong embrace.

She eased one hand up and across his broad back and laid the other on his bare chest. Closing her eyes, she allowed her hands to explore the solid reality of his body. Tears fell in never-ending rivulets down her flushed cheeks, but she didn't care if her weeping was a sign of weakness. She had been strong all the way to the hospital, and she would be strong again in a few minutes, but right now she wanted nothing more than to rejoice in the knowledge that she had not lost the man she loved.

She could feel his warm breath against her ear, her neck, her cheek. She looked up into his dark green eyes. His gaze devoured her as his big arm tightened around her, almost painfully, and drew her closer. He nuzzled her face, seeking and finding her mouth. In one savagely possessive thrust, he captured her lips, and she accepted him with eager joy as the world around them faded into oblivion. Clinging to him, she felt her strength returning, as if she were absorbing his power.

He grasped her hip with his big hand, holding her quivering body against him while he continued ravaging her mouth. Finally, he released her, gazing at her with wild hunger in his eyes.

"How the hell did you find out what happened?" he asked, his voice harsh, but he still held her close against his side.

"Ramon Carranza," she said.

"Damn that man!" Nate didn't trust Carranza. The chances were pretty good that he and Ryker were connected in some way. But what bothered Nate the most was that Carranza was obviously keeping tabs on Cyn.

Noticing Dundee standing discreetly several feet away, Nate motioned him forward. "Carranza knew about the shooting? How did he contact Cyn?"

"He sent his bodyguard," Cyn answered before Dundee had a chance to reply.

"Carranza sent his goon to get Ms. Porter. He told her Carranza was waiting downstairs in his limo," Dundee said.

"Good thing you were there," Nate said. "Why the hell did you bring her here to the hospital? The point in having you around is to keep her protected and as far away from me as possible."

"The only way I could have kept her from coming here once she found out you'd been shot was to have knocked her unconscious, and I didn't think you'd want me to do that."

Cyn wanted to scream. These two big macho men were discussing her as if she weren't standing right there. She glared back and forth from Nate to Dundee. They were of equal height and about the same size. Sam Dundee's complexion was almost as dark as Nate's, but his short hair was flaxen blond and his eyes a cold, menacing blue.

"I want you to take her back to Mimi Burnside's," Nate said, then swayed slightly, bending his body in an effort to ease the pain shooting through his side.

Cyn held her fingers out over his bandaged side, longing to touch him, to soothe his pain, but she let her hand hover over his wound. "I won't leave you. You're hurt and…" She made an unsuccessful attempt to stop crying. "How…how…bad is it?"

Giving her another crushing hug, he tried to laugh. "Not so bad." He couldn't bear the agonized look on her face. "Hey, Brown Eyes, don't you know I'm too tough and mean to kill?"

"Oh, Nate, don't joke about this." She buried her face in his shoulder, sobbing quietly, relieved that he was truly all right and angry at the injustice of life.

"Don't fall apart on me now, Cynthia Ellen Porter. I'll be okay. All I need is for you to go back to Mimi's."

"Shouldn't you be in bed?" she asked, raising her head and brushing the tears from her eyes. She completely ignored his request for her to return to Mimi's.

"No. I'm fine. The bullet only grazed my side. I admit it made a nasty mess, but I've suffered far worse."

"I can't believe they've allowed you to get up." Pulling away slightly, Cyn inspected him from head to toe, realizing, for the first time since she'd entered the emergency room, that Nate looked like a man ready to run. "You were trying to leave, weren't you?"

"I am leaving," he told her, then glanced over at Dundee. "I'm going back to Sweet Haven, and I want her to stay here in Jacksonville."

"Has the doctor said you could go? Have they released you?" Placing her hand on her hip, she glared at him.

"I told them I was going. I've got to check on Romero, then I'm getting a cab home." Nate took several staggering steps.

Cyn quickly placed a supportive arm around him. "What's wrong? Are you in pain? Mr. Dundee, find a nurse."

"Don't move, Dundee. I'm fine, dammit," Nate said, clenching his teeth. "They shot me full of painkiller. I told them I didn't need it, but they insisted."

Cyn smiled, a trembly, teary smile. Dear Lord, what was she going to do with this man, her big, brave warrior? "Mr. Dundee and I are taking you home if you refuse to stay here overnight."

"I don't want you anywhere near me." Since he held her against him with fierce protectiveness, his words were ineffectual, and totally contrary to his actions.

A petite silver-haired nurse entered the cubicle, and smiled when she saw Nate and Cyn. "I'm glad you have someone here to take you home, Mr. Hodges."

"Then it is all right for him to leave?" Cyn asked.

The nurse glanced over at Dundee. "We would prefer that he stay the night, but since Mr. Hodges has refused, he should have someone with him. We gave him a pretty high-powered injection. I'm surprised he's still on his feet."

"He won't be alone," Cyn said. "Is there anything special I need to do?"

The woman looked at Cyn. "Just keep his dressings changed, and see that he goes to the doctor for a checkup." The nurse turned to go, then glanced back at Nate. "Your friend is still in surgery. He's alive. Surgery could last several more hours."

"What about his leg?" Nate asked.

"I don't know." The nurse shook her head sadly and left.

"What happened to Nick Romero?" Cyn asked.

"He got it in the leg. The bullet severed his femoral artery. There's a chance he'll lose that leg."

"Oh, Nate, I'm so sorry."

"Well, woman, don't you see?" Realizing he was still holding Cyn, Nate released her. "Ryker plays for keeps. As long as you're with me, your life is in danger."

"My life is in danger whether or not I'm with you." She nodded toward Dundee. "Otherwise, I wouldn't need a bodyguard."

THE PROTECTORS: *This Side of Heaven*   193

Nate's knees weakened. The room began to spin slowly. He reached out, bracing himself against the wall.

Cyn willed herself not to rush to him. Maybe, just maybe, it would be better if he fell flat on his face, she thought. Then she and Mr. Dundee could just wheel him straight into a hospital bed. She watched him closely for several minutes, then realized that Nate Hodges was fighting the drug the nurse had given him, and, knowing Nate's strength and determination, he wasn't going to lose gracefully.

"Mr. Dundee, would you please call Mimi and let her know how Nate is. Tell her that we're taking him home." Cyn frowned at Nate, her hard glare daring him to protest. "Make the call as quickly as possible and bring back a wheelchair. I don't think Mr. Hodges is going to be able to stand up much longer."

Dundee nodded agreement, smiling at Cyn and then at Nate before exiting the cubicle.

"He thinks it's funny," Nate said.

"He thinks what's funny?"

"That you're bossing me around." Nate wasn't used to having anyone in his life care about him, and he certainly wasn't used to some take-charge female issuing him orders. "The last thing a man needs when he's…he's been shot is some loud-mouth feminist telling him what to do."

"Oh, shut up, Nate." Cyn scooted a chair across the room, took Nate by the arm and eased him down. "Sit down and behave yourself. As soon as Mr. Dundee brings that wheelchair, we're taking you home."

"Romero. Need to stay…see about…" Nate's words began to slur.

"There's nothing you can do for Nick. I'll keep in touch with the hospital, and you can come back as soon as you get some rest."

"And if I don't…won't…" Nate slumped in the chair, his eyelids heavy, his breathing deep.

"You're going home, and you're going to do just what I tell you to do. Understand? And I'm not leaving you. Have you got that straight?"

"Come here," he said, motioning for her to lean down close to his face.

"What?" she asked, staring directly at him as she lowered her head.

"You're a bossy wench, Brown Eyes."

Laughing and crying at the same time, Cyn kissed him on the nose. "You bet I am."

While the coffee brewed and the bacon fried, Cyn looked out the kitchen window at the slow, steady rainfall. It had been raining when she and Dundee brought Nate home a little after dawn this morning. That had been almost five hours ago, and Nate had slept the first four hours. When he had awakened, he'd refused to take any of the pain medication Cyn had found in his coat pocket, but she was determined that he would eat the hearty breakfast she was preparing in the makeshift kitchen. In her own kitchen she could have made biscuits, but since Nate's kitchen didn't have an oven, he would have to settle for toast.

She had found a wooden crate under the sink and had cleaned it to use as a tray. Laying a clean towel over the rough surface, Cyn set a plate filled with bacon, eggs and toast in the center and placed a mug of steaming black coffee to the side.

As she passed the den on her way to Nate's bedroom, she saw Sam Dundee admiring the varied array of knives that comprised Nate's extensive collection. A slight shudder passed through her at the thought of all those deadly weapons housed under one roof, indeed being proudly displayed by their owner. Perhaps she would never understand the warrior within Nate, the beast that lived within every man. She abhorred violence, but with her motherly nature, she could understand fighting to protect those she loved. She would fight to protect Nate, to keep him safe.

The door to Nate's bedroom stood open. Nate sat on the side of the bed wearing only his unsnapped jeans. For a brief moment, Cyn stared at him, at his hard lean body, at his long black hair. He was every inch a man. And that very maleness called to Cyn on some primitive level, telling her that she was his.

He glanced up, watching her as she came in and held out the crate-tray for him to take. Staring down at the tempting food, he grunted, then accepted her offering.

"Thanks, I'm starved." He gulped down the coffee, then attacked the stack of crisp bacon.

After picking up his rumpled coat and empty leather sheath, Cyn sat down in the chair beside the bed. She wondered what he'd done with his knife.

"It's still raining," she said. "Looks like it's set in for the day."

With his mouth half filled with egg, he mumbled, "Thanks for the weather report." He took another swig from the mug. "Where's Dundee?"

"Admiring your knife collection."

"Has Higdon called?" When he saw the puzzled look on her face, he said, "Nick Romero's boss. He's supposed to give me an update on Romero's condition, and…he's making arrangements to have you escorted to your father's place in Savannah."

"What?" Cyn jumped, throwing her body slightly forward. "I'm not leaving you, so you can just call this Higdon guy and tell him I won't need an escort anywhere."

"If Donna Webb hadn't been killed last night, the two of you would already be in Georgia."

"What are you talking about?"

"The woman who was with Romero last night was an agent unofficially assigned to take care of you until I finish things with Ryker. Plans were for her to drive you to your father's home and stay there with you."

Seeing the wounded look in Cyn's eyes made him hate himself for having to be so blunt with her. But dammit all, if he couldn't make her understand the real threat to her life, he'd never be able to make her leave him. "Your father has already been notified," Nate said. "He was told only what was necessary."

"Who called Daddy?" Cyn demanded, jumping up, balling her hands into fists and shaking them at Nate.

Setting the tray on the floor, Nate glanced up at Cyn. Well, she was mad as a wet cat and just as ready to spit and scratch. "If Higdon doesn't come up with some more unofficial protection for you, then I'm sending you off with Dundee."

"You're not sending me anywhere, Nate Hodges." Leaning over, she punched the center of his naked chest with the tip of her index finger. "I'm exactly where I want to be and exactly where I'm going to stay."

Nate reached out, closing his big hand around her stabbing fingers. Looking into her rich brown eyes, he saw fury and determination and...love. He couldn't remember a woman ever trying to help him, trying to take care of him. He hated to admit, even to himself, that he liked seeing her fuss and fume as she ordered him around.

Clasping her whole hand in his, he pulled her forward. Her forehead rested against his, his breath warm and coffee-scented against her mouth. "I've been shot," he reminded her. "When Ryker comes for me, I'll be at a slight disadvantage. If I have to worry about your safety, if I'm busy protecting you instead of myself, I'll be at an even bigger disadvantage."

"Nate—" She couldn't think when she was so close to him, her lips hovering over his, her body straining for contact.

"Don't you understand, Brown Eyes, if you stay with me, you'll die with me?"

Their breaths mingled as her lips touched his with whispery softness. "Yes, I understand."

She wanted to stay with him enough to die with him. The thought shot through him like a bolt of lightning. He knew she loved him, knew she didn't want to leave him and thought she understood the danger, but hearing her say that she was willing to die with him made him realize the extent of her feelings for him. This woman, his beautiful Brown Eyes, did nothing by half measures. She had a heart big enough to encompass every living creature, enough love and tenderness to soothe a thousand wrinkled brows, enough maternal instincts to try to mother the whole world. But she loved him, only him, as a woman loves a man.

Slipping his right arm around her, he pulled her to him as he pressed his lips against hers. She moaned into his mouth, opening for the potent thrust of his tongue. His kiss was frantic, wild with heady longing, ravaging with the need to possess.

Leaning into him, her slight weight toppled them over onto the bed. She fell against his uninjured side. He cradled her head on his shoulder, and buried his lips against her throat.

Dundee knocked on the open door, then cleared his throat. "Excuse me, but Higdon's here to see you."

Nate released Cyn immediately. She sat up on the bed and straightened her slightly rumpled blouse. Looking down, she realized that, somehow, Nate had managed to undo the top two buttons. She stood up, turned sideways and hastily refastened her blouse.

Nate sat up, groaning silently at the soreness in his left side. "Tell him to come on back."

"I'm staying," Cyn said, wanting Nate to know she had no intention of letting him and some government agent make plans for her without her consent.

J. P. Higdon was several inches shorter than Nate, at least twenty pounds heavier and a dozen years older. He wore a three-piece suit, parted his thinning hair at an awkward angle in an effort to cover a bald spot, and had perpetual wrinkles in his forehead.

"How are you doing, Hodges?"

"I'm fine. How's Romero?" Nate asked.

Higdon glanced at Cyn and raised a questioning eyebrow. "This must be Mrs. Porter."

Cyn stiffened her spine, tilted her chin and smiled. "I'm Cynthia Porter." She offered her hand, which J. P. Higdon accepted in greeting. "I have no intention of leaving Nate so the two of you can have a private talk." Her smile widened. She placed her hand on Nate's arm. "So you might as well go ahead and say whatever you came here to say."

Higdon glared at Cyn, his round blue eyes wide with wonder. "I assure you, Mrs. Porter—"

"I'm not leaving," she said.

"She's not leaving," Nate told the other man. "How's Romero?"

Higdon ran his pudgy fingers beneath the tight collar that bound his neck, inadvertently loosening his tie. "Looks like Romero is as tough as you. The doctors say he'll live, but saving the leg is still iffy."

"Damn!" Nate wanted to strike out at something, at someone. He wanted five minutes alone with Ian Ryker.

Cyn felt the coiled fury inside Nate as she tightened her hold on his arm. His muscles hardened beneath her fingers.

"The bullet severed the femoral artery. If you hadn't known what to do and acted so quickly, he would have bled to death long before the ambulance arrived," Higdon said.

"When can I see him?" Nate asked.

"He's in the trauma unit. No visitors except family."

"He has no one except his grandmother, and she must be over eighty." Nate knew that Romero's childhood and youth had been little better than his own. Where Nate had suffered from neglect and abuse, Nick Romero had grown up in abject poverty.

"I'll arrange for you to see him, soon, but for now, I think you'll want to know that I've commandeered someone to take Mrs. Porter to Senator Wellington's." Higdon turned to Cyn. "Your father has been informed that you and Agent Bedford will be leaving Sweet Haven at approximately seven tonight."

Cyn started to speak, but kept silent when Nate took her hand in his and gave her a cautioning glance.

"She'll be ready," Nate said.

"I guess you know that this whole business with Ryker has become personal with us now that he's attacked two of our people." Higdon paused, but when Nate made no comment, he continued. "We're going to stick to you like glue until this thing is over."

"I don't think it'll be that easy." Nate squeezed Cyn's hand, not wanting to speak so frankly in front of her, but knowing she left him no choice. "When the showdown comes, Ryker will find a way to make sure I have no help. He'll want it to be the two of us."

"We'll see," Higdon said. "Agent Bedford will pick Mrs. Porter up here tonight at seven. And you can stop wasting your money on Dundee's services. We've already got our people in place."

"What do you mean?" Cyn asked, wondering if there was a combat squad surrounding the house.

"He means that there are men, strategically placed, who will be keeping an eye on me." Nate knew that Cyn must feel as if she had stepped into the middle of a badly written spy drama.

"Carranza's been making inquiries," Higdon said. "It seems he's very interested in the state of your health."

"Probably wants to give Ryker an update," Nate said.

"I can't figure out why that old Cuban involved himself in this mess with Ryker, even if he is in tight with the Marquez family." Huffing, Higdon shook his head.

Cyn felt Nate's whole body tense at the mention of the Marquez family. "Who's the Marquez family?" she asked.

"They're the top Colombian family working out of Miami. They sort of inherited part of the action from Carranza. He retired without giving them any trouble, so he's been able to maintain ties with them." Higdon glanced down at his watch. "Good luck, Hodges. I'll keep you posted on Romero's condition."

J. P. Higdon gave Cyn a courteous nod before leaving. Dundee appeared in the doorway moments afterward.

"I suppose you heard," Nate asked, knowing full well that Dundee had been standing outside in the hallway listening to the entire conversation.

"I'm as good as gone," Dundee said. "I'll stop by the hospital and check on Romero before I leave town."

"Thanks for your help." Nate offered his hand to the other man, who accepted it in a hearty handshake.

"Anything for a friend of Nick Romero's."

Cyn waited until Dundee had walked away before tugging on Nate's hand as she looked up at him. "Why should it matter that Ramon Carranza has connections to a crime family in Miami? That shouldn't come as any surprise considering his background. I don't understand what it has to do with anything."

Nate took both of her hands in his and looked directly at her. "Ryker is employed by the Marquez family."

"Oh, my God!"

"Now do you understand?" he asked. "If Ryker has the Marquez family and Carranza behind him—"

"And I talked to Ramon Carranza about you, answered his questions. Told him things I shouldn't have. Oh, Nate."

"When Agent Bedford comes tonight, you'll go with him. You'll stay at your father's until this is over."

"I don't want to leave you."

"Cyn—"

"Hush. I...I don't want to leave you, but I will. I don't want to make things more difficult for you. I don't want—"

Before she could finish her sentence, Nate swallowed her words, silencing her with the heated passion of his desperate kiss.

CHAPTER 14

The sun, only recently visible through the haze of gray rain clouds, lay against the western horizon like an overripe peach, fat and soft and brilliantly clothed in varying shades of yellow and red. The sky, coated with an eerie golden pink glow, seemed so close. Cyn shuddered, a sense of foreboding chilling her body.

A gentle after-shower breeze stirred her hair. She had pulled it back into a large bun at the nape of her neck, but fly-away tendrils had escaped and draped her face. She ran her gaze over Nate's unkempt garden. Knee-high weeds choked the grass and overwhelmed the spring flowers which were blooming in glorious profusion. Once, years ago, Miss Carstairs had attended this garden with the passion other women would have bestowed upon a lover. Even now, the remnants of her special care showed. It saddened Cyn to think how beautiful the grounds had been only a few short years ago.

She had left Nate in his knife-filled den. Ever since Dundee's departure over an hour ago, Nate had been on the telephone. First to the hospital, then to J. P. Higdon.

Cyn knew where she was going. She'd known the minute she had left Nate to come outside. The vine-covered rooms called to her. She felt powerless to resist; indeed, she had no desire to resist. There was darkness and death and mysteries long left unsolved lurking in the shadows, but there was more. There was love and commitment and hope. The Timucuan maiden and her conquistador had been married in the mission. They had made love in those rooms. And they had died there. Cyn didn't know how she knew; she just did.

The rooms had been a part of the old mission. They had not been the chapel itself, but the priest's living quarters. He had married them, that brave man of God, and had given them his bed in which to consummate their union.

Cyn's hand trembled as she reached out and pushed open the heavy wooden door. The air was oppressive, thick with mustiness, rich with the aroma of damp earth. Weak sunlight filtered through the boarded windows, casting the entire room into cold shadows.

Dear God, what was wrong with her? She felt hot and cold simultaneously. She was afraid, and yet realized she was safe. She knew things, felt things, wanted things that were alien to her.

It's why you came here, she told herself. *They are here. Waiting. Wanting. Needing.* With slow, almost trancelike movements, Cyn made her way across the cluttered room and toward a narrow wooden door in the center of the far wall. Behind that door lay the other storage room of the old mission.

Shivers of fear and excitement spread through her, stronger than the effects of any drug. Reaching out, she laid her hand against the cool wooden surface. Applying only slight pressure, she pushed. The door opened. Slowly. Ever so slowly.

She peered inside. The room was bathed in sunlight. Dark shadows had been forced into the four corners, leaving the center of the room filled with light...glorious, golden-pink light. Cyn sucked in her breath, awed by the almost sacred beauty of the room, her eyes seeing and yet not seeing that, except for the heavenly sunshine, there was scant difference between this room and the other.

She could feel the sun's warmth despite the chill in the ancient room. Her gaze traveled upward toward the source of the light. A huge section of the old ceiling was missing, leaving a jagged gap that permitted the outside world access within the coquina walls.

Although she had never been in this room before, it felt familiar. Memories flashed kaleidoscopically through her mind. Candlelight. Moonlight. The scent of fresh flowers. A soft blanket beneath her. A hard man above her. In her. Cyn shuddered.

They wanted something from her. Needed something so desperately. What? What do you want? she cried out silently. No one spoke the words and yet she heard them.

You and your warrior must be united as we could never be.

She didn't understand. How could she and Nate be united in a way the ancient lovers had never been? The maiden and the conquistador had consummated their marriage. They had been united. She and Nate had made love. They were already united.

Shaking her head, Cyn stepped backward toward the cool, shadowy wall. Her breath came in hard, shallow gulps. She trembled when she heard footsteps in the outside room. Who was out there?

Her mouth formed one word. Nate. Before she could voice his name, she saw the man standing in the doorway. He took a step forward.

She recognized him, and yet there was something different about him. He was Nate, her beloved Nate. And yet he was more. She was more.

In that one still moment when they stood staring at each other, Cyn knew. When he came to her, when they touched, when they loved, the fulfillment they found in each other's bodies would be shared by two ancient lovers. It had been that way before, every time she and Nate had made love, but only now did she realize the truth. A truth that should have frightened her, but didn't.

The love she and Nate shared had not begun a few weeks ago when they'd first met. It hadn't even begun years ago when she'd first dreamed of him. It had been born centuries ago when an Indian maiden and a Spanish conquistador had fallen in love.

Nate felt suspended in time, as if, in entering this ancient room, he had stepped back into the past. His past, and yet not his past. Someone else's past.

And she was here. Waiting for him. For a few endless moments, all he could see were her eyes, those rich, warm, brown eyes that had haunted his dreams over the years. The eyes of the woman he loved, the woman he had loved forever.

He moved toward her, watching the way the sunlight turned her yellow hair to gold, the way her full lips parted in anticipation, the way her body hugged the wall.

He had wanted her before, more than he had ever wanted another woman. She had given him pleasure beyond his most erotic dreams, and yet he could never get enough of her. As soon as he felt sated, his heart and body fulfilled, he began wanting her all over again. He wanted her now. More than ever. His need was filled with desperation. Some unknown force within him urged him on, reminding him that life held no guarantees, that death was sure and often swift.

When he reached for her, she went into his arms, docile in her surrender. Gazing down at her beautiful face, he saw the adoration, the hunger, the love, and he was lost. Her expression mirrored his own inner feelings, passion riding him hard. Lowering his head, he sought and found her lips, taking them gently, nipping, licking, nipping again. He circled her moist lips with his tongue, then inserted the tip between her teeth. She sighed. He delved deeper. She took him inside, welcoming the marauding exploration, sharing the pleasure as her tongue raked the side of his.

With several brutal stabs, he conquered her mouth. Trembling with desire, he released her lips, burying his face in her neck, his teeth covering her delicate skin with love-bites. She clung to him, her hands searching his shoulders and back, glorying in the feel of his hard, masculine body. Reaching between their bodies, he ripped at her blouse, jerking it out of her slacks and off her shoulders. When he began working on the hook of her bra, she started unbuttoning his shirt. Two sets of eager fingers moved hastily over two hot, hungry bodies.

She wore nothing but a pair of red bikini panties, he only a pair of unzipped jeans.

"You don't know how bad I want to be inside you," he said, his chest rising and falling with the harshness of his breathing.

"I love you." She took his face in her hands, her palms covering him from cheekbones to chin.

"Come back to the house with me. I want you. Now."

"No. Here. It must be here."

He glanced around the dirty, musty room, a room stacked high with decaying boxes and littered with an assortment of furniture and old junk. "There's no place to—"

She covered his lips with her fingers. "You've been wounded. You mustn't overexert yourself."

"I've got to have you, woman. Damn my wound!"

Cyn knelt on her knees in front of him. The hard rock floor beneath her feet was damp from the rain, warm from the sun, and smooth from centuries of wear. Placing her thumbs beneath the waistband of his open jeans, she grasped the faded denim and pulled.

"What the hell are you doing?" He slapped his hands over hers where she held his jeans just below his hips. He could feel himself jutting forward, and was unable to control the fierce need eating at his insides.

"I want to make love to you." Her voice quivered with the intensity of her own arousal. "I've dreamed of this."

"Cyn…" She was offering him a precious gift, the fulfillment of a man's most carnal desire.

He allowed her to remove his jeans. He stood above her, big and strong and powerfully male, his body straining toward her, needing, begging, demanding.

Running her hands up his hips, over his lean belly and across his muscular chest, she caressed him, savoring the feel of sleek, hard smoothness. The very touch of him was intoxicating her, seducing her onward, toward a path she had never followed, into an unknown world of sensual power.

Hot, untamed sexual energy flowed through her, dominating her as surely as Nate's big body beckoned her to sample its delights. She ran her hand over him in wild abandon. Over every inch, from tiny male nipples to strong, supple calves.

When her mouth replaced her hands, he bucked forward, his manhood touching the side of her face. He looked down and saw himself caught in the web of her golden hair. He groaned, so great was his need.

Turning her head, she tasted him. He cried out, the sound a harsh, guttural shout within the ancient walls. All semblance of his control vanished as he reveled in her loving attention.

He was about to explode. He couldn't stand any more. He reached down, jerking her to her feet, swinging her up into his arms. Glancing frantically around the room, he sought and found the only suitable place he could use.

Setting her down atop a tall stack of dilapidated boxes, he spread her legs and stepped between them. If he didn't take her soon, he would die.

She surged closer, allowing her breasts to sweep across his chest as she grasped his tense shoulders. "Now," she said.

He slipped his hand between them, pinching her tight nipples until she begged him to stop. "No more."

Moving his hand downward, he palmed her. She keened, the sound thin and high and piercing. His fingers found her hot and tight and melting.

Uncontrollable in her need, she bit into the taut flesh of his upper arm. "Please, Nate, please. I'm hurting."

"So am I," he said and rammed into her like an animal intent on perpetuating his species.

The pleasure was so intense she thought she'd die. A lifetime of love consummated this mating. Cyn's love. Nate's love. The love of a Timucuan maiden and a Spanish conquistador.

Clutching her hips, he surged in and out, harder and faster, creating premonitions of ecstasy that prompted them to accept the knowledge that four hearts were beating as one.

She not only accepted the savagery of his lovemaking, but basked in his dominance, reeling with the promise each possessive thrust made, knowing that in the end, she would attain the supremacy...for it was within her body that their immortality could be created.

With a relentless, pulsating rhythm, he took her, and with equal fervor she took him. Quick and wild and hot, their bodies spiraled up, up, up into the heat of fulfillment. In one earth-shattering second, a scalding pleasure burned through them. He poured himself into her as she sheathed him, tightening her body's hold on his pulsing release.

Tremor after tremor shook her body, the untamed heat searing her. Her own flesh had become so sensitized that the mere brush of his lips against her throat was a pleasure-filled pain.

He lifted her into his arms and carried her out of the ancient rooms, through the secluded garden and into his bedroom. Laying her down atop his rumpled sheets, he stretched out beside her and pulled her damp body up against his.

Threading her fingers through his long black hair, she smiled. "I've dreamed of you since I was fifteen."

He looked down at her and saw the truth of her words in her eyes. "You dreamed—"

"I've dreamed of you for years. Oh, I didn't know it was you. Even after we met, I tried to pretend that you couldn't possibly be my dream lover."

"Your dream lover?" What was she saying? he wondered. Had she, too, been plagued by comforting dreams that ended with erotic lovemaking? "Tell me about your dreams."

He listened quietly, his heart hammering loud and strong as she told him about her dreams, when they had begun and why, and how, afterward, all she ever remembered were his mossy green eyes and the feel of his big body.

"Cyn." He kissed her tenderly. "I've dreamed of you, too. Since I was a kid. In Nam."

He felt her body tense, and ran a soothing hand over her back. "Did I bring you comfort?" she asked.

"Yes." He watched the play of emotions on her face and knew she was accepting the truth just as he must.

"And did I give you love?" she asked.

"Yes."

"And all you would remember afterward were my eyes and the feel of my body."

"Yes." He held her close, his lips against her throat.

"It wasn't just us," she said, arching into him. "It was them, too. They're a part of us. I can't explain it, but I know it's true."

"Yes, it's true." Nate realized that when a man lived as close to death as he had, he learned to believe in life.

She felt his erection pulsing against her and opened her legs to accept him. "We've loved each other forever."

He couldn't bear to think about what might lie ahead for them, the pain of separation, the agony of loss. If his most recent dreams came true, they would both die as surely as the ancient lovers had.

He thrust into her, glorying in her warmth, savoring the fact that they were both very much alive. At that precise moment, Nate knew that if only one thing survived this doomed earthly existence, it would be love.

The world outside the car blurred into one, long, endless streak of darkness punctuated by an occasional flash of light. The hum of the motor, the soft roar of the speeding automobile, the gentle whine of the night wind, all combined, lulling Cyn into a semirelaxed state. For the first hour out of Sweet Haven, she'd been tense and edgy, consumed with her need to stay with Nate, tormented by the fear that she would never see him again.

Agent Bedford had arrived precisely at seven. Nate had wasted no time in sending her away. She understood why. He loved her and wanted to keep her safe. Their goodbye, though brief, had been passionate. As long as she lived, she would never forget the feel of his arms around her, the taste of his mouth on hers, the look on his face when he pulled away from her.

Nate was probably at the hospital with Nick Romero. He'd been determined to try to see his old friend. She knew that Nate had only two real friends. John Mason, who had taken his family home to Alabama to keep them safe from Ryker. And Nick Romero, who had almost died from Ryker's ambush attack. What sort of monster was this Ian Ryker? she wondered. A man filled with hate, who lived only for revenge?

Cyn glanced over at Art Bedford, a muscular, dark-haired man with a thick mustache and wire-framed glasses. Nate hadn't known Bedford because he was a fairly new man. J. P. Higdon had assured Nate that he was fast becoming one of their best agents, and Cyn couldn't be in safer hands, not even with one of their most seasoned veterans.

They were only a few miles outside Jacksonville, on Interstate 17. Cyn had noticed the last road exit had been for Fernandina Beach. Although the Georgia line wasn't far, they still had the entire coastal expanse of Georgia to cover before reaching her father's home in Savannah. That meant a long trip lay ahead of them. She longed for rest, for sweet hours of sleep, but she was afraid to sleep, afraid of the dreams.

She closed her eyes and conjured up Nate Hodges. Sleek hard body, straight black hair, moss-green eyes, possessive words and loving touches. In a few short weeks, he had become the center of her universe, the reason for her existence. No, not in a few short weeks, she reminded herself. Love like theirs hadn't blossomed overnight, it had been growing silently in their hearts, waiting patiently in their souls for four centuries.

Even with her undeniably romantic nature, Cyn realized that if anyone had told her that she was destined to take part in the fulfillment of an ancient legend, she would have scoffed at the very notion. She would have found the idea irresistibly fascinating, but the strong, sensible part of Cynthia Ellen Wellington Porter never would have believed it possible.

But she believed now. And so did Nate. No matter what happened with Ryker, even if somehow he managed to succeed in destroying Nate, the prophecy would be fulfilled.

The prophecy…the prophecy… She could hear Miss Carstairs's soft voice recounting the tale, the romantic myth that had fired the twelve-year-old Cyn's imagination. *A troubled warrior and the woman who could give him sanctuary would come to the beach, would abide within the walls of the old mission, and discover a passion known only by a precious few. And when their lives were joined as the maiden's and the conquistador's lives could never be, then the ancient lovers would be set free, their souls allowed to enter paradise.*

When Cyn felt the car slow down, she opened her eyes in time to see Art Bedford turning off onto an exit.

"Where are we going?" she asked, puzzled by the detour.

"I've got to check in, let them know we've crossed the state line. I'll find a pay phone. You stay in the car," he said, smiling at her. "I'll lock the door and keep an eye on you from the telephone booth."

Cyn shook her head in agreement. "Would you ask if there's been any update on Nick Romero's condition?"

"Sure thing. And if you want a cola or coffee or—"

"No, thank you. I'm fine." She closed her eyes again.

Bedford pulled into an all-night truck stop, parking the car close to the pay telephones. "I won't be long. And I'll be sure to ask about Romero."

Cyn glanced around the modern, brightly lit truck stop. Even with the windows up, she could hear the roar of engines, the beat of country-western music coming from somewhere inside and the loud laughter of two scruffy men in white T-shirts, faded jeans and ball caps with Budweiser embroidered across the front. One of the men lit a cigarette while the other bit off a big plug of chewing tobacco.

Looking back toward the telephone booth, she noticed Bedford was smiling at her while he talked. He seemed relaxed and self-assured, as if he didn't have a care in the world. He must be pretty sure of his abilities to protect me, she thought. If only she could be sure that someone was protecting Nate. Her gaze searched the dark night sky, seeking and finding a bright star. With all the faith in her heart and soul, she prayed that a power far beyond any earthly force would keep Nate safe.

Cyn heard the back door directly behind her open. Jerking her head around she saw a man bending over, slipping inside. She opened her mouth to scream, but before she could emit one sound, the stranger tossed a large white envelope into the front seat, then pointed a gun in her face.

"I wouldn't cry out if I were you, Ms. Porter." His voice had a ring of familiarity. She looked at him, recognition dawning.

"Ah, yes, I see that you understand."

"You can't get away with this," Cyn told him, stealing a quick glance toward the phone booth. Bedford was standing outside, looking at her and smiling. What's wrong with him? she asked herself, can't he see the man in the back seat? Perhaps in the darkness, he couldn't. "There's a man with me. A government agent."

Bedford opened the door on the driver's side, bent over and peered inside. "You have my money?" he asked.

The man in the back nodded toward the front. "On the seat. Feel free to count it."

Suddenly Cyn felt disoriented, knowing and yet afraid to admit that she understood what was happening. She glared at Art Bedford. "You're handing me over to this man. You're betraying the agency for money."

"Smart, isn't she," Bedford said. "And pretty. You wouldn't care to share her with me before you confront Hodges, would you?"

Fear, searing and painful, choked her. The very thought that either of these men would touch her made her physically ill.

"Get in, Bedford," the stranger said. "You will drive us back to Sweet Haven, to Nate Hodges's home. And then you will leave. I suggest you disappear quickly. You can buy yourself a woman, a dozen women, with the money in that envelope."

Bedford obeyed, getting in, starting the car and pulling out onto the highway. "Oh, yeah, Ms. Porter, word is that Nick Romero has a visitor and that visitor has just received a message about you."

No, no, she wanted to scream. This was all a trap, a trap to capture Nate, and she was the bait. The man in the back seat lowered his gun, but continued holding it in his steady right hand.

"Don't think about doing anything foolish, Ms. Porter. I much prefer that you're still alive when Nate Hodges comes to me. You see, I have dreamed of the day I could take from him what he once took from me."

Cyn stared at the man, noting the sinister black patch over one eye. His other eye gleamed a silvery blue in the flash from an oncoming car's headlights. His left arm lay limp at his side. The sleeve of his expensive silk jacket, creased just above his wrist, hung loosely over the hidden stub of his hand.

"Turn around and relax, Ms. Porter. We have a long drive to Sweet Haven."

Cyn ordered herself not to tremble, not to cry, not to give this

monster the satisfaction of seeing her fear. When he reached out
and touched her shoulder, she cringed, but forced herself not to
pull away.

"I'm sorry that I've been so rude. I just realized that we haven't
been properly introduced, although I'm sure the Conquistador has
spoken of me. I am Ian Ryker."

CHAPTER 15

Nate stepped outside the intensive care trauma unit. He hated hospitals, the smell of pain and death everywhere. Although he and Nick Romero had both suffered combat injuries in Nam, they'd both been damned lucky to be part of a highly trained unit where death had been the exception instead of the rule.

Romero looked awfully rough. He was so high on medication that his speech was slurred and his thinking confused. He'd been calling for a woman, the name familiar to Nate although he had no idea who she was. Once, years ago, Romero had mentioned her name when he'd been so drunk he couldn't stand. Nate had asked him about her later, and his old friend had laughed and said that she was the one blonde he'd never been able to forget. Nate wished he knew who she was and how to contact her. If ever Romero had needed someone to care about him, it was now.

In critical condition and the safety of his leg still in doubt, Romero was as tough as they came, and if anyone could live through something like this, he could.

Nate only hoped that he would be as lucky himself and be the one still alive after his confrontation with Ryker. Life had never meant so much to him. He had always been reckless and unafraid. But that was before Cynthia Ellen Porter had entered his life in the form of a flesh-and-blood woman who loved him as he had never dreamed anyone could love him. He didn't want to die. He wanted to live.

Walking down the hall in a meditative daze, Nate accidentally bumped into someone. He looked up and saw J. P. Higdon. "Romero's still alive," Nate said. "And he's still got both legs."

"He'll make it," J.P. said. "You can't kill old battle-scarred warriors like you and Nick."

"I hope you're right." Nate noticed the strange concentrated stare Higdon gave him, the telltale nervousness as he shifted his feet repeatedly. "What's wrong?" Nate felt his heart in his throat, pounding loud and wild.

"We just received a message from Ryker."

Out of the corner of his eye, Nate saw Emilio Rivera standing several yards away near the elevators. "The message was for me?"

"Yeah, it was for you."

"Hell, man, quit beating around the bush and tell me."

"Ryker has Cynthia Porter."

Pain, intense and all-consuming, spread through Nate like high-voltage electricity. Anger more fierce than any he'd ever known claimed him. Grabbing Higdon by the lapels of his jacket, Nate shoved him up against the wall. "How the hell did this happen? You said Bedford was one of your best men."

Higdon, his eyes bright with fear, his upper lip coated with sweat, shook his head in a plea for understanding. "I have no idea what happened. Bedford could be dead for all I know. Does it really matter right now? Ryker has Ms. Porter at your place."

Nate knew immediately that Ryker had taken her to the storage rooms, to the old mission. In Nate's recent nightmares, Ryker had been in a dark, musty room when he had smiled triumphantly at Nate as he held Cyn's lifeless body.

"Ryker has threatened to kill her unless you come alone and we call off your protection," Higdon said, struggling to free himself from Nate's menacing hold.

"Then call them off." Nate loosened his grip. "And if Bedford isn't dead, he will be if I ever find him."

"You can't face Ryker alone. Your best chance of survival is to take some cover. Our boys can be discreet." When Nate released him, Higdon straightened his jacket, shirt and tie.

"Ryker is nobody's fool. I'm sure he isn't alone. He'll have lookouts just waiting for any sign of agents. He's probably got all the help he needs from the Marquez family." Nate glanced over at Emilio Rivera. "And from our friend Carranza."

"All the more reason for you to take backup," Higdon said.

"When I leave here, I don't want anybody following me. My survival isn't what's important to me. If I don't go alone, Ryker will kill Cyn." Nate knew his chances were slim, but that didn't really matter. The only thing that mattered was Cyn.

"How the hell do you think that you, one man alone, can rescue her?"

"I'm going to kill Ryker. Once he's dead, the Marquez family will have no reason to keep her, and they can do whatever they want with me once she's free."

Nate gave Higdon one last warning look before walking to the elevators. Punching the call button, he glanced over at Emilio Rivera. The big man nodded, but didn't say a word. The elevator doors opened. Nate stepped inside. Emilio stepped in beside him.

When the doors closed, Emilio spoke, his voice deep and quietly controlled. "Señor Carranza is waiting downstairs in the limo. He wants to speak to you."

"To hell with what Carranza wants!"

"You would be wise to speak with him, Nathan Hodges," Rivera warned.

Neither man spoke again as the elevator descended. The doors opened, and they stepped out onto the entry level of the hospital. Together they walked outside into the warm May night.

Nate hesitated momentarily when he saw Carranza sitting inside the back seat of the limo, the door wide open. When the old man caught a glimpse of Nate, he emerged from the black Cadillac.

Nate walked over to him, Emilio following. "I don't know what your stake in this is, Carranza, but I promise you that if Ryker harms Cyn Porter, your life won't be worth a damn."

Ramon Carranza's dark eyes clashed with Nate's unfriendly glare. "One of my former business associates is indebted to Ryker." He placed his dark, weathered hand on Nate's arm.

Instantly Nate retreated, jerking away, repulsed by the other man's touch. "What you're telling me isn't news. It's no secret that Ryker is part of the Marquez syndicate."

"You do not want to go up against these people alone."

Although the air was warm, almost balmy, Nate felt a shivering chill hit him. He hated Ramon Carranza and everything he stood for. The very thought that this man was deriving some sort of sick pleasure out of helping Ryker, by tormenting him, by threatening Cyn, made Nate want to rip out the man's heart. "Stay out of my way if you know what's good for you."

Gripping Nate's arm tightly, Carranza gave him a hard, penetrating stare. The two men looked at each other, eye-to-eye, man-to-man. "He plans to kill her regardless of what you do. He simply wants you there to witness her death."

The truth of Carranza's words ripped through Nate like one of his sharp, deadly daggers. "You've delivered Ryker's message, now you can take one back to him. Tell him that I'm on my way, and before I'm through with him, he'll be begging to die."

Releasing Nate's arm, Carranza slipped into the dark, private confines of his limo. Nate kicked the door closed with his foot. Every fiber of his being pulsated with a rage born of uncontrollable anger and a fear the likes of which he'd never known. If anything happened to Cyn...

Cyn could feel the rounded muzzle of Ryker's gun as he jabbed it into her back. Stumbling in the darkness, she steadied herself as they walked along the arched portico. Why, she wondered, had this crazy man taken her back to Sweet Haven, back to Nate's house? Where was Nate? Was he still at the hospital visiting Nick Romero? She had no idea what time it was, though she suspected it was near midnight.

When she slowed her steps, Ryker poked her in the back again. "Keep walking. We're almost there."

Cyn clutched her purse against her stomach and continued moving, praying for the opportunity to use Mimi's automatic that still lay nestled inside her leather bag. Violence had been thrust upon her, and her only chance for survival might well lie within herself. Did she have the strength and courage to fight back? Undoubtedly, Ryker hadn't even considered the possibility that she might be armed.

If she could manage to get hold of Mimi's gun, would she have the guts to use it? Was she capable of killing a man? Two men? she wondered, remembering that Bedford was still with them. Could she, to save herself, and perhaps Nate, go against her life-long beliefs?

"Where are you taking me?" Cyn asked, but she already knew. There was anger and pain and fear inside the walls of the old mission as surely as there was passion and love and fulfillment.

"Just shut up and keep walking." Ryker's voice held a nervous edge.

With Bedford standing outside in the dark shadows, Ryker pushed open the storage room door with his shoulder and shoved Cyn inside. She turned on them, irrational fear controlling her actions. Like a madwoman, she flung herself at him. With one deadly backhanded slap, he knocked her to the floor.

Scrambling to find her purse where it had landed beside her, Cyn snapped the catch and rummaged around inside, unable to see in the darkness. Her fingers encountered the cold, deadly metal. Clutching the automatic in her hand, Cyn pointed it at Ryker. In that one heart-stopping moment, she knew that, if necessary, she would kill in order to survive.

With trained instincts, Ryker intercepted her attack. He raised his leg, expertly kicking the gun out of her hand. Cyn's fingers stung from the sharp blow as she listened to the sound of metal when the gun rattled across the stone floor.

Bedford's laughter rang out loud and clear. In the semidarkness, she could barely make out his stocky form as he entered the room, bent down and picked up her gun.

"She's a gutsy broad," the DEA agent said. "She almost got you."

Ryker growled, like a wounded animal. Cyn could see him, his one malevolent blue eye sparkling in the moonlight that poured in from the open doorway. Flinging his hand backward, he brought it down across the bottom of her face. Cyn jerked from the force of his blow. Blood filled her mouth. She spit it out, then ran her tongue over her split lip.

"Be a good girl, and I'll let you live to see your lover." Ryker motioned to Bedford and the two men turned and left the room.

Once the door slammed shut, Cyn scrambled to her feet and made her way across the room. Standing between the door and the partially boarded window, she listened to the muffled sound of male voices. She could make out another voice beside Ryker's and Bedford's. Who had joined them? she wondered. How many opponents would Nate have to face when he arrived? And she knew, without a doubt, that Ryker had contacted Nate, and that Nate would come for her.

When Cyn heard the door opening, she jumped, quickly moving toward the window. Ian Ryker came in carrying a gas lantern, which he set on top of some stacked boxes. Bedford followed, but no one else. Slowly, Cyn edged her way toward the corner of the south wall. She wanted to huddle into a ball and fall to her knees. But she didn't. She braced her back against the cool coquina wall and glared at Ryker, her eyes beginning to adjust to the new light.

He watched her with the intent curiosity of a cat studying a trapped mouse. She could almost hear him smacking his lips. As cold, deadly fear raced through her, she fought to maintain some semblance of composure. She would not let this animal get the best of her.

Hearing a noise, she glanced quickly over at Bedford, who busied himself pilfering through an assortment of old furniture. Suddenly she saw that a long, thick rope lay draped over his shoulder.

"Who were you talking to outside?" she asked, her voice steady despite her ravaged nerves.

"Curious little girl, aren't you?" Ryker smiled. His mouth was broad, his lips thick and his big teeth had a wide space between the front two. "I have powerful friends who are...assisting me. As soon as the Conquistador arrives, we will be taking a little helicopter ride to a safe place where I can kill you both, very slowly."

She knew that his powerful friends must be the Marquez family, men to whom killing was as commonplace as breathing. And perhaps Ramon Carranza was another friend. If rumors were true, the charming old Cuban could be as deadly as a poisonous snake. "Nate has powerful friends, too. He has the United States government behind him."

She hated the sickening smile on Ryker's face, as if he could taste her fear and was gaining strength from it. "Nathan Hodges will come alone. He knows that I will kill you if he does not. My friends are keeping watch, even now, for any sign of betrayal."

"Nate isn't stupid. He knows you'll kill me regardless of what he does." Why are you trying to reason with a madman? she asked herself. There was no answer.

"Ah, yes, but he will play the game by my rules because he thinks he can outsmart me and keep you alive."

Ryker moved toward her. Her body hugged the wall. Cyn stared at him, trying not to react to his nauseatingly sweet smile. Reaching out, he ran his index finger over her chin, down her throat and into her blouse, stopping between her breasts. When he popped open the top button of her blouse, Cyn glared at him, reaching deep inside herself for courage. Acting on the revolt she felt, Cyn spat in his face.

Wiping away the spit with a large white handkerchief he had slipped out of his pocket, Ryker laughed, then reached out and grabbed Cyn by the shoulders. He dragged her across the room and flung her into a rickety cane-bottomed chair that Bedford had set upright.

"Tie our little hellcat down," Ryker said. "Tie her hands behind her back and secure her feet to the chair legs."

Bedford obeyed, manhandling Cyn when she tried to resist. Within minutes, Cyn was bound. Fighting the overwhelming fear of helplessness, she opened her mouth on a terrified scream.

Ryker ripped his handkerchief in two pieces and tossed them to Bedford. "Here. Shut her up."

Bending down, Bedford stuck half the moist handkerchief inside Cyn's mouth. He laughed when she gagged on the cloth. After spreading the remaining material across her lips and knotting it behind her head, Bedford looked down at her, his eyes filled with such lust that Cyn shuddered. He covered her breasts with his fat hands, squeezing painfully with his thick, pudgy fingers. Cyn squirmed, emitting hoarse groans beneath her tight gag.

"It's time for you to leave," Ryker said, coming over to where Bedford still clutched at Cyn's breasts. "If you're horny, go buy yourself a woman. As a matter of fact, I've given you enough money to buy yourself a harem."

Bedford released Cyn and stood up, facing Ryker. "Want her all to yourself, huh?"

Ryker nodded toward the open doorway, then he and Bedford went outside, closing the door behind them. Alone and uncertain, Cyn prayed. She asked for the strength to endure whatever might happen and requested, with her whole heart, that she be allowed to help Nate survive his battle with Ryker.

Please, dear Lord, watch over Nate, and, if he has a guardian angel, please send him to us now.

Suddenly Ryker burst through the door, an Uzi strapped across his chest. Cyn watched, spellbound, as he neared her. Unable to do anything except groan at his touch, Cyn had to endure the humiliation as he ripped open her blouse, exposing her lace-covered breasts.

Terrified, she closed her eyes against his nearness, against the sight of his smile. But she could not escape the shrill, menacing sound of his laughter.

"You and I, my lovely, will wait for the Conquistador." He pulled a knife from a shoulder sheath and ran the sharp tip of the blade across Cyn's breasts, from nipple to nipple. "I regret, for your sake, that I cannot kill you quickly, but I will not deprive myself of the pleasure I will derive from watching Nathan Hodges's face. Your lover will suffer the agonies of hell as he watches what I'm going to do to you."

Crouched atop the roof, Nate secured the rope to a wide, sturdy beam. Overhead, the night sky closed in around him as he dropped the other end of the rope into the gaping hole in the back storage room ceiling. He checked the sheath on his belt and the hidden one in his boot, then hoisted the M16 to his shoulder. Grasping the rope, he slid downward with silent ease.

His feet landed soundlessly onto the stone floor. Moonlight poured through the roof opening, illuminating the cluttered room. With sleek, superior, trained movements, Nate made his way to the closed wooden door that connected the two storage areas. Like a jungle cat on a hunt for nourishment, he sought out the sound of Ryker's voice.

Nate grabbed the tarnished metal handle, gave the door a tiny push and waited for any hint of sound. Silence. He nudged the door again, a bit harder. With a minute squeak, it opened wider. Leaning back against the wall, Nate peered around the corner. A bright gas lantern lit the adjacent storage room. Ian Ryker stood, cowering over Cyn where she sat, tied to a wooden chair.

Nate knew he couldn't allow himself to think about how she looked, about what Ryker might have done to her. He had to keep a cool head if he were to have any chance of saving her.

Nate slipped his Fairbairn-Sykes dagger from its sheath, and pushed the door open, listening to the ominous creaking. Ryker jerked his head around, his one blue eye glaring at the doorway where Nate stood. Swinging his Uzi around, Ryker clutched the sinister weapon. Nate lifted his hand back, released the commando dagger, then jumped behind the safety of the thick coquina wall just as Ryker opened fire. Bullets riddled the wall.

Suddenly, with swift and deadly accuracy, Nate's dagger delved into Ryker's gut. Clutching his stomach with the stub of his left hand, he continued to spray the back wall with repeated shots. Finally, he slumped over, releasing the Uzi, and spreading his fingers into the blood dripping from his wound.

"Did you see her?" Ryker screamed as he fell to his knees in front of Cyn and grabbed her by the back of her head, twisting her hair around his hand. "You should come out and take a good look. She has blood on her face. Her pretty little mouth is all swollen and her soft knees are badly scraped."

Nate listened, his heart racing with outrage and torment. Wait.

Wait, his instincts told him as he listened to Ryker's labored breathing.

Cyn wished that she could call out to Nate, to tell him that she was all right and not to let Ryker's taunts get to him. She glanced at the open doorway leading into the back storage room. How had Nate gotten in? she wondered, then remembered the roof. When she heard Ryker's harsh groans, she looked down at him just in time to see him jerk the long dagger from his stomach. Blood oozed out, turning his white shirt crimson. He held the knife up toward the heavens in a gesture Cyn knew he considered triumphant.

"I have your dagger, Conquistador." Ryker's voice held a hint of pain disguised beneath his victorious shout. "Come on out and see how I intend to use it on your beautiful lover."

Nate, his M16 on his shoulder, came through the doorway, putting himself in full view of the man sitting on the floor. Ryker held the dagger up to Cyn's chest, slicing through the sheer material of her bra. Red-hot fury seared Nate, branding every nerve within his body. Wild with the need to destroy the inhuman creature who was threatening his woman, Nate willed himself to stay in control.

Nate dragged his gaze away from Cyn's battered face, away from the look of sheer panic in her brown eyes. He studied Ryker, taking in every inch of the wounded man, noticing how profusely he was bleeding. At the rate he was losing blood, it was only a matter of time before he passed out. But Ian Ryker had the stamina of a battle-hardened soldier, and Nate knew he would fight to the bitter end. Given his strength of purpose, Ryker could well remain conscious long enough to kill Cyn.

"I'm going to take you and your woman with me," Ryker said, running the dagger's bloody blade up Cyn's throat, staining her satiny skin with the scarlet liquid. "I've got a chopper coming for us in a few minutes. They know you're here. They won't let me down."

"Who's helping you?" Nate asked, hoping to keep Ryker talking, postponing any desperate action on his part.

"I'm going to let you watch while I enjoy myself with her. When I think you've suffered enough, I'm going to kill you slowly, Conquistador, and let her watch you die." Ryker sucked in a deep breath, gasping for air, grunting with pain. "Oh, she won't be so beautiful when I've finished with her, but some of Marquez's boys will probably enjoy her for a while."

Nate stood perfectly still, never taking his eyes off Ryker. "You can't get away. Do you think a chopper can land on the beach without drawing attention?"

Ryker grinned. "You're too smart to have allowed any of Higdon's men to accompany you. You knew her life depended on your coming alone."

"Let her go, Ryker. This fight is between you and me."

"You didn't let Lian go. You and your bastard SEALs killed her."

"She got caught in the crossfire," Nate said, remembering that horrible day so long ago. "The bullet that struck her could just as easily have been fired by her own people."

"You killed my woman." Ryker rubbed the tip of the dagger up and down, from Cyn's throat to her heart and back again. "I'm going to kill yours…but not quickly. Slowly, after many, many days. The last thing you'll see is your own dagger slicing away at her soft flesh."

Nate glanced at Cyn to gauge her reaction. He had never wanted anything more than to reassure her, comfort her, promise her that Ian Ryker would never live to carry through any of his diabolical threats. "I have no intention of dying. Not to give you any kind of satisfaction and certainly not to save *her* life." Nate nodded toward Cyn, and prayed that she understood what he was trying to do and why.

Ryker looked at Nate skeptically. "It won't work, my old enemy. You can't convince me that she means nothing to you."

"Oh, she means something to me." Nate took a quick look at her, his eyes pleading with her to forgive him. "She's the best lay I ever had, but that's all. When has a woman ever meant more to me than a night's pleasure?"

Ryker let the dagger slip down the front of Cyn's body, the blade skimming over her bare stomach. "I don't believe you, but even if it's true, your sense of honor will demand that you try to save her." He scooted closer to Cyn's chair, the nub on the end of his handless arm stroking his bleeding wound. Taking the dagger away from her soft, exposed flesh, he sliced through the ropes that bound her feet to the chair. "My friends will be coming soon." He pulled her hands up and over the back of the chair, then jerked her up, draping his arm around her and pressing the dagger against her side.

"I'm taking her outside," Ryker said. "The chopper should be landing on the beach soon. You can stay here, safe for the time being, or you can come with us, with me and your beautiful woman."

Ryker hunched over in pain. His movements slow and unsteady, he ushered Cyn outside and toward the road. Nate followed. Could he take a chance on his swiftness and accuracy? he wondered. If his life alone depended upon the outcome, he'd take the risk, but Cyn's life hung in the balance. Ryker's instincts could warn him if Nate tried to use the M16. But what about the boot knife? Nate asked himself. Could he remove it from its hiding place and strike Ryker in the back before the other man killed Cyn?

Once on the beach, Ryker fell to his knees, taking Cyn with him. Nate stopped a few yards away near the old cypress tree.

"You'll never make it," Nate shouted. "You're going to pass out."

"It won't matter." Ryker flung his handless arm around his wound. "My friends will take care of me, and they'll keep both of you safe and secure until I'm ready to dispose of you."

All three people on the beach heard the sound of the automobile as it pulled to a stop on the road in front of Nate's house. Three startled gazes watched while an enormous mountain of a man emerged from the driver's side.

Pulling Cyn tightly against him and placing the dagger's tip over her heart, Ryker shouted at Nate. "I told you to come alone."

"I did come alone. I swear."

"Then who's our company?" Ryker asked, nodding toward the two men who stood beside the limo.

What the hell was going on? Nate wondered. Having Carranza show up wasn't too surprising, but Ryker pretending he had no idea who the man was didn't make any sense.

"I don't know who the bloody hell you are, but you can stop right there or I'll kill her," Ryker said.

"I suggest that if you want to live you should release Señora Porter. There are three of us, you see, and if you harm her, one of us is bound to kill you," Ramon Carranza said, never slowing his stride as he neared the beach.

Ryker laughed, the sound shrilly hysterical as it carried on the night air. "There may be three of you, but I've got friends coming. A small army of friends who'll be carrying weapons. I suggest that you get back in that big limo of yours and leave, old man."

Carranza continued moving closer and closer to Ryker. Nate wanted to reach out and grab him, but he was too far away. Carranza avoided getting anywhere near Nate.

"I'm warning you to stop." Ryker's hand trembled. Cyn could feel the knife pressing into her flesh.

"What are you doing here?" Nate, bewildered by Ryker and Carranza's conversation, knew he couldn't allow his own confusion to dull his senses or make him any less alert. This whole scene could be some elaborate hoax on Carranza's part. It was obvious the old man liked to play games. Just because Ryker didn't recognize him didn't mean they weren't on the same side in this battle.

Carranza spoke to Nate, but he never removed his gaze from Ian Ryker. "I had some important news for Señor Ryker. News that could not wait."

"What kind of crap is this?" Ryker asked. "Who are you? What sort of news have you got for me?"

"I am Ramon Rafael Carranza."

Ryker blanched, his face contorting into a frown. "What... what's the news you have for me?"

The sound in Nate's ears began as a loud buzzing, then quickly escalated into a thunderous roar. The old man had said his name was Ramon Rafael Carranza.

"My good friend, Carlos Marquez, regrets that he must sever his relationship with you," Carranza said. "He sends his apologies that he cannot assist you in this little kidnapping and murder scheme."

"You're lying. Marquez owes me. He's sending a chopper for me." Ryker's gaze searched the predawn sky as he cocked his head, listening to the silence.

Carranza took several steps forward. He was within a few feet of Ryker and Cyn. "Such a pity. In our business, a man cannot afford to put his trust in the wrong people. Marquez may, as you say, owe you, but his debt to me was far larger and much older."

Nate moved away from the trees. Good God, Carranza was going to try to jump Ryker. Was he a fool? Nate knew he had to intercede. If he didn't, Cyn would die. His nightmare would come true.

"Don't move, either of you." Ryker cursed Marquez, then dropped the dagger on the sand as he grabbed the Uzi and opened fire.

With trained instincts, Nate dropped to his belly as the shots rang out over his head. Suddenly, the Uzi's menacing roar quietened. Nate raised his head slightly and glanced around. Ramon Carranza lay on the sandy ground, blood pouring from his wounds. Ryker's lifeless body lay only a few feet away.

Nate jumped to his feet as Cyn struggled to hers, tears streaming down her face. Grabbing her, he jerked the gag out of her mouth.

"Oh, Nate."

He pulled her into his arms as he stroked her hair, kissed her face, and worked frantically to untie her bound wrists. Once Cyn was free, Nate looked down at Ryker. A small round bullet hole marred his smooth forehead. Nate could well imagine what the back of his head looked like. He didn't want Cyn to see it.

"Señor Carranza," Cyn said, her voice ragged and hoarse. "He's hurt." She tugged on Nate's arm, the gesture pleading.

Together they knelt down beside Carranza. Cyn took his head into her lap as she brushed back the strands of white hair that had fallen into his eyes. "You're going to be all right, Ramon," Cyn said. "We're not going to let you die."

Ramon Carranza looked up at Cyn as blood trickled from the corner of his mouth. "You will take care of him," he said as he gazed up at Nate.

Nate saw Emilio standing over them, the revolver that had killed Ian Ryker still in his hand.

"We must get him to a hospital," Emilio said, dropping the gun onto the sand, then reaching down to lift his employer up into his arms.

Nate helped Cyn to her feet and walked her toward the black limousine. Cyn got in first, then Nate helped Emilio place Ramon across the seat, his head resting in Cyn's lap.

Once Emilio started the engine and turned the big Cadillac around, Cyn looked over at Nate. "He saved our lives."

"I know," Nate said.

CHAPTER 16

Cyn sat beside Nate on the orange vinyl sofa. His head was thrown back, his eyes were closed, and his big arms were crossed over his chest. She wished he would allow her to comfort him as he had comforted her when they had first arrived at the hospital. While the emergency room staff had gone to work on Ramon, Nate had insisted that Cyn's scrapes and bruises needed immediate attention.

He had held her when the reality of what they'd lived through finally hit her. The nightmare was over. Ian Ryker was dead. Cyn and Nate were alive.

Cyn glanced around the surgery waiting room. A plump, middle-aged woman stood at the pay telephone, her voice hushed as she told the listener that her mother was still in surgery. In the corner chair, a teenaged boy flipped through the pages of a magazine with bored indifference. A young couple stood by the windows, his arm draped around her shoulders as he wiped her tears with a handkerchief and promised her that their little girl was going to be all right.

Two coffee machines sat on a metal table by the doorway. One glass pot was empty, the other contained no more than a cup of liquid. The wastepaper basket beneath the table was littered with dozens of foam cups, plastic spoons and empty sugar and creamer packs.

Emilio Rivera stood outside in the hallway, his back braced against the wall. No one had given comfort to the big, quiet man, whose silent eyes and hard face gave away none of his emotions.

Cyn wondered how long Emilio had worked for Ramon, how close their relationship was.

"I'm going to talk to Emilio," she told Nate. "I'll be right back."

Nate grunted an acknowledgment, but didn't open his eyes or move a muscle. Seeing Nate like this, so cold and withdrawn, broke Cyn's heart. It was as if he'd closed himself off from her, from the whole world, and refused to allow anyone near. Perhaps it was the only way he knew how to deal with everything that had happened, Cyn thought. Her kidnapping. Ryker's death. The knowledge that Ramon Carranza had risked his life to save them.

Emilio gave her a welcoming glance when she approached him. "How is Nathan?"

"I honestly don't know." Cyn touched Emilio's meaty forearm and looked up into his squinty black eyes. "Ever since they took Ramon up to surgery, he just sits there. He won't talk to me. He won't let me help him."

"*Si,* he is like his padre. A strong man who thinks he needs no one." Emilio patted her hand where it rested on his arm. "He needs you. He will accept your help, later."

As his words began to sink into her consciousness, Cyn wanted to deny her suspicions, but the facts could not be dismissed. Clutching Emilio's rock-solid arm, she asked him for the truth. "Is Ramon Carranza Nate's father?"

"*Si.*" A hint of a smile softened Emilio's battered face. "I have worked for Señor Carranza since before he met Nathan's mother. Since I was a boy of sixteen."

"You knew Nate's mother?"

"A most beautiful woman, Señorita Grace Hodges. As beautiful as you with her long blond hair and big green eyes. Señor Carranza loved her greatly." Emilio's eyes glazed over with memories.

"But Nate thought his father was dead."

"*Si,* it was his mother's wish, and they agreed it would be best for the child. Under the circumstances."

"You have to tell Nate, tell him everything. He has a right to know, and there is no one else who can tell him." She realized she was taking a chance that Nate would respond in a positive manner to the revelation that Ramon Carranza was his father. But regardless of how he would react to the news, he had to be told the truth.

"You think he wants to know?" Emilio asked, giving Cyn a skeptical look. "He is a hard man. His heart may be closed to the truth."

"There's no way to know unless we try."

Emilio nodded, the tentative smile widening as Cyn took his hand, and together they entered the waiting room. Cyn sat down beside Nate. Emilio took a chair opposite the sofa. When she touched Nate's shoulder, he flinched, but still didn't open his eyes.

Cyn felt his big body tense beneath her touch. "Nate, Emilio wants to tell you—"

"That Ramon Rafael Carranza is my father."

"You knew?"

"No, not until... Sitting here, I finally figured it out."

"He was never your enemy." Cyn couldn't tell what Nate was thinking, but she could guess, knowing him as she did. "His interest in you was personal."

"Yeah, I guess it was." Nate opened his eyes and stared up at the ceiling, then darted his gaze at Cyn. "But he was a little late in showing fatherly concern, don't you think?"

Nate closed his eyes again, and Cyn knew he was trying to blot out the truth—a truth he had yet to understand.

"Emilio can tell you about your parents," she said, longing to comfort him, to ease the pain she saw in his eyes, to remove the anger she knew was barely hidden beneath the surface of his falsely calm exterior.

Nate opened his eyes, uncrossed his arms and sat up straight. "What about them?" he asked, glaring at the huge man sitting across from him.

"You will listen, Nathan Hodges?" Emilio's dark eyes pleaded with Nate. "You will let me tell it all so that you will understand why you mustn't hate your father."

Cyn held her breath, praying for Nate's acquiescence. "Don't you think you owe it to yourself as well as your parents to know the truth?" she asked.

"So talk," Nate said, his voice brutally harsh. "I'm listening."

Bending over slightly, he let his hands drop between his knees as he looked down at the shiny tile floor.

"Señor Carranza owned a casino in Havana. He was already rich and successful at thirty-five, and had very influential friends. The most prominent friend was his father-in-law, Luis Arnaz." Emilio hesitated briefly as he watched Nate for a sign of reaction. Seeing none, he continued. "Arnaz had arranged his daughter's marriage to Señor Carranza...a business arrangement ten years before...before your mother came to Havana."

"What was my mother doing in Havana?" Nate asked, finally glancing over at Emilio.

"She had just graduated from college and came down on a holiday with some of her friends. You must remember that Havana in 1949 was a playground for the rich and famous."

"She met him at his casino?" Nate couldn't imagine the sadly beautiful woman who had been his mother as a carefree young woman jaunting off to Cuba with her friends.

"I was there...that night." Emilio's voice cracked with emotion. "It was magic between them the moment they saw each other."

The words were like a tight fist squeezing at Nate's heart. Once, he would have thought the notion of love-at-first-sight ludicrous, but since meeting Cyn, he admitted that it was possible. Hadn't she trapped him in her spell the first night he'd seen her on the beach? Had it been that way for his father the first moment he'd seen the young and beautiful Grace Hodges?

"They were very much in love," Emilio said. "He wanted to marry her, was willing to give up everything to have her."

"Then why didn't he?" Nate asked, hating Ramon Carranza for allowing his sweet mother to have gone through the shame of giving birth to an illegitimate child.

"Luis Arnaz found out about your mother. He threatened her life." Emilio placed his hands on Nate's shoulders, his thick fingers tightening. "Arnaz demanded that your father break all ties with your mother. He swore that he would have her killed. Señor Carranza knew that his father-in-law was capable of carrying out the threat."

Jerking away from Emilio, Nate stood. He felt like running, hard and fast. But he knew he couldn't run away from the truth. Ramon Carranza was his father. He had loved Grace Hodges, and had deserted her in order to save her life. All the bitterness and hatred of a lifetime churned inside Nate, his anger nearing the boiling point. He needed something to hit, some faceless enemy to pulverize.

He balled his hands into tight fists, corded the muscles in his back and neck with such tension he could feel the strain in every nerve ending. And then she touched him. Gentle, soft, loving, her touch ignited the tinderbox of emotions within him. He turned on her, his eyes fierce with a slow burning heat that became white-hot.

Cyn gazed up into the eyes of the man she loved and saw such torment, such pent-up rage, that she couldn't bear to look at him. Mindless of anything except the need to comfort him, Cyn wrapped her arms around his tightly coiled body.

Swiftly, brutally, he encompassed her in his arms, hugging her to him with the savagery of a dying man holding on to his last hope for survival. "Cyn...Cyn..."

"I'm here. I'll always be here. I'll never leave you." She felt his body shaking as she held him, her hands caressing his broad back.

They heard a woman's commanding voice ask, "Is there someone here with the Carranza family?"

Nate and Cyn turned around. Emilio stood. All three of them moved toward the nurse who was waiting in the doorway.

"I'm Ramon Carranza's son," Nate said. "How is my father?"

"They've brought him down from surgery," the white-uniformed woman said. "You may go in to see him shortly, but Dr. Brittnell wants to talk to you first."

Ramon Carranza was dying. The doctors gave them no hope. It was only a matter of hours, perhaps even minutes. Emilio had sent for a priest.

For forty-two years, Nate had wondered about his unknown father, sometimes hating him, sometimes longing for him as only a child can long for a missing parent.

In the last few minutes he had remembered everything his

mother had ever told him about his father. She had painted the man in glowing terms. Nate had never doubted that she loved his father, the mysterious man she had called Rafael. Grace Hodges had told her son that his father had been half Cuban and half Seminole Indian. That he had been a handsome man with a smile that could charm the birds from the trees.

When Nate had questioned her about why his father wasn't with them, Grace Hodges had told her son that his father was dead. As a child, he had not understood; as an adult he had accepted his mother's explanation as the truth.

"We can go in to see Ramon now," Cyn said, squeezing Nate's hand.

They entered the critical care unit together, hand in hand. Ramon looked very old and very tired as he lay on the pristine white sheets. But even surrounded by monitors and life-saving machinery, the big, dark-skinned Cuban dominated the room.

As he neared his father's bedside, Nate experienced a battle of emotions raging within him, creating uncertainty and dread. What could he say to this man? What would Ramon Carranza want from his only son?

The minute Nate and Cyn stopped by his bedside, Ramon opened his eyes. "Nathan." His deep voice was a whisper.

"I'm here." *Dammit all, I don't want to be here, Nate thought. I don't want to have to confront this man, to have to face all the ghosts from my childhood.*

Ramon tried to lift his hand, but was unable to do more than wiggle his fingers. Nate reached down and clasped the old man's hand in his.

"I promised her that…you would never be…a part of my sordid life." Each word seemed torn from Ramon, as if the utterance was painful. "I loved her so."

"It's all right," Nate said, squeezing his father's hand. "Don't try to talk."

"The day she died…" Ramon gasped for air, his lungs struggling for each breath.

"Hush, now," Cyn pleaded, her eyes filled with tears. This

shouldn't be happening, she thought. Not now, when these two had just found each other.

"She called...she was so sick. I went to her." Ramon's limp hand tightened slightly around his son's tenacious grip. "I promised to leave you...with her brother...to never tell you..."

"It doesn't matter." Nate tried to reassure the dying man. "It was so long ago. Another lifetime."

"I wanted you...my son, but she did not want you growing up...in my world." Ramon's soft grip loosened, his hand falling limp within Nate's grasp.

"Father." Nate's voice trembled, his throat tortured with unshed tears.

"I love you. Always, I have loved you...my son." And with those tender words that said far more than the sentimental confessions of a dying man, Ramon Rafael Carranza accepted death.

"Father? Father!" Not yet. Not yet, his mind screamed. We haven't had enough time.

Emilio Rivera stepped forward from his watchful position by the door. With her arms around Nate, Cyn turned in time to see the tears streaming down Emilio's battered old face.

Nate pulled out of her arms, staring at her with moist eyes, the look of a lost child on his face. "I need to be alone. Just for a while. Try to understand."

Cyn watched him walk away, stunned that he didn't want her with him, hurt that at the most traumatic time in his life, he didn't need her.

"So like his *padre*," Emilio said, placing his enormous arm protectively around Cyn's shoulder. "So much a man that he does not want his woman to see him cry."

"See him... Oh, Emilio, I didn't understand."

Emilio hugged Cyn to him, as together, Ramon Carranza's gargantuan bodyguard and Nate Hodges's woman cried for a father who had loved a son he could never claim, a mother with the courage to bear her married lover's child and a boy who had grown into a man without the love and protection his parents were powerless to give him.

* * *

Cyn slipped on her aqua robe, belting it tightly. Before leaving the bedroom, she gave Nate's sleeping body a loving glance. Quietly, she made her way to the kitchen, seeking out the coffeemaker. As she went about preparing morning coffee, she thought about the past two weeks since Ramon's funeral. It had not been an easy time—for Nate or for her.

Although Nate had spoken to her very little, preferring to keep his emotions bottled up inside him, Cyn had not left his side. Determined to carve out a future with the man she loved, Cynthia Ellen Wellington Porter was willing to wait it out, to give Nate all the time and space he needed to come to terms with his past.

She knew that Nate had already come to terms with Ryker's death, but not with her kidnapping. He still blamed himself for not being able to protect her. She realized that he probably always would. Even the fact that Art Bedford had been apprehended in flight to South America had not lessened Nate's self-imposed guilt.

Dealing with the knowledge that Ramon Carranza had been his father was difficult for a man like Nate, a man who'd spent twenty years dedicated to fighting for his country, to putting his life on the line for the principles of freedom and justice. His own father had been a part of the deadly cancer that had been eating away at the moral values of the United States for decades. And he was a part of that man, blood of his blood, flesh of his flesh. He could not deny the bitter legacy Ramon Carranza had left him any more than he could deny the vast fortune he had inherited.

Cyn's own attitudes had changed gradually since she'd fallen in love with Nate and had been thrust into the middle of his savage fight with Ian Ryker. Finally, she had come to terms with not only her own past, her husband's death and the murder of Darren Kilbrew, but she had come to terms with Nate's past. She did not condone violence, and yet she accepted the fact that violence had its place in mankind's never-ending struggle to survive. She realized that when violence is brought into your life, you inevitably have only two choices. The strong choose to fight back, to live, and hopefully restore peace. Nate was one of the strong ones, and now, she too, shared his strength.

More than anything, she wanted Nate to accept her comfort, to be receptive to the loving sanctuary she could give him. But all he had taken from her was the comfort of her body, the solace of hot, wild, frequent matings, as if making love to her could purge his soul of its torment.

Just as she poured herself a cup of freshly brewed coffee, Cyn heard the knock at the front door. Setting her mug on the table, she walked down the hall. Opening the door, she half expected to see Mimi, who had become a frequent visitor during the last two weeks. Instead of Mimi's smiling face, Cyn encountered Emilio's scowling expression.

"Good morning. May I come in, please?" Always polite and formal. That was Emilio.

Cyn stepped back and, with a gracious sweep of her hand, invited him inside. She noticed that he carried a small gray box under his arm. "Want some coffee?" she asked. "There's a fresh pot out in the kitchen."

"No, thank you. I am here to see Nathan." Emilio stood rigidly, though his expression softened when he looked at Cyn. "I have something for him. Something I found when we were packing away Señor Carranza's personal belongings."

"I see." Cyn glanced down at the small box, wondering about its contents. "I'm afraid Nate is still asleep, and I hate to wake him. He hasn't had a good night's sleep since Ramon died."

"I'm not asleep." Nate stood at the end of the hallway, his body bare except for unsnapped cutoff jeans, his long black hair disheveled, and two weeks' worth of beard covering his face. "Too much damned racket. What the hell are you doing here?" he asked, glaring at their guest.

Emilio lifted the box and held it out toward Nate. "These were your father's. They are something I know he would want you to have."

"I told you and I told his lawyers that I don't want a damned thing from him. Not one dime of his dirty, bloody money!" Nate said, his eyes burning with the conviction of his words.

Emilio handed the box to Cyn, who took it just in time to keep it from dropping to the floor. "These are letters Grace Hodges sent

Señor Carranza. The dates indicate she wrote him regularly from the time of Nate's birth until shortly before she died."

Not waiting for a reply or a response of any kind, Emilio nodded to Cyn, then turned and let himself out. Cyn held the small box against her bosom, almost feeling the warmth and love contained within the wooden box.

Letters. Love letters. Cyn looked up at Nate who had grabbed her by the shoulders. He whipped her around to face him.

"Come back to bed," he said, running his hand along the side of her leg, raising her gown and robe up to her hip.

She stepped away and thrust the box out toward him. "I think you should read these."

Nate glared at her. "I don't want to read any damn letters my mother wrote to her lover."

"To your father," Cyn reminded him. "To the man she loved."

Clenching his jaw and narrowing his eyes, Nate reached out and took the wooden box. Dammit, he didn't want to know any more about his mother's love affair with Ramon Carranza. Wasn't it enough that he had to live with the knowledge that the man who had fathered him had been a criminal, and not just any criminal, but an underworld leader?

Two hours later, Nate found Cyn walking on the beach. He knew she'd been waiting for him to come to her, giving him the time alone he needed to decide his future—their future.

He walked along beside her for quite some time before he spoke. She accepted his silent presence, as she had accepted his anger and frustration and unforgivably selfish behavior during the last two weeks. Dear God, what had he ever done to deserve a woman like Cynthia Porter, a woman who loved him enough to stand by him, giving him her support and strength while she willingly submitted her body for his pleasure?

And he had almost lost her. His hideous nightmare had almost come true. Ryker had come very close to killing her. But he hadn't. Ramon Carranza had died to save both Cyn and Nate. No matter what sort of life the man had led, no matter how sordid and sinful his past, he had atoned for some of his transgressions in one final act of love.

"She loved him a great deal," Nate said. "She wrote him regularly from the time I was a week old until shortly before her death. She sent him pictures of me, told him about my first tooth, my first word…" Nate's voice trembled.

"It's sad that they couldn't be together." She could feel the warm May sun caressing her arms and face. She felt so alive, so beautifully, joyously alive.

"He came to see her the day she died." Nate reached down and took Cyn's hand, entwining their fingers.

"He wasn't all bad. There was a private side to him that had nothing to do with his business dealings." Cyn stopped walking, tugged on Nate's hand and raised it to her lips. "You inherited his good looks, his strength, his damn macho pride…but you are your own man and you have nothing to do with the dark side of his life."

"I have a dark side to my life, too, Cyn. Perhaps just as dark as his." Nate pulled her to him, trapping their clasped hands between his chest and her breasts. "Can you accept a man with such flaws? Can you spend your life with a battle-scarred warrior whose past sins put you in danger, put you at the mercy of a madman?"

"I've accepted the fact that terrible things happen in life. The strong survive by fighting back when they're given no other choice."

"I want us to be strong and survive together," Nate said.

"Are you asking me to marry you, Nate Hodges?" she asked, smiling at him, her heart swelling with the wonder of love.

Swinging her off her feet and up into his arms, Nate laughed. "Damn right, I'm asking you to marry me. I may not be the smartest man in the world, but I've got sense enough not to lose the best thing that ever happened to me."

Clutching him around the neck, Cyn laid her head on his shoulder. "I love you, Nate. You're all I'll ever want."

Holding her up against his chest, Nate began walking back toward the house. "I may be all you want, but would you be interested in my father's millions?"

"What?"

"I've decided that Ramon Carranza's money could do a lot of good in this old world. I'm going to accept my inheritance and let you help me choose what charities need it the most. Needless to say, Tomorrow House will never have to close its doors."

"Oh, Nate, that's wonderful."

When they reached the porch, he slid her body slowly down the length of his until her feet touched the warm stone floor. Lowering his head, he brushed her lips with his in a tender, carefree kiss.

"I think Ramon would be pleased," she said.

Pressing his body against hers, letting her feel the throbbing strength of his arousal, he nipped at her earlobe. "Besides me and my father's money, I'd like to offer you something else."

Cyn laughed, swatting playfully at his chest. "You wicked man, offering me sex in broad daylight."

Rubbing his maleness into her femininity, he grinned. "The sex goes without saying, but that's not what I was talking about."

"Well, what else were you offering me?" Cyn asked.

"I think you and I would make awfully good foster parents, don't you?"

"Foster parents?"

"Bobby and Aleta. I think they need us. Bobby has no parents, and Aleta's mother has signed papers giving up any legal right to her in exchange for not bringing her up on abuse charges."

"I think," Cyn whispered into his chest, her tongue flicking over one distended male nipple, "that you will make a wonderful father."

Images of Cyn big with his child flashed through Nate's mind. The thought pleased him greatly. "Let's go inside and work on making you a natural mother."

Sunset in the western Florida sky, a mélange of colors, like the iridescent shades of a crimson-tinted rainbow. Evening of a hot summer day, the stirrings of a warm tropical breeze as purple shadows forecast the night. The ocean's heartbeat echoing along the shore as a sweet soprano voice sang, a cappella, the lyrics to "True Love."

Nathan Hodges dressed in a black tuxedo watched while the bridal procession made its way up the beach. At his side, Nick Romero, well on the road to recovery, sat in a wheelchair while John Mason and Bobby stood.

Laurel Drew Mason, wearing a tea-length dress of pale yellow satin, approached the groom, his best man and groomsmen. Aleta followed in a matching dress of a less mature design, and last but never least, Mimi Burnside, the matron of honor, strolled along the beach, unable to hide her wide smile.

The standing crowd of well-wishers held their breaths when Cyn, escorted by her father, passed by in her flowing gown of antique white satin, with Batenburg lace accenting the sweetheart neckline and butterfly sleeves. A Juliet cap covered with baby's breath sat on the back of her head and a short gathered veil covered her long golden hair, which was secured in a bun at the base of her neck. The bride carried an enormous bouquet of white orchids.

Hand in hand, Cynthia Ellen Wellington Porter and Nathan Rafael Hodges faced the minister and repeated their vows of love and lifetime commitment. Before God, their family and friends, they became one.

Nate kissed his bride so long and hard that his best man poked him in the ribs. And then the party began. Hours of food and champagne and music. Denton Wellington had spared no expense in giving his daughter the unorthodox wedding of her dreams on the Sweet Haven beach.

All the present residents and volunteer workers of Tomorrow House were in attendance as were Cyn's brother David, Bruce Tomlinson and Emilio Rivera.

While the crowd continued the revelry long after the sun had set and stars appeared in the black night sky, Nate swooped his bride up into his arms and carried her away...all the way across the street to his house.

Snuggling in her husband's arms, Cyn didn't even realize that Nate was carrying her straight to the storage rooms, to the old mission part of the house.

When he felt her tense, Nate hugged her to his chest. "All the bad memories, the pain, the ghosts of the past, will vanish tonight. From now on, these rooms will hold only happy memories."

The huge wooden door stood wide open. Cyn held her breath as Nate carried her across the threshold. The outer room was empty, swept clean, the windows unboarded and open. She clung to him, her heart beating wildly as he stepped inside the inner room. Cyn gasped at the sight.

Moonlight streamed down through the unrepaired opening in the roof and hundreds of candles glowed like flaming eyes all over the room. They flickered on the floor, in wall sconces, on a table filled with flowers, a table set with champagne and food, and they perched in the open windows like Titian-haired little guards illuminating the dark night. An old wooden bed, placed in the middle of the room, gained all of Cyn's attention. Cream satin sheets edged with delicate lace shimmered in the warm candlelight.

Nate set his bride on her feet, gazing at her with loving adoration as he drew her into his arms. "Do you have any idea how beautiful you are?"

"Am I as beautiful as you?" she asked teasingly, remembering how he'd sworn she'd never get him to wear a damned monkey suit.

"This is a once-in-a-lifetime deal, lady. You'll never see me in one of these blasted tuxedos again." He released her, pulled off his jacket and tossed it across a nearby chair.

Cyn began unbuttoning his pleated-front shirt. "You'll have to wear one when your daughter gets married."

"Aleta is only twelve, and since I'm not going to let her date until she's thirty, I won't worry about her wedding." Nate reached around and released the top button of Cyn's wedding gown.

Slowly, sensuously, with their gazes locked in the heat of a smoldering passion, Cyn and Nate undressed each other. With each garment removed, each new inch of flesh exposed, the desire within them increased until their hands trembled when they stood naked.

Nate picked her up, the feel of her bare skin exciting him, hardening his throbbing arousal. Lowering her tenderly upon the bed, he followed her down, covering her, his lips taking hers in a frenzy of wild abandon as his manhood pressed against her waiting femininity.

He had never known with any woman what he had found with Cyn, the passion, the uncontrollable thirst that could be quenched only with their heated mating, and a love that went beyond the here and now to stretch the boundaries of eternity.

She flung her arms around his neck, beckoning him to come to her. With his lips burning hotly against her neck, he buried himself deep within her. Cyn cried out from the pleasure of their joining.

With each touch, each kiss, each forceful thrust, Nate gave himself into her safekeeping, trusting her with his very soul.

"Ah, *querida, yo te amo.*" Nate spoke the words, but the sentiments belonged to an ancient conquistador as well as the modern warrior.

"And I love you," Cyn told him, her heart beating with the love of two women. "I'll love you forever."

EPILOGUE

As the last candle flame flickered into oblivion, dawn broke over the Atlantic Ocean. The first faint light of morning seeped through the windows of the old mission, covering the entwined bodies of two lovers lost in a passionate mating dance that united them for all eternity.

When fulfillment claimed them and their cries of pleasure shattered the tender silence, Nate planted within Cyn's receptive body the seeds of their immortality.

Outside, two spirits walked together along the isolated beach, their hearts rejoicing, their souls preparing for a final journey.

"It is time," she said.

"Yes, *querida*. They have set us free."

After four hundred years of waiting, the small Timucuan maiden and her big Spanish conquistador left the Florida beach where they had met and loved and died so long ago. On the day that Rafael Wellington Hodges was conceived, the souls of two ancient lovers entered paradise.

THE OUTCAST

CHAPTER 1

He was out there somewhere. Alone. Angry. Injured. And afraid he wouldn't live long enough to prove his innocence and make the guilty pay.

Elizabeth Mallory shuddered, as much from the premonition as from the chill of the February wind whipping across the front porch of her mountain cabin home. With a cup of strong black coffee in her right hand, she stood in the open doorway, gazing out over the freshly fallen snow. The first faint hint of morning painted the eastern horizon with various shades of red, from palest pink to deepest crimson. Clouds swirled, dark and foreboding in the gray sky, warning of more sleet and snow.

Elizabeth had sensed a winter storm brewing for days. She was never wrong about her weather forecasts. And she was never wrong in her premonitions. That's what bothered her. The stranger had invaded her thoughts months ago, and no matter how hard she tried to shake him, she couldn't. The first time he had come to her in a night dream. She had awakened from a deep sleep, trembling from the intensity of the vision. She had seen his hands. Big, strong hands—covered with blood. And then she'd seen his stunned face. Those fierce masculine features. Those amber eyes. She had tried to connect with his feelings, but without success. Who was this man? she'd wondered. Where was he? And why was she dreaming of him?

There was only one man in her life, if you didn't count O'Grady, a friend of her aunt Margaret's who did odd jobs around the greenhouses and kept her supplied in firewood for the long winter months high in the Georgia mountains. Sam Dundee had been her stepfather's younger brother, and when her parents had died in an automobile accident while she'd been a child, Sam had become her legal guardian. As much as she loved Sam and he her, the love they shared was platonic, the deep care and concern of family.

So there had been no one. Not in her bed. Not in her heart. Not until the past few months when she had been unable to control the visions of a tormented man pacing back and forth inside a cage. She had wanted to comfort him, but she couldn't. She could not reach him, no matter how hard she tried. Her telepathic abilities had always been somewhat untutored, not nearly as finely honed as her clairvoyant and precognitive powers, but there was more to it than that. This man, this tortured stranger, shielded his emotions, keeping everyone out, including Elizabeth.

Since childhood she'd known she was different. Her mother and stepfather had brought her to Sequana Falls, deep in the north Georgia mountains, home to her great-aunt, who also possessed psychic abilities and was the only one who'd ever been able to understand the soul-felt pain Elizabeth endured because of her powers.

Except for a brief sojourn from her mountain retreat to attend college, Elizabeth secluded herself from the world. Her abilities to predict the future, to foresee forthcoming events and read minds created problems for her from which not even Sam Dundee, with all his macho strength and loving concern, could protect her.

Cloistering herself away from the world had helped her live a somewhat normal life. She had sworn, after the terrors of living away from Sequana Falls for three years to acquire a college degree while still a teenager, that nothing and no one could ever persuade her to leave her sanctuary again.

Elizabeth allowed the hot coffee to warm her mouth before traveling downward, creating a soft heat within her body. She

THE PROTECTORS: *The Outcast*   249

breathed in the fresh, crisp air—unpolluted mountain air, air closer
to the heavens, as if it mingled with God's breath.

She tried to keep her eyes open, tried to focus on the snow-laden
trees in the forest surrounding her. But the images formed in her
mind, forcing her to see them, whether she wanted to or not. Darkness enveloped her. Night. Tonight! The stranger was running.
Running in the freezing sleet, his feet weighted down by the heaviness of the packed, frozen snow beneath him. He slipped, righted
himself, ran more slowly. Then he slipped again, lost his balance
and fell into a snowdrift.

The cup in Elizabeth's hand trembled, sloshing warm coffee
over the rim and onto her fingers. Shaking her head, she tried to
dislodge the vision, to force the images to stop. She groaned deeply,
softly. The pain of seeing the stranger's predicament and being
powerless to help him frustrated Elizabeth.

Suddenly she felt MacDatho's cool, damp nose nuzzle the hand
she held clutched at her hip. Her thoughts cleared. Nothing but
dark clouds and white snow appeared in her line of vision. Turning her head slightly, she looked down at her companion. He gazed
up at her with those serene amber eyes of his, as if he, too, had seen
exactly what she had seen, as if he knew that a stranger was about
to enter their lives.

Running her fingers through his thick winter fur, Elizabeth
crooned to the big black animal, reassuring him that she was all
right. She had raised MacDatho from a pup, his mother Elspeth,
her German shepherd pet of many years, his father a wolf from out
of the forest.

"You know, don't you, my fine lad?" Elizabeth said. "He's coming to us. Tonight."

MacDatho made a sound—not a bark, not a growl, just a rum-
bling sound. An affirmation of his mistress's words. He leaned his
head against her leg, allowing her to pet him.

"I don't know what sort of man he is." Elizabeth nudged Mac-
Datho, leading him back inside the cabin. She closed the heavy
wooden door, shutting out the cold morning.

A fire blazed brightly in the enormous rock fireplace in the living room. MacDatho followed Elizabeth to the large, sturdy plaid sofa. When she sat, he lay at her feet.

"He's in trouble and he needs me, but that's all I can sense." Elizabeth placed her mug on the rustic table beside the sofa. "I can't read him, Mac. Odd, isn't it? I can read everyone, even Sam some of the time, but I can't get past the barrier this man has put up." Elizabeth was puzzled that she could pick up no more than a tiny fraction of the stranger's thoughts or emotions. Nothing solid. Nothing complete.

Elizabeth curled up on the sofa, bending her knees so she could tuck her feet behind her. For the first time in her life Elizabeth Mallory was afraid of another human being without knowing why. Out there somewhere was a man she didn't know, a man in some sort of trouble, a man making his way to her cabin—to her. For months she had been tormented by images of this man's life. Bits and pieces of loneliness and pain. Fragments of anger and fear. If only he would allow her to see inside, to share what he was feeling. But it was obvious to Elizabeth that he shielded himself from emotions so completely that he never permitted anything or anyone past his protective barriers. Although Elizabeth knew him, would recognize him the moment she saw him, he didn't know her. When they met tonight—and they would meet tonight—he would have no idea that he was more than an invading presence in her life, that he had held a special place in her thoughts for many months, that he had become important to her even though they didn't know each other.

As much as she feared this unknown man, Elizabeth longed for him to enter her life. Anxiety and uncertainty warred with desperate need. Fear battled desire. Dread fought with longing. Elizabeth closed her eyes. The moment she envisioned his hard, lean lips forming a strangled cry and heard him pray for help, she knew she was this man's only hope—this lonely and unloved outcast.

Slouched over in the seat, his shoulders slumped, eyes downcast, Reece Landry screamed silently at the injustice that had brought him to this point in his life. He'd been screaming for months, but no one had heard him.

He had never pretended to be a saint, never considered himself a good man, and he was guilty of many sins and a few crimes. But he was innocent of the murder that had placed him in this sheriff's car, on this Georgia highway in the middle of a once-in-a-decade winter storm, being taken to Habersham County, to Alto, Georgia, to be locked away inside Arrendale Correctional Institute for the rest of his life.

No one had believed him, except perhaps his lawyer. But he wasn't even sure about Gary Elkins. His half sister, Christina had hired the man. And despite the fact that Chris professed she believed he was innocent, she couldn't disguise the doubt in her eyes. No matter how much he wanted to trust Chris, she was, after all, a Stanton, and he knew better than to trust a Stanton.

Gary had told him not to lose heart, that he would appeal the case, that sooner or later they would find the real murderer. Reece wasn't so sure. In the five months since B. K. Stanton's death, the police hadn't sought another suspect. Just about the whole town of Newell believed Reece Landry was guilty.

With his head still bent, pretending sleep, Reece glanced around inside the car. The doors were locked, opening only from the outside. A Plexiglas partition separated him from the two deputies in the front of the car. He'd known Jimmy Don Lewis most of his life, and the two had never liked one another. Jimmy Don had always been a cocky little SOB. Harold Jamison wasn't much more than a kid, red haired, freckled, with a warm, friendly country-boy grin.

Reece sat perfectly still, but in his mind he tugged on the chains binding his hands and feet, broke free and overpowered the deputies.

Hearing a chinking sound, Reece checked outside. Sleet mixed with snow peppered the windows.

In about an hour they would be in Alto. Reece could almost hear the gate closing behind him, could feel the walls shrinking to encompass him in a cage from which he would never escape.

Guilty. Guilty of murder in the first degree. He would never forget listening to the verdict being read or seeing the faces of the twelve jurors as they watched him during the trial. Not once had any of them looked at him with pity or uncertainty. He'd known, in his gut, that they would never set him free. B. K. Stanton had been the wealthiest and most powerful man in Newell, and Reece Landry had been the only suspect in his murder.

What the hell had he expected? The deck had been stacked against him since the day he was born. No one who lived on Lilac Road had a chance of gaining respectability, least of all the bastard son of a dirt farmer's daughter who had given her heart and her body to a married man.

He had grown up in Newell, in that tar-paper shack on Lilac Road, across the street from the local whorehouse and a half mile away from the best bootlegger in the county. He'd grown up hard and tough and just a little mean. Being born a bastard, raised in poverty, with a son of a bitch for a stepfather did that to a boy.

He had learned young that it didn't pay to care about anyone or anything except himself. The only person he'd ever loved, the only person who'd ever loved him had been Blanche, his beautiful, badly used and abused mother. But when he was twelve she'd died and left him with her sadistic husband.

He'd wondered why Blanche had ever married Harry Gunn. She had told him once that they were lucky to have Harry, someone to keep a roof over their heads and food in their stomachs, that not just any man would be willing to take another man's leavings.

And that's what he and his mother had been—B. K. Stanton's leavings.

The screech of tires coincided with the sudden jolt that sent Reece forward in his seat, only the safety belt stopping his headlong dive through the Plexiglas partition. The car somersaulted off the road, rolling over and over, landing right side up again as it skidded straight into the side of the mountain. A loud blast, the shattering of glass and screams of the startled deputies blended with the cry of the violent winter wind and the clink of frozen rain hitting the vehicle. The car's tumultuous movement tossed Reece about inside the back seat, despite the restraint of the safety belt. He grabbed in thin air for something to help him keep his balance as the car scraped along the side of the mountain, caving in the side of the car where Reece sat, then coming to a crashing halt as it ran head-on into an immovable object.

The pain in his head blinded Reece momentarily, a purple blackness swirling in front of his eyes. Running his hand over his face, he felt the wet warmth of his own blood. Another pain shot through his leg, the one caught between the seat and the crushed side of the car. He snapped the safety belt open, struggling to move. Tugging fiercely, he freed his trapped leg. Pain shot through his leg, and a sharpness caught his breath, sending an intolerable ache through his chest.

With his vision lost, Reece's other senses took over, intensifying the pain of his injuries, creating a sour taste in his mouth and alerting him to the sweet, sickening smell of his own blood.

What the hell had happened?

Reece's vision cleared to a blurred fuzziness. Pale light, then streaks of colors floated in front of him. He heard the deep moan of another man and wondered who else was hurt.

When he tried to move, every inch of his body protested as intense pain warned him to stay still. Slowly, with the fuzziness fading and forms taking shape, Reece's vision cleared. Trying not to jar his body or move his head, he scanned the inside of the car. The Plexiglas partition was still intact, but the front seat was now shoved several inches into the back. The side of the car where Reece had been sitting was dented, caved in enough so that the glass had shattered, but a huge limb blocked escape by that route.

Forcing himself to endure the pain, Reece turned his head, knowing his only hope was to kick out the right window. Did he have the strength? Would it matter if he did? He had no idea what condition Jimmy Don and Harold were in, whether they were dead or alive.

Reece tried to move again. Excruciating pain took his breath away. He tried again, lying down in the seat and positioning his feet. He kicked at the window. Once. Twice. Nothing. Then, garnering all his strength, Reece gave the kick all he had, crashing the window.

He eased his big body through the opening, the howling wind eating through his coveralls, the torrent of wet snow sticking to his hair and face like drops of chilled glue.

Landing flat on his face, Reece struggled to stand, but his legs wouldn't cooperate. He had to get up. He had to check on Jimmy Don and Harold. With his ankles shackled together, he found walking on the frozen ground difficult.

Reece couldn't remember a time in his life when he'd ached so badly, when every muscle in his body had cried out for relief. He wondered if he'd cracked a couple of ribs. Just how the hell was he going to escape when it was all he could do to breathe?

Knowing he couldn't leave without checking on the deputies, Reece crawled on his knees to the front side of the car. Fighting his pain and struggling against the wet, freezing sleet mixed with snow that hammered his unprotected head and face, Reece grasped the door handle and pulled himself to his feet. His leg ached like hell.

The sheriff's car had ended its wild ride with its left side butted up against the mountain, the hood crushed, like a squeezed accordion, into an enormous old tree. Snow blew into the car through the shattered windshield, covering both deputies. Reece tried to open the door, but it wouldn't budge. He called out to the men inside, knowing he couldn't leave them to die. Reece rammed his shackled fists through the window.

Peering inside he saw that Harold Jamison had been crushed by the steering wheel. He lay slumped over, his bloody face turned to one side, his sightless eyes staring off into space. Harold had been crushed to death, his body trapped.

Jimmy Don moaned, but didn't open his eyes. Reece laid his hand on the man's shoulder. "I'll get you some help. Just hang on."

Reece scanned his surroundings, seeing only the sleet and snow that obscured his vision and limited his ability to navigate. The high-way couldn't be more than a few yards away, could it? Maybe he could flag down a passing car or truck. But who in their right mind would be traveling in this weather? And if he flagged down a car for help, how would he explain not staying around until assistance arrived?

Then he remembered the radio in the car. Maybe the communication device was still operational. It was worth a try. Reece reached over Jimmy Don, checked the radio and sighed with relief when he found it still working. He radioed for help, giving the dispatch as much information as his limited knowledge permitted. When he was asked to identify himself, he cut the conversation short. He had to get away before it was too late. He'd done what he could to help Jimmy Don. It was probably more than the deputy would have done for him, under similar circumstances.

Reece winced, as much from the cynicism of his thoughts as from the constant pain in his head and body. He squeezed Jimmy Don's shoulder.

"I've radioed for help. Just hang in there."

Jimmy Don opened his eyes, his mouth trembling. He struggled to speak, but only a groan passed his lips. His body shook, then jerked. His head fell back against the seat.

"Jimmy Don!" Reece sought a pulse, but found none.

He knew what he had to do in order to survive, but he couldn't help feeling a certain amount of disrespect rifling Jimmy Don's corpse. He did it just the same, finding the keys that would free his hands and feet. Free! Free to run? Free to be hunted down and killed? No! Somehow, some way, he'd get away, he'd go back to Newell and find the person who'd killed B.K. Fate had intervened, giving him a chance to prove his innocence.

If he'd thought having the key would solve his problems easily, he'd been dead wrong. After several tries, he decided it was damned near impossible to insert the key and unlock the hand-cuffs. Cursing under his breath when he dropped the key to the ground, Reece lowered himself to his knees and retrieved it. He had to get out of these damned cuffs and chains or he'd never be able to escape.

Placing the key in his mouth, Reece lifted his hands and lowered his head. Damn but this was going to be tricky. He tried and failed, then tried again. Help should be arriving before too long. He didn't have all the time in the world to get away, but it looked like it just might take him half a day to free himself. On the fourth try, he inserted the key and said a silent thank-you to whatever higher power there might be. Clamping down on the key with his teeth, holding it as securely as he could, he turned his head, twisting the key in the lock. Reece believed the sweetest sound he'd ever heard was the lock on his handcuffs releasing.

He snapped the cuffs apart, flung them out into the snow and rubbed his wrists. Bending, he unlocked the shackles around his ankles and kicked them away.

The deputy wouldn't need his coat, but Reece would if he was to survive in this weather. He eased Jimmy Don's heavy winter jacket off his lifeless body and lifted his 9 mm automatic from its holster. Then he pulled the deputy's wallet from his pocket and removed the money inside, shoving the bills into the jacket.

Tramping through the packed snow, hearing the thin layer of forming ice crunching beneath his chilled feet, he struggled around the car, praying he could find his way to freedom.

A warm stickiness dripped down his cheek. Reaching up, he wiped away the moisture, then looked down at his hand to see a mixture of melting snow and fresh blood. God, how his head hurt!

With slow, painful steps, Reece made his way to the roadside. He had no idea where he was or in which direction he was headed. All he knew was that he couldn't stick around and get captured, get taken to Arrendale and locked away for the rest of his life. He hadn't killed B.K., but the only way he could prove it was to return to Newell and find the real murderer.

Damn, it was cold. Even in the sheepskin-lined jacket he'd stolen from Jimmy Don's dead body and the heavyweight navy blue winter coveralls issued to him at the county jail, the frigid wind cut through his clothing like a rapier slicing through soft butter.

He stumbled along the shoulder of the highway, finding it less slick than the icy road. Taking one slow, agonizing step at a time, Reece longed to run, but he did well just to continue walking.

He didn't know how long he'd been traveling away from the wrecked car when he saw the headlights of an oncoming vehicle. God, what he'd give for the warmth and shelter inside a car. If only he could sit down a few minutes and thaw out his frozen hands and feet. Trudging out into the road, Reece waved his hands about, hoping the driver would see him, and praying he wouldn't run him over.

The vehicle, an older model Bronco, slowed, then stopped, the motor running and the lights cutting through the heavy cloud of falling snow.

"What's the matter, are you crazy?" A middle-aged man, wearing what appeared to be camouflage hunting gear, got out of the Bronco.

"My car skidded off the road a ways back," Reece lied. "It's a total wreck. I need a ride to the nearest town."

"You hurt?" the gruff-spoken, ruddy-faced man asked.

"Banged my head pretty bad, bruised my leg and I could have a couple of ribs broken."

"Get in. I'm heading for Dover's Mill. Planning on getting me a bite to eat and a warm bed for the night. We can see if they've got a doctor who'll take a look at you."

"Thanks." Reece eased into the Bronco, slamming the door behind him. The warmth inside surrounded him. The comfort of sitting down spread an incredible ease through his aching body.

"I'm Ted Packard." The Bronco's driver held out his hand to Reece.

Reece hesitated momentarily, then offered the man his cold, bloodstained hand. "I appreciate the ride, Mr. Packard."

Ted eyed Reece with skepticism as he shifted gears, putting the vehicle in Drive. "What's your name, boy?"

"Landers. Rick Landers."

"Well, Rick, normally it wouldn't take us fifteen minutes to get to Dover's Mill, but with this damned storm, it could take us an hour."

Thankfully, Ted Packard wasn't a big talker or overly inquisitive. He'd seemed to accept Reece on face value, believing his story of having wrecked his car. The warmth and quiet inside the Bronco relaxed Reece, lulling him to sleep. When Ted tapped him on the shoulder to awaken him, Reece couldn't believe he'd actually dozed off.

"This here's Dorajean's," Ted said. "Best food in Dover's Mill. We'll ask inside about a doctor for you."

"Thanks." Reece opened the door, but found stepping out into the frigid afternoon air far more painful than he would have expected. He kept his moans and groans in check. "I don't think I need a doctor. At least, not right away. But I sure could use a hot cup of coffee and a bite to eat."

"Suit yourself," Ted said, exiting the four-wheel-drive vehicle. "You can call a local garage about your car, but I doubt there's much they can do until this storm lifts. If your car's totaled, it won't matter anyway, will it?"

"Right." Although his steps faltered a few times, Reece followed Ted into Dorajean's.

The restaurant buzzed with activity, obviously filled with stranded motorists. Every booth and table was occupied, leaving only a couple of counter stools free. Sitting beside Ted, Reece ordered coffee and the day's special—meat loaf, creamed potatoes and green peas.

The waitress, a heavyset, fiftyish redhead, flirted outrageously with Ted, the two apparently old acquaintances. Reece gulped his first cup of coffee, relishing the strong, dark brew as it warmed his insides. A TV attached to the wall possessed a snowy image of a newscaster. The sound had been turned down, but Reece could hear the static drowning out the broadcaster's voice. A nervous tremor shot through Reece's body. How long would it be before the sheriff's car was found and the authorities discovered that convicted murderer Reece Landry was missing? A few hours? By nightfall? Early morning?

Reece sipped his second cup of coffee, enjoying it even more than the first. He glanced around the restaurant, noting the homey atmosphere, the red gingham curtains and tablecloths, the old-fashioned booths still sporting the outdated jukebox selectors. He wondered if the contraptions still worked.

The place was cram-packed with people of various ages, sexes and races. Water from the melting snow that had stuck to customers' feet dotted the black-and-white tile floor. Reece glanced out the windows, the heavy falling snow so thick he couldn't even see Ted's car in the parking lot.

The front door swung open. Reece's heart stopped. A local deputy walked into Dorajean's. Damn! He warned himself to stay calm, but his gut instincts told him to run. Hell, he was wearing county-issued coveralls, another deputy's winter coat and carrying a gun registered to the sheriff's department. What should he do? Did he dare risk staying long enough to eat? Surely the deputy wouldn't spot one man in the middle of so many people.

The deputy walked over and sat on the empty stool next to Ted Packard. Reece clutched his hands into fists at his sides to keep them from trembling. He wasn't going to get caught. He couldn't bear the thought of going to prison. He had to stay free long enough to find out who had killed B.K.

"Here you go, sugar. Dorajean's special for today." The redhead set the plate of piping-hot food in front of Reece.

"Thanks." He was hungry. He hadn't been able to eat more than a few bites of his breakfast this morning.

"You look like you've been in a fight, good-looking," the waitress said. "You got bruises all over your face and some dried blood on your forehead."

"Wrecked his car a ways back," Ted said. "I gave him a lift into Dover's Mill."

Why didn't they just shut up? Reece wondered. The more they discussed him, the more likely the deputy would take notice.

Reece shoved a spoonful of meat loaf into his mouth, following it with huge bites of potatoes and peas. Then he felt someone watching him. Not turning his head, but glancing past Ted, he saw the deputy glaring at him.

Reece stood. He had to get away. "Where's your rest room?"

"Round the corner, to the right," the waitress told him.

"Thanks."

Reece scanned the restaurant, looking for another entrance. There wasn't one. He headed in the direction of the rest room, then made a quick turn and walked into the kitchen, hugging the wall, hoping the cook wouldn't notice him. Easing slowly toward the back door, he breathed a sigh of relief when he stepped outside. The thick veil of snow created limited visibility, so Reece wasn't surprised when he stumbled over a low stack of wood and fell headlong into a row of metal garbage cans. Dammit, what a racket they made.

A sharp pain sliced through his side, and another zipped up his injured leg. Blood oozed down the bridge of his nose. He wiped it away. Every inch of his body ached, every bone, every muscle, every centimeter of flesh.

He headed into the wooded area behind the restaurant, not daring to go back into the parking lot. Sooner or later, when he didn't come back to the counter, Ted and the waitress would wonder what had happened to him. It couldn't be helped. He had to find someplace to stay until he'd mended enough to travel home to Newell.

When Reece tried to run, the pain hit him full force. He walked as fast as the snow-laden ground would allow, then as the cold seeped into his body and he became one with the pain, he increased his speed, finally breaking into a run.

Incoherent thoughts raced through his mind. Panic seized him, forcing him onward when common sense would have cautioned him to stop. Bleeding, out of breath and disoriented, Reece felt himself falling, falling, falling. When his body hit the ground, cushioned by a good seven inches of snow, he wanted nothing more than to lie there and go to sleep. Can't do that! Got to get up. Keep moving.

Come to me. I'm waiting. I can help you.

Reece heard the voice as clearly as if someone was standing beside him, speaking. Dear God, I'm losing my mind, he thought. I'm hearing voices.

With an endurance born of a lifetime of struggle and determination, Reece rose to his knees and then to his feet. He walked. He ran slowly. He fell. He picked himself up and walked again. He sloshed through a partially frozen stream, the water rushing around chunks of ice. His foot caught on a limb and he fell, his hip breaking through the ice. Cold water seeped into his coveralls. Righting himself, he stood and tramped down and out of the stream.

Minutes ran together, warping his sense of time, until Reece had no idea how long he had trudged through the woods. The sky had turned from gray to black. Not a star glimmered in the heavens. Swollen snow clouds blocked the moon, allowing only the faintest light to filter through the darkness. Reece couldn't see a damned thing, not even his own hand in front of his face. And he was so numbed from the cold and the constant pain that he barely felt the chilling wind or the freezing dampness.

It had to be night. That meant it had been hours since he'd left the restaurant back in Dover's Mill. Why hadn't he found shelter? Surely someone had a cabin or a shack out in these woods.

Reece felt his legs give way. He stumbled to his knees. Knowing that if he lay down in the snow he would never get up, Reece struggled to stay awake, to keep moving. He began crawling. One slow, painful inch at a time.

Beckoned by an unseen force, by a comforting voice inside his head, Reece refused to surrender to the pain and hopelessness. Then suddenly a sense of excitement encompassed him. That's when he saw it—an enormous wood-and-rock cabin standing on a snow-covered hill. Lights shone in every window as if welcoming him home. Dear God in heaven, was he hallucinating? Was the cabin real? With what little strength he had left he forced himself to his feet, then checked in his pocket for the automatic. He was going to find out if that cabin was real. If it was real, then someone lived there and that person wouldn't take kindly to an escaped convict spending the night.

Lifting his feet, forcing himself to trek up the hill, Reece felt weighted down with numbness. The cabin hadn't disappeared. Still there. A warm, inviting sight. Only a few yards away. Huge steps, wide and high, awaited him. Pausing briefly, he stared up at the front porch. He'd have to break in, maybe through a window. But first he'd try the door, test its sturdiness, check out the lock.

One step. Two. Three. Four. He swayed, almost losing his balance. Can't pass out. Not now. So close. He lifted his foot up off the last step and onto the porch. The front door was so close, but somehow it seemed a mile away. If he couldn't figure out a way to pick the lock on the door, did he have the strength to smash in a window? Whoever lived inside was bound to hear the noise. He ran his hand over the bulge the 9 mm made in the coat pocket. Would he use the gun? Could he? Whoever lived inside would be an innocent victim.

Reaching out, his hand trembling, he grabbed the door handle. With shocking ease the door opened. Reece couldn't believe his good fortune. The door hadn't been locked. Who in their right mind would leave a door unlocked?

He eased the door back an inch at a time, hesitant, wondering what he would face inside the cabin. When he had opened the door completely he stared into the softly lit interior, the warmth of the house enveloping his frozen body, creating razor-sharp pricks of pain as the protective numbness began to thaw.

The smell of chicken stew permeated the air. And coffee. And something rich and spicy. Cinnamon. Maybe an apple pie.

He heard a noise, a low animal groan, then a deep growl. That's when he saw the animal. Thick black fur. Eyes like amber glass ovals. Sharp white teeth—bared. Hackles raised. What the hell was it? It looked like a damn wolf.

"Easy, Mac." The voice was gentle, soothing and captivatingly feminine. "It's him."

Reece gazed into the eyes of the most incredibly beautiful

woman he'd ever seen. She stood just inside the enormous great room of the cabin, the wolf at her side. Her hourglass figure was covered with a pair of faded jeans and a red turtleneck sweater, overlaid with a plaid jacket. Reece couldn't stop staring at her, gazing deeply into her pure blue eyes.

"Shut the door behind you." Her voice held a melodious quality. "You're letting out all the heat."

Reece slammed the door, then closed his eyes for a split second. Shaking his head to dislodge the cobwebs of confusion was a mistake. Pain so intense that he nearly doubled over shot through his head.

"You're injured." She took a tentative step toward him, the wolf following. "Let me help you."

Reece touched the 9 mm in his pocket, then glared at the woman, hoping she wouldn't do anything foolish. What could he say to her? How could he explain being here inside her cabin? Unless she was a total fool, she'd soon realize he was wearing county jail coveralls and a deputy's stolen coat. Under the best of circumstances Reece wasn't much of a sweet-talker, and now sure as hell wasn't the time to learn how to become one.

"I need food and shelter for the night." He watched her face for a reaction. "I'll leave in the morning." She only stared at him. "I'm not going to hurt you. You don't need to be afraid of me."

The wolf took several steps ahead of his mistress, stopping only when she called his name and ordered him to sit.

"You don't need to be afraid of me, either," she said. "I only want to help you. Please trust me."

Reece grunted, then laughed, deep in his chest. "Yeah, sure. Trust you. Trust a stranger. Lady, I don't trust anybody." Reece couldn't figure her out. Why wasn't she screaming her head off? Why wasn't she deathly afraid of him? Any sensible woman would have been. "I'm hungry. I need some food. A cup of coffee to start."

"All right. Please come in and sit down. I'll get you some coffee." She turned, but the wolf continued watching Reece.

"No, you don't. Stop!" She could be going to call the law, to turn him in. Reece covered the distance separating them in seconds, his head spinning, darkness closing in on him. Grabbing her by the arm, he whirled her around to face him. "I don't want you out of my sight. Understand?"

He wished the room would stop moving, wished his stomach didn't feel like emptying itself, wished the pain in his body would stop tormenting him.

"I'm not your enemy," she told him.

He heard her voice, but could no longer see her face. Darkness overcame him. His knees gave way. His hand slipped out of his pocket. He swayed sideways, then, like a mighty timber whose trunk had just been severed, Reece Landry dropped to the floor.

CHAPTER 2

Elizabeth knelt beside the stranger who had invaded the sanctuary of her home as surely as he had invaded her heart and mind repeatedly over the past few months. MacDatho sniffed the man's feet and legs, then lifted his head to stare at his mistress, their eyes connecting as they shared a common thought. This man, although weak, sick and at the moment disabled, could be dangerous. Her mind warned her to be wary of him; her heart told her to help him.

Touching his cheek, Elizabeth sensed the tension within his big body, despite the fact that he appeared to be unconscious. A day's growth of dark brown stubble covered his face, adding to his strong, masculine aura.

"He's cold, Mac. Almost frozen." Elizabeth began unbuttoning his heavy jacket. "We've got to get him out of these wet clothes and warm him up."

The man groaned. His eyes flickered open, then shut again. Elizabeth's hand stilled on his chest. She felt the hard, heavy pounding of his heartbeat and sensed the great strength and endurance he possessed.

Working quickly, she finished unbuttoning the sheepskin jacket, pushed it apart across the stranger's broad chest and tried to lift his left shoulder so she could ease his arm out of the garment.

Opening his eyes, Reece stared up at the woman leaning over him fiercely tugging on his jacket sleeve. What the hell was she trying to do, undress him? Was it possible that she was actually try-ing to help him? Well, he didn't want her help; he didn't want any-body's help. He'd learned long ago not to trust people, especially those who pretended they wanted to help you.

Reece grabbed the woman by the neck, shoving aside the thick, long braid of dark hair that hung down her back. Gasping, she stared at him, her big blue eyes filled with surprise. Then he heard the animal at her side growl as it lowered its head and bared its fangs, its hackles bristling in warning.

"Let go of me." Elizabeth kept her voice soft, even and as une-motional as possible.

"And if I don't?" Lying on his side, Reece pulled her face down next to his. There was a smell of woman about her, sweet and clean but slightly musky. He could sense that she was just a little bit afraid of him and trying her damnedest not to show it.

"MacDatho could rip out your throat if I gave him the order." She was so close to this man, only a breath away, their mouths and noses almost touching. Warmth spread through her body, a result of fear, uncertainty and sexual awareness. Some deep-seated yearn-ing within her urged her to taste his lips, to warm their cool sur-face with the heat of her mouth.

Reece reached up with his other hand, encompassing her neck completely with both hands. "And I could snap your soft, silky neck like a twig." Glancing at the woman's huge dog, he wondered if the animal would attack with or without his mistress's command.

Reece felt the woman's pulse beating rapidly in her neck. No doubt about it, she was afraid of him. Good. He needed her scared so she wouldn't do anything stupid. If he could control her, he could control her animal. But the moment he glanced from the dog back to her face, he almost regretted having threatened her. There was a wounded look in her eyes.

MacDatho growled deeply, raising his tail, his teeth still bared.

"No, Mac. I'm all right." Trying to convince herself as much as MacDatho, Elizabeth sent a message to Mac that this stranger was their friend, a friend in need of their help.

MacDatho eyed the stranger, then lowered his tail, but his hackles remained raised and his teeth partially bared in a snarl.

"You've got that animal trained pretty good, haven't you?" Keeping a tight hold on the woman, Reece raised himself up off the floor. Every bone, every muscle, every fiber of his being ached. The warmth inside the cabin sent pinpricks of pain through his body, the frigid numbness slowly replaced by nearly unbearable feeling.

"We're going to get up off the floor," Reece said, shoving himself against the soft solidity of the woman's body.

Elizabeth followed his orders, struggling to stand when he forced himself to his feet. He kept a stranglehold on her neck with one hand, the other hand biting into her shoulder. Once on his feet, he swayed. Elizabeth slipped her arm around his waist, instinctively trying to help him. He jerked away from her touch, momentarily releasing his hold on her.

She had never known anyone so afraid of human contact, so distrustful of another person's offer of help. "You need to get out of those wet clothes. You need to get warm."

Reece grabbed her by the arm. MacDatho growled again. Elizabeth sent Mac a silent message to stay calm, but she could sense his intention to attack Reece—and soon.

Elizabeth had only one choice. When she was on her feet again, she bowed her head, concentrating completely on stopping Mac from acting on his animal instincts to protect her.

"I don't want to hurt you," Reece heard himself saying and wondered why he felt such a strong need to reassure this woman. He pulled her close to his side, forcing her to walk beside him to the enormous rock fireplace.

Shivers racked his body. His hands trembled, and for a moment he wasn't sure he would be able to continue standing. When he shoved Elizabeth away from him, she almost lost her balance, but she caught hold of the wooden rocker near the wood stack on the wide hearth. MacDatho approached Reece with slow, deliberate strides.

You mustn't attack him, Elizabeth warned. Closing her eyes, she cautioned MacDatho that this stranger was an alpha male, a pack leader, the dominant animal.

Mac stopped dead still, eyeing Elizabeth as if questioning her, then he looked at Reece, dropped his tail, cringed low on his hind legs and began making licking movements with his tongue.

"What the hell's wrong with him?" The damned dog acted as if he'd suddenly become deathly afraid of Reece, and his actions didn't make any sense.

"It's Mac's way of accepting you, of letting you know he wants to be your friend." No need to explain to this stranger that she had convinced MacDatho that another male animal was the dominant one. He probably wouldn't understand, anyway.

"I don't want his friendship, or yours, either." The pain in Reece's head intensified, the tormenting aches in his body blazing to life as the numbness faded. "I'm hungry. I need some food. And some aspirin."

"If you'll come into the kitchen, I'll fix you something. Or if you want to rest in here, I'll bring out something on a tray."

"You're not going anywhere without me." Reece glanced around, looking for all the exits from the huge room. No matter what she said or how sweetly she acted, he couldn't trust this woman. He didn't dare.

He wouldn't hurt her. Hell, he wouldn't even hurt her damn, crazy dog. But he couldn't let her know that she had nothing to fear from him or she might destroy his only chance of escaping a prison sentence and proving himself an innocent man.

"Come into the kitchen. I have some leftover chicken stew from supper."

Elizabeth glanced back at the stranger as he followed her toward the kitchen. He walked on unsteady legs, his movements slow paced and lethargic. If he made it to the kitchen it would be a miracle. The man was dead on his feet.

Reece felt the dark, sinking nausea hit him. His knees buckled. He grabbed at thin air, trying to steady himself. *Don't you dare pass out again! If you do, you'll wake up in* prison! He heard the woman

say something to him, but the loud, buzzing roar in his head obliterated her words.

"Please, let me help you. You need to lie down." Elizabeth
reached out to him, trying to touch him.

Irrational panic seized Reece. The woman was lying to him, trying to catch him off guard. She didn't know him. Why would she
want to help him? He couldn't trust her.

"Stay away from me!" Clutching the gun in his right hand, he
pulled it out of his coat pocket, then shoved her away, pointing the
weapon directly at her.

He swayed toward the wall, his shoulder hitting the wooden surface with a resounding thud. Blackness encompassed him.

Elizabeth watched, feeling totally helpless as the stranger slid
down the wall, falling onto his side. Rushing to him, she knelt beside him and realized two things. He was still alive. And he held
the gun in his hand with a death grip.

"Come on, Mac. We've got to take care of him. He's probably
suffering from hypothermia and Lord knows what else." Elizabeth
wished her abilities extended to healing. Unfortunately, she didn't
have the magic touch, only a basic knowledge of herbs and the
power of the mind to restore one's health.

"I don't know how we'll ever move him. He's such a big man."
After prizing the gun from his tenacious grasp, Elizabeth pro-
ceeded to remove the stranger's coat, then his shoes and socks.
When she saw the county jail identification stamped on the dark
blue coveralls he wore, she realized that this man, this stranger who
had invaded her mind and her heart months ago, was an escaped
convict.

Her trembling hands hovered over his body. Her mind raced
through the thoughts and images that had been bombarding her for
months. She tried to sort through her feelings, to separate her emotions from logic. This man posed a threat to her. That was a certainty. But not physically. She sensed he would never harm her, that
he did not have the soul of a killer.

But he was dangerous.

"If only he'd regain consciousness." Elizabeth spoke more to herself than MacDatho, although the wolf-dog listened intently. "He's too heavy for us to move, and he needs to be in a warm bed. He could have a concussion. Look at the dried blood on his forehead and the swelling right here." Her fingers grazed the knot on his head, encountering the crusted blood that marked a line between his eyebrows and down his straight, patrician nose. She lifted a lock of brown hair, matted with blood.

Elizabeth would never have been able to explain to anyone else how she felt at this precise moment, for indeed, she could not explain her feelings to herself. All she knew was that she must help this man, that she and she alone could save him from not only the immediate physical pain he endured, but from the agony of being trapped like a caged animal, doomed to suffer for wrongs he had not committed.

With utmost haste Elizabeth divested the stranger of every article of clothing except the white boxer shorts that were plastered to his body. Where earlier the stranger had felt cold, nearly frozen to the touch, he now felt somewhat warmer.

Elizabeth rubbed his face. "Please come to, just a little. I don't think Mac and I can get you to a bed without your cooperation."

Why couldn't he have stayed unconscious when he'd first passed out in the living room? At least it was toasty warm in there, the roaring fire close. She could have made him a pallet on the floor until he'd regained consciousness. But no, he had to pass out in the cool, dimly lit hallway leading to the kitchen.

Elizabeth slapped his face gently at first, then a bit more forcefully. "Come on. Wake up."

Reece moaned. Elizabeth smiled.

"That's it, come on. All I need is partial consciousness. Just enough to get you moving."

Reece moaned again. His eyelids flickered. He heard a feminine voice issuing orders. She was demanding that he awaken, that he get on his feet. Why didn't she leave him alone? He didn't want to open his eyes. He didn't want to stand. He didn't want to move.

But she, whoever the hell she was, kept prodding him, kept insisting that he help her. Help her do what?

Elizabeth said a prayer of thanks when she had roused the stranger enough to get him to sit up. His head kept leaning sideways, resting against his shoulder. He couldn't seem to keep his eyes open. Finally, summoning every ounce of strength she possessed, she helped him to his feet. He slumped against her, his heavy weight almost sending her to her knees. She struggled against her body's insistent urging to release the burden far too enormous for her to carry.

"Come on. Help me, dammit! I can't carry you." Elizabeth encouraged him, both physically by squeezing her arm around him, and mentally by concentrating on discovering his name.

For months she had been, unwillingly, a part of this man's life. She had witnessed his suffering, his anger and his degradation at being caged, but she had never been able to delve deeply inside him. She had sensed fragments of his emotions, caught quick glimpses of his past, present and future. But nothing concrete. Not even his name.

He leaned more and more heavily against her as she tried to force him to take a step. Finally she shoved him up against the wall, bracing her body against his, trying to keep him standing. If only she could get through to him. If only he wasn't shielding his mind.

She ran her fingers over his face, gently, caressingly. Lowering her voice she spoke to him, pleadingly, with great concern. She felt the breach, the slightest opening in his mind.

"I want to help you. You need me so much. Don't fight me."

Reece! His name was Reece. He had given her that much. If he hadn't been so weak, so helpless, she doubted he would have let down his protective barrier long enough for her to have gained even that small piece of information.

"We need to get you in a warm, soft bed, Reece. You're sick, and I need your cooperation so I can help you get well."

The voice spoke to him again. So soft and sweet. The woman cared about him. She wanted to help him. Was she his mother? His mother had been the only person who'd ever given a damn about him. No. It couldn't be Blanche. Blanche was dead. She'd died years ago.

"Reece, please, take just a few steps. My bedroom is right through that door."

Her bedroom? Was she one of Miss Flossie's girls? Was she trying to seduce him? No. That couldn't be it. Miss Flossie had gone out of business ten years ago, and it had been longer than that since a woman's tempting body had been able to seduce him into doing something foolish. He chose the time, the place, the circumstances and the woman. Reece Landry was always the one in control.

"Take one step. Just one." If she could persuade him to take a step, then he'd realize he could still manage to walk, and she might have a chance of getting him to bed.

MacDatho sniffed around the discarded clothing that lay on the floor, pawing at the coveralls, his sharp claws ripping the material.

"Reece, listen to me. You're safe here with me. No one's going to put you back in a cage. Can you hear me?"

"No cage." He slurred his words, but Elizabeth understood.

"Let's walk away from the cage."

"Away from the cage," he said.

If she couldn't get him to walk soon, she'd just have to lay him back down on the floor and do the best she could for him.

Reece took a tentative step, his big body leaning on Elizabeth for support.

"That's it, Reece. Walk away from the cage."

She guided his faltering steps out of the hallway, through the doorway leading to her room and straight to her bed. He dragged his feet, barely lifting them from the floor, but he cooperated enough with Elizabeth that they finally reached her antique wooden bed, the covers already folded back in readiness. Trying to ease him down onto the soft, crochet-lace-edged sheet proved impossible. Elizabeth simply released her hold around his waist, allowing him to fall across the handmade Cathedral Window quilt she used as a coverlet.

MacDatho stood in the open doorway, guarding his mistress. Pushing and shoving, tugging and turning, Elizabeth managed to place Reece's head on one of her fat, feather pillows. His boxer shorts were as damp as his other clothing, but she hesitated removing them. Feeling like a voyeur, Elizabeth tugged the wet shorts down his hips, over the bulge of his manhood, down and off his legs. With a speed born of her discomfort at seeing him naked when he was unable to protest, and the need to warm his shivering body, Elizabeth rolled Reece over until she was able to ease the covers away from his heavy bulk. Quickly she jerked the top sheet, blanket and quilt up over his hairy legs, sheltering him from the cold. Then she reached down to the foot of the bed where a wooden quilt rack stood, retrieved the heavy tartan plaid blanket hanging alongside a Crow's Foot quilt and spread it on top of the other cover.

Sitting beside Reece, she laid her hand on his warm forehead. As long as he'd been exposed to the frigid weather there was every possibility that his injuries had created serious health problems.

He looked so totally male lying there in her very feminine bed, his brown hair dark against the whiteness of her pillowcase. Even in sleep, his face was set into a frown, his eyes squinched as if he'd been staring into the sun. His face was long and lean, his mouth wide, the corners slightly drooped, the bottom lip fuller than the top. His stubble-covered chin boasted a hint of a cleft.

Mentally, Elizabeth began sorting through her knowledge of herbal medicine, taught to her by her great-aunt Margaret, a quarter Cherokee. If only Aunt Margaret was here now, but she wasn't. The old woman was past seventy and stayed close to home during the winter months. Besides, with the roads in such deplorable condition, Elizabeth doubted she could get into Dover's Mill and back, even in her Jeep.

Reece had so many problems with which she would have to deal. His ears and nose and hands had begun to regain some of their color but still remained unnaturally pale. The best remedy to reverse the hypothermia and possible frostbite would be to keep him warm.

Reaching under the weight of the covers, Elizabeth lifted Reece's hands and laid them on top of his stomach, elevating them slightly. Then she slipped a small pillow from a nearby wing-back chair beneath the cover and under his feet.

Glancing across the room to the well-worn fireplace surrounded by a simple wooden mantel, Elizabeth realized the fire needed more wood. It would be essential to Reece's recovery to keep her bedroom warm. Just as she rose from the bed the lights flickered, then dimmed, returned to normal and suddenly flickered again, this time dying quickly. The warm glow from the fireplace turned the room into golden darkness, shadows dancing on the walls and across the wide wooden floor.

"Damn!" She'd been expecting this, knowing how unreliable the electricity was here in the mountains during a storm. She'd light the kerosene lamps and keep the fires burning in all the fireplaces and in her wood-burning kitchen stove. The generator that protected the precious environment of her greenhouses had probably already kicked on. She would check to make sure the generator was working before she gathered all the ingredients for Reece's treatment.

An antiseptic to clean his head wound would be needed, birch perhaps, along with some powdered comfrey to promote the healing. Mullein would do nicely to help with the frostbite.

Having made her mental list of necessary herbs, Elizabeth double-checked to make sure Reece was covered completely before adding another log to the fire.

"Stay and keep watch, Mac. If he needs me before I return, come for me."

The antique grandfather clock in the living room struck the midnight hour. Resting in a brown leather wing-back chair by the bed, Elizabeth tucked the colorful striped afghan about her hips, letting it drape her legs. She had done all she could do for Reece, cleaning his cuts and bruises, then applying powdered comfrey. The mullein had served several purposes in its various forms of

healing aids—as an oil to treat the frostbite, as a bactericidal pre-
caution and as a decoction to calm Reece's restlessness. While he'd
been partially awake she had persuaded him to drink the warm
mullein brew.

MacDatho lay asleep to the right of the fireplace, in a nook between the wood box and the wall. Elizabeth dozed on and off,
mostly staying awake to keep vigil, unable to refrain from staring
at the big, naked man resting uneasily in her bed. This man was a
stranger, an escaped convict, guilty of some horrible crime. In her
mind's eye she kept seeing his large, well-formed fingers dripping
with blood. Had he killed someone? Was she harboring a murderer? Obviously her visions of his being caged came from the fact
that he'd been imprisoned, locked away securely behind bars.

She had been trying unsuccessfully to break through the mental shield he kept securely in place, even while he slept fitfully. Occasionally Elizabeth caught a glimpse, a glimmer, a sliver of
emotion. She simply could not believe Reece was a murderer.

Perhaps she didn't want to believe him capable of murder. After
all, the instincts within her feminine heart pleaded with the logical side of her brain to protect him, to heal not only his body but
his soul. How could she argue with her unerring instincts? But this
was the first time she'd ever been unable to read a person, at least
partially. Even Sam Dundee, obstinate, rigid, controlled, self-suf-
ficient Sam, hadn't been able to hide his thoughts and feelings from
her all the time. Perhaps it was because Sam trusted her.

Reece was different. He didn't know her, had no reason to give
her his trust, to open up his thoughts and feelings to her. Most people had little or no control over her ability to sense things about
them, a curse for her far more than a blessing. But Reece seemed
to possess a shield that kept her out. Odd that the only man she
had ever allowed in her bed was the one man who refused her ad-
mittance into his private thoughts and feelings.

Elizabeth dozed in the chair the rest of the night, waking at dawn
when she heard Reece groaning. He had tossed the covers off and
was thrashing wildly about on the bed. Jumping up from the chair,

she placed her knees on the bed, lowered herself enough to grab his flying arms and found herself tossed flat on her back, lying beneath a naked Reece.

She stared at his face, next to hers on the pillow. His eyes were still closed. Where she had held his arms in her strong grip, trying to calm him, he now held her arms over her head, the weight of his body trapping her partially beneath him, her hip resting against his arousal.

His breathing slowed, his raging movements ceased and he lay quietly, his body unnaturally warm. Elizabeth tugged on her trapped arms. Reece tightened his hold momentarily, then when she tugged again, he released her, flopping one big, hairy arm across her stomach. Elizabeth sucked in a deep breath.

How had this happened? She was alone in her bed with a naked man—a big, strong naked man. Reece. The stranger who had invaded her heart five months ago. The stranger who was an escaped convict.

Of all the men she'd known in her twenty-six years, none of them had made her feel the way Reece did. She wanted to console him, to soothe him, to whisper words of comfort. She also wanted to be held in his arms, to be kissed by his firm lips, to be covered with his hard body, to be...

Elizabeth squirmed, trying to free herself. Reece didn't budge, the weight of his body keeping her trapped. What was she going to do? She couldn't just lie there until he rolled over. Stay calm. Don't panic. Think. Once again Elizabeth concentrated on forming a mental link with Reece. Once again his mind denied her access.

Reece covered her breast with his hand. Elizabeth gasped, totally shocked by the intimacy of his action. Although she still wore her clothes, her jeans, sweater and jacket, she suddenly felt undressed. She seldom wore a bra, wasn't wearing one now, and the pressure of Reece's hand cupping her breast made her feel naked. When his finger and thumb pinched at her nipple, it responded with immediate erectness, jutting against her sweater, answering the call of Reece's command.

No man had ever touched her the way Reece was doing now. The few young men she had dated in college had seen her as a freak once they'd found out she possessed psychic abilities, some even ridiculing her as a fraud. Despite her desire to know the pleasures of love and marriage and motherhood, Elizabeth had accepted her self-imposed solitude here in her mountain retreat—here in her grandmother's home where she was safe from the outside world.

But the outside world had invaded her privacy, had indeed burst into her life in the form of one big, angry man…a man now fondling her intimately.

She covered his caressing hand with her slender fingers, gripping his hand, lifting it from her breast. Only partially conscious, Reece moaned and curled up against her, nuzzling her neck with his nose. Shivers of apprehension raced up her spine. Spirals of inner warmth spread through her body.

"Reece?" She had to get away from him, from the power of his touch, the strength of his masculinity. She tried again to move away from him. He pulled her closer.

"Reece, please let me go. I can't stay here with you like this."

She saw his eyelids flicker, open briefly and close. He ran one hand up and down her shoulder, then caressed her waist, her hip, the side of her leg. Tremors racked Elizabeth's body, heat curling inside her, moisture collecting in preparation. This had to stop! It had to stop now! She wasn't prepared for such intense emotions, for feelings beyond any she had ever experienced.

"Reece!"

He opened his eyes, smoky amber eyes, eyes that looked right at her without seeing. She gave him a gentle shove. He turned over onto his back, closing his eyes and groaning softly. Elizabeth eased away from him. Once on her feet she pulled the covers up over his body, but not before she'd taken a good look at the man who had created such wanton desire within her.

She guessed his height at well over six feet, probably two or three inches over. He was muscular but lean, his hands and feet large and well shaped. Curly, dark brown hair covered his arms and legs, a thick mat on his chest tapering down to a narrow line across his stomach and then spreading out to surround his manhood.

Elizabeth swallowed hard, mesmerized by his masculine body, by the perfection, the sculptured beauty. Her fingers itched to reach out and touch him, to caress the very maleness of him. Hastily she pulled the sheet, quilt and blanket over him, covering him up to his neck.

His breathing seemed even, his sleep natural. She thought it would be safe to leave him alone for a while, long enough to fix herself a bite of breakfast, take a quick shower and renew her strength through a few moments of meditation. She'd have Mac-Datho stand guard. He would be able to sense any change in Reece and alert her.

Elizabeth leaned over, placing her hand on Reece's forehead. He was warm, perhaps a little too warm, even feverish.

She'd just have to rush through breakfast and a bath. Reece didn't need to be left alone for too long. Cradling his rough, lean cheek in her hand, Elizabeth gazed down at the sleeping man. Tiny, almost indiscernible flutters spread through her stomach. So this was what sexual attraction felt like. When she'd been a teenager she'd been so sure she was in love with Sam. He'd known better. Now she did, too. Sam had been comforting, reassuring, safe. Reece was none of those things, and yet...

She left him then, left him to rest, left him in order to free herself from the magnetism he possessed, a magnetism that drew her to him as she had never been drawn to another man.

After a shower and change of clothes, she allowed herself five minutes of meditation before she devoured a bowl of oatmeal and a cup of coffee. Then she bundled up to go outside and check on her greenhouses. During college when she had decided that she could never live in the outside world, she had sought a profession suitable to her personality and life-style and had chosen horticulture. She not only loved flowers and herbs, trees and shrubs, but she had a deep reverence for nature, a respect for all living things. She'd borrowed the money from Sam to install a small greenhouse behind the cabin. Her nursery business had grown by leaps and bounds, so that now she had two large greenhouses and a mail-order business that kept her knee-deep in work. Aunt Margaret and O'Grady helped out occasionally, and in the rush seasons of fall and spring planting, she often hired part-time help from Dover's Mill.

Returning from her outside trek, Elizabeth laid peppermint leaves and elder flowers on the counter. If Reece's fever rose any higher, she would prepare a tea made from equal amounts of the two ingredients. Drinking the tea would cause profuse sweating and hopefully break the fever.

Although early-morning light should have illuminated the house through the many windows, the dreary gray sky obscured the far-away sun, keeping the house in shadows, the only light coming from the fires burning in the fireplaces and the glow from the kerosene lamps. Even though the phones should be working soon, it could be days before electrical power was restored. Thank God the generator worked perfectly, protecting her greenhouses. She supposed she should have opted to hook the house up to a generator, too, but she simply couldn't justify the expense. Despite Sam's efforts to give her money, Elizabeth prided herself upon her financial independence. Her business would sink or swim on her merits as a businesswoman. She wasn't a child any longer; she wasn't Sam's responsibility.

After pouring herself a second cup of coffee, Elizabeth turned on the portable radio nestled between pieces of her prized blue graniteware collection sitting atop the oak sideboard. Picking up the radio, she ventured out of the kitchen and down the hallway. The radio music was country-western, a current Vince Gill hit. Just as she walked into her bedroom the news came on, the announcer alerting people in the Dover's Mill area of an escaped convict, armed and dangerous.

"Reece Landry, convicted murderer, escaped from a county vehicle taking him to Arrendale Correctional Institute in Alto after the car skidded off the highway and hit a tree during yesterday's severe storm. Both deputies were killed in the accident. Landry, convicted of murdering Newell industrialist B. K. Stanton, was being taken to Arrendale to serve a life sentence. Landry is six foot three, a hundred and ninety-five pounds, with medium-length brown hair and brown eyes. He is armed with a 9 mm automatic taken from Deputy Jimmy Don Lewis. Our local county sheriff is joining forces with the sheriff's department in two other counties to help in the search for Landry. The search has been hampered by the severe weather. If anyone has any information, please contact the sheriff's department immediately. Do not approach this man. He is armed and dangerous. We repeat, Reece Landry is armed and dangerous."

Elizabeth turned off the radio, placing it and her coffee cup on a corner desk. She walked over to the bed where Reece lay sleeping. He'd thrown off the quilt and blanket, leaving only the sheet covering him from the waist down.

"Did you kill B. K. Stanton?" Elizabeth whispered, not expecting an answer but hoping she could sense Reece's innocence or guilt. She sensed nothing.

Sitting in the wing-back chair beside the bed, she reached out to touch Reece's forehead. Hot. Burning hot. The fever had risen, but he wasn't sweating. His skin was dry. She went into the bathroom, drew a pan of cool water, took a washcloth from the stack in the wicker basket where she stored them and returned to Reece's bedside. Placing the pan on the nightstand, she dipped the washcloth in the water, wrung it out and began giving Reece a rubdown. If the rubdown didn't cool his fever, she would prepare the medicinal tea.

The moment the damp cloth touched his body Reece moaned, then flung his arm out, batting at the air. He hit the side of Elizabeth's shoulder. Grabbing his arm, she lowered it to his side and continued her ministrations. Time and again she dipped the cloth into the water, wrung it lightly and massaged Reece's face, neck, shoulders and chest.

Realizing her rubdown had done nothing to lower his fever, she went to the kitchen, prepared the peppermint-and-elder tea and brought the brewed medication and an earthenware mug to her bedroom. After pouring the concoction, she sat on the bed by Reece and lifted his head. As she'd done the night before, she placed the cup to his lips, shifting it just enough for the liquid to dribble. When the tea ran down his chin, Elizabeth inserted her finger between his closed lips, prizing his mouth open. She repeated the process. Reece accepted the tea. She kept her arm securely behind his head, holding him inclined just enough so he could swallow the medicine without choking. When he downed the last drop in the mug, Elizabeth sighed. Now all she could do was wait and pray.

Lowering his head to the pillow, Elizabeth turned so that her back rested against the headboard of the huge old bed her great-great-grandfather, a carpenter, had made as a first-anniversary gift for his wife. Their seven children, four of whom had grown to adulthood, had been born in this bed.

Time passed slowly as Elizabeth sat beside Reece, her hand idly brushing his shoulder, her fingers soothing the thick, springy hair on his chest. Moisture coated her fingertips when she touched his forehead. He was sweating. The fever had broken!

By noon Elizabeth had pushed and tugged Reece enough to change the bed linen after he'd stained them with perspiration. He lay sleeping peacefully, warm but not feverish, the flesh on his ears, nose and hands that she had feared frostbitten now a healthy pink. Perhaps he would awaken soon. When he did, he would be hungry. He'd probably want breakfast.

Glancing down at the man the radio announcer had called armed and dangerous, Elizabeth breathed deeply, wondering if she was a fool to trust him not to harm her. Fool or not, she could not deny the way she felt about him, the deep emotions he stirred within her. For five months this stranger had been a part of her. Without even knowing him, she had allowed him into her heart.

Elizabeth leaned over and kissed Reece on the cheek. He didn't stir. She ran her fingertips across his full lower lip. Suddenly she sensed a desperate need, a soul-felt cry for help. Laying her fingertips across his mouth, Elizabeth concentrated on zeroing in on Reece's emotions. Anger. Pain. Hatred. Fear.

"God sent you to me, Reece Landry. Somehow I'm going to find a way to help you," Elizabeth vowed.

CHAPTER 3

Warmth. Blessed warmth. Reece lay in the soft warmth, savoring the comfort, his mind halfway between sleep and consciousness. He stretched his legs, which were covered by a downy, heated weight. His muscles ached; his head felt fuzzy. Was he dead? Had he frozen to death in the snow? Was this delicious warmth coming from hell's brimstone fire? Couldn't be, he thought. This wasn't punishment; this was heaven.

Slowly and with some difficulty, Reece forced his eyelids open. He wasn't quite sure where he was, but one thing was for certain— he hadn't died and gone to hell. He gazed up at a split-log-and-plank ceiling, the wood a mellow gold. Looking around the room, he noticed the massive stacked logs of the outer walls and the rustic rock fireplace where a cheerful fire glowed brightly. Across the wooden mantel lay an arrangement of dried flowers intermingled with large pine cones and wide plaid ribbons. Several dried-flower wreaths decorated the walls, along with a few framed charcoal nature drawings of trees, flowers and even one of a wolf.

Wolf! Last night he'd broken into this cabin. No, he hadn't really broken in. Some fool had left the door unlocked. Reece shook his head. It didn't hurt! Reaching up to touch his injured forehead, he immediately realized that the dried blood had been washed away and the swelling had diminished considerably.

Had he imagined that damned black wolf, snarling, growling,

threatening, warning Reece not to harm his mistress? The woman! Had he imagined her, too? Big blue eyes. Thick dark hair lying across her back in a long braid. Full, tempting breasts. Strong arms. Comforting voice.

He could hear that voice calling his name. *Reece. I want to help you. You're safe here with me. No one is going to put you back in a cage.*

How the hell did she know his name? And why would she help him? Why had she taken care of him? Tiny pieces of his memory returned, fever-induced dreams of tender, caring hands bathing his body, stroking his face, doctoring his wounds, pouring some sort of hot, mint-flavored tea down his throat.

Reece sat up in bed with a start, the full implications of his fragmented memories hitting him. He had forced his way into the woman's home, unlocked door or not. And he had threatened her life before he'd passed out. But what had happened after that? Who had put him to bed?

The sudden realization that he was completely naked took him by surprise. Someone had carried him to this bed and undressed him. The woman couldn't have carried him. No way. Did that mean she had a husband? A father? A brother? He didn't remember anyone except the woman and her enormous animal protector.

Had the woman called the sheriff? Were deputies on their way here right now to take him to prison?

You're safe with me. No one is going to put you back in a cage.

Her words had been a promise, but Reece didn't trust promises. He'd found in his vast experience with the human race that most people lied whenever it suited them.

Reece tossed back the covers, slid his legs out of the bed and touched his feet to the floor. Although his body ached with a bearable soreness, neither his head nor his side hurt. Undoubtedly, none of his ribs had been broken in the accident—either that, or the woman who had tended his wounds had miraculously healed him.

He had to find the woman, had to ask her where he was and figure out exactly what his chances of escaping were. But he was buck naked and didn't see anything in the room that vaguely resembled his county-issued coveralls. However, he did notice a stack of folded clothes on the cedar chest at the foot of the bed.

Slowly, tentatively, Reece stood. Swaying slightly, his head spinning, he grabbed the bedpost. The faint vertigo passed as quickly as it had come. Righting himself, he walked around the bed, lifted the stack of clothing off the cedar chest and smiled when he realized he held a pair of men's briefs, a thermal top, a flannel shirt and a pair of well-worn jeans. There had to be a man in this woman's life, probably here in her home. Where else would she have gotten men's clothes? And from the look of them, the items belonged to a fairly large man, someone about Reece's own size.

But why couldn't he remember a man?

Taking his time, Reece put on the clothes, then looked around, wondering if the lady of the house had thought of footwear. Sure enough, resting on the wide rock hearth was a pair of thick socks and leather work boots.

Reece sat on the raised hearth, breathing in the aroma of aged wood burning slowly, and slipped on the socks and boots. Whoever owned these boots had a foot about a half size larger than Reece's, but the minuscule difference was of little importance. The jeans were a perfect fit, the flannel shirt and thermal top only a fraction large. The owner undoubtedly had the shoulders and chest of a linebacker.

Running his hand over his face, Reece noted the beginnings of a beard. He needed a shave, and he could do with a hot shower, even though he felt relatively clean. Memories of his ministering angel bathing him flashed through his mind. A shower and shave could wait. He needed to find his hostess. Reece laughed aloud. His hostess? For all he knew, the county sheriff could be waiting for him just beyond the half-closed door.

Reece inched the door open, peered out into the dim hallway, saw no one, but heard a man singing an old-fashioned tune, something from the forties or fifties. Following the music, Reece made his way down the hallway, noting the huge living room in the opposite direction and a massive wooden staircase leading to the second level of the cabin.

The kitchen door stood open. Bright sunshine poured in through the lace-curtained windows. Harry Connick, Jr.'s mellow voice singing "I'll Dream of You Again" drifted through the cabin from the radio-cassette player on the counter. Reece's vision took in three things in quick succession. A blue-granite wood-burning stove placed in front of a corner brick chimney, a round wooden table set for a meal, and a smiling woman holding a pan of biscuits. The smell of coffee, frying bacon and sweet spices made Reece's mouth water. He hadn't realized how hungry he was.

Then he heard a low growl and saw the big black wolf-dog he'd encountered the night before. That damned animal didn't like him. And why should he? Reece reminded himself that he had invaded the dog's home and threatened his mistress. Threatened her with his gun. His gun! Where was his gun? He'd been holding it when he'd passed out.

"Well, good morning." Elizabeth thought Reece looked rather handsome with a two-day growth of beard and wearing Sam's old clothes. "I'd about decided you were going to sleep away another day."

Reece stopped dead still in the doorway. "Lady, who the hell are you?"

The practical realist in him warned that this woman was a stranger and not to be trusted, but his male libido reacted differently, appreciating the woman's earthy beauty, the ripe fullness of her sturdy body, the basic sensuality that surrounded her like a visible aura.

Elizabeth set the pan of biscuits on a hotpad atop the counter, turned to Reece, took several steps in his direction and held out her hand. "I'm Elizabeth Sequana Mallory. You're in my home, on my mountain, in Sequana Falls."

Reece didn't make a move to enter the kitchen or to take Elizabeth's hand. Why the hell was she being so friendly? She acted as if he were a welcome guest. Was the woman crazy?

"Breakfast is just about ready. Come on in and sit down." Elizabeth turned, busying herself with preparing two plates. "How do you like your coffee?"

"Black." Reece walked into the kitchen, stopping abruptly at the table, grabbing the top of the wooden chair.

"I see the clothes and boots fit you all right." Elizabeth placed two plates of eggs, bacon and hash browns on the two blue place mats.

"Your husband's?"

"No." Elizabeth poured coffee into two Blue Willow cups.

"What did you do with my gun?" Reece clutched the back of the chair.

"It's in a safe place." Elizabeth set the cups on the table, pulled out a chair and sat down. "Aren't you hungry?"

Reece glared at her. What did she think this was, a damned picnic? Although they were total strangers, this woman was treating him like a long-lost friend.

"Don't worry, Mr. Landry, when you leave I'll return your gun to you." Elizabeth lifted the cup to her lips.

Reece watched her sip the hot coffee. Her lips were full, soft and a natural rosy pink. He remembered that those lips had touched his cheek. She had kissed him! Her small hand held the cup securely as she continued leisurely sipping the coffee. Reece noted the delicate size of her hands, but remembered their strength, remembered those slender fingers caressing his face, touching him lightly.

Dragging his eyes away from her lips and hands, Reece suddenly realized she'd called him Mr. Landry. She knew who he was. He hadn't been imagining things when he thought he'd heard her calling him Reece.

"How do you know my name?"

"Sit down, Reece. Your breakfast is getting cold."

What the hell was wrong with this woman? Didn't she have the good sense to be scared? After all, she obviously knew he was an escaped convict, a murderer on his way to a life term in the state penitentiary.

Releasing his death grip on the chair, Reece reached out, grabbing Elizabeth by the shoulders, turning her in her seat. She stared up at him with surprised blue eyes. The expression on her face was a mixture of fear, doubt, hope and supplication. This woman—Elizabeth—wanted something from him. But what?

"What's going on with you?" he asked. "If you know who I am, why haven't you called the sheriff?"

"I know who you are, Reece Landry." You're the stranger in my heart, the man who has invaded my thoughts for five months. "I heard a news bulletin on the radio yesterday morning telling about a sheriff's car that wrecked and the escape of a convicted murderer who was being transported to Arrendale."

"You heard a bulletin on the radio yesterday morning?" How was that possible? He hadn't escaped until yesterday afternoon. "What day is this? How long have I been here?"

"You came here the night before last. You were exhausted, injured and suffering from minor frostbite and exposure. Then you ran a high fever for a while."

"Son of a bitch!" Reece loosened his hold on Elizabeth's shoulders, noticing for the first time that her wolf-dog had moved to her side. "Have you notified the sheriff's department?"

"I can't. The phone's out." Elizabeth hated herself for lying to Reece, but she felt it was a necessary fabrication. The phone had been working since early this morning, but she had unplugged it, preventing anyone from calling her.

Elizabeth laid her hand atop Reece's where it rested on her shoulder. As if he'd been burned by her touch, he jerked his hand away.

"So you're stuck with me for the time being, huh?" Just because she hadn't been able to notify the authorities of his whereabouts didn't mean he was safe. From the looks of the sunshine and blue sky he saw outside the windows, the winter storm had passed. Even if she couldn't telephone for help, that didn't mean a search party wouldn't show up on her doorstep any time now.

"Why don't you sit down and eat. You've got to be hungry. You haven't eaten a bite in a couple of days." Elizabeth didn't think she'd ever seen anyone as wary, as suspicious as Reece. Didn't the man trust anybody?

Reece pulled out the chair, sat down, picked up the Blue Willow cup and tasted the coffee. The brew was warm, rich, full-bodied, with a hint of flavor he couldn't quite make out. He swallowed, then frowned, wondering exactly what the unique taste could be.

"Vanilla almond," Elizabeth said, as if she'd read his mind. "I grind my own coffee beans." She nodded at the counter where an antique coffee grinder perched on a wooden shelf alongside several other antique utensils.

Nodding in acknowledgment of her statement, Reece picked up his fork, lifted a hefty portion of scrambled eggs and put them in his mouth. Suddenly he had the oddest sensation that he'd somehow stepped into the twilight zone, that he had escaped from the sheriff's car and found his way to never-never land. Nothing about this place, this isolated cabin in the woods, or this woman—sultry, earthy and incredibly beautiful—seemed real.

Any woman, alone the way Elizabeth Mallory was, would be afraid of an escaped convict, but Reece sensed more curiosity than fear emanating from the woman sitting across the table from him.

While he continued eating, devouring the tasty breakfast, he watched Elizabeth as she broke open a biscuit, buttered it and fed small pieces to her wolf-dog. The animal ate heartily, consuming three biscuits in quick succession. Elizabeth laughed, the sound piercingly sweet to Reece's ears. There was no pretension, no coy feminine silliness to her laugh. The sound came from her heart— warm, loving and completely genuine. Any fool could see the mutual love that existed between dog and woman.

"Where'd you get him?" Reece nodded toward Elizabeth's pet.

"Mac here?" She patted the animal's back, then scratched behind his ears.

"Mac?"

"Short for MacDatho." Elizabeth sensed a minute loosening of the tension in Reece, barely discernible but evident nevertheless. "My German shepherd, Elspeth, was Mac's mother. His father was a wolf."

"I'd guessed as much. Are there many wolves in these hills?"

"Some."

"Why'd you take care of me?" Reece asked. "You should have tied me up once I passed out on you. Instead, you put me to bed and nursed me. Now you're feeding me. Woman, haven't you got any sense at all?"

Elizabeth smiled. Dear God in heaven, he wished she hadn't smiled at him like that. He wanted to capture that smile, hold on to it, keep it from vanishing.

"The newscaster said you'd been convicted of killing a man," Elizabeth said. "Did you kill him?"

"I was convicted, wasn't I?"

"I know that. But were you guilty?"

Reece finished off the last bite of bacon, downed the remains of his coffee and shoved back his chair. Standing, he stared down at Elizabeth's upturned face. "Would you believe me if I told you that I'm innocent, that I didn't kill B. K. Stanton?"

"Yes, I'd believe you."

Running his hands through his thick, wavy hair, Reece snorted. "Lady, are you that naive? Would you take the word of a stranger, someone you don't know the first thing about?"

But I do know things about you, Reece. Less than I want to know, but more than you could ever realize. "You don't have the soul of a killer."

"What makes you think I don't?"

"I can sense it. I'm very good at sensing things." Did she dare try to explain her special gifts, her God-given psychic powers? Would he believe her if she did?

"You live up here in these hills all by yourself?"

Standing, Elizabeth began clearing away the table, stacking the dishes in the sink. "Just Mac and me. My great-aunt, Margaret McPhearson, spends a lot of time up here with me in warm weather. She lives in Dover's Mill."

"How do you support yourself? Do you have a job in Dover's Mill?" Reece couldn't imagine anyone with no income being able to afford such a luxurious two-story cabin.

"I operate a nursery. I have a degree in horticulture." Elizabeth turned on the water faucet and squirted dishwashing detergent into the sink.

"What sort of nursery? Flowers?"

MacDatho followed Reece to the back door, watching him intently when he opened the door and stepped out onto the porch. The dry, frigid air cut through Reece's clothing, but the sun warmed his face when he stared up at the sky.

Walking out onto the porch, Elizabeth waited for Mac to run outside before she closed the door. She turned to Reece, instinctively reaching out to touch his arm, but she suddenly remembered his aversion to being touched and withdrew her hand.

"Look over to the right and you'll see my greenhouses. I grow roses and a fairly large variety of flowers as well as herbs and spices and a few specialty shrubs. I sell in nearby towns to both florists and gardeners, and two years ago I started a mail-order business, which has grown by leaps and bounds."

"So, you're a successful businesswoman, huh?"

"I guess you could say that."

"How are you keeping the temperatures in your greenhouses regulated without electricity? A generator?"

"Yes. The generator kicks in automatically when the electrical power fails, which is fairly often when we get a winter storm."

Reece glanced at her. The sun streaked reddish highlights in her dark brown hair and gave a golden glow to her olive skin. With the log cabin, the blue sky, the snow-covered forest as a background for her beauty, Elizabeth seemed as much a part of nature's perfection as her surroundings. Her calf-length, rust-colored corduroy skirt swayed in the cool February wind, revealing a pair of flat, plain, tan ankle boots. Her breasts swelled invitingly, not quite straining the buttons on her hunter-green-and-rust-striped blouse. Her baggy green sweater hung down past her generous hips.

Reece forced himself to look away, unable to deny his body's sexual urges. He wanted this woman. She was beautiful and sexy and caring. But who was he kidding? The last thing on Elizabeth

Mallory's mind was sex—and it should be the last thing on his mind. All he should be thinking about was getting the hell away from here before the authorities showed up looking for him. He had to find a way to get back to Newell, to hide out until he could discover who had really taken his .38 revolver and blown B. K. Stanton to hell.

MacDatho ran down the steps and into the backyard, the snow coming up to his belly.

"I wouldn't hurt you." Reece spoke the words in a low, deep voice, not much more than a whisper on the wind.

Elizabeth heard him; her heart heard him. "I know."

He saw her shiver, and realized she must be cold. "Why don't you go back inside? I didn't realize how cold it still was. The sun had me fooled."

"Are you staying out here?"

"For a few more minutes." Reece leaned over the porch railing, curling his fingers about the top wooden round.

Elizabeth laid her hand over his where he gripped the railing. When he flinched, she squeezed his hand gently. "Do you want to tell me about the murder? About what really happened?"

"What really happened was I had a motive for killing Stanton and a lifelong reputation as a town bad boy. Once they arrested me, they stopped looking for any other suspects. That's about it."

For a split second Elizabeth picked up the intense rage burning inside Reece, then suddenly he shielded his emotions, almost as if he had felt her probing.

"There's a lot more to it than that, isn't there?" Elizabeth asked. "I want you to know that I'm here for you, willing to listen when you're ready to talk, willing to do whatever I can to help you. I know you can't bear the thought of being caged again."

He stared at her as if he'd never seen her before, as if she'd appeared out of nowhere, a blithe spirit sent to taunt him. "Caged? Yeah, caged. That's exactly what it's like in jail, what it would be like at Arrendale. I nearly went nuts being locked up so many months."

"You couldn't post bail?"

"The district attorney persuaded the judge that I was a poor risk. The Stantons were generous supporters during the D.A.'s reelection bid. He owed the family a favor."

Elizabeth clutched Reece's hand. She longed to put her arms around him and comfort him. Something told her that it had been a long time since anyone had comforted Reece Landry. When she glanced at him, he was staring off into the distance.

"You won't be caged again, Reece." Tears sprang into Elizabeth's eyes. "I promise I'll do whatever I can to help you find the real murderer."

"Lady, why the hell would you do anything to help me? How can you believe that I'm innocent when you don't even know me?"

"I feel as if I know you, as if I've known you for months."

Reece turned sharply, staring at Elizabeth again. Her eyes were filled with tears. Was she crying for him? No one had ever cried for him. No one except his mother. Hesitantly, almost fearfully, Reece touched his fingertip to the corner of her eye, brushing away the tears.

"Elizabeth?" A tight knot formed in his throat.

"I'm all right."

"You're crying for me, aren't you?" He gripped her chin in his big hand, tilting her face upward. "Why?"

She gazed at him with such undisguised concern, such genuine human compassion. "Because you can't cry for yourself."

He kissed her then. He hadn't thought about it, certainly hadn't planned it. But nothing on earth could have kept him from tasting those sweet, rosy lips. Nothing short of being struck down dead would have prevented him from pulling her into his arms and devouring her with the heat of his passion. He had never wanted anything as much as he wanted to lift this woman into his arms and carry her back inside the house and to her bed. His body ached with the need for release, for the ease he knew he could find in Elizabeth's loving warmth. There was a passion inside her equal to his own. He felt it when she returned his kiss with enthusiasm, opening her mouth for his invasion, as surely as she had unlocked her door for him the other night.

He ended the kiss when the realization hit him that she had, indeed, left her door unlocked for him. How he could be so certain he didn't know, but certain he was. He grabbed Elizabeth by the shoulders, pushing her away from him and at the same time holding on to her.

"You left your door unlocked the night I came here."

"Yes."

"Do you usually leave your door unlocked?"

"No."

"Why did you leave it unlocked that night?"

Would he believe the truth or would he prefer a lie? she asked herself. "I left it unlocked because I was expecting you."

Reece glared at her, confused by her admission, wondering how the hell she could have known he was headed in her direction and why she would have left her door unlocked for an escaped convict.

"I don't understand you, lady. How could you have been expecting me?"

"Reece…" When she reached out to touch his face, he dropped his hands from her shoulders and backed away from her.

"What the hell are you, some sort of hillbilly witch?"

"Some people would call me a psychic. I was born with special abilities."

Reece looked her over from head to toe, his perusal stopping when he reached her face. "What sort of abilities?"

"I can sense things, see things. Sometimes I know things before they happen. I'm clairvoyant and precognitive. However, my telepathic abilities are limited."

"Are you kidding me?"

"I'm trying to explain why I knew you would be coming to me, and why you need me to help you."

"This is a bunch of bull, lady. If you think for one minute that I'll buy into this crap, then you've got another thought coming."

"Five months ago I began having dreams about you, then brief visions. I could see your face, sense your pain and anger and bitterness. I knew you were caged, that you were being punished for something you hadn't done. These dreams, these visions continued up until you arrived on my doorstep the night before last."

Reece stood rigid and silent, staring at Elizabeth, astonishment in his amber eyes. "Are you trying to tell me that you've been messing around inside my head?"

"I'm telling you that I can help you, that I want to help you." When he didn't respond, she went on. "Don't you see that you were sent to me because—"

"Cut the crap, lady. I told you I don't believe you." Reece held up a hand in restraint as if warning her off.

"Stay out here as long as you need to," Elizabeth told him. "I have things to do inside, then I'll have to make a trip out to the greenhouses. Make yourself at home."

Reece watched her disappear back inside the house. The frigid air began to chill him through his thermal top and flannel shirt.

He heard the back door open, then close again and realized Mac-Datho had followed his mistress inside. There was something damned strange about Elizabeth and her MacDatho. They didn't seem to belong in this century. Were they real or were they ghosts from some bygone era? Reece wondered if he was hallucinating. Could it be that he was actually lying out in the snow on the mountainside, dying slowly, freezing to death, and he had imagined the beautiful woman and her wolf-dog? Was Elizabeth a figment of his imagination? Had he dreamed her, as she claimed she had dreamed him?

If she and the wolf-dog and this cabin were real, then maybe she was a little bit crazy, living up here in the woods all alone. That would explain why she didn't lock her doors and why she didn't seem afraid of an escaped convict. Whatever the truth might be, Reece knew one thing for sure and certain—he had to find a way to get off this damned mountain and back to Newell. He wasn't going to get caught. He wasn't going to prison. Whatever he had to do to stay free, he'd do it. And if that meant using Elizabeth Mallory, if she even existed, then so be it.

* * *

Elizabeth had successfully avoided Reece Landry for most of the day, keeping busy with light housekeeping chores and necessary work in the greenhouses. His attitude toward her psychic abilities was nothing new. People who didn't know her tended to be skeptical; then once they accepted her unusual powers, people often treated her like a freak. She could never adjust in the world outside Sequana Falls. She'd learned that when she'd gone away to college.

She knew Reece had searched the house for the 9 mm belonging to the deceased deputy. He'd never find it. After sealing the gun in a plastic bag, she'd taken it with her when she'd gone to the greenhouses, finding a perfect spot for it between her two compost bins.

When Reece left, she would return the gun to him. She didn't like the idea of his using it, but knew it would offer him a small sense of security. If only he would accept her help, would open up to her and allow her to discover any possible knowledge of which he might not be aware.

Elizabeth removed the homemade beef pot pie from the oven, placing it atop the hotpad on the counter. Spooning generous helpings of the pie onto two Blue Willow plates, she laid the plates on a large tray already set with silverware and cloth napkins, piping hot coffee, small green salads and slices of made-from-scratch pound cake. Aunt Margaret had baked the pound cake before Christmas, and Elizabeth had frozen it for future use.

Picking up MacDatho's bowl from the floor, Elizabeth filled it with the remainder of the pot pie, then set it back down on the floor.

"I spoil you shamefully, you know that, don't you?"

MacDatho gazed up at her, his look telling her that he was worthy of being spoiled, then he wolfed down the warm meal.

Using her hip to shove open doors, Elizabeth carried the tray from the kitchen to the living room. Reece sat on the overstuffed plaid chair to the right of the fireplace. The sight of him sitting there, looking so at home, sent a fission of awareness through Elizabeth. A premonition? Or wishful thinking? Did she want her home to become Reece's home?

The radio-tape player, which Reece had apparently brought into the living room, rested on the floor beside his chair. The music playing was an old tape Elizabeth dearly loved, a mixed bag of cool jazz tunes. The soft, bluesy tones of saxophone and horn blended with piano, giving the listener a sensually romantic rendition of "Who Would Care?"

Reece looked up from the magazine he held in his hand, a recent copy of *Archaeology*. "I hope you don't mind, I borrowed your cassette player. Music helps me think. When I was a kid I used to sit out on my porch and listen to Willie Paul playing the piano over at Flossie's. He knew all the great jazz tunes."

Elizabeth set the tray atop the six-foot-long coffee table in front of the sofa. "Who was Willie Paul? And who was Flossie?"

Reece tossed *Archaeology* atop the pile of magazines in the big wicker basket beneath a nearby table. "Willie Paul was a black man who doubled as piano player and bouncer at Flossie's, a local night spot that also served the men of Newell as a brothel."

"Oh, I see." Elizabeth sat on the sofa, patting the cushion beside her. "I thought supper would be nice in here."

"You've been avoiding me all day, haven't you?" Reece got up, walked over to the sofa, but didn't sit down. "I guess I acted pretty ungrateful to you this morning. I've had time to think about things, and I realize that without your help, I might have died."

"Sit down and eat your supper." Elizabeth didn't look up at him, sensing the sexual arousal in Reece, knowing she wasn't ready to deal with the unnerving emotions he had created in her this morning, with nothing more than a kiss.

Reece laughed. "You sound like someone's mother. Are you always so maternal?" Sitting beside her, he lifted the coffee cup to his lips.

"You really grew up across the street from a...a house of—"

"A cathouse?" Reece tasted the coffee, then set it down on the tray, picking up a plate and fork. He wondered what she'd think if he told her that his first sexual experience had been with one of Flossie's girls. Misty, a very experienced redhead only five years older than he'd been at fifteen. "Yeah. Lilac Road was the most notorious street in Newell."

Picking up the folded white linen napkin from the tray, Elizabeth spread it across her lap. "I grew up here in Sequana Falls. My mother and stepfather brought me here when I was six, and we lived here together in my grandparents' home until my parents were killed in an automobile accident when I was twelve."

"You didn't live here on your own after they died, did you?"

"No, I lived with Aunt Margaret, my grandmother's sister. We divided our time between Sequana Falls and Dover's Mill." And Aunt Margaret taught me to accept my special abilities, not to fight them, and never to abuse the power.

Reece ate heartily, savoring every bite, and Elizabeth ate just as ravenously. Neither of them had eaten lunch. The hardwood logs burned in the fireplace. The cool jazz music filled the room, creating a mellow mood. Empty dishes lay stacked on the large tray. MacDatho snored softly on the braided rug before the hearth. Turning toward Reece, Elizabeth crossed one leg beneath the other, her entwined fingers cupping her knee. Reece rested his arm on the back of the sofa, then turned slightly, crossing his legs, his hand on his thigh.

"I'll have to leave in the morning." His words sounded loud in the peaceful stillness of the room.

Elizabeth shook her head. "You won't be able to leave."

"I'm all right. No permanent effects from the wreck or from my long trek in the snow. Just a few fading bruises and a little soreness." Reece leaned toward her, wondering why she wouldn't look at him. She had deliberately avoided any eye contact with him since their altercation on the back porch this morning. Had he hurt her feelings by not believing her claim to be psychic?

"It won't be safe for you to leave the mountain tomorrow."

"It won't be safe for me if I stay," he said. "I've been listening to radio newscasts all day. They're mounting a pretty big search for me. Since the weather seems to have cleared up, they'll be comb-ing Dover's Mill and Sequana Falls."

"They won't be able to do anything for another day or so. There's another big snow coming. It's already started. It's snowing again right now."

"How do you know?" When she didn't reply, he realized she didn't want to tell him that her powers extended to predicting the weather because she was afraid of his ridicule. "Okay, so it's snow-ing now. Being snowed-in here won't keep me safe, and it isn't get-ting me any closer to proving my innocence."

"Be patient, Reece." Elizabeth looked at him then, her eyes pleading. "Your body and mind need rest, and you need time to think, to plan a strategy for when you return to Newell."

"All I need is a means of transportation. I guess I'll have to try my hand at hitchhiking or stealing a car. Somehow I'll have to elude the manhunt and steer clear of any roadblocks."

Elizabeth reached out, her hand hovering over his where it rested on the back of the sofa. Lowering her hand, she covered his, squeezing tenderly. "I have a Jeep you can borrow. I don't keep much cash on hand, but I have a couple of hundred I can give you."

"You'll loan me your Jeep and some money?" Reece stared at her, wondering if he'd ever be able to figure her out. "Why would you do that?"

"Because I believe you're innocent. Because someone has to help you." Holding his hand firmly, she smiled at him. "Because five months ago you came to me in my dreams because you needed someone. You needed me."

Gazing directly into her pure blue eyes, Reece realized she truly believed what she was saying—there was no doubt in her mind that he had been appearing in her dreams, that she had seen visions of his captivity.

"You don't believe me, do you?"

"Elizabeth, I... Hell, I'm a realist. I don't believe in anything I can't experience with my five senses."

"It's all right. I understand. It's not necessary that you believe me in order for me to help you."

Reece lifted her hand, turning it palm up. "You're a very unusual woman, Elizabeth Mallory. And if you're willing to help me, I'm not fool enough to refuse. Maybe God has finally decided to give me a break. Maybe he did send me to you. Maybe he gave you to me as a guardian angel."

Lowering his head, Reece brought Elizabeth's hand to his mouth, kissing the center of her palm. "If your predictions about the weather come true and we are trapped up here in this cabin together for a couple more days, then you may be in real danger from me."

She gave him a startled look, her eyes widening in surprise. "What sort of danger?"

"Man-woman sort of danger."

"You want me? Want to make love to me?" The very thought warmed Elizabeth's insides, tightening her nipples and moistening her femininity. What would it be like to make love with Reece Landry, to lie in his arms and know his complete possession? Elizabeth shivered.

He'd never known a woman so brutally frank. Most females he knew were experts at playing games, saying one thing and meaning another, lying when it served their purpose.

Grinning, Reece pulled her hand to his chest, laying it across his heart. "Yeah, I want to make love to you. You're a beautiful, desirable woman, and I haven't been with anybody in nearly a year."

"We're not ready to make love. Not yet." Removing her hand from his chest, she stood and walked across the room, halting in front of the wide expanse of floor-to-ceiling windows spanning the south wall of the living room.

Reece followed her, slipping his arms around her waist, drawing her back against his chest, positioning her buttocks into his arousal.

"Oh, I'm ready. I'm more than ready." He nuzzled the side of her neck with his nose.

Elizabeth loved the feel of him. His big, strong arms draped around her body, his face buried in her neck, his lips spreading kisses up the side of her jaw, his throbbing arousal pulsating against her, beckoning her to succumb to temptation. She wanted Reece. She'd never wanted a man before. Desire was a new emotion to her, one that she realized had been growing steadily within her since her first dream of a tormented, caged man in desperate need of her help.

"You're ready to have sex, Reece." Elizabeth knew she should withdraw from his embrace, should free herself from the chains of their mutual passion, but she couldn't bear the thought of ending such sweet pleasure. "You aren't ready to make love."

He chuckled, lowering his hands to cover her stomach, then the tops of her thighs, running his palms up and down, in and out, closer and closer to the apex between her legs. "Is there a difference?"

She covered his hands where they cupped her femininity. "Yes, there's a difference between love and sex. A big difference for me. I won't have sex without the loving. When we're both ready, I'll know."

Huffing loudly, Reece released Elizabeth and walked away from her. "Another one of your psychic talents, knowing when a man is ready to make love instead of just screw?"

Elizabeth swallowed the knot in her throat, emotion creating a physical ache inside her. He was angry. Not with her, not really. Reece Landry was angry with life. If only he would let her, she would teach him to release his anger, to free himself of its destructive hold. She had another day, perhaps two, to persuade him that she could do more to help him than lend him a Jeep and some money. Maybe a day or two would be enough time.

"It's snowing," she said as she looked out the window. "It will snow all night."

"Thanks for the weather report." Reece wanted to hit something, anything that would smash into a thousand pieces and release some of the tension inside him. Sex would have worked just fine, but his hostess wasn't a woman who had sex. She *made love*. Sex and making love meant the same thing to him, and he believed any fool stupid enough to think there was a difference was deluding himself—or herself. He'd had sex with his share of women over the years, and there had never been much difference in the experiences, regardless of who his partner had been.

"There is a difference, Reece. Someday you'll understand."

He didn't respond, not even with a nod or a grunt. Elizabeth watched him walk away, entering the hallway; then he stopped, but didn't turn around. "Where do I sleep tonight? I assume I've been sleeping in your bed the last couple of nights."

"Take the stairs. I built a fire in the fireplace in the first bedroom."

"Fine." He headed for the stairs, took several steps upward, then said, "Thanks."

"You're welcome."

Elizabeth hugged her arms around her body, the chill of Reece's anger and frustration issuing her a warning. She didn't know this man, despite his invasion of her mind, her home and her heart. She had hoped that once they came together she would be able to get past the shield protecting his thoughts and emotions. But she caught only fragmented glimpses inside his mind. Not enough to trust her body to him. Her heart was another matter. She feared it was already lost.

CHAPTER 4

Reece guided the razor down his cheek. Sam Dundee's razor. For two days he'd been wearing another man's clothes, a man whose shoes he didn't quite fill, and now he was shaving with that man's razor. He'd even slept in the man's bed last night.

Elizabeth had told him that Sam was her stepfather's brother and had acted as her legal guardian when her parents had been killed in an automobile accident when she was twelve. Reece didn't like this Dundee guy, and he wasn't quite sure why. He didn't even know him, but Elizabeth knew him. Elizabeth loved him!

Hell! He had to get off this mountain. Away from Elizabeth Mallory, away from her unnatural concern about his welfare, away from her all-too-knowing blue eyes and away from the way she made him feel every time he looked at her. It had been hell keeping his hands off her. He couldn't remember a time in his life when he'd wanted a woman so badly. He'd told himself this gut-wrenching hunger eating away at him was due to the fact he hadn't been with a woman in over a year, but he wasn't so sure.

He'd been alone with Elizabeth for three nights, two of them in a semiconscious stupor, but even on those two nights he could remember her gentle touch, her soft voice, her kindness and concern. He liked Elizabeth far too much, and he didn't want to like her. Caring about her would be dangerous for both of them. He'd only wind up hurting her if he allowed her to become involved in his problems. Besides, he didn't quite trust her. He'd never completely trusted another person—not even his own mother. Blanche had betrayed him from the moment she'd conceived him, bringing him into the world a bastard, a social outcast, giving him a stepfather like Harry Gunn, then dying on him before he was old enough to defend himself. No, he'd learned early that it didn't pay to trust anyone, not even the people who professed to love you.

The snowstorm had died sometime during the early morning hours. He'd awakened to the sound of silence, to the eerie quiet left once the wind had ceased its savage moaning. The search for escaped convict Reece Landry would be on again. It was only a matter of time before someone came snooping around Elizabeth's cabin. The electricity had been restored around nine o'clock. Things were beginning to return to normal. He couldn't risk staying much longer. He'd have to leave soon. He had no other choice if he wanted to stay free.

The jarring ring of a telephone echoed through the house like a sonic boom. The razor in Reece's hand stilled on his throat. If the phone was working again, then Elizabeth could call out. She could call for help. She could turn him in to the sheriff.

Dropping the razor into the sink, Reece picked up a hand towel, wiped the streaks of shaving-cream residue off his face and ran out into the hallway. When he reached the top of the stairs he heard Elizabeth's voice, but couldn't make out what she was saying.

He took the steps two at a time, halting just before reaching the living room entrance, bracing himself against the wall. His heartbeat accelerated; the pulse in his head throbbed.

"You didn't have to worry about me, Aunt Margaret. I'm fine. Really," Elizabeth said. "Mac and I weathered the storm without any problems."

Reece glanced around the corner, watching Elizabeth while she talked. Something was bothering her. Reece noted the way her hand clutched the phone, the way she stood, her feet shifting nervously as if she couldn't stand still.

"No, don't do that!" Elizabeth's voice sounded shrill. "I mean, don't send poor old O'Grady out in this weather. I don't need anything."

Reece eased around the corner, walking silently toward Elizabeth. When he was within two feet of her, she jerked around, her eyes widening, her mouth forming an oval of surprise. She draped the palm of her hand over the bottom half of the telephone.

"Who are you talking to?" Reece asked.

"My aunt Margaret."

"Who's this O'Grady you're talking about?"

"He's—" Elizabeth removed her hand from the telephone. "Oh, Aunt Margaret, you shouldn't have done that. You're wrong. There is no one here with me. I'm not in any danger."

Reece grabbed the telephone out of Elizabeth's hand, slamming it down onto its cradle. She glared at him.

"Just what do you think you're doing?"

"What made her think you weren't alone?" Reece grabbed Elizabeth by the shoulders. "What did you tell her?"

"I didn't tell her anything." Elizabeth struggled to free herself from Reece's biting fingers.

He tightened his hold. She cried out in pain. Releasing her shoulders, Reece grasped her around the waist, jerking her into his arms. "If you didn't tell her about me, then how does she know you're not alone? Why does she think you're in danger?"

"Dammit, Reece, you're the most distrusting man I've ever known." When he pulled her closer, his face only a breath away from hers, she squirmed in his arms. "Let me go."

"I have reason not to trust people, believe me." He pulled her so tightly against him she could barely breathe.

She looked up into his eyes, those searing amber eyes so like MacDatho's. He was as much a lone wolf, as much a wild animal as Mac. But with her, Mac was a gentle beast, confident and secure in her love. Reece didn't trust her enough to be tamed. A man as hard and tortured as Reece would have to trust a woman completely, would have to love her with his very soul before he would give her the power to tame him.

"Aunt Margaret has psychic abilities. That's the reason I'm here in Sequana Falls. My mother and stepfather brought me here so that she could be my guide, my teacher."

"Are you telling me that your whole family is a bunch of gypsy fortune-tellers?"

"Believe what you will. I'm telling you that Aunt Margaret sensed I wasn't alone, that there was danger lurking about." Elizabeth wasn't sure she could make Reece understand; in the three days he'd been with her, she hadn't been able to convince him of her psychic abilities. There was no point in explaining that she had felt Aunt Margaret's worry and concern, and had plugged in the telephone so her aunt could get in touch with her without the elderly woman delving into Elizabeth's mind and discovering Reece's presence.

"What's your aunt done to upset you?" Reece asked.

"She's sending O'Grady up here just as soon as the roads clear a bit."

"O'Grady?"

"He's Aunt Margaret's gentleman friend. He works for me. Helps me around the greenhouses. He drives my nursery van and makes deliveries into Dover's Mill and surrounding towns."

"When will the roads be clear enough for him to get up the mountain?"

Elizabeth hesitated momentarily, then told Reece the truth. "By morning if he drove the van. The weather's changing pretty quickly. A warm front is headed our way. O'Grady won't try to come in the van. He'll either borrow his grandson's Explorer or he'll get the boy to drive him up here today."

"If O'Grady can make it up the mountain today, then the sheriff's deputies can make it up here." Reece shoved Elizabeth away from him. She staggered slightly, then regained her balance.

"Now that the storm is over, they'll start checking Dover's Mill and the area around Hunter's Lake again. They're setting up roadblocks at all the major intersections and will be going to all the towns close to Dover's Mill, doing door-to-door checks. O'Grady will come up the mountain today because Aunt Margaret sent him.

The local authorities won't start combing this side of the mountain until late tomorrow. They'll be looking for your frozen body."

"They think I'm dead?"

"They know that if you stayed in the mountains your chances for survival were slim. Once they've checked the few places you could have found shelter, they'll be convinced you froze to death."

"Are all these great revelations coming from shrewd female intuition or from your hocus-pocus abilities?"

"Would you believe me if I told you the truth?"

"Which is?" he asked.

"That I'm clairvoyant, precognitive and have limited telepathic powers."

Reece's gut tightened into a knot. Damn, but she talked a good game. She had him half-convinced she was a witch. After all, she had left her door unlocked for him, and she seemed to believe in him, in his innocence, with no proof whatsoever. She had nursed him back to health with astonishing speed and without the aid of modern medicine.

"Well, if you know all and see all, then you're aware that I'm planning on getting the hell off this mountain today. Before your aunt Margaret's boyfriend comes calling or before the deputies get within ten miles of this place."

"There's no need for you to leave yet." She knew he would be safe with her for another day. If only she could persuade him to stay until she'd had a chance to call Sam. In his business, Sam had contacts all over the world. It shouldn't be any big deal for him to run a check on Reece and get all the details about the murder, the trial and the possibility of other suspects.

"If you think you can persuade me to stay, then your soothsaying abilities just went haywire. No way am I hanging around here long enough to get caught. I'm not going to prison."

While they'd been talking, Reece had unconsciously backed himself against the wall. He balled his hands into fists, his whole body tightening into a rigid statue of fear and anger.

Elizabeth took slow, even steps, moving toward Reece with the unwavering certainty that she had to get through to him, she had to reach his mind, convince him that she wanted to help him, that he could trust her.

Reece glared at her. She came closer and closer. He wanted to warn her to stay away from him, but he didn't say a word. He simply watched as she stood in front of him, reached out and placed her warm hands on each side of his face. She shut her eyes.

Reece swallowed. A sensation of tender concern seeped into his mind. What the hell? She held his face, tracing his bones with her fingertips. He didn't know what she was trying to do, but he wanted her to stop.

When he wrenched his face out of her grasp, turning his head to the side, Elizabeth opened her eyes and smiled.

"I can't read your mind, Reece. You won't let me."

"Good for me!"

"But I can sense things. Just little things."

"Like what?"

"I can sense your loneliness. You're completely alone. Or at least, you think you are." Reece's inner turmoil stirred within Elizabeth, the great sense of bitterness almost overwhelming her. "You resent others. Your mother. Your father. Everyone who has touched your life in any meaningful way. You won't let anyone close to you for fear of being hurt."

"Shut up, dammit!" Reece turned his back on her and walked away, out into the hallway.

Elizabeth followed him, placing her hand on his back when he braced his open palms on the wall and leaned his forehead against the wooden surface.

He tensed at her touch, but she did not withdraw her hand. "You've been locked away for five months. All I could sense was a cage. But now I know it was a jail cell. The first time I saw you, I saw the shock and pain on your face. I saw the blood on your hands."

Reece whirled around, grabbing her by the shoulders, his eyes wild with the realization that Elizabeth knew things she couldn't possibly know.

"How the hell did you know I had blood on my hands? That was never in the newspapers, never on television or radio. How did you know?" He shook her soundly.

"Reece, stop it!"

He stared into her pure blue eyes, and the truth came to him as surely as if he'd been struck by a bolt of lightning and survived the ordeal. "I didn't kill him. I heard the gunshots. I ran into the library and found him. I tried to stop the bleeding, but it was too late. He died. Damn him, he died and his blood was all over my hands."

"It's all right, Reece. I believe you. I understand."

"How the hell could you understand? I'd hated him all my life, prayed for his death, but when the moment came, I didn't want him to die. I tried…I tried…."

Elizabeth felt the tears inside Reece, choking him, constricting his breathing, squeezing his heart. But his eyes remained dry, his face set in tense agony. She reached into his mind, but he shut her out. He wouldn't allow her entrance, refusing to accept her mental comfort.

Elizabeth slipped her arms around his waist. He was rock solid, his body rigid with control. "You're right, I don't understand. But I could, if you would tell me about him. About B. K. Stanton."

Reece felt her strong, supportive arms around him. Elizabeth Mallory was as sturdy and solid as the rock-and-log cabin in which she lived, as hardy and vigorous as the mountain she called home. He'd grown up mothered by a weak woman. Reliability and responsibility hadn't been Blanche's strong points. She'd been a fragile, needy woman who hadn't been able to take care of herself, let alone a child.

In his mind's eye he could see Blanche. Small, frail, her gray eyes looking to him for help, the only color in her pale face were the bruises left by Harry Gunn's big fists. Even though he'd been a scrawny kid, she'd expected him to help her. And God knew he'd tried. But in the end he hadn't been able to help her. All he'd gotten for his efforts were bruises and broken bones of his own.

He'd had no one to depend on, no one to defend him, and he'd learned not to care, to never expect anything from anyone. He'd lived his whole life alone, shielding himself from emotions, priding himself on the fact that he needed no one.

Elizabeth's embrace seemed to surround more than just his body. He felt cocooned in safety. Without thinking about what he was doing, without second-guessing his motives, without giving his doubts and uncertainties time to take control, Reece pulled Elizabeth into his arms, holding her against him, absorbing the power of her generous heart.

He'd been alone all his life, long before his mother had died. He had taught himself not to need anyone, not to depend on anyone. And here was this woman, this beautiful, unique woman offering him her comfort and her trust. Would he be a fool to accept what she offered, or would he be a fool to refuse?

Elizabeth tightened her hold around Reece, easing her hands up his back, stroking him, caressing his tight muscles. He lowered his hands from her waist to her hips, cupping her buttocks, dragging her into his arousal, telling her without words what she was doing to him.

She looked up at him with those trusting blue eyes, eyes that smiled at him, eyes that offered so much.

"You shouldn't look at a man like that. You're liable to give him ideas."

She opened her mouth on a sigh, her lips parting. Her face bloomed with color. Her fingers bit into his neck as she lifted her arms around his shoulders. "I want you to know that I care, that I can help you."

She could not, would not admit that she wanted him as a woman wants a man. The feeling was new to her, far too new for her to accept the desire and allow herself to act upon it. If making love with Reece was meant to be, and in her heart of hearts she believed that it was, then she and Reece would become lovers. But not now. Not yet. He wasn't offering anything except sex; she wanted nothing less than love. When he was prepared to make love to her, she would know. Her heart and her instincts would tell her.

Reece could not resist the temptation Elizabeth Mallory repre-
sented. She was comfort and safety and pleasure. He wanted all
three. Lowering his head, he brushed his cheek against hers. She
smelled like flowers—sweet, so very, very sweet.

"You smell good, sweet Lizzie. Like roses." He nuzzled her neck
with his nose, breathing in that flower-garden scent.

"My perfume." She breathed deeply, succumbing to the heady
intoxication of his touch. Turning her face upward, she offered him
her lips. "I make my own perfume from roses."

Never having been a romantic man, Reece was stunned at his
own thoughts. Her mouth looked like a rose, opening its pink pet-
als just for him. And her eyes, half-closed now, were as deep and
dark a blue as sparkling sapphires.

His lips touched hers, tentatively at first, and then as she responded, he took her mouth with total possession, savoring the feel
of her body molded securely to his. She fit him; he fit her. Their
bodies had been formed to entwine perfectly. Her full breasts
pressed against his chest, her feminine softness centered on his male
strength, her arms claiming him as surely as his did her, and their
lips mating with the fierceness of lovers preparing to join in a
more intimate fashion.

Reece ran his hand down her hip, lifting up her leg, pressing her
to him. Elizabeth moaned into his mouth, clinging to him, squirming against him.

"If you want to help me, Lizzie, then be my woman. Now. For
today." He kissed her again, taking both their breaths away.

She held on to him, but broke the kiss, laying her head on his
chest. She heard and felt his wild heartbeat. "I can't have sex with
you, Reece."

The instant tension in his body notified Elizabeth that he had understood only too well what she was telling him. He released her
abruptly, turned and walked into the living room.

Elizabeth waited a few minutes, willing her raging senses to
calm. It would have been so easy to give in to his needs and the
needs of her own body. For the first time in her life she wanted to

be with a man, to offer herself to him. But there was too much standing in the way, keeping them from the union of hearts and souls as well as of bodies.

She found him sitting on the sofa, bent over, his clasped hands resting between his knees. He didn't look up when she walked over and stood in front of him.

"Talk to me, Reece. Tell me about B. K. Stanton."

"You're damned and determined to hear the whole sordid story, aren't you?"

MacDatho, who'd been asleep in front of the fireplace, reared his head, focusing his amber gaze on Reece and Elizabeth. He stretched, then lowered his head, keeping his eyes open.

Elizabeth knelt in front of Reece, taking his hands into hers. "My knowledge of your life is limited. I really can't read your mind, and I can't help you if I don't know what we're dealing with."

"I don't see how you can help me, anyway, but if you want to hear my version of Reece Landry's life story, then I'll tell you. Once you've heard the truth, you may not be so eager to help me, after all."

Lifting Reece's right hand, Elizabeth sat on the sofa beside him, entwining their fingers, giving his hand a tight squeeze. "I want to know whatever you want to tell me."

Leaning back on the sofa, Reece closed his eyes. He didn't want to rehash all this old misery, but his gut instincts prompted him to share his past with Elizabeth.

"My mother, Blanche, was a beautiful woman. Blond and china-doll pretty. She worked at Stanton Industries years ago. A minimum-wage job. Anyway, to make a long story short, she had an affair with B. K. Stanton himself, who was a married man with children. When my mother discovered she was pregnant, good old B.K. offered to pay for her abortion."

Elizabeth sensed his anger. She tightened her hold on his hand. "But she didn't get an abortion."

"No, she decided to have me. I don't know why. All of us would have been better off if she'd just gotten rid of me."

"Don't say that, Reece. It isn't true."

Opening his eyes, he glanced at her and saw the tears caught in her thick, dark lashes. Sucking in a deep breath, he pulled his hand out of her grasp. "My mother didn't have anyone to take care of me, so she had to quit work. Stanton gave her a little money so he could keep on sleeping with her. But when his wife found out about Blanche and me, she made a lot of threats. I was six years old. That was the last time my father came around. Then about a year later my mother married Harry Gunn."

Silence hung in the room like a threatening black cloud promising a killer storm. Elizabeth shut her eyes, absorbing Reece's pain, a child's pain. In her mind she saw clearly a man's big, broad hand striking a little boy's face. The child fell to the floor, his amber eyes filled with hate.

As suddenly as the vision had appeared, it faded away. Elizabeth knew Reece had closed his mind to the memory. She tried to prize her thoughts back into his mind. She couldn't. He had, once again, safely shielded himself from his emotions.

"Your stepfather was abusive." She made the statement as unemotionally as she could, but she could not conceal the tears escaping from her eyes.

"Yeah, he was a real son of a bitch. Knocked me and Blanche around whenever the mood struck him." Reece placed his knotted fists atop his thighs.

"What a horrible life for the two of you."

"Blanche died when I was twelve, and things got worse. I was fifteen before I grew big enough to defend myself properly. The beatings stopped. I found trouble everywhere I looked, and I was always looking for trouble. I've had problems with the law since I was a kid."

No wonder Reece was such a hard man, such a loner. Elizabeth wanted to know more, wanted him to share all of his past with her. Her instincts told her that he had never told anyone else the things he was telling her.

"All those years, you knew B. K. Stanton was your father?" Elizabeth asked.

"Yeah, I knew the richest and most powerful man in town was my father. And I knew he didn't give a damn whether I lived or died." Reece closed his eyes, shook his head and groaned. "Damn, I wish I'd left that town—his town—before he decided to take an interest in me."

"When was that?"

"When I was sixteen he stopped me on the street one day. Just like that—" Reece snapped his fingers "—B.K. grabbed my arm and asked me if I was Blanche Landry's boy." Reece's stomach churned. A sour taste coated his tongue. Hot, bitter anger rose in his throat. "He offered me a part-time job. I had quit school, and he said if I'd go back to school he'd give me a job after school and full-time in the summer. We made a deal, my old man and me. Then when I graduated high school, I joined the marines, did my time and came out determined to make something of myself. My only mistake was going back to Newell."

"Why did you go back?"

"Damned if I know, unless..." Reece slammed his fist into the sofa arm.

MacDatho rose from the floor, watching Reece intently.

"I'm not going to hurt her, Mac," Reece told the wolf-dog. "You should know that by now."

"He knows." Elizabeth placed her hand on Reece's arm. "You went back to Newell because you had something to prove, didn't you?"

"I guess. I suppose I wanted B. K. Stanton to know I was going to college, that no matter what I'd come from, I was going to be somebody."

"You had a lot of mixed emotions about your father, didn't you?"

"I hated him. Plain and simple." Reece stood, stretching, exercising his muscles.

"Did you hate him enough to kill him?"

Reece turned sharply, glaring at Elizabeth. "I thought you believed me, believed that I didn't murder him?"

"I do believe you."

"Then why ask me if I hated him enough to kill him?" Reece

walked to the windows, staring out at the sunshine spreading over the snow, glistening on the velvety white surface as if it were scattering crushed diamond particles everywhere it touched.

"What happened when you returned to Newell after the marines?" She should have known he'd been in the marines. Sam had been a marine. Reece Landry and Sam Dundee shared some common traits.

"I went to college, worked at Stanton Industries in my old job as a machine operator to help supplement Uncle Sam's financial aid. When I got my B.S. degree the old man offered me an office job. That's when I got to know the rest of the family."

"Your father's other children?"

"Yeah, my big brother, Kenny, the heir apparent, and my sister, Christina. Kenny and I hated each other on sight. I liked Christina, and she liked me. She's the one who hired a lawyer for me when I was arrested for the old man's murder."

Elizabeth longed to put her arms around Reece, to offer him the care and support he'd never known. But she knew he wouldn't accept her comfort right now.

"Your sister believed you were innocent?" Elizabeth asked.

"She wanted to believe I didn't kill our father, but she had her doubts. I could tell every time she looked at me, she was wondering if I'd done it."

"Why did the sheriff arrest you? What evidence did they have against you?"

He glanced at Elizabeth and suddenly realized how much he wanted her to believe him. "The gun was mine. I'd reported the .38 stolen a couple of days before somebody used it to kill the old man. They didn't find any fingerprints. Whoever used it had wiped the gun clean. And the usual paraffin test for powder residue was inconclusive because my hands had been covered with dried blood."

"Motive and weapon. You hated your father and the gun that killed him was yours."

"That's right, only there's more. B.K.'s wife, Alice, and the family lawyer found me leaning over my father's body with blood all over my hands and the gun at my side."

"Oh, Reece." She touched him then, unable to prevent herself. He tensed at her touch, but when she hugged up against him, he relaxed and slipped his arm around her waist.

"B.K. had called and asked me to come to his home. He said he had something important to tell me. When I arrived, the front door was standing wide open, so I walked in. I called out. B.K. told me to come on back to the study. Then I heard my father arguing with someone, but I couldn't make out the other voice. Couldn't even tell if it was male or female. B.K. was shouting, saying he could do whatever he damned well pleased, that nobody could tell him what he could and couldn't do.

"Before I reached the study I heard gunshots. I rushed inside and someone hit me from behind. They didn't knock me unconscious, but everything went black for a few minutes and I was pretty shaken up. I didn't see who had hit me. When my vision cleared, I staggered over to where B.K. lay on the floor. He was bleeding like a stuck hog. I knelt down, covering his stomach wound with my hands. He called my name. And then he died."

Elizabeth held Reece in her arms, trying to absorb some of his pain, longing for him to accept what she offered, knowing he had never shared as much of himself with another human being.

"Motive, weapon, opportunity." Elizabeth sighed. "They didn't believe you, of course, about the person who hit you over the head. And the authorities never looked for another suspect."

"Brother Kenny and his mother had their lawyer, Willard Moran, use all the influence the Stanton family had in Newell, and believe me, it was plenty. I spent five months in that damned little jail cell, feeling like a trapped animal, knowing I was doomed."

Elizabeth held him. He hugged her fiercely.

"During the trial my lawyer pointed out that if I'd shot B.K., I'd have hardly had time to wipe the gun clean before Alice and Willard found me. And there was no proof that I'd actually fired the gun. I was convicted on circumstantial evidence."

"The Stantons must be very powerful to possess that much control over the sheriff's department and the district attorney."

"The Stantons own Newell, and if the Stantons say I killed B.K., then the town has no choice but to agree."

"You were framed," Elizabeth said.

"You do believe me, don't you?"

"Yes, of course I do. Did you think I wouldn't?"

He buried his face in her shoulder, breathing her sweet rose scent, accepting her loving warmth as she held him.

Abruptly she pushed him away. The sense of loss overwhelmed him.

"O'Grady! My God, Reece, go upstairs and wait. O'Grady will be here in a few minutes."

"How the hell do you know…" Reece grinned. "I've got to get used to this sixth sense of yours."

"When O'Grady leaves, I want to talk to you about our calling Sam to help us," Elizabeth said.

"No way. This guy may be your stepuncle, your family and friend, but I don't know him from Adam."

"Sam will help us."

"I said no." Grabbing her by the shoulders, he gazed into her eyes. "Understand me, Lizzie. I don't want you calling Sam Dundee."

"You can trust him."

"I don't trust anybody, lady, you should know that by now."

"Even me, Reece?"

He hesitated momentarily. "I'm not sure, Elizabeth. I want to trust you, but——"

The sound of a horn alerted Elizabeth to the fact that O'Grady had arrived. "Go upstairs and stay there until I come and get you."

Reece followed her instructions, and Elizabeth opened the front door, stepping out into the frosty wind, waving at O'Grady as he exited the passenger side of his grandson's Ford Explorer. An eighteen-year-old Rod O'Grady waved at Elizabeth but made no move to leave the warmth of his vehicle. The deafening *boom boom boom* of the boy's stereo system threatened to bring the icicles down from the roof overhang.

Elizabeth gave O'Grady a big hug, then rushed him inside to the warmth of her cabin. "I told Aunt Margaret that there was no need for you to come all the way up here with the roads so bad."

Elizabeth motioned MacDatho out of the open doorway, then closed the front door.

"You know Margaret. She got one of her notions. Thought somebody was up here with you." O'Grady glanced around the hallway before venturing into the living room. "There's an escaped convict on the loose. I think hearing about the man sent Margaret's imagination into overdrive."

"Did you say there's an escaped convict around Dover's Mill?" Elizabeth asked.

"Reece Landry. Young fellow. Killed a guy down in Newell. Escaped after the sheriff's car took a bad spill off the road and into the side of a mountain near Deaton Crossing."

"Are you staying long enough for coffee?" Elizabeth nodded in the direction of the kitchen.

"No, child, I can't stay. Rod's itching to get back home. Got a date tonight, I guess. He's been cooped up during the storm."

"Are the authorities looking for this Landry man?"

"They used bloodhounds, but didn't have much luck. They figure the guy's probably frozen to death in the woods somewhere by now. The day he escaped they tracked him to the falls, but they didn't figure there was much point going on from there since the storm was getting worse. They saw where he'd fallen through the ice in the stream, but had no idea where he went once he got out of the water. Snow was falling so hard they couldn't see two feet in front of them, and the dogs seemed to be losing the scent."

"Do you suppose they'll be coming up this way soon?"

"Why are you asking me? I figure you already know the answer if you want to know."

Elizabeth smiled. "Humor me, O'Grady."

"Well, your aunt Margaret says they'll be at your door by tomorrow evening. And my guess is she's right. I heard they planned to search the woods for his body tomorrow, and they're already setting up roadblocks on all the major roads and doing a house-by-house search in Dover's Mill. If they don't find his body, they'll keep searching until they wind up in Sequana Falls." O'Grady removed his brown checkered wool cap with dangling earflaps. "Why are you so interested in what the sheriff's doing to find this Landry fellow?"

"Just curious." Elizabeth smiled.

O'Grady scratched his partially bald head, mussing the thin strands of white hair that stuck out around his ears. "I figure I can get back up here with the van in a few days and get deliveries back on schedule. Anything you need me to take down the mountain today? I can get Rod to help me load the back of his Explorer."

"No, there's nothing that urgent. Deliveries can wait a few more days."

"Any message you want to send Margaret?" O'Grady warmed his hands by the fireplace, then turned to face Elizabeth. "She sent you a message."

"Did she?"

"Yep. She said to tell you that you wasn't to leave Sequana Falls without letting her know."

Elizabeth stood deadly still, a chilling sense of foreboding rushing through her body. If Aunt Margaret had seen her leaving Sequana Falls, then there was every possibility that she would be going. She'd made no plans to leave the sanctuary of her home, and had no premonitions about her future travel plans.

"Tell Aunt Margaret that I'll call her if I decide to take a trip."

O'Grady gave Elizabeth a fatherly pat on the back. "Well, I'll report in to your aunt. You sure you're alone here?"

"I'm never alone with Mac around."

As he walked out of the living room, Elizabeth following him, O'Grady glanced at MacDatho, stretched out on the rug in front of the sofa. "Yeah, I guess he's a good guard dog. Don't figure nobody could get past Mac, could they? Not unless you gave him the okay."

Elizabeth opened the front door, waving goodbye to O'Grady as he crossed the porch, went down the steps and got into his grandson's Explorer. She watched until they disappeared down the road, then she turned and went back into the cabin.

Standing at the foot of the stairs, Elizabeth called Reece's name. When he answered, she told him that O'Grady was gone and it was safe for him to come down.

"I'm going to finish that shave I started earlier when I heard the phone ring," Reece told her. "I've still got a lot of beard left."

"I'll put on a fresh pot of coffee. Take your time."

Elizabeth hurried into the kitchen, ground some coffee beans and put them on to brew. Knowing what she had to do and that there was no time like the present, she went back into the living room, picked up the telephone and dialed Sam's Atlanta business number. As soon as she gave her name, she was put through directly to Sam.

Maybe Reece didn't trust Sam, but she did. Sam would never do anything to hurt her, and if she told him she believed Reece Landry was an innocent man, Sam would listen to her.

"Elizabeth, is everything all right?" Sam asked. "I've heard a bad winter storm hit the mountains. I tried to call, but your phone was out. I finally got in touch with Aunt Margaret."

"Did you also hear about an escaped convict named Reece Landry?"

"I'm afraid that bit of information hasn't been on the Atlanta news. What's this Landry guy got to do with your calling me?"

"Reece is here with me, at the cabin. He nearly died getting to me, but I took care of him and he's—"

"Dammit all, Elizabeth, are you telling me you're harboring a fugitive? Have you lost your mind? Has the man been holding you at gunpoint? Get off this phone now and call Howard Gilbert."

"I don't need to call the sheriff," Elizabeth huffed, shaking her head with disgust. Sam wasn't being as reasonable as she'd hoped he would be. "As a matter of fact, I'm trying to prevent the authorities from capturing Reece."

"Elizabeth, tell me what the hell's going on?"

"I've been trying to do that. If you'll just calm down and listen,

I'll tell you what I want you to do." Elizabeth told Sam every detail of Reece's life that he'd shared with her up to the point where the sheriff's car had wrecked in the winter storm. "Reece never stood a chance, Sam. The sheriff's department never tried to find any other suspects."

"What makes you think this man is innocent?"

"My instincts."

"You've looked into his mind, is that it?"

"I've had visions about Reece for the past five months, but I didn't tell anyone. Not you or Aunt Margaret, although I think she suspected something." Elizabeth paused, taking a deep breath. "Reece has been in my heart and mind since the day his father was murdered. I know he's innocent, Sam. He needs your help."

"What do you want me to do?"

"Get as much information as you can about B. K. Stanton's death. We've got to prove who killed Reece's father, or he'll be put in prison for the rest of his life."

"Elizabeth, what are you not telling me?"

"I don't know what you mean."

"I asked if you knew Landry was innocent because you'd read his mind. You didn't answer me," Sam said.

"I can sense certain things about Reece, and pick up on some of his emotions, but…well, I can't read him the way I do most other people. He's able to form some sort of shield around his mind, around his emotions."

"Good God, Elizabeth, you're taking this guy on faith? You're risking your life without knowing for sure whether or not he's really innocent."

"He's innocent, Sam. I know he is. Please help us."

"I'll run a background check on Landry and I'll—"

"I thought I told you not to call Sam Dundee!" Reece stood in the doorway, his face flushed with anger, his amber eyes wild with fear.

"Reece, please try to understand…." Elizabeth gazed at Reece with compassion and a plea for understanding in her eyes.

"Elizabeth!" Sam shouted into the telephone. "Is that Landry? If it is, put him on the phone."

"Wait just a minute, Sam." Elizabeth held out the phone to Reece. "Sam wants to talk to you."

Reece stared at the phone as if it were a slithering snake ready to strike, then glared at Elizabeth. "I thought I could trust you, but the minute my back was turned you called Dundee."

Elizabeth shook the phone at Reece. "I didn't betray you. I'm trying to get Sam to help you prove your innocence. Sam has contacts everywhere. He owns a private security agency in Atlanta. His sources are unlimited."

Reece walked into the room slowly, glancing back and forth from Elizabeth to the phone in her hand. She shoved the phone at him.

"Talk to Sam," she said.

Reece took the phone. "Yeah?"

"Landry?"

"Yeah."

"I don't know exactly what's going on there," Sam said, "but I want to warn you that if you harm Elizabeth, you're as good as dead. Do I make myself clear?"

"Crystal clear."

"If Elizabeth believes you, then I'm willing to give you the benefit of the doubt. I'm checking you out, Landry, and if I find out you've been lying, I'll personally cut your heart out."

"And if you find out I've been telling the truth?"

"Then I'll do whatever Elizabeth wants me to do to help you. Now put Elizabeth back on the phone."

Reece handed her the phone. "He wants to talk to you again."

"Sam?"

"I'll call you tomorrow and let you know how much I've been able to find out. Until then, for God's sake, be careful."

Elizabeth breathed a sigh of relief. Sam was going to help them. "Thank you, Sam. You can't know how much this means to me."

"What I want to know is how much Reece Landry means to you."

"I'm not sure, but…" Elizabeth glanced at a scowling Reece. "Just call us tomorrow with whatever information you can find. Reece is going to have to leave soon, and he needs something to go on."

Returning the telephone to its cradle, she faced Reece. "Sam is going to help you."

"I think I should leave as soon as possible." Reece glared at her, the distrust glowing in his eyes. "I don't dare trust Dundee. For all I know he's calling the sheriff to turn me in right now."

Elizabeth grabbed Reece by the arm as he turned from her. "You don't have to leave. Sam isn't going to call the sheriff. He would never break a trust. He's an honorable man."

"I'll stay until morning," Reece said, all the while damning himself for a fool for taking a chance by trusting his beautiful witch. "On one condition."

"What condition?" Elizabeth asked.

"I want my gun back."

Elizabeth nodded agreement. "If I go get your gun and give it to you, you promise you'll stay until Sam calls tomorrow?"

"I'm probably a fool for agreeing, but I agree."

"I'll need to put on my coat. I hid your gun outside, between the compost bins." Elizabeth walked out of the living room, through the kitchen and onto the back porch. When she reached for her coat on the rack by the door, Reece grabbed her by the shoulders, twirling her around. She stared at him, uncertain what he intended to do.

"I would never hurt you. You know that, don't you? The gun is for my protection against the police."

Elizabeth swallowed the knot in her throat, but she couldn't slow the rapid beat of her heart. "I understand."

Reece traced the lines of her jawbone with his fingertips. "I don't want you to be afraid of me."

"I'm not afraid of you, Reece. I'm only afraid of what might happen to you."

Elizabeth pulled away from him, put on her coat and went out into the cold February afternoon alone. It was at that moment she made her decision. When Reece Landry left her mountain, she was going with him.

CHAPTER 5

"We're not going to discuss this anymore!" Reece stuffed cans of soup and sandwich spreads into the duffel bag Elizabeth had given him. "When I leave this mountain, I leave alone."

"But you don't know the back roads. If I'm with you, you're less likely to get caught. We could even get through the roadblocks with me driving. I could fill the back of the Jeep with flowers from the greenhouse and tell the police that I'm on a delivery run. You could hide under a blanket or something." Elizabeth handed Reece a loaf of bread and a carton of saltine crackers.

"You've seen too many movies. This isn't a game. This is for real. If you go with me, you could get yourself killed." Reece eyed the 9 mm lying on the kitchen table.

"And without my help, you could get yourself killed," she said.

Reece looked at Elizabeth, the woman who had saved his life only a few days ago, the woman who wanted to join him in his fugitive's journey. She wasn't small and fragile. She wasn't a whining, helpless female. Mother Nature had put Elizabeth Mallory together like a work of art—round, full-bodied, solid. She possessed an inner strength as well, a strength that attracted Reece as much as her physical beauty. Braless and with her hair tumbling freely down her back to her waist, Elizabeth presented a picture of earthy sensuality.

Elizabeth was the type of woman who could plow a field, cook three meals a day from scratch, shoot and skin her own game, give birth to a baby and be ready to fight off an Indian attack the next morning. Pioneer stock.

"Why are you looking at me like that?" she asked.

"I was just picturing you fighting off an Indian attack," Reece said.

"What?"

"Just thinking about how much you're probably like your ancestors who settled these mountains." Reece stuffed the stack of clean clothes Elizabeth had given him into the duffel bag. More of Sam Dundee's clothes.

"For your information, my ancestors didn't fight off the Indians. My Scots-Irish ancestors married Indians, they didn't kill them." Elizabeth laid her hand atop Reece's where he gripped the handle of the duffel bag. "If you let me go with you, I can get you to Newell safely, and...and I can help you find your father's murderer."

Reece looked her directly in the eye. "What do you intend to do, go through the whole town reading everyone's mind?" Reece pulled away from her, dropping the duffel bag to the floor.

"I could meet the people who knew your father. Possible suspects. Members of his family."

Picking up the gun, Reece slid it into the pocket of the leather jacket Elizabeth had given him. "I need to check the Jeep." He walked toward the door leading to the back porch. "You said it has a full tank of gas. That means I shouldn't have to stop on the way."

"Reece, please don't leave until after Sam calls." Elizabeth followed him to the back porch.

"I won't, if he calls in the next hour." Reece opened the door. A puff of cold air hit him in the face. Turning, he smiled at Elizabeth. "How will you explain about your Jeep being gone?"

"I'll think of something."

Elizabeth stood on the screened-in back porch, watching Reece until he rounded the side of the house. He would never agree to her going with him. She had to think of an alternative plan. Without her, Reece didn't have a prayer of finding B. K. Stanton's killer.

Reece could never understand the type of sacrifice she was willing to make for him, and it was probably best that he didn't know. Leaving the sanctuary of her home in the mountains meant having to face the world, to be bombarded with people's thoughts and feelings, to see into the futures of strangers. She had spent her entire life trying to control her abilities, and to some degree she had achieved that goal—but only to a degree. Often she had no control whatsoever over the visions, over the intense emotions coming from others, over the premonitions that sometimes only a look or a touch from someone triggered within her mind.

Her special talents were as much a curse as a blessing. Thank God her family had brought her to Aunt Margaret instead of trusting her future to scientists who would have used her as a guinea pig, or to charlatans who would have used her in money-making schemes.

She had chosen her solitary life here in her ancestors' Georgia mountains. Surrounded by nature, shielded from the thoughts and emotions of a town filled with people, Elizabeth found peace and purpose. Nothing and no one had ever tempted her to venture far from Sequana Falls since her college years, except one necessary visit to Sam six years ago to bring him home from Atlanta—a trip she wasn't eager to repeat.

And now she was preparing to go back out into the world, to follow a man she barely knew, to expose herself to the trauma of mixing and mingling with people. How could Reece Landry have come to mean so much to her in such a short period of time? But five months wasn't a short period of time, was it? For some people it was a lifetime. She had known Reece in her heart far longer than the few days he'd spent at her cabin.

A higher power had sent Reece to her. She knew that fact as surely as she knew Reece Landry was her destiny, and she his. No one had ever needed her the way Reece did. Not only did he need her to help him prove his innocence, he needed the warmth and caring she could give him to vanquish the loneliness he had endured his whole life.

Just as Elizabeth heard the telephone ring, she saw Reece coming around the house, heading for the back porch.

"That's Sam calling," she told Reece, then ran inside, racing toward the living room. Breathless and nervous, she picked up the telephone. "Sam?"

"You sound funny. Is something wrong?" Sam asked.

"I was on the back porch. I ran." Elizabeth took several deep, soothing breaths. "What did you find out?"

"You've gone and gotten yourself involved with a real bad boy. Reece Landry's been in trouble since he was a kid."

"I know that. Reece told me all about his childhood run-ins with the law. So what else did you find out?"

"Look, kiddo, there's a possibility that Landry murdered B. K. Stanton. A lot of people who know him agree that he has a real killer instinct."

Elizabeth sighed. How could she persuade Sam that he was wrong? "Reece may have a killer instinct, but he doesn't possess the soul of a killer. You, of all people, should understand the difference."

Sam didn't respond. Elizabeth felt the hesitation, knew he was having difficulty accepting a truth he could not deny. Finally he said, "Point well taken."

Elizabeth sensed Reece's presence behind her before she turned to face him. She mouthed the words "It's Sam." Reece nodded.

"There are other suspects, aren't there?" Elizabeth asked. "You must have found out something."

"Hey, I've had less than twenty-four hours to dig up information," Sam said.

"So tell me what you've found out."

"There's a chance Landry is innocent."

Smiling, Elizabeth glanced at Reece, the trust and confidence she felt showing plainly in her expression. "Go on. Tell me more."

"The whole thing was too neat, too pat to suit me. Landry's gun, no fingerprints on the gun, some of the tests were inconclusive, eyewitnesses who caught him at the scene, a motive of hatred and revenge and the strange coincidence that Landry had been invited to Stanton's home that night, for the first time in his life." Sam paused for a moment. "I'd say the man was framed."

"Who could have framed him?"

"Now, that's the sixty-four-thousand-dollar question. But I'd say other members of Stanton's family are prime suspects. Especially the son, Kenny. Seems he and his father didn't get along, and Kenny hates Landry."

"Sam, Reece is going to need your help. He's planning on leaving today to go back to Newell. I want to go with him, but—"

"Dammit, Elizabeth, you aren't putting your life at risk by going with that man! Do you hear me?"

"The elephants in India can hear you."

Reece grabbed the phone out of Elizabeth's hand. "Dundee, you don't have to worry. I'm not taking her with me."

"Damn right you're not!"

"I'm borrowing Elizabeth's Jeep, but I'll make sure she gets it back, somehow. I don't want her involved in this any more than she already is. If you've found out anything that can help me, I'd appreciate you telling me now."

"From what little I've found out, I'd say there's a good chance you were framed. A smart man would turn himself in to the law before they shoot first and ask questions later. Your lawyer can appeal the case."

"What good would an appeal do if we don't have another suspect?" Reece asked.

"What chance do you have of discovering anything while you're on the run?"

"I'm not turning myself in," Reece said.

"Then you're a damned fool!"

"Would you turn yourself in if you were me?"

Sam grunted. "No."

Reece handed the phone to Elizabeth. "Sam, I'll call you back. Reece will be leaving soon, and I…we'll talk later and I'll explain things."

Hanging up the phone, Elizabeth turned to Reece. He stared at her, hoping she wouldn't ask again to go with him. As bad as he hated leaving her, he hated even more the possibility of anything happening to her because of him.

She stood there looking at him, those big blue eyes of hers pleading. She'd left her coffee brown hair loose today instead of French braiding it, and its dark, silky mass hung to her waist. She wore a pair of old, faded jeans that fit her round hips and legs like a second skin. Her nipples pressed against the ribbing of her beige sweater. Her golden skin glowed with youthful vibrancy and good health.

The temptation to scoop her up in his arms and carry her away with him became unbearable. He broke eye contact with her, wondering if she was messing with his mind, sending him subliminal messages of persuasion.

Reece took several tentative steps toward Elizabeth; she moved forward, reaching out for him. MacDatho inched his big body between them, accomplishing his obvious objective of separating them.

Elizabeth reached down, petting MacDatho's head, soothing him with her touch. She relayed a mental message to him that she needed a private goodbye with Reece. Mac nuzzled Elizabeth's leg, then removed himself from between Reece and her. Seating himself by the door, the wolf-dog waited patiently for Reece's departure.

Reece drew Elizabeth into his arms. She clung to him, running her hands up and down his back. "Don't go yet. Stay."

"I can't." He kissed her forehead. "If I stay here any longer, I not only jeopardize my own life, but yours, too. You've done more to help me than I could have ever asked of anyone."

Elizabeth wrapped her arms around his waist. "Since you won't allow me to go with you, to lead you off the mountain and safely back to Newell, I'll draw you a map of the back roads. The police won't have any idea that you'll know about the back roads."

Reece held Elizabeth away from him. "Draw me the map, but do it quickly."

She dashed over to the desk beneath the windows, fumbled inside the middle drawer and pulled out paper and pencil.

"If the deputies find any evidence that I've been here with you, tell them I held you at gunpoint. Tell them I threatened your life."

She held up the completed map, tears forming in the corners of her eyes. "Don't worry about me. I won't have to talk to any deputies. Besides, they'd never believe you held me at gunpoint for four days. Not in the shape you were in, and not with MacDatho around."

Reece took the map out of her hand, shoved it into his jacket pocket, then grabbed her by the waist, drawing her up against him. "Take care, huh, Lizzie. And don't shed any tears over me." He wiped the tears from her eyes with the tip of his finger. "I'm not worth crying over. I'm not worth anybody caring about me."

"You're wrong about that." She kissed his chin. "You are worth somebody caring." She kissed his jaw and then his cheek. "You deserve someone's tears." She kissed him lightly on the mouth. "You deserve to be loved, Reece Landry."

"Damn you, Lizzie. Don't do this to me!" His kiss consumed her with his brutal need, with his savage passion. All the loneliness, the pain, the anger that had been building inside him since the day he'd been born verged into one obsession. To have Elizabeth Mallory be that somebody. The somebody who'd care. The somebody who'd cry for him. The somebody who'd love him.

Feeling his desperation, Elizabeth tried to give him what he needed, to respond with an open heart. As her tears clouded her vision, she clung to him, whispering his name over and over again as he buried his face against her neck, his nose nuzzling her hair.

Mustering all the control he possessed, Reece released Elizabeth and stepped away from her. "Say a prayer for me, Lizzie."

More afraid than she'd ever been in her life, she stood motionless. She watched Reece walk to the door, pat MacDatho on the head and pick up the large duffel bag from the floor before opening the front door.

When he walked out onto the porch, Elizabeth forced her legs to move. She lingered in the doorway while he got into the Jeep and drove down the road, away from Sequana Falls.

MacDatho waited patiently at her side, finally circling her as a signal that he thought it was time for them to go inside. Elizabeth glanced down at Mac, nodding in agreement, suddenly feeling the frigid air seeping through her clothing.

Twirling around, she ran inside, MacDatho at her heels. She knew what she had to do. If she hurried, Reece wouldn't have more than an hour or so head start. And it didn't really matter because she knew what roads he would be taking off the mountain, past Dover's Mill and all the way into Newell.

She was not going to let Reece face this ordeal alone. She was going to be at his side, offering him all the support she could give him. And Sam, even if he didn't know it yet, was going to help them uncover the real murderer.

Within twenty minutes she had packed her suitcase, doused all the fires in the fireplaces, checked both greenhouses, sacked a grocery bag filled with MacDatho's food and pulled Sam's antique car out of the barn they used as a garage and parked it in front of the cabin.

She dialed Aunt Margaret's number, mentally preparing herself to lie about her plans. "Aunt Margaret, I wanted to let you know that I've decided to go to Atlanta and spend some time with Sam."

"Is that so?"

"It's been a couple of years since I've been any farther than Dover's Mill, and I think now's the time to test the waters, so to speak, to see if I still have the same problems dealing with the enormous influx of thoughts and emotions I usually get from being around huge crowds of people." This is only a half lie, Elizabeth told herself. Maybe her aunt wouldn't see past the pretense.

"I suppose you'll be bringing that wolf of yours by here for me to take care of."

"I thought O'Grady could take care of him. Mac and O'Grady are old friends."

"Bring Mac by here on your way out of town and I'll see that O'Grady picks him up. And leave whatever instructions O'Grady will need to keep things running smoothly in the greenhouses until you return."

Elizabeth sighed. "Thanks, Aunt Margaret. I'm not sure how long I'll be gone."

"I suppose you'll be gone until you're either arrested for aiding and abetting a criminal or until you've helped the man prove himself innocent."

Why had she ever thought she could get away with lying to Aunt Margaret? The woman's psychic abilities were as keen as they'd ever been. No one kept secrets from Margaret McPhearson.

"He is innocent," Elizabeth said. "And he's out there all alone, with no one on his side."

"Be careful, Elizabeth. I feel great danger for you and for your man."

"Pray for us, Aunt Margaret. Please pray for us."

"I've been doing that since the night he came to you," Margaret told her niece.

"I love you."

"I love you, too, child."

After hanging up the phone, Elizabeth swallowed, wiped her eyes and said a brief prayer of her own. Aunt Margaret had understood. She wasn't so sure about Sam Dundee.

She dialed the Atlanta number and waited to be put through to Sam. Somehow she had to make him understand why she was going to follow Reece, and why it was imperative that he meet them in Newell.

"Elizabeth?" Sam's deep voice was brisk and a bit harsh. "Has Landry left?"

"He left almost thirty minutes ago. I let him take my Jeep."

"Thank God he's gone. You've done some crazy things in your life, but this has to be the craziest."

"Sam, I want you to listen to everything I have to say before you start screaming at me. Promise?" Elizabeth hated it when Sam made her feel like a naughty child. She supposed that came from his having had the responsibility of her guardianship for so many years. He couldn't stop acting like a big-brother protector.

"I don't like it already. What are you up to?"

"I'm going to follow Reece to Newell, and I'm going to have to—"

"The hell you are! Now listen to me, young lady, you are not to leave Sequana Falls. Do you hear me? I don't care what all your special powers tell you about Reece Landry. The man is an escaped murderer, and whether he's guilty or innocent, the police aren't going to take that into consideration if he tries to resist arrest when they catch up with him."

"I want you to meet me in Newell. Tomorrow. I'll call you in the morning and tell you where to meet us."

"Elizabeth, don't do this!"

"My mind is made up. I've already packed my bags, told Aunt Margaret and made plans for Mac to stay with O'Grady."

"If Landry took your Jeep, how do you plan on following him? You aren't taking that old delivery van you let O'Grady keep, are you?"

"O'Grady will need the van for deliveries and to make trips up the mountain to keep check on the greenhouses while I'm gone." Elizabeth sucked in a deep breath, calling forth all her courage to tell Sam about her chosen mode of transportation. "I'm taking your old Thunderbird."

"You're what?" Sam bellowed.

"You can pick it up tomorrow when you fly into Newell. I promise I'll take good care of your baby."

"You are not going to take my '65 T-Bird down the mountain in weather like this. The roads will still be icy in spots. You could wreck the car and kill yourself."

"I'll call you in the morning and let you know where to meet Reece and me. In the meantime, do whatever you can from Atlanta to get the ball rolling. We're going to discover who really killed B. K. Stanton, and we've got to do it as quickly as possible. Reece can't stay on the run forever."

"Elizabeth, listen to me. Don't do this. It's crazy. You're asking for trouble. You're—"

Elizabeth laid down the phone, cutting Sam off mid-tirade. He'd rant and rave for a while, but he'd eventually calm down, and when she called him in the morning to tell him where he could meet Reece and her, he would come prepared to help them.

"Come on, Mac. You're going to visit Aunt Margaret and O'Grady. And I want you to be a good boy for them."

Reece had followed Elizabeth's map and directions down to the last detail. He couldn't remember a time when he'd put so much trust in another human being, enough trust so that he literally put his life in her hands. She hadn't been kidding when she'd said she knew all the back roads off the mountain and through the surrounding towns. He hadn't run into one roadblock or seen anyone who even vaguely resembled a policeman, highway patrolman or sheriff's deputy. He'd pulled off the road halfway between Dover's Mill and Newell to relieve himself and enjoy one of the ham sandwiches Elizabeth had packed for him, along with coffee from a thermos she had prepared.

The sun eased lower and lower on the western horizon. Reece guessed the time was around three or three-thirty in the afternoon. With clouds building steadily in the sky, blocking part of the sun's last rays, night was sure to fall early today. He was less than fifteen miles from Newell. He couldn't risk going into town, taking a chance that someone might recognize him.

He knew where he'd spend the night. Flossie, the madam who'd once run the local brothel and had been his mother's friend, now owned a sleazy motel on the outskirts of Newell. Nobody would recognize the Jeep, and the type of clientele Flossie got at Sweet Rest Motel wasn't likely to call the police if they did recognize him. He'd be safe at Flossie's motel tonight, and he could make a few phone calls in the morning before he left. He needed to talk to his lawyer. Elkins was bound to be wondering where the hell he was, but he wouldn't risk telling Gary his exact location. Not yet. As much as he wanted to trust the man, he wasn't one hundred percent sure his lawyer wouldn't turn him in to the authorities.

He needed to call Chris. He didn't trust her entirely, either, but she was his half sister and she did profess to care about him and believe in him. She'd paid for his attorney, and would have posted bail if the judge had been willing to set bail.

And he would call Elizabeth. He'd call her tonight to let her know he'd made it home to Newell without a hitch. She'd be worried about him. It felt odd knowing someone actually cared about his well-being.

Maybe he'd give her another quick call in the morning before he went out to B.K.'s hunting lodge. It would be nice to hear the sound of her voice one last time.

Brushing aside the cotton-candy thoughts, Reece concentrated on the drive ahead. He turned off onto a dirt road that led through the woods and some unused farmland. It was the long way around to Sweet Rest Motel, but it was the safest. He'd be unlikely to run into any other vehicles.

He pulled the Jeep to a halt in front of the door marked Office in the parking area of the motel. The buildings were old, built of concrete blocks recently painted a rather nauseous shade of pink, the doors to each unit bright turquoise. Flossie didn't seem to be doing much business. Only one truck and one older model station wagon were parked in front.

Reece reached into his pocket for the money Elizabeth had given him. Two hundred dollars. It was all she'd had in cash, and she'd insisted he take it.

The woman behind the register wasn't Flossie but some young girl with huge breasts and frizzy, bleached-blond hair. He'd never seen her before, and he knew just about everybody in Newell. Hopefully she was a newcomer who wouldn't recognize a face that had been in all the newspapers and on TV.

"You need a room, handsome?" she asked.

"Yeah. Just for tonight. How much?"

"Thirty-five bucks. Local phone calls are free. And there's a TV in your room, with a pay-for-view box. Checkout time is eleven." She handed him a key. "You're in number nineteen."

Reece laid thirty-five dollars on the counter, then turned to leave.

"Hey, mister, you forgot to sign the register."

"You sign for me, honey."

"What's your name?" she asked, smiling.

"Whatever you want it to be." Reece opened the door.

"If you get lonesome later on, *Mr. Jones,* stop back by. I get off duty at nine. I could show you a real good time." She looked him over from head to toe, stopping to gawk at the way his jeans fit across his crotch.

"I'll keep it in mind." Reece went outside, looked around for number nineteen, then got into the Jeep. He parked in the slot in front of his room, got out, grabbed the duffel bag and locked the Jeep.

Unlocking the door to number nineteen, he flipped on the light switch. Two purple ceramic lamps, one on the nightstand, the other on the right side of the dresser, came on, casting a lavender glow over the mismatched furnishings.

Reece found the room to be pretty much what he'd expected. A double bed with an orange-and-purple flowered spread dominated the small space. A single chair rested under the window, which boasted curtains that matched the spread. Atop the left side of the dresser, an oak-veneer box that didn't match the bed's maple headboard or the metal rounds on the chair, sat the TV.

Reece dropped the duffel bag on the floor, removed the leather jacket he wore, tossing it on the chair, then fell across the bed sideways. The mattress sagged. The box springs moaned under Reece's weight. Within minutes he'd fallen asleep.

The ringing telephone wakened him. For a couple of seconds he wasn't quite sure where he was, then a quick look at the motel room reminded him all too vividly that he was back in Newell, already hiding out. Who the hell would be calling? No one knew where he was. He grabbed the receiver.

"Yeah?"

"Hi, there, Mr. Jones. This is Luanne, in the office. I thought I'd call and remind you that I get off work in about an hour."

Sitting up in the bed, Reece combed through his hair with his fingers. The image of huge breasts and red lips flashed through his mind. He needed a woman, but he didn't need one badly enough to risk having sex with someone who'd have no qualms about turning him over to the law in the morning. Besides, his taste in women had far surpassed Luanne's type years ago.

"Look, honey, I appreciate the offer, but——"

"I could run over to the State Store, get us a fifth and we could watch one of those sex movies on the TV."

"Luanne, I'm bushed. I'm afraid I wouldn't be much fun tonight. Some other time, okay?"

"Sure thing, Mr. Jones. You know where to find me. I work the evening shift here five nights a week."

Reece hung up the phone, crawled out of bed and went into the bathroom. What he needed more than anything else, even a woman, was a shower, a shave and a good night's sleep. Tomorrow his life as a fugitive would start all over again. For a few hours he could relax, here at the Sweet Rest Motel, under the guise of Mr. Jones. In the morning he'd head out for B. K. Stanton's hunting lodge. None of the family ever used the place during the winter months, after hunting season. And now that B.K. was dead, he doubted anyone would ever use the place again. Since Kenny hated hunting, he'd probably sell the place, with no objections from his mother or sister. As far as Reece knew, neither Alice nor Christina had ever set foot in the lodge.

Reece came out of the shower, dried off quickly, briskly rubbing his hair. He walked out of the bathroom, turned back the covers and sat on the bed. His stomach growled, reminding him that he hadn't eaten any supper. He didn't dare risk going out somewhere for food. Rummaging around in the duffel bag, he pulled out a pimento cheese sandwich and the thermos. The sandwich was soggy, the coffee lukewarm. Finishing both quickly, he lay down and closed his eyes.

He couldn't remember ever feeling so alone. Strange thing was that he'd spent most of his life as a loner, needing no one, wanting no one. Even the months he'd spent in jail before, during and after the trial, he'd never felt such intense loneliness. Anger. Frustration. Hatred. And even pain. But not overwhelming loneliness.

He knew damn well what was wrong with him. He'd spent a few days with a woman who had surrounded him with attention, a woman who'd cared for him when he was sick, who'd fed him and clothed him and shared her home with him. Elizabeth Mallory had pierced the barrier that protected him from loneliness. She'd made him want things he knew he could never have. She'd shown him life's goodness, when all he'd ever known was its evil.

He pictured her in his mind. That strong, sturdy body of soft, feminine curves. That mass of dark brown hair. Those pure blue eyes that looked inside him, as if they could see his very soul.

He heard her voice saying his name. *Reece. Reece. Where are you, Reece? I can't find you.*

His eyelids flew open; he sat upright in bed. What the hell was that all about? He'd felt her presence inside his head, felt her frustration at not being able to find him. Had he lost his mind? Elizabeth Mallory was over a hundred and fifty miles away, safe and secure in her mountain cabin.

Reece's hands trembled. Sweat beads dotted his upper lip. He found himself thinking about where he was, heard himself repeating the name Sweet Rest. Saw himself driving along the back road to arrive at Flossie's sleazy motel.

He flopped back down onto the bed. Dragging the lumpy pillow out from under his head, he turned on his side, beating the pillow with his fists.

He tossed and turned for what seemed like hours, but when he checked the electric alarm clock on the nightstand, he realized it was only nine-thirty.

He heard what sounded like a soft knock, but dismissed the noise as nothing more than another motel patron in the room next to his. The knock grew progressively louder until he realized that someone was knocking on his door. Damn, crazy woman! Luscious Luanne was no doubt standing outside with a fifth in a brown bag, her motor running and determined not to take no for an answer. He jerked a pair of clean jeans out of the duffel bag, slipped them on and zipped them. He glanced over at the 9 mm on the nightstand.

"I told you not tonight, honey," Reece said as he opened the door a fraction, keeping the safety chain latched. "Why don't you—"

Reece stared at the woman standing outside his motel door. She wasn't some cheap blond floozy carrying a fifth of whiskey. She was a blue-eyed brunette carrying an overnight bag.

"Elizabeth!"

"It's freezing out here. Let me in."

Removing the safety chain, he opened the door enough for Elizabeth to enter the room.

"What the hell are you doing here?" Reece asked, his voice a low growl.

"Well, hello, Elizabeth, so nice to see you. Glad you followed me over half the state of Georgia. Come in and make yourself at home."

"Don't get smart with me, Lizzie. What do you mean, you followed me?" Reece closed the door, locking it securely.

Elizabeth set her overnight case on the floor beside Reece's duffel bag. "I appreciate your letting me know where you were. I'd made myself crazy going all over Newell looking for my old Jeep. If you hadn't shown me how to get here, it could have taken me till morning to find you. I didn't dare ask anyone how to get to Sweet Rest Motel."

"I didn't let you know where I was. What the hell are you talking about?"

"You were thinking about me, weren't you?"

"You read my mind?"

"You let me read your mind, Reece. You opened up. You lowered your shield enough to let me in."

"I don't want you here. I told you that you couldn't come with me, didn't I?" Reece fumbled in the duffel bag, dragging out a pine green flannel shirt.

"Won't you sit down, Elizabeth?" she said in a mocking tone. "Why, thank you, Reece, I believe I will." She sat in the only chair, crossing her arms under her breasts.

Reece put on the shirt, leaving it unbuttoned, then grabbed

Elizabeth by the shoulders, jerking her up out of the chair. His fingers bit into the plush material of her heavy wool coat.

"You're getting out of here, right now," Reece told her. "I don't want you here."

"Yes, you do. You want me and you need me." Elizabeth stared him directly in the eye, her look daring him to deny her statement.

"I can't let you stay with me! I'm running from the law, goddammit. If you stay with me, you could get killed."

"And if I leave you, you'll be all alone."

When she tried to touch his face, he released his hold on her and shoved her away from him. "I've been alone all my life. I like it that way. I don't want you around. You'll just get in the way. You'll be more trouble than you'll be worth."

"No matter what you say or do, I'm not going to leave you, Reece." Elizabeth tried again to touch him. He dodged her seeking hand.

"Get the hell out of my life, lady. Can't you get it through that screwy head of yours that I don't want you, I don't need you and I'm better off without you?" Reece saw her face pale, saw her jaw clench, noted the wounded look in her eyes. He couldn't allow himself to feel guilty about hurting her feelings. He had to think of Elizabeth, put her safety first, before his own needs. Every word he'd said to her had been a lie, but he'd lied to her for her own good.

Reece lifted her overnight case off the floor, handed it to Elizabeth and unlocked the motel door. "Go back to Sequana Falls where you belong. Forget you ever knew me."

Elizabeth accepted the overnight case. Reece opened the door. Cold night air swept into the room. Elizabeth quivered. Reece stood by the door, his gaze riveted to the floor.

Listening for her footsteps, he waited for her to walk past him. He waited and waited and waited. Then he heard the bathroom door close.

He slammed shut the outside door. "Elizabeth!"

CHAPTER 6

She ignored his constant beating on the door, dismissed his ranting words and made no effort to remove herself from the bathroom. Reece gave up, flipped on the television and sat at the foot of the bed. What the hell was he going to do with her?

He had never met anyone like Elizabeth Mallory. She was an enigma to him, a riddle without an answer. He'd left her in Sequana Falls, back where she was safe. He'd thought he'd never see her again. But here she was, in his motel room, locked in the bathroom and not listening to reason.

She was so damned sure she could help him, was determined to stay with him until they found B. K. Stanton's real murderer. Despite the fact that Elizabeth insisted that she possessed special psychic talents, Reece had his doubts. He was a man who didn't believe in anything if he couldn't see it, feel it, smell it, taste it or touch it; she expected him to believe that she could read minds, forecast the future and sense events occurring miles away.

One thing was for sure, she'd found him at this godawful motel on the seedy outskirts of Newell. But that feat hadn't necessarily taken any psychic powers. Maybe she'd simply gotten lucky. That's what he wanted to believe.

But he could not dismiss the nagging sense that Elizabeth had spoken to him from miles away, that she'd called out his name, that she had asked him where he was and told him she couldn't find him.

Hell, when she'd showed up at his door he'd accused her of reading his mind. He didn't want to think she'd gotten inside him, that all this hocus-pocus stuff she'd been telling him was true, but dammit, he couldn't get the sound of her voice out of his head.

It didn't matter whether or not Elizabeth was psychic and might be able to use her powers to help him. He could not allow her to stay with him. He was a fugitive on the run, a convicted murderer. If she stayed with him, her life would be in danger. He wouldn't let her take the risk.

Besides, she'd just get in the way, he told himself. The woman didn't mean anything to him. He couldn't allow himself to care. He couldn't indulge in any weakness, and that's what caring about another person was—a weakness. His mother had loved B. K. Stanton. The man had been Blanche's weakness, and her mindless love for another woman's husband had destroyed her. No one, other than Blanche, had ever held a place in Reece's heart. He had never loved anyone, and he never would. That was a promise he'd made himself a long time ago, one he intended to keep.

Elizabeth took her time in the bathroom, dreading the thought of facing Reece again. He hadn't been happy to see her. No doubt he was out there now thinking of ways to make her leave. What he didn't know was that there was nothing he could say or do to make her go away. She had every intention of staying with him and helping him, whether he wanted her to or not.

She'd hung her heavy coat on the door rack, then stripped out of her jeans, sweater and shirt, peeling away the layers until she got down to her thermal underwear. She wasn't a femme fatale by any stretch of the imagination; her experience with men was quite limited. A more worldly wise woman would have come prepared with a slinky black negligee and a bottle of wine. She would have used her feminine wiles to seduce Reece, and thus bring him around to her way of thinking.

Elizabeth glanced down at her underwear. A splattering of tiny peach flowers gave the soft, beige cotton knit material a feminine appearance, but she certainly didn't look sexy covered from neck to ankles in her long johns. Well, it didn't matter how she looked because she had no intention of seducing Reece.

Regardless of what he said or did, she would not allow him to send her back to Sequana Falls. She had risked too much coming to him. No one knew he'd spent four days in her home, no one except Aunt Margaret and Sam, and they weren't going to tell anyone. If she hadn't followed Reece, she would have been safe—safe from the police if they caught him, and safe from the outpouring of emotions that always bombarded her whenever she went out into the world. Coming through Newell had been difficult, sensing random feelings, picking up fragments of thoughts, looking out the window at a middle-aged couple and knowing the woman would lose her husband in less than a year.

Come what may, whether he wanted her or not, she could not leave Reece. He needed her. Even though she couldn't see into his future any more clearly than she could reach into his mind, she knew she was meant to save him. Her own instincts told her that much. Aunt Margaret had sensed the same.

"You must save him, Elizabeth. No one else can," her aunt had told her when she'd left MacDatho in the old woman's care. "Only you can save him from himself."

Elizabeth washed her face, scrubbing away the light makeup she wore. Picking up her clothes, she eased open the bathroom door and glanced at Reece sitting on the edge of the bed. She couldn't hide in the bathroom all night; sooner or later she would have to face him. Now was as good a time as any.

A soft rapping on the outside door halted Elizabeth's first step out of the bathroom. Reece jerked around, his body tense, then he got up, walked to the window and pulled back the curtain. Elizabeth heard him laugh. He swung open the door.

"You're late," Reece said. "I expected you earlier."

Elizabeth didn't see the visitor until Reece moved out of the way, revealing a curvy blonde in a hot pink jumpsuit dotted with rhinestones, and with a white fake-fur jacket hanging around her shoulders. Holding up a brown paper bag, the woman pulled out a bottle of whiskey and offered it to Reece.

"Come on in out of the cold…er…uh…Luanne." Reece closed the door behind the woman, then accepted the liquor, slipping his arm around her waist and drawing her up against him.

"Now this is the kind of reception I was hoping for, Mr. Jones." Dropping her jacket on the floor, Luanne rubbed herself against Reece, her dark pink lips curving into a self-satisfied smile.

Elizabeth walked out of the bathroom, took several tentative steps across the carpeted floor and stopped to stare at Reece and the woman in his arms. Who was the woman and why had she come to Reece's motel room? Anger combined with jealousy, totally annihilating Elizabeth's sixth sense.

Elizabeth noticed that the blonde had caught a glimpse of her. Dropping her clothes on the floor, Elizabeth smiled and nodded her head. The woman Reece had called Luanne widened her eyes, staring at Elizabeth as if she thought she might be seeing an aberration.

"Look, honey, I'm interested in spending the night with you, but—" Luanne blinked several times when Elizabeth waved at her.

"And I'm interested in the same thing," Reece said. He knew that sooner or later Elizabeth was going to come out of the bathroom, and if she caught him in a compromising situation with another woman, she was bound to storm out of the motel and get her butt back to Sequana Falls and out of his life.

"Well, I'm not into these threesome deals, honey." Luanne kept staring at Elizabeth.

Without releasing his hold on Luanne, Reece pivoted just enough to catch sight of Elizabeth in his peripheral vision. "I wondered if you planned to stay in the bathroom all night. Come on out and meet a friend of mine. Lizzie, this is Luanne. Luanne, Lizzie."

The two women sized each other up, each taking in every inch of the other's face and figure. Reece tried not to make comparisons, but the obvious stared him in the face. Elizabeth was a bigger, taller woman, with broader hips and shoulders. For all her bustiness, Luanne was small, with a fragile quality, whereas Elizabeth's body proclaimed her vitality and strength. Luanne wore heavy makeup, her hair was bleached almost white and her long fingernails were painted a bright pink to match her jumpsuit. Elizabeth's face was scrubbed clean and her long dark hair hung around her shoulders, hitting her at the waist. Her thermal underwear hugged her body, revealing every round, feminine curve. Her clear blue eyes glared at him, demanding an explanation.

Luanne was smoke; Elizabeth was the fire. Luanne was like a gaudy trinket that could be bought at the dollar store and discarded the moment it turned your skin green. Elizabeth was jewel-studded gold, priceless, and once possessed, the owner would rather die than ever part with it.

"Don't get in a huff, honey." Reece returned Luanne's endearment. "Lizzie showed up a while ago, uninvited."

Luanne grinned, first at Reece and then triumphantly at Elizabeth. "Is that right? Well, why don't you send her on her way? 'Cause I'm not staying if she does."

Reece set the whiskey bottle on the nightstand, then turned to Elizabeth and shrugged. "Well, Lizzie, you see how it is, don't you?"

Yes, by golly, she did see how it was. She saw clearly. Ms. Luanne Evans was a new acquaintance, not one of Reece's old friends. Luanne's mind was quite uncomplicated, and was wide open for anyone to pick up her rather raunchy thoughts. The woman certainly had plans for Reece. Elizabeth had no intention of allowing those plans to come to fruition. If any woman shared a bed with Reece Landry tonight, it was going to be Elizabeth Mallory.

Elizabeth sat on the bed. Reece frowned. Luanne pulled away from Reece, planting her hands on her slender hips.

"Look, Lizzie, maybe you're deaf or something, but the man said he wants me." Luanne glared at her rival.

Elizabeth scooted up in the bed until her back touched the headboard. Raising her arms behind her head, she stretched and yawned.

"Well, the only problem with that, Lu, is sometimes Mr. Jones says one thing when he means another."

Taking a few steps over to the bed, Reece reached down and grabbed Elizabeth by the arm. "I mean what I say, Lizzie. Get dressed, pick up your clothes and get the hell out of here. I've got plans for tonight."

Turning her nose up, Luanne smiled, then shook her head just enough to toss about her thick, teased hair.

Elizabeth slapped away Reece's hand. "I'm not leaving." She glanced over at a smug Luanne. "Besides, Luanne can't stay all night. When her boyfriend gets home from work around one in the morning, she'll have to be there or he'll come looking for her."

Luanne's mouth fell open. "How do you know when Joey gets home from work?"

"He's going to get home early tonight. From his job on the assembly line at Stanton Industries," Elizabeth said. "Around eleven-thirty. He's sick with a stomach virus."

"How do you know where Joey works and that he's going to get sick?" Luanne backed up against the wall, staring at Elizabeth with round, dark eyes. "What are you, some kind of fortune-teller?"

"I'm a witch. *Honey.*" Rising up on her knees, Elizabeth sat in the middle of the bed and pointed her finger directly at Luanne. "And if you stick around here, trying to put the make on my man, I'll cast a spell on you."

Luanne picked up her coat off the floor and hurriedly slipped into it. "I'm outta here. Just forget you ever knew me. Okay?" Glancing at the whiskey bottle, Luanne hesitated, then opened the door. "The drinks are on me." She rushed outside, slamming the door behind her.

Reece leaned over, bracing his hands on each side of Elizabeth where she sat on the bed. "You think you're cute, don't you?"

"I think I did what any sensible woman would have done under the circumstances." Tilting her head just a fraction, Elizabeth smiled at Reece. "I eliminated my competition."

"I had plans with Luanne. Plans that included getting rip-roaring drunk with her and—"

Elizabeth covered his lips with the tip of her index finger. "You didn't have any plans with that woman. You turned her down when she offered. She showed up here all on her own, just the way I did."

"How do you know?" Glaring at Elizabeth, Reece lowered his head until they were face-to-face, their breaths mingling. "You didn't read my mind!"

"No, I read hers. Minds like Luanne's are easy to read, but not very interesting."

"Damn you, Lizzie! I don't want you here with me. What do I have to do to make you understand?" He was too close to her. He needed to back off, to get away from her big blue eyes, her soft pink lips, her flowery scent, her womanly heat.

"Why are you so afraid of me?" Elizabeth slipped her arms up and around Reece's neck. "I would never hurt you. All I want to do is help you."

"I don't want your help." He prized her arms from around his neck and shoved her away from him.

Elizabeth fell back across the bed. She lay there staring up at Reece. "You don't want to need me, do you? You're afraid to want me, to need me, to care about me."

She wasn't reading his mind or picking up anything with her sixth sense, only with her feminine intuition. Reece was afraid of her, of the way she made him feel. And she had to admit the truth to herself—she was every bit as afraid of the way he made her feel. She couldn't remember a time in her life when she'd acted so irrationally, even when her actions were prompted by her psychic revelations. She had never felt so connected to another human being, never felt so essential to another's very existence. She had opened her home and her heart to a stranger, a man accused of murdering his own father, and she had followed that man halfway across the state of Georgia, determined to save him, not only from a wrongful conviction but from the pain and anger slowly destroying him.

"Don't send me away, Reece. Don't shut me out of your life."

Reece didn't want to think about what she'd said, about the truth of her words. Dammit, she was right. He was afraid of her, of the way she made him feel. That was the whole problem—Elizabeth Mallory made him feel more than anger and hatred, and Reece didn't want to feel anything else. He'd built his life on those two emotions. The thought of ever caring about another person scared the hell out of him.

For both their sakes, he had to get rid of Elizabeth. He had to make her see reason. Maybe the only way to do that was to show her what kind of man she was dealing with, what kind of man Reece Landry really was—a white trash bastard who didn't give a damn about anybody but himself.

"All right, honey, if you want to stay, stay." Grabbing her around the waist, Reece jerked her up off the bed, bringing her body tightly against his. "I had planned to enjoy Luanne's company all night, but you'll do just as well. After all, a woman's a woman."

Elizabeth stared at Reece, her blue eyes focused intently on his face as she tried to make sense of what he'd said. "Why would you say something so utterly ridiculous?"

Reece rubbed himself against her, his arousal hard against her softness. The feel of her, the scent of her, the warmth of her body created a heady seduction, prompting Reece's reaction to her nearness. He cupped her buttocks in his big hands, lifting her up and into the need pulsing between his legs.

Elizabeth squirmed, trying to free herself, but her movements ignited a strong reaction in Reece. Fondling her hip with one hand, he grasped the back of her neck, pulling her mouth to his, kissing her with bruising force. Moaning, Elizabeth opened her mouth for his invasion as she clung to his shoulders.

Reece devoured her lips. He pillaged her mouth with his tongue, all the while exploring her body with one hand as the other held her captive.

When he ended the kiss, Elizabeth laid her head on his chest, her arms draped around his neck. "Would...would it have felt like this with Luanne?"

Hell, no! Kissing had never made him feel the way he did right now. Women liked to be kissed, so Reece had learned the art of kissing quite young, but kissing had never meant more than part of the pleasant, necessary foreplay to entice a woman into bed. But after kissing Elizabeth, he was a minute away from exploding. If he hadn't ended the kiss, he would have taken her right where they stood. Hard and fast and hot.

"Like I said, a woman's a woman. Kissing is kissing." Reece grinned. "If you liked the feel of my tongue in your mouth, you'll love the way I'm going to feel inside you."

Elizabeth clutched Reece's shoulders. "I...I won't be used. If you think I'm willing to be just another woman in a long line of women, then you'd better think again."

"Nobody's forcing you to stay, Lizzie." Reece slid his hands into position under her breasts, lifting them. "All I'm saying is that I'm horny as hell. I need a woman, and if you stay, you're going to be that woman."

Elizabeth swallowed hard, wondering if Reece could possibly mean what he was saying. Swaying slightly, she closed her eyes, trying to focus, to concentrate on Reece's thoughts. Her mind ran into a solid wall of resistance.

"What's it going to be, honey?" Reece asked. "Are you going or staying?"

What was he trying to do? Scare her off? Make her dislike him? Despite the fact that she couldn't read his thoughts, Elizabeth felt certain that Reece would never do anything to harm her, and most certainly would never force her to have sex with him.

Pulling away, she turned her back to him and clasped her hands together. She couldn't allow Reece to run her off. She had to find the courage within herself to overcome whatever obstacles he put in her way.

"Go on home, Lizzie." Reece wanted to take the few steps that separated them and pull her back into his arms. He wanted to hold her and kiss her and find comfort in her embrace. He wanted to lay her down on the bed and make slow, sweet love to her all night. He wanted to wake in the morning and see her smiling at him, hear her saying his name.

Elizabeth turned to face him. "I won't allow your fear to keep me from helping you."

"Dammit, woman!" Anger. He knew and understood that emotion only too well. If he allowed the anger to consume him, to control his actions, he could drive her away. He couldn't let any other feelings influence him. Not now. Not when Elizabeth's life could depend on what happened between them tonight.

Without saying another word, Reece walked toward her. Elizabeth saw the anger and determination in his eyes, and for one split second she sensed something else in Reece—sorrow—and she held on to that fleeting emotion when he lifted her into his arms and tossed her down on the bed. She had no time to adjust her body or focus her mind before Reece came down on top of her, his big, hard body pressing her into the mattress. He gave his hands free rein to explore her body. He squeezed her breasts. He delved his hand between her tightly clenched legs, rubbing the side of his hand against her intimately. When she tried to roll away from him, he straddled her body, placing a knee on each side of her hips.

Elizabeth looked up at his hard face, into those lone-wolf amber eyes, and knew there was no way she could control this man, that she was completely at his mercy. "Don't do this, Reece. Stop trying to make me hate you."

Reece slipped his fingers beneath the edge of her thermal top, shoving it up over her stomach to the swell of her breasts. She grabbed his hands, momentarily stopping him, but he manacled her wrists in his grasp and lifted her hands over her head, flattening them on the pillow.

"I don't want you to hate me, honey. I want you to love me and love me and love me. All night long."

"No, Reece. Stop it. Now!"

He nuzzled her tummy with his nose, nudging the edge of her thermal top higher and higher until her round, full breasts were exposed. Elizabeth sucked in her breath, a surge of uncertainty and sensual longing combining within her. She hated the way Reece was acting, but despite his deplorable behavior, her body ached with wanting, with the need for his touch.

"Great boobs, Lizzie. Just the way I like them. Big and firm." Leaning over her, he flicked one of her nipples with his tongue.

Groaning, she twisted and turned, struggling against his hold. "Don't, Reece. Please. Not like this."

Ignoring her pleas, he suckled her breast. She cried out from the pleasure of his touch and the pain in her heart. He released her trapped hands, ran his fingertips down her throat, over her breasts and into the waistband of her thermal bottoms. He eased the bottoms down enough to expose her navel and hips.

Reece forced himself to look at Elizabeth, to endure the hurt he knew he would see on her face. She stared at him, tears trapped in the corners of her eyes. The sight of those tears weakened him, but he forged ahead, sure he was right in what he was doing—saving Elizabeth from Reece Landry.

"You see how it is with me, Lizzie. I'm a sorry bastard who doesn't give a damn how you feel. I take what I want, and to hell with the consequences." He unzipped his jeans, lowered himself atop her and gave her a hard, forceful kiss. "I'm mean, honey. Mean enough to kill. I'm no good through and through."

Elizabeth tried to speak, tried to tell him that she didn't believe him, that somewhere buried beneath all that pain and anger and bitterness was a good man. A man who had been unloved and abused all his life, a man in desperate need of someone to care. But she couldn't form the words, couldn't get the sound past the knot of tears lodged in her throat. All she could do was cry.

Reece watched the tears well up in her eyes and spill over, streaming down her cheeks. Her chest rose and fell in quick, jerky undulations. Her mouth opened to release her gasping sobs.

He couldn't bear the sight of her tears. He knew she wasn't crying for herself, but for him. After the way he had treated her, she still cared. Damn her! He hadn't frightened her; he had hurt her. He hadn't run her off; he'd made her cry.

She lifted her hands up to him, touching the side of his face with her fingertips. Her touch burned him, like a cleansing fire cauterizing a wound. The pain surged through him. He fought the healing effects of her pure, loving concern. He couldn't care about this woman. He wouldn't!

Reece jumped off the bed, zipped up his jeans and reached for the bottle of whiskey on the nightstand. Opening the liquor, he tilted the bottle, placed it to his lips and took a choking swallow. He coughed several times.

"You're a fool to stay with me. Why the hell don't you leave while you still can?" He took another gulp of the whiskey, wincing from the impact as it seared a path down his throat.

Wiping away the tears she could not control, Elizabeth pulled up her thermal bottoms and jerked down the top, then got out of the bed. How could she ever make him understand that she couldn't leave him even if she wanted to? No one else could save him. Aunt Margaret knew and so did she. Even if someone else could prove his innocence and set him free, no one else could free him from the anger and hatred that had ruled his life. Only she could do that.

She laid her hand on his back. Every muscle in his body tensed.

Not turning around, Reece lashed out at her. "I could have raped you, Lizzie. Why the hell are you still here? Aren't you afraid to be in the same room with me?"

She wrapped her arms around his waist, holding him. His body remained rigid. "Don't you think I knew what you were trying to do?"

He covered her hands with his own where she held him tightly at the waist. "I was trying to get me some, honey, but you weren't cooperating." Prizing her hands from his body, he pulled away from her.

Elizabeth sighed. "You were trying to scare me away, trying to prove to me what a rotten, no-good skunk you are."

Reece turned around slowly. "You think you're so damned smart, don't you?"

"I'm not leaving, so you might as well cut the rest of this macho-idiot act!"

"You have got to be the most stubborn, bullheaded woman I've ever known!" Reece unzipped his jeans, pulled them off and tossed them on the floor.

Elizabeth stared at his naked body.

"If you want to stay, then stay." Reece lay down on the bed. "I've had a long, strenuous day and things are bound to be worse tomorrow. I'm going to get some sleep." He punched one of his pillows several times, bunched it into a wad and stuck it under his head. "You can do whatever the hell you want to do."

Reece turned out the nightstand lamp, pulled the covers up over himself and closed his eyes. Elizabeth stood in the middle of the motel room, her gaze riveted to Reece Landry. Why, of all the men on earth, had the good Lord in heaven sent her a man like this? A man who could shield his heart and his mind from her. A man who fought her efforts to help him every inch of the way. A man so scarred by his past that he was afraid to trust another human being.

Elizabeth turned back the covers and crawled into bed beside Reece, then pulled the covers up to her neck. Lying there quietly and unmoving, all she could think about was the way Reece looked naked. Big, tall, muscular. His arms, legs and chest covered with dark brown hair. He possessed an aura of strength and ruggedness, from his thick, overly long brown hair to his wide chest, to his impressive manhood.

Elizabeth shuddered at the thought of the way Reece had touched her, the memory of his lips at her breasts, his hands fondling her to the point of arousal. As the minutes passed, Elizabeth relaxed, her mind centered on the big, naked man lying beside her. She drifted off into sleep, succumbing to dreams of Reece Landry. His smile. His amber eyes. His naked, aroused body covering her.

Reece lay awake for hours, feigning sleep but unable to rest knowing that Elizabeth lay next to him. She'd fallen asleep quite some time ago. The sleep of the innocent. A clear conscience and a pure heart.

He'd done some damn fool things in his life, but his actions with Elizabeth tonight had to top the list. Had he actually been stupid enough to think she'd fall for his rapist act? He had spent four days alone with her in her cabin and had allowed her to get to know him, the real Reece Landry, the man he barely knew himself.

She hadn't bought the story of his rendezvous with Luanne and she hadn't believed him capable of brutalizing her. He had to face the facts. Elizabeth Mallory, for whatever misguided reasons, was determined to stand by his side, to march head-on into disaster, to go the limit to help him prove his innocence. What had he ever done to deserve the loyalty and trust of a woman like Elizabeth?

Did he dare believe what she believed? That they were predestined to meet? That she and she alone could save him?

Whether he believed or didn't wasn't the point. The point was that Elizabeth was in his life and in it to stay. Now, the question was, what the hell was he going to do with her?

Elizabeth snuggled against him, resting her head on his shoulder, cuddling her body into his. Swallowing, Reece opened his eyes and looked at her. She was asleep, and practically in his arms. Strange thing was that as many women as he'd bedded over the years, he'd never slept the whole night with one. Not ever.

A narrow ridge of illumination filtered through the window where the flowery drapes didn't quite meet, a combination of moonlight and fluorescent motel sign. Rising up on one elbow, Reece gazed down at Elizabeth. For a split second his heart stopped. She was so incredibly lovely, and he wanted her desperately.

Her dark hair looked like black silk in the shadowy room. Reece lifted a strand and brought it to his lips, then dropped it, watching it fall back to her shoulder. Her eyelashes were long and thick, her cheekbones high and only slightly rounded. And her lips—those full, luscious lips. The memory of how those lips had felt when he'd kissed her was enough to arouse him.

When she nestled more snugly against him, Reece slipped his arm under her, lifting her even closer to his side. Still asleep, she laid her arm across his chest, her fingers curling around his hair. He sucked in a deep breath.

He touched her cheek with his fingertip, tracing the lines of her face, slowly, lovingly. She moaned in her sleep, pressing her body into his. He leaned over and kissed her tenderly on the lips, then drew her securely into his arms.

Whatever tomorrow brought, Reece knew one thing for certain. He wasn't going to let anything or anyone hurt this woman. Not ever. And that included him.

The jarring ring of the telephone woke Reece instantly. Instinctively reaching toward the nightstand, he grabbed the phone. Suddenly he realized that there was a woman in the bed with him, a woman lying there beside him, her head resting on his arm. Elizabeth! She opened her eyes and smiled at him.

"Answer the phone," she said.

Glancing from her sleep-fresh face to the phone in his hand, Reece growled at the caller. "Yeah?"

"It's Flossie, sugar."

"Flossie?" Reece sat upright in the bed.

"Look, you've got to hightail it out of there as fast as you can. Luanne just called me and said she remembered where she'd seen you—that Mr. Jones in number nineteen was that Landry fellow who killed old man Stanton."

"Dammit!" Reece jumped out of bed. "Can you trust her to keep her mouth shut?"

"Not hardly," Flossie said. "Not where there's money involved. Guess you didn't know that your half brother has put up a fifty-thousand-dollar reward for information leading to your capture."

"Hell!" Reece held his hand over the bottom half of the phone and turned to Elizabeth. "Get our stuff together. Quick. We're leaving."

"Look, sugar, I tried to persuade Luanne that she was wrong, but she said she planned on calling the sheriff just in case she was right. They're liable to show up here any minute now. I'll do whatever I can to stall them, but—"

"Thanks, Flossie. I owe you one," Reece said.

"You don't owe me nothing, sugar. I just wish you hadn't come back to Newell. They're all out to get you, and the Stantons won't rest until you're back behind bars."

"I won't let that happen."

"You got some place you can go?" Flossie asked.

"B.K.'s old hunting lodge."

"I wouldn't go there. The sheriff might not check it out, but you don't need to take any chances. Kenny's liable to remember you've been to the lodge. You need some place the law would never look."

"What about your old place on Lilac Road?" Reece asked.

"That place has been condemned for nearly a year," Flossie told him. "Besides, the sheriff is bound to check out any place you've ever been connected with."

Reece hadn't thought beyond his plan to hide out at B.K.'s cabin, but he realized that Flossie was right. Any place the law could connect him to would be suspect.

"I've got it! The Burtons' summer house up at the lake in Spruce Pine."

"Perfect," Flossie agreed. "Get going, boy, and good luck. If there's anything I can do to help you, just let me know."

"I've got a friend with me." Reece watched Elizabeth stuff their belongings into their bags. "If she ever needs anything, Flossie, I'd appreciate your looking out for her."

"Sure thing, sugar. What's her name?"

"Elizabeth." Reece hung up the phone, grabbed his jeans and shirt as Elizabeth threw them across the bed, and dressed hurriedly. By the time he was fully clothed, she was pulling on her boots.

Reece grabbed her by the shoulders. "Do you still feel the way you did last night? Are you still determined to stay with me and help me prove who killed my father?"

"You know I am."

"Okay, then, listen carefully. I'm going to take your Jeep and drive out to Spruce Pine. An acquaintance of mine took me to her parents' summer house up there once. No one ever uses the place in the winter." At least, he hoped no one would be using it while he and Elizabeth were there. Tracy Burton Stanton occasionally used her parents' summer cottage during the off-season as a hide-away to take her lovers. She'd taken him there once.

"I'll follow right behind you," Elizabeth said.

"The place is pretty isolated, so we should be safe there, at least for a few days." Reece knew Tracy would never tell a soul that her brother-in-law knew where her parents' summer house was located. After all, she'd have to explain why she'd taken him there. "Don't follow me right away. Just in case. Do you understand?"

Elizabeth nodded her head.

"After I leave, you drive around to the office and tell Flossie who you are. She'll give you directions to the Burtons' summer place. She's been up there a few times herself, entertaining old man Burton and his friends."

"Can you trust this Flossie?" Elizabeth wondered what sort of woman the former madam was, and why Reece was acting out of character by letting the woman know his whereabouts.

"A man would be a fool to trust Flossie with his money or his heart, but he can trust her not to turn him in to the law." Reece cradled Elizabeth's chin in the curve of his thumb and index finger. "We'll need some supplies. Stop at a store on the way and get whatever you think we'll need to last a few days. Once we're safely hidden away, we'll plan our strategy."

"I'll follow your instructions." Elizabeth threw her arms around him, hugging him fiercely. "I'll meet you as soon as I can."

Reece pulled out of her embrace. "I've got to go, Lizzie." He threw his bag over his shoulder, opened the door and walked outside.

"Please be careful." She stood in the doorway, watching him get into the Jeep and drive away.

Elizabeth closed the motel door behind her, walked out to Sam's vintage T-Bird and put her bag in the trunk. She glanced toward the office, near the main entrance to the motel. Four sheriff's vehicles screeched into the driveway. A man she assumed was the sheriff emerged from the first car and went inside the office. Elizabeth got into her car and drove around toward the office, parking and waiting until the sheriff came out and walked around to the car directly behind him. Elizabeth was too far away to hear what was being said, but she knew they were discussing Reece. She sensed the high tension, the raised level of adrenaline in the officers forming the search party.

She kept hearing the words *murderer, Landry, own father, dead or alive* tumbling around in her mind, and knew the officers were intent on capturing Reece at any cost.

The sheriff led the pack as they pulled up outside room nineteen, several men emerging from their vehicles, their guns pulled, as the sheriff lifted his bullhorn and called for Reece Landry to surrender.

Elizabeth's mouth felt dry, her hands damp. Her stomach twisted into knots. Hatred. The sheriff's deputies hated Reece Landry. They hated him not only because he had escaped but because they thought of him as a bad seed, a man capable of murdering his own father.

Clasping the key to number nineteen in her moist hand, Elizabeth marched into the office. The woman behind the desk glanced up at her.

"You checking out, sugar?" the six-foot redhead asked.

"Are you Flossie?" Elizabeth stared at the woman whose striking burgundy red hair had been draped into a French twist.

Flossie eyed Elizabeth, raising her black-lined, thinly tweezed eyebrows. "Yeah, sugar, I'm Flossie."

"Then, yes, I'm checking out." Elizabeth laid the key on the counter and waited for a response from Flossie.

Flossie picked up the key, then dropped it into the wastebasket under the counter. "What's your name?"

"Elizabeth."

"Elizabeth, huh? Well, has our friend left yet?"

"Only a few minutes ago." Elizabeth looked at Flossie, wondering if she dared trust her.

"Are you in a hurry or you got time for a cup of coffee?" Flossie nodded toward the coffee machine sitting at the end of the counter. "Might be a good idea for us to talk, and you could wait around and see what happens when Sheriff Bates finds out his man has slipped through his fingers."

"Luanne saw me last night," Elizabeth said.

"Well, we'll just skip the coffee, but I don't think you have to worry about Luanne telling the sheriff much about you. I don't know what you said or did to her last night, but you convinced her you were a witch. She won't tell anybody but me because she's afraid they'll think she's crazy." Flossie's wide red lips spread into a big grin.

"Thanks for everything, Flossie."

"You'd best be leaving, sugar."

Elizabeth reached out across the counter, taking Flossie's age-spotted, ring-adorned hand into hers. The two women exchanged knowing glances.

I've got to help this girl get away. She's important to Reece, and that's a first. Maybe she'll stand by him and he'll get himself out of this mess. Sensing Flossie's thoughts, Elizabeth breathed a sigh of relief.

"You know he's on his way to the Burtons' summer house by the lake. I need directions so I can go to him after I pick up some supplies."

Flossie looked past Elizabeth, out the glass front of the office. "They're busting in room nineteen right now."

Turning her head, Elizabeth watched as the deputies broke down the door and stormed inside.

"Tell me how to get to Spruce Pine, to the summer house."

"Take Highway 40 until you get to Midget Creek. There's a four-way stop. Take a left and keep going until you see a sign that says Oden's Bait and Tackle Shop. About a mile past Oden's is a turnoff on the right. Take it and stay on that gravel road until it forks in two different directions. Take another right. It'll turn into a dirt road before you reach the cottage. The house is pretty well hidden in a grove of trees."

"I'll find it. Thanks."

Flossie came out from behind the counter, sizing up Elizabeth. "I hope you love that boy, sugar. I hope to God you love him, 'cause if ever a man needed to be loved, Reece Landry does."

Did she love him? Elizabeth asked herself. Did she? She cared about him, longed to be with him, was willing to suffer going out into the world to help him, was taking a chance on being arrested for aiding and abetting a criminal.

"I care about him. I care a great deal." Elizabeth rushed outside into the cold morning air. Glancing toward room nineteen, she saw the sheriff and other officers standing around in a circle, discussing Reece Landry's second escape.

She slipped into the T-Bird, started the engine and drove out onto the highway. Within five minutes she turned onto Highway 40 and began looking for a minimart of some kind, one that had a pay telephone. About two miles up the road she pulled off at Joe's Market, asked the attendant at the full-service pump to fill the T-Bird and went inside to shop for supplies. Only a few customers wandered around, most of them people who'd stopped for gas. Elizabeth filled a hand basket with sandwich fixings, canned soups, milk and cereal and coffee, along with assorted items she thought they could use. She placed the basket on the checkout counter, then retrieved a six-pack of beer and a six-pack of cola from the wall cooler.

The middle-aged woman at the checkout counter smiled as she added up Elizabeth's purchases. "You new in town or just passing through?"

"Just passing through right now, on my way to meet a friend." When Elizabeth heard the bell hanging above the door tinkle, she turned to see a highway patrolman entering.

"Hey, there, Pete," the checker said. "Are you here for your regular?"

"Just coffee right now, Carolyn." The patrolman poured himself a cup from one of the two pots behind the counter, handed the checker the correct change and took a sip of the hot liquid. "I haven't got time for lunch. They've called an all-points bulletin for us to be on the lookout for Reece Landry. The night clerk over at the Sweet Rest thinks a customer who came in yesterday evening was this Landry guy."

"You mean he's here in Newell?" Carolyn rolled her big brown eyes heavenward. "Didn't know the man personally, but I can't imagine anybody in his shoes being fool enough to come back here, knowing he'd be recognized."

"Well, whoever this Mr. Jones was that spent the night in room nineteen, he got away this morning, and so did the woman who spent the night with him."

Carolyn grinned at Pete while she continued checking Elizabeth's groceries. "Yeah, well, I heard that Landry had a way with the ladies. Good-looking guy...uh...from what I could tell from his pictures in the paper. I remember something coming out during the trial that Kenny Stanton's wife said Landry was after her hot and heavy."

"Kenny Stanton's wife is a real looker. Can't blame Landry for giving it a try." Pete laughed, tipped his hat to Carolyn and Elizabeth, then walked toward the door, his disposable coffee cup in his hand.

"Do y'all know who the woman was with Landry?" Carolyn called out just as Pete opened the door.

"Got no idea, and the only description is sketchy. A brunette."

"Probably some hooker, if he was at the Sweet Rest."

"Yeah, more than likely."

Elizabeth watched the patrolman get into his car and drive away. Turning to the checker, she forced a smile. "Is this Landry man in trouble with the law?"

"Child, Reece Landry's been in trouble with the law all his life." Carolyn began sacking Elizabeth's groceries. "But he's an escaped convict now. He was convicted of murdering his own father, but he escaped on his way up to Arrendale less than a week ago."

"Why would he come back here?" Elizabeth picked up amusement in the woman's mind and heard words like *framed* and *innocent* and *inheritance* in her thoughts.

"I'd say he's a fool." Carolyn handed Elizabeth two sacks, then picked up the third. "I'll help you to your car with this one."

"Thanks."

Carolyn followed Elizabeth toward the door. "Reece Landry claimed he was innocent, and a few folks around here believed him. He wasn't old B.K. Stanton's legitimate son, if you know what I mean."

Elizabeth opened the door. "Weren't there any other suspects?"

"Plenty, but the sheriff didn't follow through on anything once they arrested the man the Stanton family wanted out of the way." Carolyn followed Elizabeth to the T-Bird and handed her the third sack after Elizabeth placed the others on the back floorboard. "If you come through this way again, stop by."

"I'll do that." Elizabeth slid behind the wheel of Sam's antique T-Bird, turned and waved at Carolyn.

Her round cheeks rosy from the winter wind, Carolyn waved back as she curved her lips into a friendly smile. Elizabeth had the oddest sensation that Carolyn knew she was somehow connected to Reece Landry, and like Flossie, Carolyn hoped that Elizabeth truly cared about Reece.

Elizabeth drove the car to the edge of the parking area where a pay telephone was located. Glancing back toward the market, she saw that Carolyn had returned inside. Elizabeth rummaged in her purse for a quarter.

Dialing the operator, she gave Sam's phone number and asked that the charges be reversed. Within seconds Sam came on the line.

"Are you in Newell?" he asked.

"I'm at a minimarket outside town at a pay phone," Elizabeth told him.

"Where's Landry?"

"We're in separate cars. He's taken the Jeep on out to a summer house in Spruce Pine. He thinks it's a safe place to hide out while we're searching for the real murderer."

"Are you all right, Elizabeth?"

She smiled, knowing full well that Sam wanted to ask about his precious '65 Thunderbird. "I'm fine and so is your car. It could get muddy when I drive out to the cottage. The place is located on a dirt road."

"Give it up, kiddo, and go home. I promise I'll do everything I can to help Landry."

"I want you to come to Newell, today, and meet us at the cottage. We have to form some sort of strategy. Reece is confused and not thinking straight or he never would have come back here. A woman at the motel recognized him and called the sheriff this morning."

"What motel?" Sam asked.

"The motel where Reece and I stayed last night."

"My God, Elizabeth, tell me you're not sleeping with that man!"

"I'm not sleeping with Reece." She grinned, remembering waking this morning in Reece's arms. "Well, I did sleep with him last night, but—"

"I'll kill him!"

"Calm down, Sam. We just shared the same bed. I'm still as pure as the driven snow."

"This is no joking matter. Landry may not have killed his father, but he's no saint. As a matter of fact, he's a real bad boy and has the reputation to prove it."

Elizabeth sighed. Sam should know better than to try to convince her to do anything she didn't want to do. "I'm not leaving him."

"What's going on, Elizabeth? Really?"

"I think I may be falling in love with Reece."

Sam groaned. "Do you think he loves you?"

"No," Elizabeth admitted. "Reece doesn't know what love is, but he will. He needs me, Sam. Even Aunt Margaret says I'm his only hope, that no one else can save him from himself."

"Why do you need Aunt Margaret to read Landry's mind, to see into his future? Isn't your crystal ball working?"

"Now who's trying to be funny?" Elizabeth asked. "I can't see into

Reece's future. I haven't picked up any images about what's going to happen to him. And I told you I can't get inside his head, except every once in a while. When he lets me."

"Well, I'll be damned. A mind you can't read and a future you can't predict. You really are taking him on faith, aren't you?"

"I care so much about Reece, about what happens to him. He's lived a very hard life. He deserves some happiness."

"Look, kiddo, you've got yourself involved in this man's problems and you're sexually attracted to him. But don't just assume you're falling in love with him." Sam cleared his throat. "Sexual attraction isn't love, and neither is caring about someone. You could easily be mistaking your desire to set things right in Landry's life with love."

"I know." Elizabeth realized far better than Sam did that she was totally confused where her feelings for Reece Landry were concerned. "That's why I said that I think I'm falling in love with him. I've never been in love before, and I'm not sure."

"Take things slow and easy."

"Sam, please fly out of Atlanta as soon as you can. We really need your help. I'll give you the directions to the cottage."

"Even if Landry is innocent, we may not be able to prove it," Sam told her. "Have you ever considered that possibility? Are you willing to stay on the run for the rest of your life?"

"Reece *is* innocent, and together the three of us are going to prove it."

"Have you told Landry that you're involving me in this, that I'm coming to Newell?"

"No, not yet. Why?"

"Because he may not like the idea of me trying to help him," Sam said. "I don't think Landry trusts me any more than I trust him."

"Well, that's plain stupid. You trust me and Reece trusts me, and I trust both of you, so it stands to reason that the two of you should trust each other."

"Yeah, sure. Now give me the directions to that summer house."

Elizabeth gave him the details and wished him a safe trip.

"Kiddo, you be careful."

"I will, Sam. I promise."

She replaced the telephone slowly, her hand lingering on the cool plastic. She'd loved Sam all her life. He was her brother, her uncle, her father figure and her friend. She wanted Sam to like Reece, to trust him. And she wanted Reece to feel the same way about Sam.

Reece paced back and forth on the front porch of the Burtons' summer house, the February sun warming him as surely as the winter wind chilled him. Where the hell is she? he wondered. She'd had more than enough time to pick up a few supplies and get to the cottage. What if the sheriff had picked her up? What if she'd been in an accident? What if she'd changed her mind and decided not to join him?

If she had any sense at all, she was on her way back to Sequana Falls and as far away from him as she could get. In the cold light of day she might have realized what a mistake she'd made following a fugitive, a man balanced between life and death.

A hard knot formed in his gut. He slammed his fists down on the pristine white wooden banister surrounding the porch. Dammit, he didn't want to care whether she was on her way to him or on her way back to Sequana Falls. He didn't want it to matter, but it did. There was something addictive about Elizabeth Mallory, about the way she looked at him, the way she put her strong arms around him, the way she said his name. In less than a week she'd gotten under his skin. She'd made him want her near. No other woman had ever done that.

Reece glanced up at the blue-gray sky, heavy white clouds floating past, the sun noonday high. In the distance he heard a car. His heartbeat accelerated. Maybe it was Elizabeth; maybe it was the sheriff. He went inside the cottage, positioning himself beside one of the huge front windows, and waited for the car's approach. Peering around the side of the window, he saw the black '65 Thunderbird round the curve in the dirt road.

Elizabeth! She'd come to him. She hadn't deserted him. A spiral of sweet, unadulterated joy sprang up inside him and spread through his body and mind, and even invaded his heart.

Swinging open the front door, he rushed out onto the porch, but stopped himself from running into the yard to meet her. His heartbeat roared in his ears. Excitement raced along his nerve endings.

He wasn't alone.

Elizabeth flung open the car door, stepped outside and waved at Reece. Dear Lord, he was so handsome, so big and virile and utterly beautiful standing there on the gingerbread-trimmed porch, Sam's old jeans clinging to his lean, muscled hips and legs. She wanted to run to him, throw her arms around him and tell him how glad she was to be with him.

Did she love Reece Landry, a man she'd met less than a week ago, yet a man she'd known in her heart for months? Her feelings for Reece were complicated, her empathy for him, her desire to help him and the sexual attraction she felt all mixed together. She knew one thing for certain—she had never felt about another man the way she felt about Reece, and the intensity of those feelings frightened her.

Reece headed straight for her. "I was beginning to wonder if you'd come to your senses and gone back to Sequana Falls."

For one brief instant Elizabeth felt Reece's fear—he'd been afraid that she had left him. Swallowing down the overwhelming emotions choking her, Elizabeth smiled, secure in her knowledge that, despite how much Reece protested, he truly wanted her at his side.

"It took a while to get the supplies. The checker was talkative. And a highway patrolman came in the store and they started discussing you and your second escape."

Reaching inside the car, Elizabeth picked up a grocery sack and handed it to Reece. "Can you carry two?" she asked.

Nodding, he accepted the second sack. Elizabeth took the third and they walked toward the cottage. She glanced around, taking in the two-story white frame house with dark green shutters and roof. A wraparound porch, graced with carved banisters, circled the house.

"Why did you decide to come here instead of your father's hunting lodge?" Elizabeth asked, wondering who owned this lovely summer cottage.

"Flossie pointed out that the sheriff might have the hunting lodge under surveillance, since Kenny would alert them that I knew how to locate the lodge."

"You spent time with your father at his hunting lodge?"

"Yeah. Once. B.K. liked roughing it, liked hunting. He took Kenny and me up to his lodge to do some hunting last year." Reece led Elizabeth up the porch and inside the house.

Just as she had suspected, the interior had been perfectly decorated by someone with good taste and money. Pastel, spring colors dominated the living room. Fragile lace curtains had been pulled back to expose the row of French windows facing the front porch. Sturdy white wicker furniture held thick cushions and pillows covered in blue, rose and cream floral prints. A brass screen stood in front of the fireplace, which had been painted a pale cream and was adorned with a simple wooden mantel. A cheerful fire burned brightly in the fireplace.

Elizabeth followed Reece into the kitchen, an open area adjacent to the living room. The stainless steel appliances were modern and matched the sink and countertops. White hexagonal tiles covered the floor and glass-fronted white cabinets lined the walls. "I didn't realize that you ever socialized with your father and his family."

Reece helped Elizabeth unsack the supplies and place them in the empty cupboards, storing the beer and colas in the double-wide refrigerator.

"I didn't socialize with the family. Not really. I was never invited to their house, but B.K. saw to it that I attended some of the same social functions." Reece retrieved one of the beer bottles, snapping the lid with a decorative metallic opener attached to the side of the refrigerator. "The hunting trip wasn't socializing. It was a contest B.K. contrived to see which one of his sons was as rough and tough and mean as he was."

Elizabeth watched Reece put the beer bottle to his lips and pour the liquid into his mouth. "Are you saying that your father deliberately encouraged a rivalry between you and his other son?"

After downing a third of the beer, Reece set the bottle on the counter and wiped his mouth. "I'm saying that B. K. Stanton's legitimate son was a disappointment to him. Kenny lived the good life. Never had to get his hands dirty. He's a spoiled, weak mama's boy."

"Everything you're not."

"Everything that B.K. and Alice Stanton's wealth and social positions made him, and yet, he wasn't what B.K. wanted." Looking toward the front of the cottage, Reece gazed out the windows. "Are your bags in the trunk of your car?"

Elizabeth nodded. When Reece walked past her, she reached out, laying her hand on his chest. "Your father discovered that you were more of a man than his other son, is that it? He found that you possessed the qualities he admired, the qualities he couldn't find in Kenny."

Reece glanced down at her hand. "Yeah. I'm the exact opposite of my big brother. And our father finally saw how he could use those differences to his advantage. He thought that if he threw me up in Kenny's face often enough, Kenny would eventually grow a backbone and become the son B.K. wanted." Reece walked away from Elizabeth and out onto the porch.

A stinging warmth of pain spread through her when she realized how deeply Reece had been affected by his father's manipulation. She met him at the door when he returned with her bags.

"There is one bedroom downstairs and two upstairs. They're all pretty much the same. I'll put your bag in here." Opening the door to the downstairs bedroom, Reece walked in, tossed the bag on the old iron bed and turned quickly, his body colliding with Elizabeth's. He grabbed her by the shoulders to steady her.

"Looks like we won't need to share a bed tonight," she said. The memory of waking in the early-morning hours to find herself snuggled into Reece's arms warmed Elizabeth with the hope of what lay ahead for them.

"Not unless you ask me real nice," he said.

"Oh?"

Reece laughed. "I'll have to hunt up some more firewood, since our only source of heat is the fireplace. There used to be some electrical heaters the Burtons kept for cool autumn nights, but since they use this place mostly in the summer, I don't think they keep the heaters around anymore. If you get cold in the night, you can always come get in bed with me."

"I'll keep that in mind." She smiled, trying to imitate his jesting. But talking about sharing a bed with Reece reminded her just how much she had liked awakening in his arms this morning. Reece was a virile man, and if they shared a bed again, he would probably expect them to have sex. Was she ready for such an important step in their relationship? More importantly, was Reece ready?

"Did you have any problems finding this place?" Reece asked.

"No problems. Flossie's instructions were perfect."

"The sheriff didn't try to stop you or question you, did he?"

"I left before they gave up searching the motel for you."

Reece turned toward the fireplace, warming his hands. He'd thought twice about building a fire in the fireplace, since a helicopter might spot the smoke, but he'd been listening to news on the radio and there had been no mention of a search outside Newell. Roadblocks had been set up and a manhunt begun, but the law figured Reece Landry was either on his way out of town and they'd catch him at a roadblock or that he was hiding out in one of his old haunts and a door-to-door search might reveal his whereabouts. The police had no reason to come snooping around Spruce Pine, no reason to connect him with Tracy Burton Stanton's parents or their summer house.

"Lizzie, you shouldn't be here with me. You shouldn't be involved in this."

"I thought we'd already settled that argument once and for all," Elizabeth said. "I'm staying and that's all there is to it."

"I'm no good, Elizabeth." Reece kept his back to her, his focus on the fire in front of him. "If you stay with me, I could get you killed, or at the very least, break your heart."

Elizabeth refused to acknowledge the possibility that Reece was right. Together they would prove Reece's innocence and come through this nightmare. And she would save Reece, save him from himself. If he broke her heart in the process, she would survive.

"Are you hungry?" she asked. "I'm starving. I haven't had a bite to eat since I stopped for a hamburger on the way to Newell yesterday."

Reece slapped his hands against his hips, then rubbed them up and down his thighs. He turned to face her. "Yeah, sure. I'm hungry."

"Let's fix lunch. I can open a can of tomato soup and make some grilled cheese sandwiches."

"I'll do the soup," Reece said. "You fix the sandwiches."

Elizabeth spread out the bread, cheese and margarine on the stainless steel counter. "Whose place is this, anyway?"

"It belongs to Albert and Edna Burton." Reece placed the can of soup under the can opener.

"How do you know these people?"

"What difference does it make?"

"Just curious, I guess." Elizabeth spread margarine on the bread. "I have a feeling you're hiding something from me."

Reece jerked a metal pot from a bottom cupboard. "I know the Burtons' daughter."

"Is she one of your old girlfriends?"

"No." Reece poured the soup into the pot, then filled the empty can with water and added it to the mixture.

"Why are you being so secretive?" Elizabeth laid the sliced cheese on the bread.

Reece set the soup pot on the stove, adjusted the heat and turned to face Elizabeth. "Albert and Edna Burton's daughter married Kenny Stanton."

"This house belongs to your sister-in-law's parents?"

"Yeah."

"How did you know about this place? Did Flossie tell you about it?" Elizabeth remembered what Carolyn, the checkout clerk at the minimart, had said about Tracy Stanton accusing Reece of coming on to her hot and heavy. Had Reece had an affair with his brother's wife? Had they shared a secret rendezvous at her parents' summer house?

"Like I told you, Flossie had entertained Albert Burton and some of his friends out here when Mrs. Burton was otherwise occupied."

Reece handed Elizabeth a frying pan he'd pulled out of the cupboard where the cooking utensils were stored.

"What about you? Obviously you know your way around this kitchen. You've been here before, haven't you? You've been here with Tracy Stanton."

"I checked the kitchen out while I was waiting for you. As a matter of fact, I gave the whole house a once-over." Reece placed his hands on Elizabeth's shoulders. She laid the sandwiches in the skillet and placed the skillet on the stove.

"What kind of relationship do you have with your brother's wife?"

"I don't have a relationship with Tracy."

"Then why did she make the statement at your trial that you were after her, and I quote, 'hot and heavy'?"

"Because she was still angry with me for turning her down." Reece released Elizabeth's shoulders. "Tracy was after *me* hot and heavy. She invited me up here to her parents' summer house one weekend over a year ago."

"You met her here?"

"Yeah. I was curious. I knew what she wanted, and I have to admit that the idea of cuckolding Kenny tempted me."

"What happened?"

"We kissed." Reece closed his eyes, remembering how close he'd come to carrying his brother's wife to bed. "We both got pretty steamed up, but then I put a stop to things. Tracy Burton Stanton might have money and education and generations of blue-blooded breeding, but I realized that she wasn't any different from the girls who used to work for Flossie." Reece laughed, the sound a mirthless grunt. "The only difference was she gave it away for free."

"You didn't make love to Tracy Stanton?"

"I don't make love to women," Reece said. "I have sex with them. But I didn't have sex with Tracy."

"I'm glad," Elizabeth said. "I'm very glad."

"Yeah? Well, funny thing is, Lizzie, so am I."

Thirty minutes later Elizabeth and Reece sat at the small kitchen table, an oak antique flanked by four Windsor chairs, and sipped on second cups of coffee and nibbled on oatmeal raisin cookies.

"One of the reasons it took me a while to get here is that I stopped at a pay phone and called Sam." Elizabeth glanced at Reece. He stared at her, his amber eyes void of any emotion.

"Even when you're on the run with another man, you still have to check in with Dundee?" Reece set down his cup with a resounding thud, warm coffee spilling out onto the tabletop. "What sort of hold does that guy have over you?"

Elizabeth stared at Reece in disbelief. He was jealous. Reece was jealous of Sam. She suppressed her laughter. "Sam's family. He's been like a big brother to me most of my life." She reached across the table, placing her hand atop Reece's fist. "Sam was a DEA agent for years, then something happened that made him want out, and he formed his own private security agency in Atlanta. He knows a lot about investigating people and protecting them."

"Sounds like good old Sam is the answer to our prayers." Huffing, Reece jerked his hand away from Elizabeth.

"Sam's coming to Newell. Today."

"What the hell for?"

"He's already set things in motion to investigate B. K. Stanton's death and discover other suspects. He'll have his first real report for us this afternoon."

Tightening his jaw and clenching his teeth, Reece breathed deeply. "It may have slipped your notice, but we don't have a telephone out here."

"Sam isn't going to phone me. He's coming out here to the cottage."

Reece jumped up, knocking his chair backward in the process. "You told Dundee where we were? You gave him directions to this place?"

"Yes, I did. And I don't see why you're so upset."

Reece glared down at her. "You don't see why I'm..." Reece's amber eyes glowed with yellow fire. "You betrayed me, Lizzie. Surely you aren't stupid enough to think that Dundee wants to help me. All he wants is to get you away from me, to keep you safe. He's probably already called the sheriff."

Elizabeth scooted back her chair and stood. "I would never betray you, Reece. Never. Sam won't call the sheriff, and he will help you."

"Because he loves you!"

"Yes, because he loves me, and he knows my instincts are seldom wrong."

"I hope you're right about Dundee, because if you're wrong..." Reece walked out of the kitchen, through the back door and into the small clearing behind the house.

If he had any sense at all, he'd take Elizabeth's Jeep and get the hell out of Newell. He'd leave her behind, her and her big brother Dundee. Did he dare stay and trust a man he didn't even know, a man whose primary interest in him was the woman they had in common? And could he really trust Elizabeth? Just because every time he looked at her, he wanted to take her didn't mean he could trust her.

What the hell was he going to do? Would he be a fool to stay and put his life and his freedom in Elizabeth Mallory's hands? Or would he be a bigger fool to run away from his one chance to prove himself innocent and from the one woman who'd ever really cared about him?

CHAPTER 8

Elizabeth sat alone inside the Burtons' summer house. Reece had been outside for the past couple of hours. First he'd parked Sam's '65 T-Bird at the back of the house, beside the Jeep, then he'd taken off into the woods, saying only that he was going to take a walk down by the lake.

For the twentieth time she checked her watch, wondering when Sam would arrive and how long Reece was going to stay outside sulking. She wasn't accustomed to being alone; MacDatho was nearly always at her side. She wished she could have brought him with her, but where a lone woman might go practically unnoticed, no one would forget a huge black wolf-dog.

The back door creaked. Elizabeth tensed. Turning her head just a fraction, she saw Reece enter the kitchen.

"It's getting colder out there," he said. "I thought I'd make some fresh coffee, but it looks like you've already done that." He glanced at the freshly filled coffeepot.

"It's going to snow before dark." Elizabeth turned back around, focusing her attention on the fire.

"Does that mean Dundee will be snowed in here with us?" Reece picked up a clean coffee mug from the dish drain, grabbed a dish towel off the wall rack and lifted the coffeepot.

"There will be a light snow, just an inch or two. Sam should be here soon."

"Maybe he couldn't get a flight out of Atlanta." Reece poured the mug full of coffee, returned the pot to the coffeemaker and walked into the living room, sitting in a chair to the left of the wicker sofa where Elizabeth sat.

"Sam flies his own plane. A small twin-engine Cessna. He probably rented a car at the airport and is on his way here now."

"Quite a man, our Mr. Dundee." Reece leaned over, resting his hands between his spread knees, the warm mug secure in his grasp. "Former DEA agent, owns his own business, flies his own plane. I can hardly wait to meet this guy."

"He's anxious to meet you, too." Tilting her chin up, Elizabeth glared at Reece. "You see, you're the first man I've ever run away with, and Sam doesn't trust you any more than you trust him."

"Sounds like he's very protective when it comes to screening the men in your life." Reece sipped his coffee. "Does he warn off all men you show an interest in or just the ones who are escaped convicts?"

"There haven't been any men in my life for Sam to screen." Elizabeth bowed her head, looking down at her lap where she'd laid her clasped hands. "You're the first."

Reece strangled on his coffee. The mug in his unsteady hand hit the wooden floor. "Damn!"

Elizabeth jumped up, rushed to the kitchen for a towel and returned to mop up the spilled coffee. Reece knelt beside her, picking up the broken pieces of the ceramic mug. He threw the shards into the fireplace. Elizabeth wiped the floor clean.

She rested on her knees in front of him. He laid his hand on her shoulder. She froze at his touch.

"Clarify things for me, will you, Lizzie?" Taking her hands in his, Reece lifted her to her feet, took the soaked towel from her and threw it across the room toward the kitchen area. "My mind has gone into overdrive here and I'm thinking some pretty crazy thoughts. I don't think you said what I thought you said. Or at least, I don't think I understood you right."

"What didn't you understand? That Sam has always considered

himself my protector? That Sam doesn't trust you? That there have never been any men in my life for Sam to screen?" Elizabeth's hands trembled.

Reece pulled her to him, holding her hands between their bodies. "How old are you, Elizabeth?"

"Twenty-six."

Reece sighed. "Well, you've had boyfriends, dated, had a few experiences over the years. Right?"

"I dated some in college."

Reece grinned. "Good. Then I did misunderstand when you said I was the first."

Elizabeth looked into his eyes, those lone-wolf amber eyes. They were so warm, so intensely inviting. "I dated several silly boys who were scared off once they found out I could read their minds. Sam worried about me when I went away to school, but he didn't worry about me getting in trouble with boys. He knew how difficult it would be for me to control all the energy I'd receive from other people. He doubted any boy could sweet-talk me into something I didn't want to do, since I would be able to perceive his motive."

"Okay, so you dated silly boys in college who couldn't deal with your hocus-pocus routine. What about after college? There had to have been men who didn't give a damn that you were psychic."

"Does it bother you, Reece? That I'm psychic? That usually I can predict the future, that sometimes I'm aware of events occurring miles away, that often I can read people's minds?"

Dropping her hands, Reece grabbed her face and pulled her to him. "I'm on the run with a virgin, aren't I, Elizabeth? There really hasn't been another man in your life, has there?"

"You're the first, Reece."

Looking at her face, flushed and glowing with emotion, gazing into those pure, honest blue eyes was almost more than Reece could bear. "Of all the men on earth, baby, why me?"

"You came to me, Reece, in my mind. I felt your pain and anger and hatred. I sensed your loneliness. I could see you locked in a tiny cage. You invaded my life." Tears filled her eyes. "You became the stranger in my heart."

"Elizabeth?"

"It was meant for me to save you. I'm the only one who can. Aunt Margaret knows it. I know it." Tears spilled from her eyes, streaking her cheeks. "You know it, too, Reece. In your heart."

"Can you read my mind? Can you see into my future?"

"I can't see your future, Reece. I've tried. Something is blocking my vision. Aunt Margaret says it's because our futures are entwined and I have never allowed myself to look into my own future. I've been too afraid." She slipped her arms around his waist. "And I can't read your mind. I told you that you shield your thoughts and your emotions from me most of the time. Every once in a while I pick up on a few things."

"Do you know what I'm thinking right now, Lizzie? What I'm feeling?" His lips took hers in a wild yet tender kiss, his mouth covering hers, tasting, licking, savoring the sweetness of her innocence.

He cradled her head in one hand and ran his other hand down her back, pushing her forward, holding her against his arousal. Elizabeth clung to him, her arms lifting, her hands caressing the corded muscles in his back. When he slipped his tongue inside her mouth, she moaned, bunching the material of his shirt into her fist.

Reece ended the kiss quickly, his body still throbbing with need. He heard a car. Gulping for air as she pulled away from him, Elizabeth glanced toward the windows. The afternoon sun hung low in the cloudy sky. A gray Buick Regal stopped in the driveway in front of the cottage. Sam Dundee, all six feet four inches of him, emerged.

"It's Sam." Elizabeth wiped the loose strands of her hair away from her face, took a deep breath and rushed to the front door.

Reece followed her, halting directly behind her when she opened the door and stepped out onto the porch. So that is Sam Dundee, Reece thought. About an inch taller than me, fifteen pounds heavier and a good five or six years older. And by the looks of his suit, overcoat, shoes and gold watch, a hell of a lot richer.

When Elizabeth started to go to Sam, Reece grabbed her by the shoulders, holding her in place on the porch in front of him. She stopped immediately, relaxing in his grasp.

Reece stared at Sam when the other man reached the bottom of the porch steps. Their gazes locked. Steel blue-gray eyes met cold gold-amber. Reece recognized the look in Dundee's eyes, the expression on his face. One strong warrior always recognized another.

"Come on inside, Sam," Elizabeth said. "It's freezing out here." She pulled away from Reece's hold; he let her go.

Sam walked up the steps, reached out and took Elizabeth into his arms. The blood ran cold in Reece's veins. He didn't like seeing Elizabeth in another man's arms, especially a man like Dundee. It took every ounce of his willpower not to jerk her away.

"Thanks for coming." Elizabeth hugged Sam, thankful, as she had always been, that he was a part of her life.

"You knew I would." With his arm around Elizabeth, Sam turned to Reece. "You must be Landry."

"Yeah. And you must be the guy that Lizzie thinks can walk on water."

Sam grinned, squeezed Elizabeth's shoulder and held out a hand to Reece. Reece accepted the greeting, a quick, hard handshake, each man putting the other on notice. *Elizabeth Mallory is important to me.*

"Lizzie, huh?" Sam laughed. "Never thought of you as Lizzie."

Elizabeth laughed. "Come on, you two, let's go warm ourselves in front of the fire."

Reece waited for Elizabeth and Sam to enter the cottage, then followed them. After laying Sam's overcoat on the back of the wicker sofa, Elizabeth motioned for him to sit.

"Would you like a cup of coffee?" she asked him.

Sam sat down, then glanced over at Reece. "Let's talk business, Landry."

"Now, Sam." Elizabeth sat beside her big-brother protector.

"I don't like Elizabeth being here. Every minute she's with you, she's in danger," Sam said. "I'll do everything I can to help you prove your innocence, but your best bet is to surrender to the sheriff and let me find some evidence that will warrant your lawyer getting you an appeal."

Reece crossed the room to stand in front of the fireplace. "Have you already called the sheriff? Told him where he can find me?"

"I don't work that way, Landry. For whatever reason, Elizabeth has taken on your problems. She's determined to help you, and I'm determined to help her and protect her."

"The last thing we need is for you two to argue," Elizabeth said.

"I think Landry needs to know where I stand." Sam unbuttoned his charcoal gray pin-striped coat, exposing the pristine whiteness of his shirt, his tie a crimson stain against the purity. "If Elizabeth believes you're innocent, then I'm willing to do whatever it takes to find the real murderer. I think you should turn yourself in, but I haven't betrayed you and I won't. I don't like Elizabeth's involvement with you because I think you can get her in big trouble. I don't want her to stay with you. I want her to leave here with me this afternoon."

"I'm not leaving." Elizabeth placed her hand on Sam's where he'd rested it on the back of the sofa. "Tell us what you've found out, and then we'll all work together to figure out where we go from here." She glanced up at Reece. "Sit down."

Reece took the chair to the left of the sofa, the one closest to Elizabeth. Leaning back, he folded his arms across his chest. "Let's hear it. What has the great man found out?"

Elizabeth scowled at Reece. "Go ahead, Sam. Don't pay any attention to Reece. I haven't had a chance to work on his manners yet."

"How much have you told Elizabeth?" Sam asked Reece.

"About what?" Reece widened his eyes, a mocking grin on his face.

"About your past. About your life."

"She knows I'm a worthless bastard who's been convicted of murdering his father," Reece said.

"I know the whole story." Elizabeth felt torn between her need to comfort Reece and her need to make Sam understand her feelings.

Sam glanced at Elizabeth, then at Reece. "All right. Then it's safe to say it won't come as a surprise to hear that Reece Landry has a few enemies in Newell, enemies with money and power who are very pleased that he was convicted of B. K. Stanton's murder."

"That's all you've found out?" Reece chuckled.

"You've also got a few friends, including your sister. She's the one person who might be able to help us." Standing, Sam shoved his hands into his pants pockets. "Just from my preliminary inquiries I think there's a good possibility that you were framed, and I think your brother and his mother could be our prime suspects. After all, they, and your sister, Christina, stood to lose a lot of money if you weren't convicted of murder."

"What do you mean?" Elizabeth asked.

"My old man made a new will shortly before he was killed," Reece said. "But he didn't bother telling anyone, including me. The only person who knew, other than B.K. himself, was the family lawyer, Willard Moran." Reece tossed his head back, blew out his breath and looked up at the ceiling. "I think that's the reason B.K. asked me to come by his house that night. The night he was shot."

"He named you in his will?" Elizabeth wanted to put her arms around Reece, to comfort him, to share the pain he felt.

"B. K. Stanton left Reece one-third of everything he possessed." Sam paced back and forth in front of the fireplace. "After thirty-two years he was finally acknowledging Reece as his son."

Reece sat up straight, looked across the room and out the windows, his gaze not really focused. "Damn generous of him, wasn't it?" Reece laughed. "The really funny thing is that I think he did it because he knew how furious it would make Kenny and Alice."

"Look, bottom line here is that Stanton's whole family had reason to kill him," Sam said. "He and Kenny never got along. B.K. completely controlled his son's life. He even handpicked Tracy Burton for Kenny's wife.

"The man had been betraying Alice with other women most of their married life. It was no secret that she despised her husband." Sam glanced over at Elizabeth, never slowing as he paced back and forth. "And the whole town knows that Christina Stanton never forgave her father for paying off her fiancé to dump her about ten years ago because B.K. didn't think the man was good enough for his daughter." Sam stopped pacing, then looked down at Reece. "And your stepfather had motive to kill Stanton. From what I've learned, Harry Gunn had threatened to kill his wife's former lover on more than one occasion."

"Good old Harry." Reece shook his head. He didn't know who he'd hated the most over the years—B. K. Stanton or Harry Gunn.

"So, it looks like we've got ourselves a full cast of suspects," Sam said. "I've set up an appointment with Gary Elkins in the morning. He's eager for us to work together. Your lawyer believes you're innocent."

"Does he?" Reece asked, glancing up at Sam. "Since Christina's money paid for his services, I was never quite certain where his loyalties lay."

"You don't trust anybody, do you, Landry?"

Reece stood, facing Sam. Two big, tall men sizing up each other. "Something tells me you're not the trusting sort, either, Dundee. You sure as hell don't trust me with Elizabeth, do you?"

Elizabeth jumped up off the sofa, standing in front of Reece and Sam, her body separating the two men, the three of them creating a human triangle. "We're going to have to trust one another. It's the only way we can prove Reece's innocence."

Sam turned, taking Elizabeth by the arm. "He's right about my not trusting him with you, kiddo. You shouldn't be in the middle of this mess. I want you to come with me, today. We'll both stay in Newell, if that's what you want, and I'll do whatever it takes to find Stanton's killer."

"Why don't you two talk this over," Reece said. "I need some fresh air." He grabbed his coat off the rack by the door and went outside.

Elizabeth turned to Sam. "Why did you have to ask me to leave again? I'd already told you that I'm staying with Reece." Never before had she been forced to choose between Sam and another man. Never before had she had reason to go against Sam's wishes.

Sam took Elizabeth by the shoulders, pulling her into his arms, stroking her hair the way a parent would comfort a child. "I'm worried sick about you, kiddo. I'm scared something really bad might happen."

Elizabeth hugged Sam, feeling, as she always had, safe and secure in his arms. "I understand how you feel, but I want you to understand how I feel. I really do think I'm falling in love with Reece. I know it's crazy for me to love him, but——"

"Elizabeth, Elizabeth." Sighing, Sam took her by the shoulders again.

"He needs me, Sam. There's just so much pain inside him. Anger, pain and fear." Reaching up, Elizabeth cradled Sam's cheek in her palm. "Remember the agony you were in six years ago when you came off your last assignment for the DEA? That's the shape Reece is in now, but for different reasons."

Elizabeth felt Sam flinch, saw the memories glaze his eyes. "It wasn't your fault, Sam. You didn't have a choice. You did what you had to do. But I have a choice. I'm not leaving Reece."

Sam swallowed, squeezed Elizabeth's shoulders and forced a smile. "He doesn't deserve you, kiddo."

Elizabeth flung her arms around Sam, hugging him fiercely. "I love you, you know that, don't you?"

"And I love you, too, little girl."

Reece stood on the front porch, the afternoon sun dimmed by the clouds, small, damp snowflakes beginning to fall. He had meant to stay out here, to give Elizabeth time alone with Sam Dundee, but the more he'd thought about the possibility she might leave him, the more determined he'd become to ask her to stay. He'd opened the door just a fraction and had seen Elizabeth in Sam's arms. He'd heard her tell him she loved him.

A knot of intense agony sprang to life in Reece's gut. Why the hell should he have trusted this woman any more than he'd ever trusted another?

She'd leave with Dundee. She loved Dundee. He didn't care,

dammit! It didn't matter! He had lived his whole life without Elizabeth Mallory. He'd be just fine without her. He didn't need her. Reece gripped the top rail of the porch banister, his knuckles turning white from the strength of his hold.

The front door swung open. Sam Dundee came outside alone. Reece waited for the second set of footsteps, then, when he didn't hear any, decided Elizabeth was probably getting her bags.

Sam walked over and stood by Reece. "It's snowing."

"Y'all better leave soon, otherwise, you and Lizzie could get snowed in here with me."

"Elizabeth says there won't be more than an inch of snow." Sam bent over, clasping the banister with both hands.

"You believe in her psychic abilities?" Reece asked.

"Yeah, I believe," Sam said. "I've known Elizabeth since she was six years old and my brother married her mother. They moved to Sequana Falls, into Elizabeth's grandparents' home, so that she could be near her great-aunt, who also has psychic talents."

"Aunt Margaret?"

"Margaret has been Elizabeth's guide, her teacher and her protector."

"I thought being her protector was your job!"

"Margaret's and mine." Sam turned to Reece.

Reece faced Sam. "If you've got something to say to me, then say it."

"Elizabeth has risked more than you know to follow you, to stay with you, to help you."

"So, when she leaves with you, she won't be risking herself anymore, will she?"

Sam grinned. "She's not leaving with me."

"What?"

"You chose the wrong time to walk in on us," Sam said. "And you misunderstood what you saw and heard. I noticed you standing in the door. Elizabeth didn't. Odd that she can't read you clearly."

Reece held his breath, wanting to believe and yet afraid to believe what Sam was saying. "She's not leaving with you?"

"Elizabeth and I are family." Sam grasped Reece's shoulder in his big hand. "Elizabeth and I are not lovers. We aren't in love."

Reece nodded his head, acknowledging what Sam had said. "She shouldn't stay with me."

"She won't leave you."

"You couldn't persuade her to go with you?"

"No. She's staying with you because she believes she's the only one who can save you," Sam said. "She'll risk being caught with you and charged with aiding and abetting a criminal, she'll risk the possibility of being killed if she gets caught in the cross fire if the law finds you, and she risks her sanity by going into town and facing people whose thoughts and emotions she can't control."

"What do you mean, people's thoughts and emotions she can't control?" Reece stared at Sam, noting the concern in his expression.

"Elizabeth reads minds, she picks up on the energy that comes from people's thoughts and from their emotions. Often she can predict their futures or see into their pasts just by touching them. Sometimes she can control these energies. Other times she can't. When she can't control them, can't shield herself, then she's bombarded with too much input."

"That's the reason she lives secluded in the mountains, isn't it?" Reece asked. "So she won't be exposed to too much psychic energy coming from other people."

"She almost had a nervous breakdown when she went away to college. We learned then that she didn't dare risk living in a city or even a large town."

"Will she be all right out here? Away from town?"

"She probably would be if she stayed, since she only occasionally picks up anything telepathically at distances, the way she did with you. But she doesn't intend to stay out here," Sam said. "She's meeting me in town tomorrow at Gary Elkins's office."

"Why?"

"She knows it's possible that if she can meet everyone involved with B. K. Stanton, she might be able to read them and discover which one of them is the murderer."

"No, I can't let her do that," Reece said. "I won't let her put herself at risk for me."

Elizabeth opened the front door and stepped outside. "You two finished with your man-to-man talk?"

"Just about." Sam released the banister, stood up straight and smiled at Elizabeth.

"It's too cold out here for y'all to stay much longer. For goodness' sakes, it's snowing." Elizabeth walked over and stood between Sam and Reece.

"I'll see you in town in the morning." Sam gave Elizabeth a quick peck on the cheek, then walked down the steps and out to his rental car. "You take good care of my T-Bird."

"We could swap," Elizabeth suggested.

"No need to do that, kiddo. You keep the Thunderbird." Sam opened his car door, glanced up at Elizabeth and then over at Reece. "She's worth a king's ransom, Landry. Remember that."

Sam got in the Regal, started the engine and drove away without a backward glance. Elizabeth slipped her arm around Reece's waist. He pulled her close. She laid her head against him.

"You should have gone with him, Lizzie."

"I couldn't leave you."

A sharp, breathtaking pain hit Reece straight in the gut. He couldn't let this happen—he couldn't let Elizabeth care for him, and he didn't dare feel anything more than sexual attraction for her. He wasn't a man accustomed to women like Elizabeth—honest, caring and loyal, with a purity of soul that frightened him.

"You're putting yourself in danger by staying with me." Reece pulled away from Elizabeth, turning to look down into her crystal-clear blue eyes. Eyes that spoke so eloquently without words. Eyes that told him how much she cared, how deeply she longed to share his misery and lighten his burden.

"You don't really want me to leave, do you?"

"Besides the fact that you could get injured accidentally if the law finds me, you're sure to be in big trouble unless we can convince them that I kidnapped you." Reece walked the length of the porch, leaned back against the wall and gazed out at the forest, trees and brush blanketed with a light dusting of newly fallen snow.

Elizabeth stood near the steps, looking across the porch to where Reece rested his back against the house. Why was it so difficult for him to accept the fact that she wanted to stay with him, to help him, to comfort him? Surely the good Lord wouldn't have sent Reece to her if he hadn't meant the two of them to be together.

Reece kept his gaze focused on the scenery. "Sam told me what you're risking, emotionally and mentally, by leaving Sequana Falls, by exposing yourself to so many other people's thoughts and feelings."

"Sam told you?"

"He thought I had a right to know."

"He shouldn't have told you."

Reece turned around slowly, admitting to himself that he had to face Elizabeth and yet not wanting to look into those all-too-knowing blue eyes of hers. Why now, God, why now? he asked himself. Why send someone so special into my life when my whole world has crumbled around me? Why offer me something that I can never have, something I'm not worthy of, something I didn't dream could ever be mine?

"You're going to wind up getting hurt, one way or another, because of me." When he saw her take a tentative step forward, he held up a hand to warn her off. "I can't give you what you want. I'm no good for you, Lizzie. What do I have to say or do to get through to you?"

"I thought we'd settled this argument." She wanted desperately to run to him, throw her arms around him. She couldn't; he wouldn't accept her. Not now.

"When you go into Newell and meet with Gary Elkins, you're going to be exposed to hundreds of people, maybe thousands. How can you deal with that kind of attack on your mind?"

"It's not as bad as Sam led you to believe." Elizabeth knew she was trying to convince herself as much as Reece. "When I went away to college I was only in my teens and I hadn't been able to train my mind to shield itself."

"Can you shield your mind now?"

"To some extent," Elizabeth said. "Every living thing gives off energy. I read the psychic energy people emit. Sometimes that energy is so strong I can't block it."

"Can you read everybody? Do you pick up on everybody's psychic energy?"

"Almost everyone. Some people shield their minds and their emotions without realizing they're doing it. But no one can shield themselves all the time."

"You can't read me all the time, can you?"

"No, I can't. You won't admit your true feelings even to yourself. You won't allow anyone to get close to you. You've closed your mind and your heart to others because you're afraid."

Reece walked toward her, his gaze locked with hers, his amber eyes hypnotizing her the way an animal often does his prey as he moves in for the kill. Elizabeth stood perfectly still—waiting—her heart racing wildly, her breathing shallow and quick. He reached out, circling the back of her neck with his big hand, drawing her forward until her lips were at his throat. She tilted her head, staring up at him, excitement and uncertainty shining in her eyes.

"Why is it that you can read other people so clearly, that you can see into other people's futures, but not mine?"

Tears formed in Elizabeth's eyes. Her bottom lip trembled as she forced herself not to cry. "I told you that I can't read your future because our futures are entwined, and I have always refused to look into my own future. You see, Reece, I have my own fears."

He brought her face closer to his, their lips almost touching. "You can get inside my head, Lizzie. You've done it before. I heard you calling my name when I was at the motel and you were trying to find me. I told you where I was and how to get there, didn't I? And I realize now that all those months I stayed in jail, before and during the trial, I kept getting these odd feelings that someone was trying to talk to me, to comfort me, to let me know I wasn't alone. I thought I'd been caged for so long I was going crazy."

Tears escaped from Elizabeth's eyes, falling like life-giving raindrops. Reece kissed her eyes, kissed her tears, tasting her heart's blood. Dear God in heaven, forgive me, he thought, but I can't be strong any longer. I can't walk away from this precious gift. I'm only human.

"What am I thinking, Elizabeth?"

Sweet, tingling warmth spread through her, quickly turning to hot excitement. Desire poured from Reece's mind, desire so intense she felt it in every cell of her body. She shivered from the power of his thoughts.

"You…you want to make love to me." Elizabeth trembled, her body softening, her legs weakening. She swayed into Reece. He covered her mouth with his, taking her with tender fury. Wanting as he had never wanted in his life. Hungry for love. Desperate to claim this woman as his own.

Reece lifted her into his arms, his lips caressing her throat. Wrapping her arms around his neck, Elizabeth gave herself up to the moment, to the destiny neither of them could deny.

CHAPTER 9

Carrying her into the cottage, Reece held her close, secure in his arms, as he marched straight through the living room. He kicked open the partially closed bedroom door. Elizabeth tightened her hold around his neck, a sudden sense of fear mingling with the anticipation she felt.

Reece was going to make love to her. Now!

He lowered her slowly onto the old iron bed, laying her on top of the crocheted lace bedspread. With her arms still around his neck, she beckoned him downward. He spread his legs, placing his knees on each side of her hips, towering above her, gazing down into her flushed face.

Elizabeth had never known true desire before, had never wanted a man with desperate, mindless passion. Removing his coat, Reece threw it on the floor. Her feelings frightened her, making her wonder if she was prepared to give herself to Reece, to not only abandon her body, but to place her heart and soul into his safekeeping. By his own admission, he was not a man who knew much about love. Would he use her and then discard her after she'd served her purpose?

Elizabeth looked into his eyes, focusing, trying to connect with his mind. She perceived a need and a longing so incredibly intense that her own mind reeled from the power. Whatever else Reece felt was overshadowed by his masculine need to possess, to take, to dominate.

Elizabeth's hand trembled when she reached up to touch his face. "I'm afraid, Reece. I'm so afraid."

No! his mind screamed. Don't be afraid of me. Don't deny me. Not now. I'll die if you don't let me love you.

Shuddering from head to toe, Elizabeth blinked back tears. Dear God, she'd heard his thoughts!

"I'm not going to deny you anything," she told him. "Not now or ever. I want you to make love to me. I want to become yours. But…I haven't…this is my first…"

Circling her wrists, Reece lifted her hands from around his neck and lowered them to the pillow resting above her head. She trembled, her body arching up against his.

"I want to take you right now. Hard and fast." Reece rubbed his arousal into her aching femininity. "I hurt with wanting you, Elizabeth."

Desire, fear, love and uncertainty swirled around inside her. She nodded her head in understanding, giving him permission to do with her as he would.

Tightening his hold around her wrists, he lowered his head to her breasts, nuzzling her through her sweater. When her nipples beaded, he bit them through the heavy cotton material.

"I could do anything I wanted to do to you and you couldn't stop me." Reece stared down at her, his face void of emotion. "I'm bigger than you. Stronger than you. And folks around here will tell you that I can be a mean son of a bitch. You have every reason to be afraid of me."

Elizabeth opened her mouth to speak, but no words came out, only a gasping breath.

He released her hands. "But I don't want you to be afraid of me. I want you to believe me when I tell you that I'd never hurt you. I'd never do anything you didn't want me to do."

She did believe him. She knew in her heart of hearts that Reece Landry would never harm her, that despite all the pain and bitterness inside him, he wanted and needed the love only she could give him.

"I trust you," she said.

He groaned, covering her body with his, burying his face in her neck. "Ah, Lizzie, I want to wait, to take my time, to make it good for you, but I don't know if I can. I'm close to losing it right now."

"It's all right, Reece. We have all night, don't we? The first time won't be the best for me, anyway, will it? So let me do the giving this time and you do the taking. Then next time, you give to me. You can—"

He covered her lips with a hot, hungry kiss, his body moving urgently against hers. She felt his hands at her breasts, kneading her through her sweater, then lifting the garment with great haste. Trying to help him, she rose up enough to accommodate the removal of her sweater. His mouth descended, taking one nipple, sucking, savoring, tormenting, while he pinched at the other nipple with his fingertips. Elizabeth moaned into his mouth, writhing as a savage warmth unfolded deep within her.

While Reece fought with the zipper on her jeans, Elizabeth unbuttoned his shirt, spreading it away from his body. She ran her hands over his chest, loving the feel of his springy chest hair, his tight male nipples, his hard muscles, his hot flesh.

Reece brought her zipper down, then tugged on her jeans until he pulled them over her hips and down her legs. He tossed them on the floor. He removed her panties with such haste that he ripped the thin cotton lace.

All the while he removed her clothes, he kept kissing her, tasting her mouth, running his tongue over her naked body, suckling her breasts, delving into her navel. Elizabeth explored Reece from neck to waist, glorying in the joy she found in his very masculine body, covering him with hot, excited little kisses.

Reece unbuckled his belt, unzipped his jeans and jerked them off, throwing them atop Elizabeth's on the floor. She slipped her hands beneath his shirt, scoring his back with her fingernails, delving beneath the waistband of his briefs to cup his buttocks. Reece groaned, his swollen manhood pulsating against the triangle of dark curls guarding her femininity. He jerked his briefs off and kicked them onto the floor.

"I can't wait, baby. I can't wait!" Reece clenched his teeth, grabbed her hips and lifted her up, seeking and finding the heaven between her thighs.

Elizabeth clung to his shoulders, her body arching to accept his invasion, welcoming him. Reece plunged into her, hesitating when he felt her tightness; then when she clasped his buttocks and pushed him into her, he completed his possession, taking her completely. She cried out, the sound an indrawn gasp. Reece stopped, waiting for her to accept him. Nothing had ever felt this good. Nothing!

Elizabeth was his now. She belonged to him. No other man had ever known the ecstasy of her sweet body.

"I hurt you, didn't I?" Despite the winter chill that filled the house, sweat beaded across Reece's forehead and on his upper lip.

Elizabeth rose enough to kiss his chest, his neck and then his chin. "I'm fine. You're the one who's hurting. Please let me take away that hurt, Reece."

On the brink of orgasm, Reece needed no further inducement. Her words prompted him to action, his big body tense as he thrust deeper and deeper into her satiny, gripping heat. Within seconds he cried out, spilling himself into her, shuddering with release.

Elizabeth ached with need, with wanting something she had never known with a man, wanting Reece to be the first and the only one to give her pleasure. When he fell to her side, holding her against him, Elizabeth stroked him, petting his chest, his hips and his thighs.

"Thank you, Lizzie."

She snuggled against him, unable to speak, unable to do anything more than cling to Reece.

Evening shadows fell across the room. Only the dreary gray gloom of cloud-obscured light came through the windows. She could see his body, naked except for his shirt, big and hairy and muscled, his flesh a natural light olive hue. His partially erect manhood lay nestled in a bed of brown hair. She had an irresistible urge to touch him, to circle him and discover the feel of his masculinity. When she reached for him, Reece grabbed her hand, bringing it down on his stomach, trapping it beneath his own.

They lay side by side, their heads resting on the pillows. Glancing over at him, she smiled. "Reece?"

"Are you all right, Elizabeth?"

She saw the concern in his eyes, the fear. "Yes, I'm all right. It's just that I want more. I want to touch your body, to taste you. I'm aching inside, Reece."

Reece lifted himself up on one elbow. "Keep talking like that, Lizzie, and I'll be ready in a couple of minutes."

She ran her hand down his chest, stopping just a fraction above his manhood. "My breasts are so tight and heavy."

Reece looked at her large, firm breasts, noting how rigidly her nipples stood out, as if begging for his mouth. He flicked one nipple with his tongue. Elizabeth squirmed, moaning and reaching out, circling Reece.

Reece clasped her hand, covering it with his own, showing her how he liked to be touched, what movements gave him the most pleasure.

"My whole body throbs," Elizabeth said. "I have this tingling sensation down here." With her unoccupied hand she covered herself, indicating the area. "I took away your pain, Reece, now I want you to take away mine."

Reece removed his shirt, tossing it atop their other clothes on the floor, then reached up and tugged down the spread and blankets. Elizabeth lifted up as Reece pulled the covers down enough so that they could slip underneath. He slid his arm behind her back, dragging her up against him.

"Warm?" he asked.

She nodded.

"Comfortable?"

"I would be if I weren't hurting so much."

"Do you want me to take you again, right now?"

"Yes."

Reece laughed. "The first time was for me. The second time is going to be for both of us."

Elizabeth kissed his chest. Reece shoved her slightly away from him, turning her over on her side.

"What are you doing?" she asked.

He rubbed her shoulders, lifting her long hair aside to kiss her neck. "I'm making love to you, Lizzie. Slow, sweet, passionate love."

"Oh."

"Just relax, baby, and let me take you where you want to go."

He kissed and licked and caressed every inch of her back side, from her neck to the heels of her feet. Elizabeth squirmed and moaned and begged Reece to stop tormenting her, but he continued with his magic foreplay, teaching her what an incredibly sensuous woman she was. Her body, though tense with need and anticipation, became pliant in his hands, warm, quivering putty to be molded to his specifications. By the time he turned her around to face him, she was crying with her need, pleading with him to take her, to ease the agony that had built inside her.

Reece spread her legs, positioning himself between them, but he did not take her. Instead, while she clung to his shoulders, biting her nails into his muscles, he lowered his head and took one of her nipples into his mouth. She arched up off the bed, her femininity open and waiting for his possession. With every stroke of his tongue, every touch of his fingertips, Reece brought Elizabeth closer and closer to the brink.

"Please, Reece. Please…"

"You're almost ready."

"I *am* ready!"

His fingers sought and found her moisture, hot and dripping with desire. "You are ready, baby. So very, very ready."

When he entered her with one swift, firm plunge, she took him into her, accepting him fully, clinging to his shoulders, wrapping her legs around his hips. She met him thrust for thrust, giving and taking in equal measure, reveling in the feel of him buried deep within her, savoring the fullness of him that made her complete.

"Ah, Lizzie…so good, baby. You're so good."

"Love me, Reece. Love me!"

He took her hard and fast then, with a frenzy she equaled with her acceptance, her raging hunger to find fulfillment. Their bodies moved in unison, to the undulating rhythm of mating. The tightness within her released, exploding shards of breathtaking pleasure through her whole body, the throbbing spasms of her climax continuing on and on until satiation claimed her. Reece followed her over the precipice, falling headlong into an earth-shattering climax, his body jerking as he jetted his release into her receptive body. He groaned with pleasure, falling on top of Elizabeth, whose own body still pulsed with the aftershocks of such a fierce loving.

He rested heavily atop her, his big body damp with sweat, even though the covers lay at their feet. Elizabeth clung to him, her own body damp from their lovemaking. She felt as if she were still a part of him, still connected. She could not bear to let him go.

Reece eased off her, cradling her in his arms, never wanting to release her, wanting to keep her at his side forever. Reaching down, he pulled the covers up and over them. He kissed Elizabeth on the forehead.

"I don't think I could bear to lose you, Lizzie. Not now." He hadn't even realized he'd spoken aloud until he heard the sound of his own voice.

Draping her arm across his stomach beneath the covers, she cuddled closer to his side. "I'm yours. Now and forever. Don't you know that, Reece?" *Don't you know that I love you?*

She felt his body go rigid, and knew only too well that he wasn't ready for her confession of love.

"It's all right," she told him. "I won't leave you."

They lay there together, in each other's arms, as evening turned to night. Elizabeth slept, warm, safe and content, protected in the embrace of the man she loved. Reece lay awake for a long time, thinking about his life and wondering if there was any chance that he could change. Was it possible for a hard-hearted, cold bastard like him to ever learn to love, really love, the way Elizabeth deserved to be loved?

Finally Reece allowed sleep to claim him, but even in his dreams he could not escape the fact that Elizabeth Mallory cared for him. And more than anything, yes, perhaps even more than revenge against the Stantons, he wanted to be able to return her feelings.

Elizabeth awoke to the sound of the winter wind whipping around the edge of the cottage, creating a keening whine. Opening her eyes to the morning sunlight filling the room, she glanced at the empty side of the bed and wondered where Reece was. The silence in the house chilled her far more than the frigid temperature in the room. Holding the covers around her to protect her from the cold, Elizabeth crawled over to the edge of the bed, leaned down and picked up her jeans and shirt from the floor, leaving her panties. She slid the garments under the covers and dressed as quickly as possible, then sat on the side of the bed to put on her shoes.

She glanced into the kitchen when she emerged from the bedroom. Coffee brewed in the coffee machine; two clean cups waited on the counter. When she entered the living room Elizabeth felt the warmth from the roaring fire and also a distinct chill coming from across the room. She saw that the front door stood wide open, freezing air pouring into the cottage.

Approaching the door, she noticed Reece standing on the porch, his back to her. She walked across the room and out the door, stopping just inches away from Reece.

"It's a beautiful morning," he said, not turning around. "But it's damned cold. Are you wearing your coat?"

Elizabeth eased up behind him, slipping her arms inside his coat and around his waist, hugging him to her. "You can keep me warm."

In an instant he whirled her around and into his arms, opening his coat to pull her up against him. She smiled at him, loving the look she saw in his eyes, those lone-wolf amber eyes that told her how glad he was to have her near.

"What time is it?" she asked, wrapping her arms around him, burying her face in his chest.

"Probably around seven-thirty." He rubbed her back with up-and-down strokes, warming her with his touch.

"How long have you been up?" She kissed his neck.

"Not long. About twenty minutes." He nuzzled the side of her face with his nose. "I've made coffee." Reece turned her around so that they stood with her back to his chest, facing the front of the cabin. "You were right about the snow. There's less than two inches."

Elizabeth glanced at the white-glazed scenery, a light dusting of snow producing a fairyland effect on the bare trees and brush, tipping the evergreens with a thin layer of ice. The wind howled, blowing snow in every direction, creating the illusion that it was still falling from the sky. Like tiny, delicate diamonds, translucent in the sunlight, the snow danced in the wind.

"It is a beautiful morning." Turning in his arms, Elizabeth looked at Reece, absorbing the pure pleasure of being so near to him. "The most beautiful morning of my life."

He took her face in his hands, gazing into her eyes, his look pleading with her for understanding. Then he kissed her, soft, delicate, gentle kisses.

"Morning always comes, doesn't it?" She smiled at him. "I understand. No matter how magical the night might have been, today we're back to reality."

"I'm sorry, Lizzie. I wish—"

She covered his lips with her fingertips. "It's all right, Reece. I know what lies ahead of us, what we'll have to face. I suppose I just wanted a few more minutes of pretending everything is the way I want it to be."

"Come on back inside." He ushered her across the porch and into the cabin, closing the door behind them. "You're freezing, babe." He brought her cold hands up to his lips, cupping them and then blowing his warm breath over them.

"How about breakfast? Toast and some scrambled eggs?" She pulled away from him.

He caught her around the waist, pulling her up against him. "What time are you supposed to meet Sam at Gary Elkins's office this morning?"

"Ten o'clock."

Releasing Elizabeth, Reece shrugged off his coat and tossed it onto a nearby chair. "Toast, eggs and coffee sound good." Reece sat on the sofa.

"Fine. I'll go fix breakfast." She started toward the kitchen.

"Breakfast can wait." Reece glanced over his shoulder at Elizabeth, who turned and looked back at him.

"I suppose it could, but if we're both hungry, why should we wait?"

"I'd say that depends on what we're hungry for, wouldn't you?"

Elizabeth swallowed hard, wondering if she could dissolve the knot in her throat. She took several tentative steps across the room, halting directly behind the sofa.

"What are you hungry for?" she asked.

Before she knew what was happening, Reece reached out, grabbed her and pulled her over the back of the sofa and into his arms. She squealed. He sprawled out the full length of the long wicker couch, resting her body atop his.

"I'm hungry for you, Elizabeth. I didn't get enough of you during the night."

She straddled his lean hips, pushing one of her knees into the padded sofa back and balancing the other on the edge of a seat cushion.

"I'd rather devour you first and save the eggs and toast until we've worked up a real appetite for food." Elizabeth unsnapped his jeans and released his zipper, finding him naked beneath his pants.

Reece undid her jeans and tugged them down her hips. She lifted her body up enough from him to jerk the jeans past her knees and down to her ankles. Just as she started to kick them onto the floor, Reece tumbled them both onto the heavy, braided rug in front of the fireplace.

"Reece!" Her jeans fell off her feet.

He eased his own jeans down over his hips, anchoring them at midthigh, then he pulled Elizabeth on top of him, positioning her just where he wanted her. She adjusted her knees on each side of his hips, lowering herself onto his arousal. He surged up and into her as she took him into her body.

He urged her breasts toward his mouth, taking one nipple between his teeth, nibbling, then stroking it with his tongue before suckling greedily. He allowed her to set the pace, to create the rhythm. Elizabeth took charge, building the tension higher and higher not only in herself but in Reece, allowing the primeval woman within her to dominate, to take her own pleasure as surely as she gave it to her mate.

There before the blazing fire, Elizabeth took Reece, glorying in her own feminine power and accepting the fact that he possessed equal dominion over her. When their bodies burned with a fire hotter than the one that warmed the cottage, they shattered into simultaneous releases so intense that the aftershocks rocked them again and again.

Elizabeth lay on top of Reece's sweat-damp body, exhausted from appeasing a hunger far greater than any she'd ever known. After endless moments Reece helped her to her feet and led her to the bathroom, where they shared a long shower, making love again before dressing and returning to the kitchen for breakfast.

Elizabeth waited for Sam outside the renovated nineteenth-century antebellum cottage on Main Street where Gary Elkins's office was located. She felt a bit underdressed in her jeans, sweater and winter coat, but she'd packed light when she'd left Sequana Falls, thinking of nothing except following Reece.

At precisely ten, just as the town clock struck the hour, Sam Dundee stepped out of his rental car. Elegant in his dark suit and overcoat, Sam approached Elizabeth, giving her a quick hug.

An attractive young receptionist greeted them when they entered the office, which had been decorated by someone with excellent taste and a flair for making an office practical and at the same time pleasantly appealing. "May I help you?" The reception- ist smiled at Sam and Elizabeth, her warm brown eyes revealing her genuine friendliness.

"We have an appointment with Mr. Elkins. I'm Sam Dundee." Sam assisted Elizabeth in removing her coat, then took off his over- coat and hung both items on a wooden rack near the entrance.

"Yes, sir. Mr. Elkins is expecting you." Getting up from her tidy desk, the young woman led Sam and Elizabeth toward a heavy wooden door to the right of the reception room. She knocked, then entered, announcing Mr. Elkins's ten-o'clock appointment.

Gary Elkins rose from a button-tufted hunter green leather chair, rounded his enormous antique oak desk and held out his hand to Sam.

"Won't you come in, Mr. Dundee? I'm eager to find out how you can help me prove Reece Landry innocent of B. K. Stanton's murder. You said that you were contacted by a psychic who claims she had a vision about Reece, that she believes in his innocence."

Elizabeth watched Gary Elkins as he shook hands with Sam and motioned for the two of them to sit, his gaze scanning Elizabeth quickly before he offered his hand to her.

"And is this lovely young lady the psychic you told me about?" Elkins asked.

Gary Elkins's white-blond hair was thin, his blue eyes pale and his complexion ruddy. Standing beside Sam, he looked like a kid, but then few men were as big as Sam Dundee.

"This is my niece, Elizabeth," Sam said. "She's quite involved in this situation."

"I see." Gary Elkins released Elizabeth's hand, motioned for them to be seated in the two Queen Anne wing-backs that flanked his desk, then returned to his chair.

Elizabeth felt immediate warmth, honesty and good-heartedness coming from Gary Elkins. She sensed that not only were the man's credentials as a lawyer irreproachable, he was also a decent human being. She knew that she and Sam wouldn't be putting their trust in someone who might betray Reece.

Sam glanced over at Elizabeth. Smiling, she nodded, reassuring Sam that they could confide in Gary Elkins. Sam returned the smile and the nod, then faced Reece's lawyer.

"Not only do Elizabeth and I believe that Reece Landry is innocent, but we think he was framed for his father's murder," Sam said.

Gary Elkins's eyes widened. "I see. Well, I agree with you, but I'm afraid that there's no evidence to substantiate that fact."

"I intend to uncover that evidence, Mr. Elkins." Sam leaned back in the chair, crossing his legs as he relaxed.

"Is your niece the psychic who had a vision about Reece?" Elkins glanced at Elizabeth.

"I am psychic, Mr. Elkins, but...I...I know Reece, personally," Elizabeth said. "And I know he didn't kill his father."

"I'm afraid I don't understand." Elkins frowned. "I thought I'd met all of Reece's friends during the trial."

"Look, Elkins," Sam said, "what I'm about to tell you will remain confidential. Understand?"

"Yes, I understand."

"When Landry escaped after the wreck nearly a week ago, he broke into Elizabeth's cabin in Sequana Falls—"

"He didn't break in," Elizabeth said. "The door wasn't locked."

Sam gave Elizabeth a hard stare, then turned his attention back to Reece's lawyer. "Landry was in pretty bad shape. Elizabeth nursed him back to health and the two of them became friends. He told her the facts about Stanton's murder and the trial. Elizabeth believed him, and so do I."

"Why didn't you go to the sheriff?" Elkins asked. "Why did you come to me?"

"Because Reece doesn't trust the sheriff's department, and I believe he's right in his distrust. But he wasn't sure about you, and I decided to find out for myself whether or not you were truly on Reece's side." Elizabeth scooted to the edge of her seat, clasping her knees with her open palms.

"Do you know where Reece is now?" Elkins looked directly at

Elizabeth. "If you do, then I urge you to contact him and tell him to turn himself in. If the local authorities find him, they'll kill him."

Icy chills pelted Elizabeth's body. "They'll—"

"Landry isn't going to turn himself in," Sam said. "I've talked to him, tried to convince him to give us a chance to dig up some new evidence, to wait for his appeal to go through."

"Look, I don't know who you people are or why you've chosen to believe Reece, but he needs all the help he can get. So do I." Elkins slammed one hand down atop his desk. "Dammit, the Stantons possess a great deal of power in Newell and the local sheriff knows the family wants Reece apprehended dead or alive."

The outer door swung open and a tall, slender brunette entered. "Not all the Stantons want Reece dead."

"Christina!" Elkins jumped up, rounded his desk and rushed over to the woman who'd just entered his office.

"Is this the man who has information about Reece?" Christina Stanton asked. "Is she the psychic?"

Gary Elkins slipped his arm around Christina's shoulders, closed the office door behind her and led her into the room. Sam stood, offering the woman his seat. She shook her head and turned her attention to Elizabeth.

"Chris, these people say they want to help Reece. They know where he's hiding," Elkins said.

Elizabeth held out her hand. "I'm Elizabeth Mallory."

Christina stared at Elizabeth's hand for a few seconds before accepting it in greeting. The moment Elizabeth touched Reece's half sister, she felt the woman's anguish and frustration.

"You really do want to help your brother, don't you, Ms. Stanton?" Elizabeth asked.

Looking directly at Elizabeth, Christina pulled her hand away. Her eyes glazed with tears. She nodded her head. "Yes, I do. I know my mother and brother are convinced that Reece killed Daddy, but I don't think Reece is capable of murder."

"Neither do I," Elizabeth said.

Christina glanced from Elizabeth to Sam to Gary Elkins.

"Reece broke into Ms. Mallory's cabin when he escaped after the wreck," Elkins said. "They became acquainted and she and her uncle, Mr. Dundee, want to help Reece."

"Do you know where Reece is?" Christina asked.

"I'm afraid I can't tell you where he is." Elizabeth sensed Christina's fear. "But I can tell you that he's all right."

"Chris, honey, please sit down." Elkins led her to the empty chair Sam had just vacated. "When I spoke to Mr. Dundee yesterday, he told me that he owns a private security agency in Atlanta and he has a great deal of experience in preventing crimes. He's a former DEA agent." Elkins glanced up at Sam. "I've got all that straight, haven't I, Mr. Dundee?"

"You've got it right." Sam sat on the edge of Gary Elkins's desk. "Ms. Stanton, what we need is another suspect, someone else who would have had motive and opportunity to kill your father."

"Oh, Mr. Dundee, my father had a lot of enemies. Personally, I think Reece's stepfather, Harry Gunn, killed Daddy. The man hated Daddy."

"Ms. Stanton, do you believe in psychic abilities?" Sam asked.

"What?"

"Elizabeth is a psychic," Sam said. "She can read the psychic energy from people."

"Are you saying she can read minds?" Gary Elkins asked.

"Sometimes." Sam stood, towering over Christina Stanton. "If Elizabeth could meet your family and others who knew your father, then she might be able to pick up on something that could help us. She might be able to clue us in on a suspect."

"This is crazy!" Gary Elkins walked between Sam and Christina, boldly glaring up at Sam. "We want to help Reece, but if you think we're going to be fooled by some charlatan act—"

"You and Christina are in love." Elizabeth stared directly at the couple. "Neither of you have had the courage to admit your feelings to the other."

Gary's mouth fell open; Christina gasped, tears springing to her eyes.

"Gary is afraid you don't find him attractive," Elizabeth said. "And, Christina, you're afraid to trust another man after what happened with your fiancé."

"I don't believe this!" Elkins said.

Standing, Elizabeth walked over to Christina. Gently pushing Gary Elkins out of the way, she took Christina's hand. "The two of you will marry someday, and you'll be happy."

"Now, see here!" Elkins said.

Christina held fast to Elizabeth's hand. "No, Gary. I believe her." Christina looked up at Elizabeth. "What can I do to help you help Reece?"

Gary Elkins slumped down beside Sam on the edge of his desk.

"I want to meet your family," Elizabeth said. "Introduce me to them as a psychic who has had a vision about your father's murder and tell them that I'm convinced Reece is innocent. They mustn't know that I've met Reece, that we're personally acquainted."

"When do you want to meet my family?"

"As soon as possible."

"This evening," Christina said. "You can have dinner with us."

"Why don't you and I leave Sam and Gary to discuss what they can do, and in the meantime, you and I can become better acquainted." Elizabeth squeezed Christina's hands, then helped her stand.

Christina glanced at Gary Elkins, a weak smile trembling on her lips. "Gary, I think you and I need to have a nice, long talk very soon."

Elkins's ruddy complexion flushed a blotched pink and red. "Yes, Chris, we do."

Christina turned to Elizabeth. "Do you have your car with you, Ms. Mallory? I'm afraid I had Mother's chauffeur drop me by here."

"Call me Elizabeth. May I call you Chris?"

"Yes, please do."

Elizabeth waved goodbye to Sam, and ushered Chris out the door.

Three hours later Elizabeth sat across the table from Chris at Calahan's, a downtown restaurant located in a restored building. Their table was on the second floor, in the nonsmoking section by the windows looking down on Main Street.

In the time since they had left Gary Elkins's office Chris had given Elizabeth a tour of Newell, including a ride down Lilac Road where Reece had grown up. Elizabeth had felt an instant rapport with Christina Stanton, and had no doubts that the woman was sincere in her desire to help her brother.

Elizabeth watched Chris play with the piece of apple pie on her plate. "Are you sure it's a good idea for me to go home with you after lunch?"

"I'm sure," Chris said. "Mother had some sort of charity do at the country club, so she'll be out until around four. Kenny's at work, trying to keep things going at Stanton Industries, and finding out he can't fill Daddy's shoes."

"You want to run Stanton Industries, don't you, Chris?"

Chris turned her head sharply, staring at Elizabeth with round eyes. "How did you... I forgot, you're psychic. You really did read my mind, didn't you? You knew exactly what I was thinking."

Elizabeth wiped the corners of her mouth with the white linen napkin, then laid it on the table beside her empty dessert dish. "Your father must have been a very old-fashioned man, one who didn't believe his daughter should be left in charge of his business."

"Daddy didn't have any problem with me working at Stanton Industries, giving me an honorary position to pacify me." Chris scissored through her piece of pie with the prongs of her fork. "But he wasn't too thrilled when I started coming up with ideas, making suggestions, actually taking my job seriously."

"I'd bet you have a degree in business. Right?"

"Can't you just read my mind?" Chris smiled.

Elizabeth picked up her coffee cup. "I only pick up on strong emotions, usually, and I try very hard not to tune in to every thought of the person I'm with."

Chris laughed. "Yes, I have an M.B.A."

"And Kenny?"

"Kenny didn't go for his M.B.A. after getting his B.S. because

Daddy thought it best for him to learn to run the business by running the business."

"What happened?"

"Reece happened."

Elizabeth sipped her coffee. "Reece worked at Stanton Industries, and he and Kenny didn't get along."

"That's the understatement of the year. Reece and Kenny hated each other. Kenny was so jealous of Reece he couldn't see straight."

"Why? Because he knew Reece was your father's illegitimate son?"

"Oh, it went a lot deeper than that." Chris shoved her pie plate away from her, dropping her fork on the table, the edge hitting the plate with a clink. "Daddy was a manipulator. He deliberately pitted Reece against Kenny. He saw that Reece was smart and quick to learn, that he was hungry for acceptance and success. He used that against Reece, and against Kenny."

Elizabeth had wondered how much his inheritance would mean to Reece, how deeply his need for revenge against the Stantons ran. Once the real murderer had been found, would Reece stay on in Newell, accept his share of Stanton Industries and seek his place as a member of society? If he did, was there any hope for her to have a future with Reece? She couldn't live in Newell. She could never become a part of the world he would live in as part of the Stanton family.

"Do you think Reece would like to be in charge of Stanton Industries?"

"I'm not sure," Christina said. "I know he feels cheated by my father's unwillingness to recognize him as his son. I think Reece wanted Daddy's acceptance more than he's willing to admit."

"I understand that your father changed his will shortly before his death," Elizabeth said. "Who knew that your father left Reece one-third of his estate?"

"As far as Gary could find out, no one other than Willard Moran, our family's lawyer, knew about the new will."

"How long before his death did your father have his lawyer draw up a new will?"

"Three days."

"Reece thinks that your father asked him to your house the night he was killed because he planned to tell him about the new will."

Sighing, Christina rubbed her forehead. "Uncle Willard suggested to the sheriff that Daddy had told Reece before...that Reece actually killed Daddy for the money. The district attorney tried to use Uncle Willard's testimony at the trial."

"When can I meet Uncle Willard?" Elizabeth asked.

"He will be dining with us tonight. He's been very supportive ever since Daddy died. I'm not sure Mother would have survived half as well without him."

"So, I'll not only meet your mother and brother, but Uncle Willard, as well."

"And don't forget Tracy!"

How could she forget Tracy? After all, she and Reece were hiding out in the woman's parents' summer house. "You don't like your sister-in-law, do you?"

"You didn't have to read my mind to figure that out, did you?" Chris laughed.

"How did Tracy get along with your father?"

"Tracy got along better with Daddy than she does with Kenny. Daddy handpicked Tracy, you know. Old family. Old money. But Daddy didn't realize the good breeding that was supposed to come along with old families and old money was sadly lacking in our dear Tracy."

Elizabeth reached across the table, touching Chris's hand where she clutched her napkin. "Do you think a member of your family could have killed your father?"

Chris breathed deeply, letting out her breath on a long sigh. "As much as I despise Tracy, she had no motive. Kenny feared Daddy and sometimes hated him, but he also worshiped him. And Mother...well, Mother and Daddy lived separate lives. She knew he had his women, and she chose to look the other way. I suppose she hated him for it, but I doubt she would have killed him, not after all these years."

"And we know that Reece didn't kill him," Elizabeth said.

"I'm not sure how much good it will do for you to meet the family this evening."

"If I can pick up on anything, something I learn might help Reece."

"Let's go, then, and we'll see what we can find in my closet that might fit you. Mother would die if you came down to dinner wearing jeans."

Elizabeth grinned. "Thanks, Chris. I'm afraid I left Sequana Falls in such a hurry I didn't consider I'd need anything to wear other than jeans."

Chris stood, placing the straps of her bag over her shoulder. "Lunch is on me."

"I'll leave the tip."

When Elizabeth opened the driver's side door of Sam's '65 T-Bird, she saw a note lying on her seat.

"What's that?" Chris asked as she got inside the car.

Elizabeth picked up the note and opened it. A key fell out. Holding the key in her hand, she read the note silently to herself. Sam had left her the name of his motel, the room number, a key and a message to meet him after her dinner with the Stantons.

"It's from Sam."

Elizabeth started the engine and drove down Main Street. The bright sun had melted most of the snow, leaving a grimy slush along the roadside. Following Christina's instructions, Elizabeth maneuvered the car out of town and toward the highway. Glancing in her rearview mirror, Elizabeth noticed an older model Chevrolet, the paint faded, rust splotching the surface and the vinyl top ragged. The car had been behind them since they had pulled out of the parking lot at Calahan's.

Elizabeth turned left onto the highway; the Chevy followed. She couldn't make out the driver's identity, but she could tell that he was the sole occupant.

"Chris, do you know someone who drives an old, ragged blue Chevrolet?"

"Why?" Chris started to turn around.

"Don't look right now, but I think somebody's following us."

"Who would be following us?"

"I have no idea." Elizabeth speeded up just a little. The car behind her speeded up enough to keep them in sight. "Turn toward me and act as if you're talking, then catch a quick glimpse of the car behind us."

Chris followed Elizabeth's instructions. Gasping, she jerked around quickly. "It's Harry Gunn!"

"Reece's stepfather?"

"The man is scum. No, he's worse than scum. He makes my skin crawl."

"Why would he be following us?"

"I have no idea…unless—"

"Unless what?" Elizabeth asked.

"Unless he's been following me to see if I'd lead him to Reece. He knows that I hired Gary to defend Reece, that I offered to put up bail for him before the judge denied bail. Harry Gunn knows that I'm one of the few people in Newell who believes Reece is innocent."

"So Mr. Gunn thinks if he follows you, you'll lead him to Reece, and he wants Reece handed over to the sheriff. Right?"

"Harry Gunn would like to see Reece dead." Chris pulled her shoulder bag across her stomach, holding it close to her beige wool coat. "I think Reece's stepfather killed Daddy and framed Reece. He hated Daddy even more than he hated Reece."

"I want to talk to Mr. Gunn," Elizabeth said.

"No! You mustn't. He's dangerous!" Chris clutched Elizabeth by the arm.

Elizabeth pulled the car off the road into a service station located in the middle of a minimall. Killing the engine, she opened her door. The old Chevy pulled in on the opposite side of the service station.

"Stay here," Elizabeth said. "If I can get close enough to him, I should be able to sense something. If he killed your father, maybe I can pick that up."

"Elizabeth!" Flinging open the door, Chris jumped out, following Elizabeth as she marched toward Harry Gunn's old car.

The man was slumped down in the seat, the bill of a ball cap covering his eyes. Elizabeth knocked on the window. Harry Gunn shoved the ball cap up and looked out the window at Elizabeth. Her stomach flip-flopped. The man, probably no more than his mid-fifties, appeared much older. His gray hair had thinned to baldness in the front, his complexion was sallow and a week's growth of scraggly beard covered his face.

Harry Gunn rolled down his window. "Yeah? Something I can do for you?"

Overwhelmed by the smell of liquor and stale body odor, Elizabeth stepped back, bumping into Christina.

"I don't know where Reece is," Chris said. "Stop following me or I'll call the police."

When Harry Gunn laughed, he showed a mouthful of yellowed, chipped teeth. "Go ahead and call 'em. I'll tell them you're hiding that bastard half brother of yours."

Elizabeth sensed the hatred. She felt the evil, the cruel, malevolent energy surrounding Harry Gunn. Seldom, if ever, had she felt such wickedness. She could not probe past the wickedness into Harry's thoughts.

"Reece Landry is an innocent man," Elizabeth said. "He has friends who will not allow him to pay for a crime he didn't commit."

"Who are you, sister? You don't look like any of the Stantons' highfalutin friends or any of Reece's good-time gals."

"She's my friend, and...and a psychic who had a vision about Daddy's murder. She's come to Newell to help us find the real murderer," Christina said. "She believes in Reece's innocence."

"Well, then, she's as big a fool as you are." Gunn grinned, tobacco spittle dripping from the side of his mouth. "Reece is no good. He never was. I tried my best to beat some sense into him, but all he ever gave me was trouble. He killed B.K., all right. The whole town knows it. And I'm just sorry they didn't give him the death sentence."

Harry rolled up his window, started the old Chevy's engine and backed out of the service station.

Chris grabbed Elizabeth by the arm. "Can you imagine being raised by a man like that? Reece's life must have been a living hell."

Elizabeth covered Chris's hand, patting her gently. "I believe that man is capable of anything, even murder!"

CHAPTER 10

Elizabeth felt uncomfortable wearing Christina Stanton's designer dress, and even more uncomfortable surrounded by the emotions of a family who despised Reece Landry. A sense of panic began growing inside Elizabeth during the formal dinner when Christina introduced her as a new friend and a psychic who had predicted she would marry Gary Elkins. Tracy and Kenny had seemed amused, Alice Stanton disgusted at the thought and Willard Moran unconcerned.

Dinner conversation had been light, inconsequential and unrevealing as far as Elizabeth was concerned. Everyone seemed curious about exactly who she was and why Christina had invited her into their home.

After-dinner coffee was served in the elegant, austere living room, where Alice Stanton sat on the gold brocade Sheraton sofa and stared at Elizabeth.

"Where do you live, Ms. Mallory?" Alice asked, her faded blue eyes shaded by half-closed lids. "Would I possibly be acquainted with any of your people?"

"Elizabeth is——" Christina said.

"I'm from a small town in the northern part of the state." Elizabeth didn't have to be psychic to sense Mrs. Stanton's snobbery or her discomfort at having an undesirable stranger in her home. "And I'm quite sure you wouldn't know anyone in my family."

"How long have you been practicing this psychic stuff?" Tracy Burton Stanton, long and lean, with huge brown eyes and a halo of strawberry blond curls, smiled at Elizabeth, who wondered how someone with such a sharp, hawk nose could turn it up with such expert ease.

Christina gasped, then glared at her sister-in-law, silently chastising her for being rude to a guest.

"I've been psychic all my life, Ms. Stanton, but my abilities became very apparent when I was about six years old." Elizabeth held the delicate china cup and saucer in her hand, wishing she had declined the offer of coffee.

"How did you and Chris meet?" Kenny sipped his coffee with the same precise movements his mother used, an almost feminine flair to his actions.

"In Gary's office," Christina said, glancing at Elizabeth for approval. "She...Elizabeth had a vision recently. A vision about Daddy's murder."

"What?" The cup in Alice Stanton's trembling hand quivered.

Murmurs rose around the room. Kenny set his cup on a nearby table. Tracy sat up straight, her eyes widening, her face turning pale. Seated beside Alice on the sofa, Willard Moran placed his arm around her shoulders.

Overwhelmed by the whirlwind of emotions Christina's revelation had stirred up, Elizabeth gripped the arm of her Queen Anne chair and very slowly set her cup on the marble-topped mahogany coffee table. She tried desperately to sort through the myriad feelings coming from the people in the room, but the strength of their emotions collided, creating chaos in Elizabeth's mind.

Standing beside Elizabeth's chair, Christina glanced down, then leaned over and whispered, "Are you all right?"

"I can't separate their emotions. Their energies are mingled together." Elizabeth breathed deeply, willing herself under control. The bombardment began to ebb as she shielded herself.

"What sort of vision did you have about Daddy's death?" Kenny, short and squarely built like his mother, stood behind the sofa, stroking the fine brocade cloth with the tips of his perfectly manicured fingernails.

"I won't have this sacrilege in my house." Alice Stanton, her sagging, hound-dog cheeks flushing profusely, straightened her spine and shrugged off Willard Moran's comforting arm. "This psychic business is evil and I'll have none of it."

"Calm down, Alice." Tracy laughed, obviously amused at her mother-in-law's discomfort. "You're overreacting a bit, don't you think? After all, we know what happened to B.K. What could this woman—" Tracy glanced over at Elizabeth, a smug smile on her face "—possibly tell us that we don't already know?"

"Tracy's right, my dear." Grasping Alice's hand, Willard patted her tenderly. "We all know that Reece Landry killed poor B.K."

"I don't want that man's name mentioned." Jerking her hand out of Willard's, Alice entwined her fingers in a prayerlike gesture. "He's caused this family more than enough grief. And now he's running around free, possibly still in Newell."

"Don't fret so, Mother. The authorities will apprehend him, and he'll spend the rest of his life rotting in Arrendale." Kenny clutched the back of the sofa, his fingers biting into the cushion.

"Reece Landry didn't kill B. K. Stanton." Elizabeth saw, heard and felt an immediate reaction. Disbelief and fear dominated the room. Elizabeth tried to zero in on the fear. She felt it strongly, emanating from the area around the sofa where Alice Stanton sat beside Willard Moran, and Kenny stood behind them.

"Of course he did," Willard said. "Alice and I walked in on him only moments after he'd shot B.K. We discovered him kneeling over B.K.'s body. His hands were covered with blood."

Very slowly, as if she were in a trance, Elizabeth stood, her eyes slightly glazed as she stared across the room at the fireplace. "B. K. Stanton was shot twice while he was standing behind his desk in his study. I can't see the murderer, but I can see Reece Landry rushing into the room, after the shots were fired. I can see him being struck over the head and falling to his knees."

"Those are the lies he told in court!" Kenny shouted. "The man's a conniving, money-hungry bastard! He hated Daddy. He hates this whole family."

Elizabeth felt Kenny's hatred—intense, all-consuming, bitter, resentful. She also felt his fear. A little boy's fear that his father didn't love him, didn't approve of him, that another brother might prove to be the father's favorite.

"Not all of us hate Reece," Christina said. "And not all of us believe he killed Daddy."

"Is that what this is all about, Chris?" Tracy asked. "You're so determined to prove Reece innocent that you've hired some phony psychic to say that she's had a vision about who really killed B.K.? Don't you think it's odd that she can't see who the murderer is?"

"Each time I have the vision, I see more and more," Elizabeth lied, and prayed her deceit didn't show on her face.

"What do you mean, you see more and more?" Willard Moran stood, his sharp blue eyes narrowing as he glared at Elizabeth.

"I believe it is only a matter of time before the real killer's identity is revealed to me." Elizabeth sensed more fear, greater fear—a mother's fear. She glanced down at Alice Stanton. The woman was afraid Kenny had killed his father!

"That's nonsense, and no court of law would take anything you have to say under consideration." Bespectacled, ruddy-faced Willard Moran smoothed his thick white mustache with his thumb and index finger. "Reece Landry was tried and convicted and that's all there is to it. The man will be apprehended and punished."

Elizabeth focused on the Stanton family's lawyer. Finding him in complete control of his very logical mind, she prodded harder. Sensing only a determination to protect Alice Stanton, Elizabeth probed his emotions. Moran's emotions were so totally centered on his devotion to Alice that all other feelings were subdued and thus shielded from Elizabeth's search.

"You shouldn't be doing this." Alice frowned, shaking her head sadly as she stared at her daughter. "Reece Landry…killed B.K. and we all know it. You betrayed this family by hiring Gary Elkins to defend that man, and now you're so desperate to free your father's murderer that you've hired some woman to pretend she's had a vision that can prove Reece innocent."

"I haven't hired Elizabeth," Christina said. "She does possess psychic abilities and she does know that Reece is innocent."

"I will not listen to another word," Alice said, tears forming in her eyes. "I do not wish to be rude, young woman, but I want you to leave." She glanced at Elizabeth briefly, then focused on her clasped hands resting in her lap. "Immediately!"

"I'm sorry that my presence has upset you, Mrs. Stanton." Elizabeth nodded to Christina. "I'll say goodbye now."

Chris escorted Elizabeth out into the foyer, halting at the front door. "I'm sorry. I guess I was hoping—"

"Don't apologize." Elizabeth squeezed Chris's hand. "I didn't sense anyone's guilt, but I was able to shift through all the emotions whirling around tonight and conclude several things."

"Like what?" Chris asked. "Anything that can help Reece?"

"I'm not sure, but perhaps." Elizabeth wondered just how honest she should be with Chris. "Your mother is afraid Kenny killed your father."

"Oh, God! I have to admit that I've had the same doubts myself, but I still believe Harry Gunn killed Daddy. That man is an animal."

"What about Mr. Moran?"

"Uncle Willard?"

"He loves your mother. He's quite devoted to her." Elizabeth opened the front door. "He'd do anything for her. Anything."

"But why would Uncle Willard kill Daddy? He had no motive."

"Well, someone killed your father, and we know it wasn't Reece. That leaves your brother, sister-in-law, mother and Willard Moran."

"And Harry Gunn."

"Yes, Harry Gunn."

Elizabeth glanced down at the mauve silk dress she'd borrowed. "I'll have Sam return the dress to Gary Elkins's office tomorrow."

"Don't worry about the dress." Chris followed Elizabeth outside onto the front portico. "When you see Reece...tell him...well, tell him that..."

"He doesn't accept love easily, does he?" Elizabeth smiled at Reece's sister. "I think he knows you love him. It's just that he's known so little love in his life that he doesn't trust the emotion. Not in himself, and most definitely not in anyone else."

"You know Reece so well to have met him only a week ago."

Ah, but I've known him for months. "We won't give up on him, will we?" Elizabeth hugged Chris, then walked down the brick steps and toward her car.

"Your coat," Chris called out. "Did you leave it upstairs?"

"I put it in the car with my jeans and sweater before dinner." Elizabeth waved goodbye, then hurried quickly to her car, the winter wind chilling her.

Just as she grasped the door handle on the T-Bird, she felt a tap on her shoulder. Whirling around, she came face-to-face with Tracy Stanton.

"Ms. Stanton! You startled me."

"If Chris hired you, then I'll pay you double for telling me the truth."

"Chris didn't hire me." Sensing Tracy's bitterness and anger, Elizabeth braced herself against the side of Sam's antique car. "I am a psychic, and I honestly do believe that Reece Landry is innocent."

"Damn that man!"

"Why do you dislike your brother-in-law so much, Ms. Stanton?"

Tracy's shrill laughter scraped across Elizabeth's nerves. "I don't dislike Reece. As a matter of fact..."

Tension coiled inside Elizabeth like a deadly snake waiting to strike. A green snake filled with jealousy. Tracy Stanton cared about Reece. She loved him, in her own selfish way.

"You love Reece."

"You said his name as if you know him." Tracy scanned Elizabeth's face. "Is that what this is all about? You're one of Reece's women?"

"I can assure you, Ms. Stanton, that I'm not one of Reece Landry's women." Liar! Liar! Her conscience screamed at her. You've lain in his arms. You've kissed his hard mouth. You've known the pleasure of his possession.

"Then let me warn you, Elizabeth Mallory. Reece Landry is deadly to the female sex. He's the kind of man we all dream about."

When Elizabeth stared at Tracy, showing her confusion, Tracy laughed. "He's all man, if you know what I mean. I used to lie up there——" Tracy nodded toward the second floor of the Stanton mansion "——on my silk sheets and dream about what it would be like to have Reece Landry make love to me."

"Ms. Stanton, I really don't think——"

Tracy manacled Elizabeth's wrist, her sharp fingernails biting into Elizabeth's flesh. "I wish I'd known that B.K. was leaving Reece a big piece of the golden pie. I wouldn't have ended our affair so quickly. I would have chosen him instead of Kenny. Stanton Industries is what Reece has always wanted, you know."

"Either you're lying to me or to yourself," Elizabeth said, jerking free of Tracy's hold. "You never had an affair with Reece Landry. He wouldn't have sex with you. He wouldn't betray his brother."

Her brown eyes wild, Tracy glared at Elizabeth. "You really are psychic, aren't you?"

"And you're very good at lying, aren't you, Tracy? You lied to the police and you lied in court, didn't you?"

"You can't prove a thing." Tracy backed away from Elizabeth, her walk unsteady. "Uncle Willard told us that nothing you say is evidence. Isn't that what he said?"

"I feel very sorry for you, Tracy Stanton." Elizabeth opened the door and got inside her car. As she drove away, she didn't look back at either Tracy or the Stanton mansion.

Elizabeth turned her car into the parking area of the Plantation Inn, an expensive motel on the outskirts of Newell. She parked the T-Bird near the entrance. With trembling hands she opened the car door and stepped outside, her legs unsteady. The confrontation with Tracy Stanton had topped off the evening to perfection, weakening her considerably. There would be no way she could keep her condition from Sam; he would detect the symptoms immediately, having seen them in the past.

She knew he would be furious, but that couldn't be helped. She had to give Sam her impressions of the people she had met tonight, several of the most likely suspects in B. K. Stanton's murder. Although she hadn't picked up on specific guilt from anyone, the only person she had completely ruled out was Christina.

A sense of relief washed through her when she realized that Sam's room was on the ground floor. Fumbling in her purse for the key, Elizabeth heard voices coming from inside and wondered if Sam wasn't alone. Listening carefully, she realized that the voices were coming from a television newscast.

Inserting the key, she turned the lock and opened the door. The room lay in semidarkness, the only light coming from the television screen and the bathroom. She scanned the room quickly. Sam was nowhere to be seen.

"Sam," she called out, closing the door behind her.

The bathroom door opened; Reece Landry stood in the doorway.

Already weak from her ordeal with the Stantons, Elizabeth swayed, clutching at thin air as she felt her knees give way.

"Lizzie!" Reece rushed across the room, grabbing Elizabeth just as she crumbled onto the floor. Lifting her in his arms, he carried her to the bed.

She stared up into his worried face, reaching for him, barely able to lift her arms. "What are you doing here?"

"Waiting for you." Reece laid her gently on the bed, sitting beside her, holding her hand. "What's wrong? What happened?"

"Nothing's wrong. I'm fine." She tried to sit up, but her head began to spin. This was all her fault. She had overreacted to the venom inside the Stanton home, the riot of emotions ranging from hatred to desperation. She had tried to shield herself, but in her zealousness to discover any possible leads, she had allowed herself to become too immersed in her psychic readings.

"You're not fine. Something happened. I want to know." Reece ran his hands up and down her arms, grasping her shoulders and anchoring her to the bed.

"Where's Sam?"

"He's not here." A twinge of anger shot through Reece. Why did she need Sam? What could Dundee do for her that he couldn't? "What's wrong, Lizzie? Tell me. I want to help you."

Elizabeth smiled at Reece, recalling the numerous times she had pleaded with him to allow her to help him. Now the situation was reversed, if only temporarily. Lifting her hand, she stroked his cheek.

"I'm exhausted...from trying to read their thoughts, from trying to pick up on anything that could—"

Reece covered her lips with his fingertip. "You never should have gone home with Christina. My gut instincts told me it was dangerous. Damn, Lizzie, this is my fault. Sam tried to tell me what could happen to you."

"I'm all right, Reece. I was just trying too hard. I didn't protect myself."

"You shouldn't be in the middle of this mess. You should be home in Sequana Falls all safe and sound."

"And I will be home all safe and sound, once we find out who really killed B.K." Elizabeth tried to sit up; Reece shoved her back down on the bed.

"I don't want you to do anything except lie there and rest. Sam should be back in a few hours." Reece kissed her on the forehead, then stood. "I have to go see somebody before I go back to Spruce Pine. I want you to stay here with Sam tonight. You'll be safe."

An old Western movie came to life on the television. Blurs of vivid color danced across the screen. The beat of Hollywood-style Indian war drums echoed through the room.

"Where is Sam?"

"He's following up a lead I gave him." Elizabeth widened her eyes, questioning Reece. "I had told Sam that Tracy was Kenny's alibi and vice versa, but my bet was Tracy wasn't with Kenny when B.K. was shot. I figure she was with some guy."

"She spends more time with her lovers than with her husband, doesn't she?"

"I didn't sleep with Tracy. I told you that. I was tempted, mainly because she belonged to Kenny, and then when it came right down to it, Kenny was the reason I didn't."

"You hurt her deeply when you rejected her." Elizabeth sat up on the edge of the bed, removed her coat and tossed it on a nearby chair. "She thinks she's in love with you."

"Did you two have a nice little chat tonight?" Reece surveyed Elizabeth from the top of her head to the tips of her mauve pumps. "Where did you get those clothes?"

"Yes, Tracy and I had a *nice* little chat. And these clothes belong to Christina. The shoes are a little loose, but a close fit." Elizabeth kicked off the high heels. "So Sam is trying to find the guy you think Tracy was with when B.K. was shot?"

"He's already found him. He's meeting him tonight and going to try to persuade him to admit the truth."

"Sam has been very busy." Elizabeth rubbed her temples, willing the tension to subside, breathing deeply as she relaxed.

"Sam came out to the cottage this afternoon to tell me what he'd found out. He knew I'd be going nuts waiting around out there. He understood why I needed to come into Newell with him, why I needed to see you after you met Chris's family."

"I can't believe Sam let you take such a risk!"

"Sam understood, dammit! He advised me against coming, but he knows I've got to be involved in solving my own problems, that I can't sit out there in Spruce Pine while you and he take all the risks."

Standing, Elizabeth walked slowly toward the bathroom. Reece hurried to her side when she leaned against the doorpost. "Where the hell are you going?"

"I need to wash my face and get something to drink."

"Come on and sit down." Reece led her back to the bed. "I'll get you a washcloth and a glass of water."

"How does Sam think he'll be able to persuade Tracy's lover to admit she was with him the night B.K. was murdered?" Elizabeth asked, sitting down on the bed.

"By paying him to tell the truth, the same way I'm sure Tracy paid him to lie," Reece called out from the bathroom. "Sam said he'd cover the expense and I could pay him back out of my inheritance."

"By all means, you and Sam be sure to keep tabs on who owes what. You wouldn't want to be indebted to each other," Elizabeth mumbled.

"What?" Reece came out of the bathroom carrying a damp washcloth and a glass of water.

"Nothing. I was just talking to myself."

Reece set the glass on the nightstand and handed Elizabeth the washcloth. "Will you be all right here by yourself until Sam gets back?"

"Where are you going?" Elizabeth ran the washcloth over her face, savoring the feel of the cool moistness on her skin.

"B.K.'s secretary, Claire Roberts, lied under oath during the trial. When Gary questioned her about a fight Kenny and B.K. had the day B.K. died, she claimed Kenny and his father hadn't argued, that the two got along beautifully."

"Hadn't anyone else heard their argument?"

"Yeah. Me."

"So it was your word against this Claire Roberts's. Why would she have lied?"

"All I can figure is that Kenny threatened her somehow, probably threatened to fire her. I know Claire liked me. She's a good, decent woman. If I can talk to her, I might be able to persuade her to tell the truth."

"You can't mean you're going to see her tonight!"

"She'd never admit the truth to Sam, but she just might be honest with me. It's worth a try." Taking the washcloth from Elizabeth, Reece handed her the glass of water.

Clutching the glass, Elizabeth stared at Reece. "What makes you think she won't call the sheriff the minute she sees you?"

Reaching out, Reece tilted the glass up to Elizabeth's lips. She drank several sips, then set the glass down on the nightstand. "Besides, you shouldn't be out running around all over Newell. Have you forgotten that the authorities are in the middle of a manhunt for you?"

Reece flipped off the television. "If I stay in Newell, sooner or later I'll get caught. I've got to do everything I can before that happens to find some sort of evidence to clear myself, or at least to throw suspicion on someone else."

"Let Sam do the investigating. He's an expert. And he's not an escaped convict the police can shoot on sight."

"Sam and I can do twice as much working together."

Elizabeth slid off the bed, standing in her bare feet. "Then the three of us should be able to get three times as much done, shouldn't we?"

"Stay out of this, Lizzie. You've done more than enough for me already. Look at yourself. You're wiped out. You need to rest, to steer clear of people."

Elizabeth slipped Christina Stanton's mauve pumps back on and reached for her coat. "I'll drive you to Claire Roberts's house. You can lie down in the back seat. Maybe no one will stop us."

"You're staying here."

"I'm going with you."

"Dammit, what do I have to say or do to convince you that I don't want you in danger because of me? Not only is the law apt to take potshots at me, I've got dear old Harry scouring Newell trying to find me. Sam told me that folks are laying odds that Harry finds me before the sheriff does."

Elizabeth walked over to Reece, placed her hand in his and looked him in the eye. "I'm all right. I can't stay here, waiting and wondering. Please understand. I want to help you."

Reece brought her hand to his lips, kissing her knuckles. "What did you think of the Stantons?"

"They're all afraid of you," Elizabeth said. "Chris wants us to prove your innocence. She considers you her brother. Kenny hates you, and Tracy wants you. Alice Stanton is afraid Kenny killed his father, and Willard Moran would do anything for Alice."

"The Stantons in a nutshell." Clutching her hand, Reece brought it to his chest, holding it against his heart. "All my life I wanted to be a part of that family. I wanted everything that Bradley Kenneth Stanton had, and if we can prove my innocence, everything I ever wanted can be mine. A big house. An expensive car. Stanton Industries."

"Your revenge would be complete if you could claim your inheritance, wouldn't it?" Elizabeth knew only too well that if Reece claimed what was his and stayed in Newell, they would have no future together. She could never exist in an artificial world of power and prestige. Even if she could control her psychic abilities, she would never fit into the Stantons' wealthy life-style. And she'd found out tonight that she still didn't possess the power to completely shield herself, that other people's thoughts and emotions could harm her, even eventually destroy her.

"The sweetest revenge against Kenny and Alice, but especially old B.K. himself, would be to walk into the Stanton Industries boardroom and tell them that I'm taking over. With Chris behind me, I could do it."

"Chris would back you. She would think the family owed it to you." Elizabeth felt a sense of uneasiness, remembering how much Chris wanted the CEO job herself. What would Reece do if he realized that the job Kenny now possessed and he longed for himself was destined to belong to their sister?

"I need to talk to Claire, to see if she can help. If I can't prove my innocence, I can never claim my inheritance."

"Then let's go see Claire Roberts," Elizabeth said.

"Please stay here."

"I'll drive," she said. "You lie down in the back seat. Just give me the directions."

Within fifteen minutes Elizabeth parked Sam's '65 Thunderbird in Claire Roberts's driveway in front of her neat, redbrick house. They hadn't met another car along the tree-lined street.

"There's a light on in the front of the house and a station wagon parked under the carport." Elizabeth glanced over her shoulder at Reece, who sat up in the seat.

"You stay out here." Reece shoved up the seat on the passenger side and opened the door. "I'm not sure what kind of reception I'll get, but if I could persuade Claire to tell the truth about Kenny's fight with B.K., the sheriff might think about reopening the case."

"I'll be all right." Elizabeth tried to smile. "You do what you have to do."

"If you see anything suspicious or if the police drive by, then just back out of the driveway and ride around for a while. I don't want you—"

"Getting in trouble because of you." Elizabeth shook her head. "This conversation is getting ridiculous."

"I'll be back as soon as I can."

Reece couldn't shake his guilt. Elizabeth Mallory had no business smack-dab in the middle of his problems. If the police caught her with him or found any proof that she was involved in keeping his whereabouts a secret, she was sure to be brought up on charges.

But what was a man to do with a woman like Elizabeth? He'd never known anyone like her. She was determined to help him. She had convinced herself that she was destined to save him, and the funny thing was, she'd half convinced him.

Of course, once they found out who killed B.K. and everything had been set right, she'd go back to Sequana Falls. And he would claim his inheritance.

Reece rang the doorbell. The porch light came on. Claire Roberts, short and matronly plump, eased open the door. Her expressive brown eyes widened. She clutched the storm door handle.

"I need to talk to you, Claire. Please." Reece saw the fear in her eyes and hated that she was afraid of him.

"What are you doing here, Reece? The sheriff's department, the police…everyone's looking for you." Lowering her eyes, staring down at the floor, Claire bit into her bottom lip. "You have to go. I can't talk to you."

Reece clasped the outside door handle. "I don't know why you lied in court about Kenny and B.K.'s argument, but I need you to tell the truth. I know you don't want to see me spend the rest of my life in prison for a crime I didn't commit."

"Oh, Reece, I'm so sorry. I...I..." Tears welled up in Claire's eyes.

"Did Kenny threaten you?" He shouldn't be feeling sorry for Claire, considering that her testimony at the trial proved him to be a liar, but he knew she was a good person.

Claire unlocked the storm door, opening it slowly. "I had no idea that my testimony would hurt your case. Kenny said that he wanted to protect his family, his mother in particular, from any more sordid news coverage. He said...he was under no obligation to keep me on as his secretary when he took over the reins at Stanton Industries."

"He threatened to fire you?" Reece glanced around, wondering how long he could stand on Claire's porch without one of her neighbors noticing.

"I have two daughters in college. I've raised them all on my own since my divorce when they were small. I have to have a job."

"Claire, could we talk inside?" Reece asked.

"What? Oh, yes, Reece, come in. I'm sorry that I lied, but I did what I felt I had to do."

Claire opened the door and allowed Reece inside her house. He closed the door behind him.

"Your older daughter is attending college on a Stanton scholarship, isn't she?" Reece wondered how many Stanton employees' sons and daughters had been awarded a full-tuition scholarship paid for by Stanton Industries. He'd been B. K. Stanton's son, but he'd put himself through school.

"Kenny could have taken away Shelly's scholarship and could have seen to it that Lauren didn't get one. He made himself very clear when he told me that he didn't want anyone to know about the argument he'd had with his father."

"Claire, I understand the predicament you were in, and I can't really blame you, but...I need your help." Reece stood in the living room, only a couple of feet away from the front door. He didn't want to push his way into Claire's home. He didn't want to frighten her.

"I know you didn't kill Mr. Stanton," Claire said. "In the years I worked with you at Stanton Industries, I had a chance to see what sort of man you are. You aren't a murderer. But then, neither is Kenny."

"I'm not asking you to accuse Kenny of murder," Reece said. "All I'm asking is that you tell the truth."

"Kenny warned me only this morning about keeping quiet." Claire clasped her hands together. "He's out of his mind with worry since you escaped."

"Kenny won't be calling the shots at Stanton Industries if I'm proven innocent of B.K.'s murder. Christina and I will have the majority shares. We'll make sure your job is protected and your daughter's scholarship."

"Hearing you put things like that makes me so ashamed." Claire wiped the tears from her face with her hand. "I knew I should have told the truth. I wanted to go to your lawyer and tell him what I'd done after the trial, but I was so afraid."

Reece took Claire by the shoulders. She stared at him, wringing her hands, her chin quivering. "Will you go to the sheriff tomorrow and tell him the truth?"

"I...I..."

They both heard the car pull into the driveway. Reece released his hold on Claire's shoulders. "Are you expecting someone?"

"No, I..." Claire eased back the sheer curtains over the picture window and peered outside. "Oh, my goodness, it's Kenny. He just got out of his car, and he's talking to some woman."

Every nerve in Reece's body tensed. Some woman. Hell, the woman had to be Elizabeth.

"What's he doing here?" Claire trembled, her hand clutching the sheer curtains.

"He's checking up on you. Making sure you keep your mouth shut."

"Who's the woman with Kenny?"

"She's not with Kenny. She's with me. She drove me over here to see you tonight."

"Oh, dear. How will she ever explain being at my house?"

Standing directly behind Claire, Reece glanced out the window. Elizabeth stood beside Sam's T-Bird. He heard her voice, loud and strong and clear.

"Well, hello, Mr. Stanton. What are you doing here?"

"Ms. Mallory, our visiting psychic." Kenny surveyed Elizabeth from head to toe. "I'm here on business, to pick up some papers from my secretary. What are you doing here? I wasn't aware that you were acquainted with Claire Roberts."

"I'm not acquainted with Mrs. Roberts." Elizabeth glanced toward the house, hoping Reece was aware of Kenny's arrival. "I had another vision. One that involved the woman who lives here."

"What sort of vision?" Kenny asked.

"A vision of a terrible argument between you and your father. Mrs. Roberts witnessed the argument. I came here to question her about my vision, and find out what she knows."

Even in the darkness, Elizabeth saw Kenny's face collapse, but she couldn't help admiring his control. He didn't move a muscle.

In her peripheral vision Elizabeth noticed the front door of Mrs. Roberts's house open. Surely Reece wouldn't be foolish enough to walk outside at this precise moment.

"Mr. Stanton, is that you?" Claire Roberts stood on her porch, staring out at the two people in her driveway.

"Yes, Claire, it's me." Turning around, Kenny faced Claire. "I've stopped by to pick up those papers I need for tomorrow morning's meeting, but it seems I'm not your only visitor."

"Who's that with you?"

"Elizabeth Mallory, some young woman who claims to be a psychic and says she's had visions about B.K.'s death. Christina brought her to the house for dinner tonight."

"Why did you bring her here with you?"

"I didn't," Kenny said. "She was here when I arrived."

"I see. Well, I'm afraid those papers you want aren't ready yet. Perhaps if you can come back in an hour."

Kenny walked up the sidewalk, stopping at the bottom of the

front steps. "I'll just come inside and wait for you to finish up with that report if you don't mind, Claire. There's no need for me to drive all the way back home, is there?"

"I'd like to speak to you tonight, Mrs. Roberts." Elizabeth rushed over, stepping in front of Kenny. Reece had to be inside the house, and undoubtedly Claire Roberts had no intention of telling Kenny. Did that mean Reece had persuaded B.K.'s secretary to tell the police the truth, to admit that she had lied under oath?

"Couldn't this wait until tomorrow, Ms. Mallory?" Kenny glared at Elizabeth, his round, full face slightly flushed.

"It's all right," Claire said. "Why don't you both come on in."

Once inside the house, Elizabeth glanced around the living room, wondering if Reece had exited through a back door or if he was hiding in another room. She could tell that Claire Roberts was nervous simply by the hesitant way she walked, the way she kept wringing her hands, the way she repeatedly glanced toward the darkened hallway.

Reece was at the end of that hallway, impatiently waiting. Elizabeth sensed his unease. She tried to reassure him by sending him a telepathic message, hoping he would open his mind to hers. She could almost hear him saying, "Be careful, Lizzie. Be careful."

"I really won't take up too much of your time," Elizabeth said. "Like Mr. Stanton told you, I'm a psychic, and I've had several visions concerning B. K. Stanton's death. I am convinced that Reece Landry is an innocent man."

"I agree," Claire said. "I've never, not for one moment, thought Reece capable of murder."

"Who are we to say?" Kenny balled his meaty hands into tight fists. "After all, Reece was convicted of Daddy's murder. He was the only real suspect. The only one with a motive. Everyone knew he hated Daddy, that he hated our family."

Ignoring Kenny, Elizabeth turned all her attention on Claire. "You were present when B. K. Stanton and Kenny had a terrible argument the day Mr. Stanton was killed, weren't you?"

"How did you—" Claire gasped.

"This is utter nonsense!" Kenny's baritone voice sounded overly shrill in the stillness of Claire Roberts's living room. "Don't say another word, Claire."

Elizabeth glanced at Kenny. "By threatening Mrs. Roberts, you make it appear that you have something to hide."

"Why the hell did you have to show up?" Kenny's hound-dog cheeks, so similar to his mother's, sagged. His thin lips drooped at the corners. "Everything is as it should be. Reece Landry is a worthless bastard. He hated Daddy."

"But he didn't kill him." Elizabeth's voice was a mere whisper, but the conviction of her words filled the room.

"Yes, he did!" Glaring at Elizabeth, Kenny walked toward her slowly. "Landry killed Daddy. He killed him!"

"You may hate your brother, Mr. Stanton, but you know he wouldn't have been the only suspect if your family hadn't bribed and threatened witnesses to keep quiet. Somehow you persuaded Mrs. Roberts to lie about an argument you had with your father." Elizabeth sensed the fear and anger building to a boiling point within Kenny Stanton. "You…you threatened to kill your father that day, didn't you?" Elizabeth was as shocked by the realization as Kenny was by her pronouncement. The memory had been crystal clear in Kenny's mind.

"He might have threatened to kill his father," Claire said, "but he didn't any more kill Mr. Stanton than Reece did."

"No, you mustn't!" Kenny's eyes glazed over, his vision unfocused as he stared off into space. "We've always been good to you, Claire. Why would you betray us?"

"I'm not betraying anyone anymore." Claire slumped down on the sofa. "I lied in that courtroom because I was afraid, but I can't keep quiet any longer if I can help Reece by telling the truth."

"What are you saying?" Kenny staggered about as if he were drunk.

"I'm going to the sheriff in the morning and tell him what I did."

"You can't!" Kenny turned quickly, his eyes fixed on Elizabeth. "This is all your fault. You and your damned visions. No one is going to do anything to help Reece. I won't allow it. Do you hear me? I won't allow it!"

"Did you kill your father?" Elizabeth backed away from Kenny, slowly but surely easing toward the front door.

"Did I... Is that what this is all about?" Kenny opened his clenched fists, then reclosed them. "Is that what your crazy visions showed you? That I killed Daddy?"

"Mr. Stanton...Kenny..." Easing herself up off the sofa, Claire held out her hand. "No one is accusing you of anything."

"She is!" Kenny pointed at Elizabeth. "You're no psychic. You haven't had any visions. You're in this with Reece, aren't you? You're just another stupid woman who fell for his tough-guy image, aren't you?"

Sensing Kenny's deep frustration, Elizabeth backed up against the door, uncertain how close he was to losing control. "You're talking about your wife, aren't you? Reece Landry didn't have an affair with Tracy, despite what you may think or what she might have said. Don't let your jealousy blind you to the truth about your brother."

"That man is not my brother." Kenny reached out for Elizabeth, grabbing her by the shoulders, jerking her forward. "You're as big a fool as every other woman I know when it comes to Reece Landry, but you've made a big mistake trying to help a convicted murderer." Grabbing Elizabeth around the waist with one fleshy hand, Kenny circled her neck with his other hand, pressing his fingers against her windpipe.

"If the police don't catch Landry, then Harry Gunn will," Kenny said. "And that old man's crazy enough to kill anyone who gets in his way. You know how crazy he is? He's been taking turns following Chris and then Tracy all around Newell. Ever since he heard Reece was back in town, he figured Chris or Tracy would lead him to Reece."

"Kenny, please let Ms. Mallory go." Claire took a tentative step forward. "She may want to help Reece, but that doesn't mean she wants to harm you."

Kenny tightened his hold on Elizabeth, his fingers biting into her neck. She tried not to panic, but she felt Kenny's desperation, all his pain focused on her because she was Reece Landry's woman.

"Kenny, please..." Elizabeth said. She knew what was going to happen, and wished she could prevent the inevitable. Reece would never allow Kenny to harm her. At this precise moment she sensed Reece preparing himself to attack. And when he did—

"I was Daddy's only son," Kenny said. "Everything was mine. Daddy, Stanton Industries and Tracy. Then Reece came along."

"I know how difficult it must have been for you, but surely you realize that your father played you and Reece against each other for his own perverse reasons. You mustn't blame Reece—"

Kenny roared with laughter, the laughter of a man on the edge of a breakdown. "Don't blame Reece for sleeping with my wife, for taking my father away from me, for stealing part of my inheritance." Kenny shoved Elizabeth up against the wall. "When I found out about Tracy and Reece, I should have killed her. I should have killed them both."

Kenny's fingers closed around Elizabeth's throat, choking her. She grabbed at his shoulders, shoving him, at the same time kicking his leg. If only Reece would stay put, she could handle this situation. Kenny didn't have a weapon, and she felt certain she was strong enough to fight him off.

Just as she raised her leg, aiming directly for Kenny's groin, he released her. Reece jerked Kenny away from Elizabeth, tossing him to the floor as easily as he would have thrown a pillow. Kenny glared up at his brother, pure hatred in his eyes. Elizabeth slumped against the wall, coughing several times, then gulping in air.

"You slimy little son of a bitch!" Reece stared at Kenny, at his father's firstborn, at the soft, pampered, weak and spoiled heir to the throne.

Lying flat on his back on the floor, Kenny looked toward Elizabeth. "I was right, wasn't I? You're just one more of Reece Landry's conquests." Then Kenny grinned as he stared up at Reece. "What's the matter, Landry? You don't want me to touch your woman? That's not fair, is it, since you've done a lot more than touch my wife?"

Reece, his legs spread apart, clenched his hands open and closed as he stood over his brother, wanting more than anything to beat the hell out of Bradley Kenneth Stanton, Jr. "You're too blinded by hate to see the truth. God, I feel sorry for you. To think I envied you all my life."

Elizabeth grabbed Reece by the sleeve of his jacket. "Don't do what you're thinking. He's not worth it."

"You'd better listen to your lady friend," Kenny said, shoving himself up into a sitting position. "Unless you intend to kill me and Claire both. After all, she'd be a witness to my murder."

Elizabeth tugged on Reece's sleeve. He glanced at her quickly, exchanging a brief message of understanding, then looked back down at Kenny. "Claire is going to tell the sheriff the truth about your fight with B.K.," Reece said. "And the man Tracy was with when B.K. was killed is going to blow your alibi, so, big brother, you'd better be prepared to do some explaining."

"You think you're so damned smart, don't you?" Kenny's mouth widened into a self-satisfied smirk. "Well, I didn't kill Daddy. And Claire isn't going to tell the sheriff anything, and neither is that muscle-bound twenty-year-old Tracy was screwing the night you murdered Daddy."

Elizabeth saw Claire pick up from the end table a heavy brass flower vase filled with an arrangement of silk roses. Elizabeth glanced at Reece, and knew he was aware of Claire's movements.

"The Stantons own this town," Kenny said. "We make the rules. Nobody goes against a Stanton and wins. You should know that, Landry."

Claire Roberts walked up behind Kenny, who sat on the floor smiling at Reece and Elizabeth, a cocky glint in his eyes. Lifting the large brass vase, Claire brought it down on top of Kenny's head. He fell sideways, unconscious. The brass vase thumped silently onto the floor; the peach silk roses scattered across the sea of blue carpet.

Claire knelt beside Kenny, feeling for a pulse. "He's fine. I just knocked him out."

"You most certainly did," Elizabeth said, slightly stunned by the other woman's actions.

"Reece, you have to get away as fast as you can," Claire said. "I'll have to call the police before Kenny comes to, but I'll wait as long as I can to give you a head start."

"Claire?" Reece stared at B. K. Stanton's secretary.

"I'll tell the police everything. The truth about Kenny's quarrel with his father, the fact that he threatened to kill B.K. And...and I'll tell them that you were here tonight. I'm through with lying. For Kenny or for you."

"That's fair enough," Reece said. "Thank you, Claire."

"Go on. Get out of here." Bracing her hand on a recliner at her side, Claire lifted herself up from the floor.

Slipping his arm around Elizabeth, Reece led her out the front door and to Sam's T-Bird.

"Get in the back and lie down," Elizabeth told him. "I'll drive us to Spruce Pine as quickly as possible."

Reece opened the car door. "We need to talk to Sam before we go back to the cottage. He should know what happened here, that Kenny's going to tell the police you're helping me. And I need to find out if Sam was able to persuade Tracy's lover to admit the truth."

"It's too dangerous to go to Sam's motel. Once Kenny comes to—"

"We're going to the motel," Reece said. "And Sam's going to get you out of Newell as fast as he can."

"No! I won't go. I won't leave you."

"Dammit, Lizzie. This time you'll do what I tell you to do."

CHAPTER 11

"Dammit, what a mess." Sam Dundee paced back and forth at the foot of the bed in his motel room. "You should turn yourself in, Reece. Tonight."

"I don't know," Reece said. "My gut instincts tell me that now isn't the time, that we aren't any closer to finding the real killer."

"Look, you've got Claire Roberts willing to admit that she lied under oath because Kenny Stanton threatened her, and I persuaded Neil Colburn to tell the police that Tracy Stanton paid him to keep quiet about being with her when your father was murdered. That shoots holes in Kenny's alibi."

"We have no proof that Kenny killed B.K.," Reece said. "If I turn myself in, they'll pack me off to Arrendale, and appeal or no appeal, my chances of ever being set free are slim if we can't prove who really shot B.K."

"The real murderer is going to reveal himself or herself." Elizabeth's gaze softened when she looked at Reece. If only he would allow her to comfort him. No matter how close he let her get, he kept a barrier between them—a barrier of fear and distrust.

"Is that a psychic prediction or just a wild guess?" Reece knew he wasn't being fair to Elizabeth, but, dammit all, he'd had just about enough. He didn't know how much longer he could withstand the temptation to lower his guard completely, to let Elizabeth inside his head and inside his heart. He'd be a fool to keep her with him; she'd be an even bigger fool to stay.

"Neither prediction nor guess." Elizabeth swallowed the tears trapped in her throat. Even knowing where Reece's anger and bitterness came from, she couldn't keep herself from being hurt by his words. "Whoever killed B.K. knows you're innocent, and he or she will soon know that I'm helping you and I've claimed to have a psychic vision of the murder. I don't think they'll wait too long before they make their move."

"She's right," Sam said. "If the real murderer finds you and Elizabeth, he'll do whatever it takes to silence both of you."

"Don't you think I know that." Reece narrowed his eyes, giving Sam a hard look. "I want you to get Elizabeth out of Newell as fast as you can. Tonight, if possible."

"I would agree with you, except for one small problem you've overlooked," Sam said. "The sheriff will be looking for Elizabeth as soon as Kenny Stanton tells them that she's aiding and abetting you. There's no way I can get her out of Newell once that happens."

"What the hell are we going to do?" Reece hated the thought of Elizabeth being in trouble with the law because of him.

"Turn yourself in tonight." Sam nodded toward the telephone. "Call Gary Elkins and tell him to meet you at the sheriff's office. I'll go with you and Elizabeth, and we'll see if we can hoodoo them into believing that Elizabeth isn't involved, that Kenny Stanton is lying."

"I'm not ready to give up my freedom." Reece couldn't bring himself to put his life in anyone else's hands. Not Gary Elkins's or Sam Dundee's. Not even Elizabeth's.

"Wherever you go, whatever you do, I'm going with you." Elizabeth walked over to Reece, clasping his arm in her strong grip.

Reece jerked away from her. "Don't be a fool, Lizzie. You've done everything you can do for me. I don't want you following me around like some lovesick puppy. Just because I'm the first man you ever—"

"Shut the hell up!" Sam bellowed, punching Reece in the chest with his index finger.

Elizabeth placed her hand on Sam's shoulder. "It's all right, Sam. Reece's bark is a lot worse than his bite. He's tried this tactic before and it didn't work. Obviously he doesn't learn from his mistakes."

"Obviously," Sam said.

"How you've been able to put up with her all these years, Dundee, I'll never know." Grinning sheepishly, Reece shook his head. "You can't tell her anything. She knows too damn much. She can look through a guy like he's made of glass. And no matter what you say to her or do to her, she just keeps on caring."

"That's called love and loyalty." Sam placed his arm around Elizabeth's shoulders. "A couple of qualities that were obviously missing in your life, Landry."

"Yeah, so it would seem."

"If you don't intend to turn yourself in tonight, then I suggest that you and Elizabeth go back to Spruce Pine for the time being," Sam said. "If you don't get out of Newell pretty quick, you'll be trapped here."

"You want Elizabeth to go with me?" Reece asked. "I thought you, of all people, would see how dangerous her being with me is."

"I've known since the day she called and told me she was hiding you in her cabin that she was in danger because of you. But she didn't listen to my warnings then. And now it's too late to take her away from you."

"Keep her here. Take her to the police. Make them believe that Kenny's lying, that her only involvement with me is through her visions."

"That won't work," Elizabeth said. "Claire Roberts will tell the sheriff the truth. Besides, Sam is right. I won't leave you. He believes me when I say that somehow, some way, I'm the only person who can save you."

"How?" Reece asked. "By having the real killer come after you?"

"Perhaps. I'm not sure."

"Time's a-wasting," Sam said. "You two go back to Spruce Pine. In the morning Gary Elkins and I will meet y'all at the Burtons' cottage. Be prepared to turn yourself in to the sheriff, Landry, or be a hundred miles away from here."

"I don't like ultimatums."

"And I don't like Elizabeth's life being in danger."

"All right," Reece agreed. "You get in touch with Gary. Give him all the information we've uncovered, and meet us at the cottage first thing in the morning. That will give me all night to sort through things, to decide what to do."

"If you leave, don't take Elizabeth with you."

"She'll be waiting for you at the cottage, whether I'm there or not."

"Hold on just one minute," Elizabeth said. "Nobody's making any decisions for me."

Reece grabbed Elizabeth's arm. "If I run, Lizzie, I'll be running for the rest of my life, and you won't be going with me."

Elizabeth wanted to protest, to tell Reece that she didn't care where he went, she *was* going with him. But she realized that Reece was right. If he didn't trust her enough to accept her help, to believe that Sam and Gary Elkins and Chris Stanton were all on his side, then there was no hope for Reece and her. She couldn't force Reece to trust her or to love her. There was no way she could reach his mind or his heart if he continued denying her entrance.

Elizabeth turned to Sam, pulling free of Reece's hold on her arm. "I'll be waiting for you in the morning. We'll go to the sheriff and tell him everything. The complete truth. And then I'll face the consequences of my actions."

Sam hugged Elizabeth. "Ah, kiddo, why did you have to grow up?"

"He'll do the right thing," Elizabeth whispered to Sam. "I have to believe that he'll decide he can trust us."

"If you're going with me, let's go." Reece swung open the motel-room door.

Elizabeth followed him outside. A slow, steady drizzle fell from the sky. Raindrops pelted her face as she stood gazing out into the dark night.

"Please, dear Lord, please take care of Reece," Elizabeth prayed silently. "Set him free. Give him the peace he's never known."

When Reece prodded her to move, she turned to him, staring into his hard, lone-wolf eyes. He had shut her out. Not one sign of emotion showed on his face.

Elizabeth stepped out of the shower, dried herself off quickly and slipped into clean panties, jeans and a sweater. After towel-drying her long hair, she combed it away from her face. A weariness she had seldom experienced encompassed her, a bone-tired weariness, a heartsick weariness.

In less than a week her whole world had turned upside down, thanks to Reece Landry, thanks to her own obsession with saving him—saving him not only from a wrongful conviction but from a life that had almost destroyed him.

No matter how hard she tried to get through to him, he would allow her only so close and no closer. He had made love to her with a passion she'd never known existed, but he had given only a portion of himself to her, holding in reserve his heart, not trusting anyone enough to share his soul.

Elizabeth felt as if she had lost control of her life, of her thoughts, of her emotions. Reece Landry had become her whole world. She had become so wrapped up in helping him that she'd lost herself.

Elizabeth opened the door to the bedroom she had shared with Reece only last night. It might as well have been a million nights ago. He had been so cold and distant since their return to the cottage. She had no idea where he was. Outside, in the living room or in an upstairs bedroom. Of course, she understood that he, too, had some soul-searching to do. Would he be able to put his trust in others, to accept the advice of his lawyer?

Sitting down at the antique dressing table, Elizabeth ran a comb through her damp hair. She glanced into the mirror, seeing her own image, the wide blue eyes, the mane of dark wet hair, the sad expression she could not banish.

Laying down the comb, she closed her eyes, extinguishing her own image, closing out the world. She hadn't meditated in several days. At home in Sequana Falls, daily meditation was a part of her life, helping her center her energy and focus her abilities. Aunt Margaret had taught her that meditation was the only way she would ever learn to control the great talent with which she had been blessed, the only way her soul could derive true peace.

The day would come when she would be able to shield herself, to protect herself from the psychic energy of others. Aunt Margaret had explained how many years it had taken her to reach a point of self-protection, where she could, at will, block out the bombardment of the energy others emitted.

Elizabeth repeated the word *angel,* using it as her mantra, seeking sanctuary and inner peace in her prayerlike state of meditation.

"An-gel. An-gel. An-gel." As she chanted, her voice became a low whisper, her mind gradually clearing as utter calmness encompassed her.

Reece eased open the bedroom door, stopping dead still when he saw Elizabeth sitting at the dressing table, her eyes shut, her lips moving repeatedly as she whispered a single word. Angel.

What the hell was she doing, his loyal, loving little witch? Casting a spell? Going into a trance? Calling on the heavenly hosts to come to their aid?

The best he could make out, she was praying or something along those lines. He couldn't remember a time since he was a kid that he'd prayed, that he'd asked for someone else's help. He'd begged and pleaded for someone—anyone—to save his mother and him from Harry Gunn. He supposed, in a way, God had answered his prayers, but he had taken his own sweet time doing it. Blanche's death had freed her from Harry; Reece's physical strength had emancipated him from his stepfather's brutality.

Even knowing he was witnessing a private moment in Elizabeth's life, one he had no right to share, he could not turn and walk away. He couldn't stop staring at her, listening to her, absorbing some of the radiant peace she emanated, like a deep spring bubbling forth pure, clean water. A warmth spread through his body, accompanied by a calmness he had never known.

What was happening to him? he wondered. Was Elizabeth delving into his mind? Was she manipulating his emotions?

She looked so serene sitting there at perfect peace with herself and with the world around her. She was offering that same peace to him. Did he dare believe in its existence? And if he did believe, did he have the courage to accept her precious gift?

He wasn't sure how long he stood in the doorway, transfixed by Elizabeth's beauty, both physical and spiritual. Perhaps it was only minutes. Perhaps longer.

Complete quiet settled over the room. Elizabeth opened her eyes and turned slowly toward Reece. He saw that she started to lift her hand to him, but stopped abruptly.

"How long have you been standing there?" she asked.

"Don't you know?"

"Yes, I know, but do you?"

"I don't think I'm ready to accept what you're offering me." Reece walked into the room, his gaze fixed on Elizabeth. "I want to trust you completely. I want to believe that my life can be… That I can put the past behind me. All the anger and pain and hatred. But I can't."

"You don't want to let go of the emotions that have dominated your life." Elizabeth turned all the way around on the velvet bench. "You're afraid of the unknown. Of trust and loyalty and love."

Reece sat on the edge of the bed. Raking his hand down his face, he wiped his mouth. "You want me to turn myself in, don't you? You want me to hand myself over to the sheriff and trust you and Sam and Gary and Chris to save me."

She smiled at Reece. Tears gathered in her eyes, obscuring her vision. "I know it's difficult for you to accept the fact that there are people who care about you, but—"

"I didn't ask anybody to care about me." Bent over, his hands clasped together between his spread knees, Reece stared at the floor. "I didn't ask you to help me and I didn't ask you to care about me."

Such anger! Elizabeth felt the resurgence of hostile emotions growing inside Reece. He was fighting an inner battle, yearning for something he didn't quite believe in, afraid to relinquish his hold on the old demons that had haunted his life since childhood—the familiarity of their ugly but constant presence the only thing he'd ever been able to count on.

"What if you allowed me to see into your future? If I could promise you that B.K.'s real murderer would be brought to justice and you would be cleared of all charges, would you trust me and the others who want to help you?"

Jerking his head up, Reece stared at her, his amber eyes gleaming with uncertainty. "I thought you said that you couldn't see my future, that our futures were entwined and you would never look into your own future."

"If it's the only way to help you, then I'm willing to try." Elizabeth stood.

Reece glared at her. "No. Don't do it, Lizzie. Don't break one of your sacred rules for me. I've taken enough from you as it is."

Elizabeth walked across the room, knelt in front of Reece and laid her head on his knee. "You're afraid of the future. Even if you're cleared of B.K.'s murder and claim your inheritance, you won't be free. You'll stay in Newell, you'll take over Stanton Industries, you'll avenge yourself against Kenny and Alice and even Chris. But nothing you do will ever change the past. B. K. Stanton is dead. You can't hurt him. Blanche is dead. You can't help her."

Reece stroked Elizabeth's head, threading his fingers through her damp, silky hair. "How the hell can you know me so well? You say that I shield myself from you and yet you seem to see inside my head."

Tears burned in her eyes. A warm, tingling flush of pain spread through her. "It doesn't take a psychic to figure you out." Turning her face just a fraction, she looked up at him. All it takes is a woman who cares about you, Elizabeth thought.

Reece's breath caught in his chest, creating an agonized constriction. She was, without a doubt, the most beautiful thing he'd ever seen. Radiant and warm. Tender and caring. He wanted her in a way he'd never thought it possible to want another human being. Not only did he want to possess her body, to make love to her until he was spent, he wanted to cherish all that she was—the goodness that made Elizabeth Mallory unique in a world of lesser women. He wanted to protect her from every harm, to ease her pain, to see her smile, to hear her laugh.

He wanted her to open her arms to him, to call his name, to bring him out of the darkness in which he existed into the warm, pure light of her life.

The truth hit him full force, like a lightning bolt out of the blue. A truth he knew only too well. A truth he had allowed himself to momentarily forget.

Reece placed his hands at Elizabeth's waist, helping her to her feet as he stood, then shoving her gently away from him. Why had he, for one minute, thought he was good enough for Elizabeth? What could he offer her? Nothing. Absolutely nothing she wanted or needed. Right now, as an escaped convict on the run, he offered her danger and uncertainty. If and when he was cleared of B.K.'s murder and could offer her the wealth and power his inheritance would afford him, he could offer her anything money could buy. But Elizabeth would not want material things; she would want his love.

They stared at each other, lone-wolf amber mating briefly with angelic blue innocence. Elizabeth knew he was going to leave her, that no matter how much his soul longed for all she offered him, his inner demons demanded a battle to the death.

He walked away, halting briefly to turn partially toward her as he neared the doorway. "I'll sleep in one of the upstairs bedrooms tonight."

"Yes. I understand."

"Whatever I decide…I want you to know how grateful I am for all your help. I probably owe you my life. I'll never forget—"

"It's all right, Reece. You don't have to thank me. I did only what

I wanted to do—what I had to do." But I've failed, haven't I? Even if we can save you from prison, will I be able to save you from yourself?

Reece had no idea what time it was, how close to midnight, how close to dawn. All he knew was that he hadn't been able to sleep, that he had spent what seemed like endless hours fighting the demons in his soul. How did a man who had spent his life taking care of himself, never trusting or counting on anyone else, give in to the weakness of putting himself in someone else's care?

Was that his problem? Reece wondered. Did he see trust and caring as weaknesses? Why couldn't he consider them strengths? After all, it would take far more courage for him to willingly turn himself over to the sheriff and put his trust in others than it would to keep on running.

He slipped into his jeans, zipping them but leaving them unsnapped. The chill in the upstairs bedroom cautioned him against walking around bare chested. Lifting his shirt from the foot of the bed, he put it on and walked out into the hall. The cottage was pitch-black, including the stairway, except for the shimmering stream of moonlight flowing through the glass panes of the French door that separated the tiny foyer from the front porch.

Reece made his way down the stairs, his booted feet creating a soft, steady beat against the wooden steps. There was no point in his turning and tossing the rest of the night. What he needed was a shot of whiskey if he could find some in the house, and knowing Tracy's tastes, he figured the liquor cabinet in the living room was stocked.

The living room lay in darkness, the moonlight filtering through the sheer curtains, forming soft, wavy shadows across the floor. Low, golden-crowned orange flames danced atop disintegrating logs in the fireplace. A hushed stillness, the winter peace of nature, the blessed quiet of aloneness permeated the room like a giant sponge that had soaked up a wellspring of tranquillity.

He felt her presence before he saw her. The very idea of sensing Elizabeth without seeing her sent shock waves through Reece.

Before he'd met her, he hadn't believed in much of anything, certainly not in anything he couldn't experience with his five senses. But since coming under her spell, he had learned to believe. He had learned to trust. He had learned to care. He didn't know exactly how she'd done it, but Elizabeth Mallory had begun to perform a miracle inside him. A half-formed miracle—incomplete, but the beginning was there.

He stood in the arched opening leading from the foyer to the living room. His heart beat steadily. He heard its thumping rhythm pounding in his ears.

And then he felt Elizabeth's loneliness, the deep sadness that filled her heart. Her quiet, gulping sobs blasted like trumpets when he heard them. She was crying for him. Crying because he could not cry, just as she had done before, the day they had stood on her back porch in Sequana Falls and he had shared a part of his past with her.

He crept into the room with silent steps, wanting to be nearer yet afraid to confront what he knew he would face once he'd touched her. She sat curled up in the white wicker rocker by one of the windows, a flowered afghan draped around her, her legs hugged up against her body, her chin resting on her knees.

She wore her thermal underwear, the ones with the tiny flowers printed on the cotton fabric. Her hair had dried and hung loosely around her shoulders, down her back, the tips almost touching her waist.

The moonlight spread over her, coating her like a sheer, radiant veil. She glowed, lighting the darkness the way stars illuminate the night sky.

Reece wanted to run, but his feet didn't move. If he stayed, he wouldn't be able to resist her. Even now, without touching her, he felt the power of her enticement, calling to him, offering him everything and more, so much more than he'd ever thought possible.

"I'm going to turn myself in to the sheriff in the morning." He heard her gasp softly and swallow her tears.

"I won't desert you," she told him, her voice a tender whisper in the darkness. "I'll stay with you and help you. We'll get through this together."

She eased her legs down, touching her feet to the floor. Draping the afghan across her breasts, she stood. Reece hesitated for one brief second, then he held open his arms. Elizabeth stared at him, her breathing slow and heavy. She walked toward him, each step measured, giving herself time to accept the inevitable.

When she stood less than two feet in front of him, she looked at him, then closed her eyes. Once done, some things can never be undone, she told herself. Be sure you are prepared for this, be certain that, if need be, you can go on without him. Know in your heart that you are willing to raise his child alone—the child he will give you tonight if you make love with him.

The knowledge that she had glimpsed her future shook Elizabeth to the very core of her soul. Never had she allowed herself the freedom to see into her own future. But she had not allowed herself to do so this time. It had simply happened.

She shivered, every nerve ending in her body alive with the knowledge that she was destined to love Reece Landry, that he had been sent to her, in her dreams, in her visions, a gift from the gods.

Reece pulled her into his embrace. The afghan slipped off her shoulders, falling at her feet like a pastel flower bed. She trembled as she slid her arms up around his neck, relaxing her body against his. Accepting. Trusting. Yearning. Loving.

The very nearness of him, the hard, demanding strength of him, the heady, masculine aura surrounding him sucked Elizabeth into a vortex of desire, a whirlpool of passion that demanded she surrender herself.

Reece shuddered with a fierce need to possess the woman in his arms, to lay her down and cover her with his body. He inched his hand up her back, under the fall of silky dark hair, lifting the coffee brown strands, burying his face against her neck, gripping the back of her head with his open palm. She smelled of fresh sweetness, clean and pure.

Elizabeth clung to him, losing herself in the moment, in the feel of him, the hard, lean-muscled feel of a man. Her heart fluttered inside her, like a trapped bird fighting to escape. Her heart longed to escape, to soar, to join with his and become a part of him.

She felt the wild, racing beat of his heart as she laid her face against his chest. She heard the loud, strong pounding. Her whole body throbbed with a need so intense she wanted to scream, to cry out for release, to plead for the exhilarating torment to end.

Reece lifted her head, turning her to face him, lowering his mouth over hers, laying claim to her lips. Elizabeth greeted his kiss with hungry anticipation, relief shooting through her. The tension mounted higher and higher when he thrust his tongue inside, devouring her with his need.

Elizabeth's fingers bit into his shoulders. Reece's free hand roamed down her back, grasping her buttocks, caressing her with a tender fury. He held her head immobile, drinking deeply from her sweetness, wanting—desperately needing—all she had to give.

Their bodies pressed together, her breasts crushed to his chest, his maleness throbbing against her stomach.

Reece tried to speak, tried to tell her how much he wanted her, but words seemed redundant. He raised her thermal top, easing it slowly, inch by inch until it lay in a fat roll under her arms. Her full, round breasts, the nipples jutting into sensitive hardness, beckoned his touch. Reece delved one hand down the back of her thermal bottoms, then reached out with his other hand, covering her breast, kneading softly, then playing with her nipple, pinching it between his thumb and forefinger.

The sheer, agonized delight of his touch spiraled through Elizabeth like fire along a thin trail of kerosene, flames burning higher and higher, quickly out of control. She writhed against him, moaning with a pleasure close to pain.

Shoving back his unbuttoned shirt, she caressed his chest. She loved the feel of his tight muscles, the thick mat of curling chest hair, the tiny male nipples tight with desire.

"I want you," she told him on a breathless sigh. "Make love to me."

She knew what she was asking—all that she was asking. Reece

knew only part. He could not know that, tonight, he would give her his child.

She could have turned from him, said no, refused them both the unequaled pleasure of loving each other. She could ask him to use protection, but in her heart of hearts she knew that she did not want to refuse him, she did not want to prevent his seed from creating a new life within her body.

She loved Reece Landry. And she wanted his child.

Reece pulled the thermal top over her head, tossing it to the floor, then lowered the bottoms down her legs and over her feet. She stood before him totally naked, the moonlight creating a halo around her body. Reece shrugged out of his shirt, letting it fall where it would. When he unzipped his jeans, Elizabeth stilled his hands, covering them with hers.

She dropped to her knees, burying her face against him as she clutched the waistband of his jeans and tugged them over his hips. The faded jeans dropped slowly down his legs, landing in a pile of denim at his feet. Reece kicked his pants out of the way.

Elizabeth caressed his stomach, then spread her arms around him, cupping his buttocks, squeezing them.

Reece moaned. She smelled the heady fragrance of his arousal and breathed deeply, savoring the elemental maleness that was uniquely Reece's own. When her lips touched him, he trembled, sighing, almost crying with pleasure.

Her inexperience brought out her insecurities, but the depth of her love overcame her innocent shyness. She made love to Reece, drunk on the power she possessed over him, reveling in the wanton groans she elicited from him. When she took him into her mouth he grasped the back of her head, guiding her, teaching her with his touch.

Unbearable pleasure rocketed through Reece, spilling out of him, saturating the very air he breathed. His chest rose and fell with each labored breath. Slowly withdrawing himself and dropping to his knees, he lifted her face to his, tasting himself on her lips.

Smiling, she shut her eyes, giving herself over to him, allowing him free rein of her body. He deepened the kiss. She clasped his shoulders. He caressed her, his big hands roaming over her back, her waist, inching upward to lift the weight of her throbbing breasts. He kissed her lips, then her chin, gliding his tongue down her throat. Stopping his pilgrimage in the hollow between her breasts, he gazed at her and smiled.

"You certainly know how to bring a man to his knees, Lizzie."

Laughter erupted in her chest, bubbling up and out of her. "Oh, Reece, I—"

He silenced her with his mouth, obliterating her words, keeping her from declaring her love for him. She didn't have to say the words. Her actions spoke for her.

Taking her hands in his, Reece stood and lifted her to her feet. He led her out of the living room and down the hall, pausing every second or two to kiss her. When they entered the bedroom, she lay on the bed and opened her arms, inviting him into the warmth, the passion, the love he could know only with her.

Reece could no more deny her than he could will the sun not to rise or the earth to stop revolving. He came down on top of her, covering her body with his. He made a banquet feast of her, nibbling, tasting, sampling every inch of her, devouring her with his fierce desire.

Elizabeth squirmed beneath the mastery of his hands and mouth, learning exactly how much pleasure a man can give a woman if he chooses to do so. And Reece Landry chose to take her to heaven that night, to give her abundant sensual joy.

Her breasts begged for his attention, then ached with throbbing need when he touched them, kissed them, suckled them. She felt herself drifting in a sea of ever-increasing awareness, finding herself on the brink of drowning in rapture when Reece spread her legs and pleasured her with his mouth. She cried out as her body shook with release.

He lifted himself over her, gazing down at her damp face, her flushed cheeks, her lips moist and open.

"You're an angel, Elizabeth. My angel."

He took her then, before she could respond, before she could proclaim her love. He filled her completely, her body, her heart, her soul. As surely as she knew she loved Reece Landry, she knew this moment was meant to be.

They loved with a wild abandon that neither had ever known or would ever know again, except in each other's arms. It was madness. It was ecstasy.

And when they reached their climaxes, she first and he following quickly, they lay in each other's arms, in the cool, dark stillness of the night, neither of them speaking. He listened to her breathe; she listened to him breathe. Reece pulled the covers up over them. He kissed Elizabeth on the forehead. She snuggled against him.

Smiling, she laid her hand on her stomach. No matter what tomorrow brought, she knew she would never lose Reece. She carried his child in her body. He would be a part of her forever.

Reece sat straight up in bed, the sheet and quilt falling to his waist. Adrenaline pumped through his body like floodwaters from a broken dam. Something had awakened him. He ran his hand over his face, blinking his eyes. Listening intently, he heard only the sound of his own heartbeat, and Elizabeth's soft, steady breathing as she lay nestled at his side.

He heard a car door slam, and then another. Laughter. Silly, drunken laughter. Tracy Stanton's laughter.

"Dammit!" He muttered the word under his breath as he threw back the covers and got out of bed. What the hell was she doing here in February? He'd had no idea that she used her parents' summer cottage as a trysting place in the winter months. She'd brought him here in May.

The keys to the Jeep and the T-Bird were on the nightstand. If they hurried, they could be out of the house before Tracy and her lover came inside.

Suddenly Reece remembered that his and Elizabeth's clothes were scattered on the living room floor. Damn! Making his way out of the dark bedroom, he eased open the door and dashed down the hallway, bumping into the edge of a small oak table in the foyer. He stifled a vivid curse, damning the table silently.

He could hear Tracy's voice outside, but not yet on the porch.

454   BEVERLY BARTON

She laughed again, then a deep male voice said something Reece couldn't quite make out.

Thankful that so many windows graced the living room, allowing in the moonlight, Reece scrambled around on the floor, picking up the clothing Elizabeth and he had discarded so carelessly only a few hours ago.

As he made his way back into the foyer, he heard footsteps on the porch, then a loud, heavy thud.

Tracy's laughter echoed in the black stillness. "What's the matter, Jeffie-pooh, are you drunk?"

"Hell, yes," Jeffie-pooh said. "Come on, Trace, give a guy a hand."

"You got down there all by yourself, lover. You can pick yourself up. I'm going inside. It's freezing out here."

Reece heard the key sliding into the lock, and saw two shadows outside the French door. Careful to avoid the foyer table, he rushed back to the bedroom. He pulled on his jeans and shirt, then slipped on his boots, not worrying about his socks. Finding Elizabeth's bag at the foot of the bed, he pulled out a pair of jeans and a sweater, then stuffed her thermal underwear into the bag. Leaning over the bed, he gave Elizabeth a gentle shake.

Elizabeth opened her eyes and smiled at Reece, assuming he had awakened her for more lovemaking. She reached out for him, but instead of encountering his sleek, naked body, she felt her clothes thrust into her arms.

"Get dressed as quickly as you can, Lizzie," Reece whispered. "Tracy Stanton is here. She's brought one of her lovers. They're on the porch, and they're both drunk."

Elizabeth jumped out of bed, pulling on her clothes as quickly as possible. "What's she doing here? Did you know she used this place in the winter?"

"There's no time for questions. We've got to get out of here." Reece pulled Elizabeth into his arms, slipping the keys to the Thunderbird into her hand. "I'll take the Jeep and go straight to the sheriff. You go to Sam's motel and tell him what's happened."

"Oh, God, Reece, they'll hear us when we drive off."

"Probably." He gave her a quick kiss. "No matter what happens, just keep driving. Don't look back. Don't think about me. Don't worry about me."

"What about our bags, our food?" Elizabeth didn't hesitate to follow Reece when he pulled her out of the bedroom and into the hall.

"We'll take our bags." Reece lifted both bags off the floor. "We won't need the food."

"They'll call the sheriff as soon as they hear us. They'll think we're burglars."

"My guess is that Tracy won't call the sheriff. If she did, she'd have to explain what she was doing out here."

"What if we can't get out without their seeing us?"

"Hush. Listen." Reece stopped dead still just before entering the foyer. Keeping Elizabeth behind him, he glanced out into the entrance hall. The front door swung open. The overhead light came on. Tracy Stanton stood in the doorway, her slender body wrapped in a gray fox jacket.

"Come on, Jeffie. Make us a fire in the fireplace so we can warm up."

A tall, lanky young man came up behind Tracy, grabbing her around the waist. "I can warm you up just fine without building a fire."

Pulling out of her lover's embrace, Tracy headed straight for the living room. "You get a fire started, and I'll pour us some drinks."

Elizabeth peered around Reece's side, watching as the other couple went into the living room.

"We'll go out the kitchen door," Reece told her. "We'll have to squat down behind the counter. Be as quiet as you can."

Elizabeth nodded agreement, the roar of her heartbeat drumming inside her head.

"Look, Trace, there's already a fire in the fireplace," Jeffie said.

Elizabeth froze. Reece nudged her. Together they walked out into the foyer and toward the kitchen, Reece carrying their bags, hers in his hand, his over his shoulder.

"So there is," Tracy said. "Isn't that odd. I didn't see a car out front. Wonder who's been here."

"Maybe your parents," Jeffie said.

"They're in Gatlinburg skiing all this week."

Knees bent, Elizabeth squatted beside Reece behind the kitchen counter and they did a quick duck-walk toward the back door. Reaching up in the darkness, Reece grabbed the doorknob, turning it until he heard the lock release.

The lights came on in the living room. Reece jerked open the back door, pulled Elizabeth to her feet and ushered her outside.

"Reece!" Tracy screamed his name.

"Keep running," Reece told Elizabeth. "Get in your car and go straight to Sam."

"She saw you. She knows it's you!"

"Go, Lizzie. Go, now!"

Obeying, Elizabeth made a mad dash through the backyard, but before she could get to Sam's Thunderbird a car pulled up behind her, the headlights blinding her.

"What the hell?" Reece said, turning sharply when he heard the vehicle.

The driver kept the motor running. The bright headlights cut through the darkness, trapping Elizabeth and Reece in their glare.

"Lizzie, come here to me." Reece's gut instincts told him that whoever the driver was, he wasn't the sheriff or any law officer. A shiver of apprehension raced up Reece's spine.

Elizabeth began walking away from the T-Bird and toward Reece. A car door slammed.

"Stay right where you are, witch-woman. Reece's little psychic whore. He can't help you, and you can't help him anymore."

Reece dropped their bags to the ground. Sweat beaded his upper lip and forehead, despite the cold air whipping around him. The sharp, metallic taste of fear coated his tongue. Harry Gunn!

"Let her go, Harry," Reece said. "This is between us. She's got nothing to do with our fight."

Dammit all, why hadn't he remembered Kenny saying that Harry had been following Tracy around? If only he had remembered, he might have been prepared. And Elizabeth. Why hadn't she sensed Tracy's arrival or Harry's? Had she been so consumed by their lovemaking that all else had been obliterated from her mind?

Elizabeth breathed deeply, uncertain what to do. Harry Gunn had come to kill Reece. There was no doubt in her mind about that one fact. But why hadn't she sensed that Tracy Stanton would bring a lover to the cottage, and Harry Gunn would follow her? Only the strongest thoughts and emotions could have blocked out her precognitive powers. Making love to Reece had consumed not only her body, but her mind and her heart. And all her thoughts of the future had centered on the child Reece had given her.

Tracy Stanton ran out the back door, Jeffie following her. "My God, Reece! I had no idea you'd ever come here to the cottage."

"Yeah, pretty good hideout," Harry Gunn said, his voice loud and clear. "I knew if I kept following your brother's wife around, sooner or later she'd lead me to you."

"Are you crazy, old man?" Tracy screamed. "Do you think I'd have helped Reece?"

"When a woman's got the hots for a guy as bad as you do Reece, she'll do anything for him." Harry Gunn stepped around the front of his car, out of the direct glare of the headlights. He held a gun in his hand—an old .38 caliber revolver.

"What are you going to do?" Tracy asked.

"Hey, man you can't—" Jeffie said.

"Hush!" Tracy gave Jeffie a sharp jab in the ribs.

"I'm going to kill Reece," Harry said. "Then I'll call the sheriff and collect that big reward your husband is offering."

"No." The word escaped from Elizabeth's lips like a whisper on the wind.

"Look, Harry, I know you hate me, and if you're determined to kill me, then so be it." Reece took a tentative step toward Harry. "But there's no need to involve anyone else. Let everyone else leave and you and I will settle this between ourselves."

"Stay where you are." Harry pointed the gun directly at Reece.

"Nobody's going anywhere. I'm ready to kill the lot of you, if I have to."

"You don't have a quarrel with anyone else," Reece said.

"Maybe I do and maybe I don't." Harry waved the gun in the air, then aimed it at Reece. "He was a smart-mouthed kid." Harry glanced over at Elizabeth. "Always trying to stick up for his mama. His sweet, whore of a mama. How the hell was she supposed to forget about B. K. Stanton when the man's bastard was around all the time?"

Elizabeth sensed an unnatural hatred for Reece emanating from Harry Gunn. She shuddered at the thought of the man's rage. He wanted to see Reece dead. Nothing else would satisfy him.

"Yeah, Blanche never could get over being in love with Stanton," Harry said. "She never loved me. It was always B.K."

Elizabeth knew with certainty that Harry Gunn had hated B. K. Stanton enough to kill him, but she could not sense his guilt or innocence. Harry was too consumed with his hatred for Reece, his determination to kill his stepson.

Harry stood several yards away from Reece, who was only a few steps from the back door where Jeffie held Tracy in his arms. Reece heard Tracy speaking to her lover in a quiet, quick voice.

"Go back inside the house and get to my car. I've got a cellular phone. Call the sheriff's office and tell them what's going on."

Harry jerked his head around, his gaze momentarily leaving Reece to focus on Tracy and Jeffie.

Now, while Harry was momentarily distracted, might be Reece's best chance for jumping him. If Harry was intent on killing him, he might not be able to stop his stepfather, but there was a chance that he could save Elizabeth, as well as Tracy and Jeffie, if he could wrestle the gun away from Harry.

"What are you mumbling about?" Harry asked, staring at Tracy. "You cooking up some scheme to save your old lover? Well, don't try nothing. Harry Gunn ain't no fool."

Tracy glanced over at Reece, then back to Harry. "You're wrong if you think I give a damn whether you shoot Reece full of holes or not. He doesn't mean a thing to me. Hell, if he's dead or rotting in prison, he can't collect his share of B.K.'s fortune, can he?"

"You're lying." Harry turned completely around, grinning at Tracy. "You think I don't know all that boy's talent is between his legs. Women been chasing him all his life. If he was a girl, he'd be a whore just like his mama."

All the anger, the pain, the uncontrollable hatred Reece had felt boiled up inside him. In one, quick calculated move, Reece rushed Harry Gunn, who turned sharply, the gun in his hand gleaming in the glow from his car's headlights.

"Now!" Tracy cried out. "Go now, Jeffie."

Jeffie rushed inside the cottage. Tracy leaned forward, her feet unmoving as she opened her mouth in a silent cry. Just as Reece lunged forward, Harry turned, aiming his gun. Elizabeth ran between Reece and Harry. The gunshot exploded, the sound echoing over and over again in Reece's ears. Somewhere, as if at a great distance, he heard the sound of a woman screaming. Tracy.

Elizabeth felt the impact of the bullet when it entered her side. Searing hot pain gripped her. The world began spinning around and around. Slumping over, clutching her side, she fell to her knees.

Reece slammed into Harry Gunn with deadly force, like the bullet that had wounded Elizabeth. Knocking his stepfather to the ground, Reece grabbed for the gun that Harry held tightly. Reece swung his fist into Harry's face, then lifted the man's head and beat it against the cold, hard earth. Harry's hand opened. The gun fell onto the damp grass.

Mindless, feeling nothing except pure hatred, Reece hammered his fists into Harry Gunn's pale, wrinkled face, then sent several hard blows into Harry's midsection.

Tracy ran out into the yard, kneeling beside Elizabeth. "Jeffie's calling the sheriff. They'll get you to the hospital."

Elizabeth clasped Tracy's arm. "Stop Reece. Please stop him from killing his stepfather."

"Why the hell would you care?" Tracy stared down at the blood covering Elizabeth's side. "The guy shot you."

"I don't care about Harry Gunn," Elizabeth said. "I care about Reece. No matter how much he hates Harry, he would never forgive himself if he killed him. Please, Tracy. Stop Reece."

"All right. I'll try."

Reece drew back his fist to strike again. Tracy grabbed his arm. "Don't hit him anymore, Reece. He's unconscious."

"I'll kill the son of a bitch! I'll kill him."

Tracy circled Reece's arm with both of her hands, tugging on him, trying to pull him away from Harry. "He can't hurt any of us now. He's unconscious. Do you hear me? Elizabeth…Elizabeth wants you to stop."

Reece tensed at the mention of her name, suddenly realizing where he was and what he was doing. "Elizabeth."

"She doesn't want you to kill Harry."

Reece glared down at his stepfather, a crumpled heap of flesh and bones, a dirty, stinking, sick old man. Reece stood, his whole body trembling. He saw Elizabeth huddled on the ground, her life's blood seeping out of the bullet wound in her side.

God in heaven, don't let her die. Reece fell to his knees beside her, then sat on the ground, lifting her into his arms. "Elizabeth?"

Gazing up at him, she tried to lift her hand. "Don't worry. I'll be all right."

"Sam knew this would happen. This was what he was afraid of." Reece held her close, tears forming in his eyes. "It's my fault. You shouldn't have been with me. Oh, God, Lizzie, don't die, sweetheart. Please don't die."

"I'm not going to die," she told him. "Not for a long, long time."

"Are you looking into your future?" He kissed her forehead.

"I did that…last night." Despite the pain and weakness, Elizabeth felt a great sense of peace. How could she tell Reece that she knew she wasn't going to die because she had to live to give birth to their child?

Jeffie ran out the kitchen door, halting abruptly when he saw Reece sitting on the ground, holding Elizabeth. "What happened? When I heard a gunshot, I thought old Harry had killed Reece."

"Elizabeth ran between Harry and Reece," Tracy said.

"Damn! Is she hurt bad?" Jeffie walked out into the yard and slipped his arm around Tracy.

"I don't know."

"She's going to be all right," Reece said, cradling Elizabeth in his arms, holding her close. Tears streamed down his face.

"I called the sheriff," Jeffie said. "I told him to send an ambulance."

Elizabeth closed her eyes. She felt herself drifting. Reece kept repeating her name, calling her Lizzie. She opened her eyes and lifted her hand to his face. She touched his wet cheek.

"You're crying," she whispered. "Oh, Reece." Then Elizabeth closed her eyes again, drifting into unconsciousness.

Reece had no idea how long he sat on the cold ground, holding Elizabeth in his arms—five minutes, ten minutes. Finally Tracy touched him on the shoulder.

"Let's take her inside where it's warmer."

Reece lifted Elizabeth in his arms and carried her into the cottage. He laid her down on the bed they had shared only hours ago. Reece clenched his teeth at the sight of her bloody sweater. Lifting her sweater, he used it to wipe away the blood. The bullet had entered her upper left side and exited from the front, at her waist.

Tracy stood in the doorway, Jeffie directly behind her, both of them looking into the bedroom.

"Is there anything we can do?" Tracy asked.

"Yeah, go back outside and make sure Harry doesn't come to."

"I'll handle that," Jeffie said.

"I don't know what to do to help her." Reece sat on the side of the bed, holding Elizabeth's hand to his chest. "If it was the other way around and I was lying there, she'd know what to do. She'd go outside and pull up some weeds and grass and perform a miracle."

"You really care about her, don't you?" Tracy walked over, standing by the bed.

"She believes in me." Reece lifted Elizabeth's limp hand to his lips. "She's gone through hell for me because she wants to help me.

Me," Reece said with a laugh, the sound an anguished cry, "B. K. Stanton's worthless bastard."

"She loves you, Reece. She risked her life to save you." Tracy laid her hand on Reece's shoulder.

Reece jerked away from her touch. "Where the hell is that ambulance?"

Reece looked up to see the medics carrying a stretcher into the bedroom. Sheriff Bates walked in behind them, two deputies following.

Reece kissed Elizabeth, then moved out of the way. The medics lifted her gently onto the stretcher and carried her outside to the waiting ambulance. He stared at Simon Bates, who aimed his automatic directly at Reece.

"You won't need that." Reece held his hands over his head in a sign of surrender.

The deputies cuffed him, both young men moving quickly to accomplish the task. Reece heard the sheriff speaking, talking to him, barking out orders, but he couldn't distinguish the words. All he could think about was Elizabeth. She filled his mind and heart completely.

Elizabeth opened her eyes to see Sam Dundee looking down at her. She smiled at him. If Sam was with her, then she was safe. Her mind felt fuzzy, her body weightless. What was wrong with her? Why did she feel so strange?

With sudden clarity she remembered the events that had brought her here. She was in a hospital. She glanced around the room, a private room, her bed the only one.

"Hey, kiddo." Sam brushed her hair away from her face with a gentle hand.

"Reece?" Was he in jail? Yes, of course, he had to be. He had promised he'd turn himself in to the sheriff.

"Landry's in jail," Sam said. "They took him there yesterday morning while they were bringing you to the hospital."

"He's all right, then?" Elizabeth tried to lift herself up in the bed.

"Stay calm, honey." Sam laid a restraining hand on her shoulder. "You've got a pretty big hole in your side. The doctors stitched you up, but it'll take a while for you to recover. You'll probably be in here for a few days, maybe a week."

"Is Reece all right? Y'all told the sheriff that he planned to turn himself in, didn't you?"

"Gary Elkins is taking care of everything, so stop fretting."

"What about Harry Gunn?" Elizabeth could see Harry's warped smile, could visualize the gun he'd aimed at Reece, could feel the bullet enter her body. She trembled.

"Are you all right?" Sam took her hand in his.

"Reece didn't kill Harry, did he?" Elizabeth looked up at Sam with pleading eyes. "I can't sense anything. I can't get a handle on… Oh, Sam, please tell me. I…I…"

"Harry Gunn is under guard here at the hospital. He's got a broken nose, a concussion and several fractured ribs, but he'll live."

"Harry hated B. K. Stanton enough to have killed him." Elizabeth held tightly to Sam's hand. "And he is capable of murder. I sensed that about him. And he hated Reece enough to have framed him. That way he could have destroyed the two people he hated most."

"Yeah, you're right, kiddo." Sam stroked the back of Elizabeth's hand, making circles around her knuckles. "The only problem with that theory is that I don't think Harry Gunn was smart enough to have planned the frame-up. Whoever framed Reece was as shrewd as he was devious."

"What about Kenny Stanton? He has no alibi, and we can prove he threatened to kill his father the day of the murder."

"Elizabeth, will you stop upsetting yourself. It's not good for you. You've done all you can to help Reece. Leave the rest up to me and to his lawyer."

"I want to see him."

"Honey, you can't. He's in jail and you're in no shape to go traipsing over there."

Elizabeth read the worry in Sam's mind, picking up on his fear that she would do something irrational when she found out about—

"They're taking Reece to Arrendale today, aren't they? Why? Couldn't they wait a day or two?"

"Reece was arrested yesterday morning. Although the sheriff is willing to reopen the investigation into B. K. Stanton's murder, the fact remains that Reece was convicted of the crime and sentenced to prison."

"Reece will go crazy locked up in a cell." Elizabeth swallowed her tears. "Sam, we've got to find the person who really killed B. K. Stanton."

"We will. I promise. You know you can count on me." Sam released her hand, then sat in a chair beside her bed. "As soon as you're released from the hospital, I'll drive you up to Alto, to Arrendale for a visit with Reece."

"Isn't the sheriff going to arrest me for aiding and abetting a criminal?" Elizabeth asked.

"Looks like the sheriff is going to buy Tracy Stanton's story that she brought you out to her parents' summer house yesterday morning. She said that you were a psychic who'd had a vision about B.K.'s death and you'd come to the family with the news that Reece was innocent. She and Christina decided you should stay on in Newell in case you had any more visions."

"The sheriff didn't actually believe her, did he?"

Sam grinned. "Hell, no, but he's not about to call Mrs. Bradley Kenneth Stanton, Jr., a liar."

"I see. Reece was right about the Stantons' power in Newell, wasn't he?"

"In this case, let's be thankful. You can rest easy now, kiddo. Just get better so I can take you home."

Elizabeth placed her hand on her stomach, reminding herself that she was responsible for the new life inside her. She relaxed against the pillows, breathing softly, suddenly aware of the pain in her bandaged side. She closed her eyes, concentrating on Reece, trying to transmit a message of love and hope to him. As she lay there sending love out into the atmosphere, a dark sense of fore-boding surrounded her.

Someone was afraid of her—afraid she knew the truth about B. K. Stanton's murder. He wanted to prevent her from helping Reece, but knew he couldn't risk coming to the hospital.

"Are you in pain?" Sam asked.

"No...not really. Why?"

"You're frowning."

"The person who killed B. K. Stanton is a man." Elizabeth opened her eyes and looked at Sam. "He's afraid I'll be able to identify him."

Sam leaned over the bed, gently grasping her face in his hand. "Turn it off, honey. Shield yourself. You're not strong enough for this right now."

She raised her head, nodding, knowing Sam was right. But without any warning the vision came. She could not stop the flow of color, the formation of images, the whirling, spinning sensation that enveloped her mind.

A huge crowd of people lined the sidewalk. Flanking Reece, two deputies brought him outside the building, hurrying him through the throng of observers.

Someone's thoughts screamed inside Elizabeth's head. *Reece Landry must die. He's caused enough pain. Even if I must sacrifice myself, I won't allow Landry to inherit any of his father's estate. I'll protect...I'll protect...I'll do whatever it takes.*

Bracing her body with her hand, Elizabeth pushed herself into a sitting position, then reached out and grabbed Sam's arm.

"He's going to kill Reece. Today. When they bring Reece out of the jail. He'll be hiding in the crowd."

"Calm down." Sam tried to make Elizabeth lie back down, but she refused.

"Please, Sam, you've got to stop them from taking Reece out of jail today."

"The sheriff isn't going to listen to me, honey."

"You can't let him kill Reece!"

Sam took Elizabeth's shoulders in his strong, gentle grasp, pushing her down on the bed. "I'll go to the jail and see what I can do. If nothing else, I'll keep watch. I'll guard Reece."

Elizabeth took a deep breath. "I wish I could see the man's face, but I can't. He hates Reece. He's willing to sacrifice anything to keep Reece from going free."

"Everything will be all right," Sam said. "Whoever this man is, if he tips his hand today, I'll be there to catch him."

"Are you sure Harry Gunn is well guarded?" Elizabeth asked. "And what about Kenny Stanton?"

"Harry Gunn isn't in any shape to walk out of this hospital, but even if he was, the deputy would stop him. As for Kenny Stanton, I don't have any idea where he is, but I can find out."

"Don't let anything happen to Reece. I love him."

"Yeah, kiddo, I know you do."

CHAPTER 13

The nurse came in shortly after Sam left and gave Elizabeth an injection. She protested the shot, but the nurse insisted. She had a sneaking suspicion that Sam had suggested they give her something to calm her down a little.

She didn't want to sleep, but the medication overcame her resistance. When she awoke, she rang the nurses' station and asked for the time. It was eleven-fifteen. Surely by now Sam had persuaded the sheriff not to move Reece today. What difference could one day make to the local authorities? Maybe Sam had gone to Gary Elkins and Reece's lawyer had contacted a judge about delaying the transfer.

Elizabeth tried to focus her energy on Reece. Where was he? How was he doing? What was he thinking? With a sudden, sharp clarity, the vision of Reece being led up the sidewalk appeared in Elizabeth's mind. The crowd was pushing closer and closer. Newspaper reporters where shouting questions. Photographers were snapping shots of the prisoner. Sam Dundee and Gary Elkins followed Reece and the deputies. Elizabeth scanned the crowd. Christina Stanton stood beside her brother, Kenny, and his wife, Tracy. Willard Moran stood alone on the opposite side of the walkway. The sun reflected off the muzzle of a gun—a gun aimed directly at Reece. Breaking through the crowd, Elizabeth hurried toward Reece. She saw the startled look on his face, then heard him call her name.

The truth of what would happen hit her with full impact. She and she alone could save Reece. Only she could zero in on the killer. Only she could read a person's mind. She had to go to the jail and stop the killer before he shot Reece.

Elizabeth eased the intravenous needle from her hand. When she tried to sit up, her head spun around and around. Slow and easy, she told herself. You can't pass out. Not now. Taking her time, she slipped out of bed and stood, holding on to the bed rails.

Glancing down at her open-backed hospital gown, she wondered where they'd put her clothes. Damn, they would be covered with blood. Taking tentative steps, gauging her strength as she walked across the room, Elizabeth opened the closet. She sighed with relief when she saw her bag lying on the floor. Bending over, she gasped when the pain in her side sliced through her like a sharp rapier.

She knelt, undid her bag and pulled out a clean pair of jeans and a heavy peach wool sweater. Her shoes lay beside her bag. She dressed as quickly as she could, but each movement came with pain. Pulling her purse out of the bag, she slung it over her shoulder.

Easing open the door, she peered out into the hallway. She didn't see anyone, not even one nurse. She made her way along the corridor to the elevators, punched the Down button and waited. She wondered how close the hospital was to the jail. If necessary, she'd call a cab when she got downstairs.

Once on the ground level, she stopped at the reception desk and inquired about the location of the local jail. She couldn't believe her luck when the young woman told her that the county jail was only two blocks away, directly behind the courthouse.

When she walked outside, the winter wind bit into her heavy sweater, chilling her. The wound in her side ached, and she still felt a little light-headed from the medication. Her pain didn't matter—nothing mattered except saving Reece. With each step she took, she knew she was one step closer to keeping the man she loved alive.

She could hear the crowd several minutes before she

rounded the corner and saw them. Reece Landry's capture and transport to Arrendale had to be the media event of the year in Newell, Georgia. The sidewalk leading to the jail was lined with people, so many people that Elizabeth couldn't even see the sidewalk.

She made her way through the fringe crowd that waited around near the street, dozens of people who were there simply to see the spectacle. Directly in front of her, toward the back of the crowd, stood Kenny Stanton, Tracy at his side. Elizabeth glanced to their right and to their left, searching for Christina. Then she saw her, standing directly in front of Kenny. The whole Stanton family was here to see Reece off. Everyone except Alice.

Kenny was the most likely suspect. No one could hate Reece more than Kenny, unless it was Harry Gunn. Elizabeth tried to connect with Kenny, but found it impossible. The psychic energy coming from the crowd mixed and mingled, making it nearly impossible to pinpoint the exact location of a thought or feeling.

If only she could touch Kenny, she might be able to separate his energy from the energy of those around him. And if he saw her, he would know that she was on to him, and might not make a move against Reece. Regardless of what Kenny might or might not do, she had to approach him.

Breathless from her two-block walk from the hospital, Elizabeth made her way through the crowd, nudging between the curious men and women waiting for a glimpse of Reece Landry. Christina saw her, her eyes widening, her mouth forming a circle. Elizabeth shook her head. Christina nodded.

Elizabeth brushed up against Kenny. Turning quickly, he stared at her. Her knees trembled. She gripped Kenny's arm. Glaring at her, he looked down at her hand clutching his coat sleeve.

She could sense doubts in Kenny's mind—grave doubts. He was no longer certain that his half brother had killed their father.

Kenny looked Elizabeth in the eye, then placed his hand atop hers. "You shouldn't be out of the hospital, Ms. Mallory."

Tracy jerked her head around. "What are you doing here?"

Elizabeth pulled her hand off Kenny's arm, willing herself to find the strength to stand alone. "Please, I have to find him. It isn't you."

"What are you talking about?" Kenny asked.

"You aren't the murderer. You didn't come here to shoot Reece."

The crowd's rumble grew louder. Elizabeth shoved past Kenny and Tracy to see the front doors of the county jail swing open. The sheriff walked out first, followed by two deputies who led Reece down the steps. Sam Dundee and Gary Elkins were only a minute behind the others.

Elizabeth closed her eyes, trying to concentrate, trying desperately to pick up on any kind of signal the killer might be emitting. She couldn't rush in front of Reece this time and take the bullet for him. She had no idea from which direction the bullet would come; the crowd circled Reece.

Hatred. Deep, soul-wrenching hatred. She felt it so strongly that she almost doubled over in pain. And the hatred was directed at Reece—because he was B. K. Stanton's illegitimate son. Because Reece's existence had caused Alice Stanton unbearable shame and heartache. Reece could not be allowed to live, to lay claim to a fortune that didn't belong to him.

"Oh, dear God," Elizabeth said, her voice inaudible in the boisterous racket coming from the crowd. She glanced across the sidewalk. There in the front row stood Willard Moran, dressed in a conservative blue suit, his charcoal gray overcoat unbuttoned, his hand in his pocket.

She looked up the sidewalk. The sheriff was only a few feet away, Reece and the deputies directly behind him.

Reece saw her then, saw her pale face, noted the fear in her eyes. What the hell was Elizabeth doing out of the hospital? When Reece halted, the deputies slowed enough to accommodate him.

Reece called out to Sam. "I thought you said Elizabeth would have to stay in the hospital a few days. What's she doing here?"

Elizabeth's gaze met Sam's, then she looked over at Willard Moran, knowing she and she alone could stop him. He was holding a gun in his pocket, waiting for the moment Reece would pass him, waiting to kill Reece.

Elizabeth nudged her way between two reporters calling out questions to the sheriff and to Reece. Willard Moran stepped onto the sidewalk, between the sheriff and his deputies. Elizabeth ran forward, throwing herself into Willard. The gun in his hand fired, the bullet sailing into the air over their heads. When Willard's body hit the ground, the gun flew out of his hand, falling with a clang onto the edge of the sidewalk.

Reece tried to run to Elizabeth, but the chains around his ankles slowed his gait. Startled by what had just happened, the deputies didn't instantly realize that their prisoner had pulled away from them. They grabbed Reece tightly, jerking him back. He fought them, trying desperately to reach Elizabeth, calling out her name.

Sam Dundee rushed past Reece, shoving everyone in his way aside. The blood surged through Reece's body, his heart pumping wildly as he strained in the confines of his cuffs and chains.

Willard Moran knocked Elizabeth off him. She rolled over onto the sidewalk, blood oozing through her sweater. Before Willard could stand, Sheriff Bates grabbed him, jerking him to his feet. Sam knelt beside Elizabeth, lifting her into his arms.

She felt Sam holding her, heard Reece crying out her name. She wanted to get up, to go to Reece and tell him that she was all right, but she couldn't make her body cooperate. Raising her head, she struggled to sit up.

"Reece…Reece…" She barely recognized her own voice. So raspy. So whispery soft.

"Reece is okay. He's just fine," Sam said. "Take it easy. We've got to get you back to the hospital."

"Elizabeth!" Reece's tortured voice drowned out the crowd's clamor.

Deputies began ordering the bystanders to move away from the scene, to disperse and leave the situation to the authorities. Reporters buzzed around like busy bees; photographers snapped shot after shot—of the crowd, of the sheriff cuffing Willard Moran, of the deputies holding back the crowd, of Reece Landry's tortured face, of Sam Dundee holding Elizabeth in his arms.

"Clear this crowd out of here," the sheriff ordered. He shoved Willard Moran toward a deputy. "Take Mr. Moran inside and detain him until we have things under control out here."

"Reece. I want to see Reece." Elizabeth pleaded with Sam.

The sheriff motioned at the two deputies holding Reece. "Bring Landry over here. Now!"

Reece couldn't get to Elizabeth fast enough to suit him. Kneeling, he cursed the cuffs that bound his hands, that restricted his movements. More than anything he wanted to take Elizabeth out of Sam's arms, to hold her close to him.

"Elizabeth." Tears streamed down Reece's cheeks. He couldn't remember ever crying in front of people, or even crying alone. Not until Elizabeth Mallory had come into his life.

"Willard Moran killed your father," Elizabeth said.

Reece and Sam exchanged knowing looks. "And he was going to kill me, wasn't he?" Reece leaned over, brushing his lips across Elizabeth's forehead. "You risked your life coming here." Reece choked on the tears in his throat. "You've risked your life twice to save me."

"You'll be free now, Reece. Free to live the life you've always wanted." Elizabeth lifted her hand, touching the side of Reece's face with her fingertips.

"God, Lizzie. Dear God!" Reece crumbled, his body shaking with sobs, his head resting on Elizabeth's chest.

She stroked his hair, caressing him with loving fingers. "I won't ever have to cry for you again, will I, Reece? You...you can cry...for yourself now."

Reece jerked his head up. He saw Elizabeth's eyes close and felt her hand drop away from his head.

"Lizzie!"

"Come on, Reece, get up!" Sam ordered. "Get out of the way. I've got to take her back to the hospital."

The deputies lifted Reece to his feet. He watched, helpless to do anything else, as Sam lifted Elizabeth in his arms and carried her down the sidewalk.

"Get Landry back inside," the sheriff told his deputies. "Looks like we're definitely reopening the B. K. Stanton murder case."

Elizabeth sat in the chair beside the hospital bed she had occupied for the past few days. Her bag was packed, and she was dressed in jeans, a blue silk blouse and a brown suede vest. She and Sam were driving home to Sequana Falls today, but before she left, she had to see Reece.

Although Sam had kept her abreast of the events following Willard Moran's arrest, she regretted that she hadn't been at Reece's side to see him through the painful process and to share in the jubilant relief when Gary Elkins had completed the legalities that set Reece free.

Christina had stopped by yesterday to thank Elizabeth for all the help she'd given Reece and to tell her that no one in the family had suspected Willard Moran was capable of murder. The man had been B. K. Stanton's lawyer for over thirty years, a trusted friend. Chris and Kenny had called the man Uncle Willard all their lives.

Willard Moran had loved Alice Stanton with a mindless devotion. By destroying B.K. and eliminating Reece, he had thought to protect Alice from any more hurt and make sure her children's inheritance wasn't squandered on her husband's bastard son. In the end, Willard had been willing to sacrifice himself to achieve his goal.

Elizabeth heard a soft knock at the door. "Come in." She turned to see Sam standing in the doorway, Reece behind him.

"You're all dressed and ready to leave," Sam said.

"The doctor told me to take it easy for a few days, and not to do anything that might reopen my wound again." Elizabeth smiled at Sam, deliberately not looking at Reece.

Sam grabbed Reece by the arm, hauled him to his side, then stepped back into the hallway. "I'll go get a cup of coffee or something while you two visit. I'll be back to get you in a little bit, kiddo."

Reece stood in the doorway, staring at Elizabeth, his expression grave. "You look a lot better than the last time I saw you."

"I feel a lot better." Every nerve in her body came to full alert, tingling with excitement and fear. "Come on in, Reece."

Reece ambled into her hospital room, his gaze traveling over the walls, the ceiling and the floor. Standing beside Elizabeth's chair, he cleared his throat.

Elizabeth stared at Reece, noting how different he looked from the man who had passed out in her cabin less than two weeks ago. He'd had a haircut, his glossy brown hair neatly styled, and he was freshly shaved. He wore dark brown slacks and a camel tan wool jacket, his tie a conservative beige-and-coral-striped silk.

"You look very handsome," she told him. "Like a successful young businessman."

Reece knelt beside Elizabeth, resting his big body on his haunches. "I owe you my life and my freedom, Lizzie. How does a guy repay someone for giving him so much?"

"You'll repay me by making your life count for something, by living well and being happy."

Reece gripped the metal armrest on her chair. He wanted to touch her, but couldn't bring himself to reach out and take her hand. He wasn't sure how she would accept the news that he planned to stay in Newell and claim his inheritance.

"Sam told me he's going to follow you back to Sequana Falls today." If only he could ask her to stay here in Newell with him. If only he could tell her what she wanted to hear. If only he could repay her for everything she'd done for him.

"My life is in Sequana Falls. Aunt Margaret. MacDatho. My business." She couldn't read his mind, but she knew that despite all he'd gone through and all he'd learned, Reece wasn't prepared to give up his lifelong dreams and start a new life with her.

"I don't suppose you'd consider staying on in Newell." He could offer her the world now, the whole world on a silver platter. Wealth, power, social position—all the things he'd been denied because of his illegitimate birth, all the things he'd dreamed of having for as long as he could remember.

Elizabeth willed herself not to cry; she had done too much crying lately. She laid her hand atop his on the armrest. "I wouldn't be happy in Newell. I don't think you will be, either, but you'll have to find that out for yourself."

"Ah, Lizzie, you mean so much to me." Taking her by the hands, he helped her to her feet, then pulled her into his arms. "I've never cared about anyone the way I care about you. You don't know how grateful I am that you came into my life when you did."

She laid her head on his chest. "I don't want your gratitude, Reece. I want your love."

He tensed, every muscle in his body going rigid. "I…uh…I'm not sure I know how to love anybody, especially someone as special as you."

Wrapping her arms around his waist, she hugged him. "There's an old saying, one I've heard Aunt Margaret quote. Something about all the love we come to know in life comes from the love we knew as children."

Reece kissed the top of her head, breathing in that sweet rose scent that would forever remind him of Elizabeth. "Well, that puts it in a nutshell, doesn't it? I don't know how to love because no one ever loved me."

"That's not true." Tilting her face, she gazed up into his amber eyes, those lone-wolf eyes that still proclaimed him an untamed animal. "Despite what you think, your mother loved you. You know she did."

"Yeah, well, maybe she did. In her own way."

"And now you have my love." She ran her fingertips across his jaw. "I love you."

Reece closed his eyes, shutting out Elizabeth's face, protecting himself from the glow of love that surrounded her. Damn, why couldn't he just tell her that he loved her? What made it so impossible?

He couldn't change his past. Not the circumstances of his birth, not B. K. Stanton's denial and rejection, not the years he and his mother had suffered at the hands of his sadistic stepfather. And no matter how much he wanted to be free from all the pain and anger and hatred inside him, he wasn't ready to forgive and forget. He had an inheritance to claim, a company to run, a sister he wanted in his life and a brother with whom he'd have to deal.

If Elizabeth would settle for the man he was, scarred and bitter and hungry for retribution, then he could offer her anything money could buy. He'd give her an engagement ring the size of a dime. He'd build her a mansion as big as the one Alice Stanton lived in.

"Thank you," Elizabeth said.

"For what?"

"For letting down your shield." The tears she had tried to control gathered in the corners of her eyes. "Thank you for sharing your thoughts with me."

He hadn't realized that he had opened himself up to her, allowing her to read his mind. "Stay here with me, Lizzie. Marry me. Teach me how to love."

"You're right, you know, Reece. You can't change the past. But you can let it go. You'll never be happy until you can do that."

Reece clasped her shoulders. "How do I do that? How do I let go of the past when the past has made me who I am? If I let go of the past, I won't have an identity."

"You'll always be Blanche and B.K.'s illegitimate son. You'll always be an outcast in the Stanton family, even if you own controlling interest in Stanton Industries. The only way you can ever let go of the past is to make peace with it, starting with the Stanton family."

"How the hell do you suggest I do that?" Reece ran his hands slowly up and down her arms. "Alice Stanton has every right to despise me. And Kenny hates my guts."

"They don't have to love you or even like you. They'll have to make their own peace with their lives."

"So what should I do, Lizzie?" He held her from him, his big hands shackling her wrists. "Should I walk away and let them have it all? Do you have any idea how much I wanted B.K. to acknowledge me as his son? Do you know how badly I wanted everything that belonged to Kenny?"

"I know, Reece. But are you sure, really sure, that what you once wanted so desperately is what will make you happy now?"

Reece dropped his hands, releasing Elizabeth. "I don't know. I don't know anything anymore. Give me some advice, Lizzie. Look into my future and tell me what you see. Are our futures still entwined?"

Yes, Reece, our futures are still entwined. I'm going to have your child. You'll always be a part of me. "Your future will be what you make it. You should stay here in Newell. Claim your inheritance. Make peace with the Stantons. And if you discover that you don't really want to take over Stanton Industries, then give that job to your sister and come live with me in Sequana Falls."

"Come live with—"

"I love you, Reece. I'll love you as long as I live. I've done all I can to help you, to save you from yourself. The rest is up to you. You have to stay here in Newell and come to terms with your past. When you've done that, and if you decide that you can love me, then come to me. I'll be waiting."

"Elizabeth?"

"You're free, Reece. Free from the past, if only you'll allow yourself to be. You're a man, not a child. You have choices to make. No one else can make those choices for you. You decide what you want from this life, and how much you're willing to give in order to get it."

Several loud, hard knocks sounded at the door, then Sam Dundee walked in, glancing back and forth from Elizabeth to Reece to Elizabeth.

"If we're going to get home in time for supper, we'd better be leaving." Sam picked up Elizabeth's bag. "O'Grady's taking Aunt Margaret and MacDatho up to the cabin, so they'll all be there to meet us."

Elizabeth leaned into Reece, circling his forearm with her hand. She kissed him on the cheek. "You take all the time you need to decide. We...I'll be in Sequana Falls."

CHAPTER 14

"You can't be serious," Kenny Stanton said. "Daddy would be appalled at the very idea of a woman running Stanton Industries."

"Well, Daddy isn't making the decisions." Rearing back in the tufted-leather chair behind B.K.'s desk, Reece placed his hands on his hips and glanced around his father's former office. "Chris and I own two-thirds of the stock in this little family company, and we agree that she's the most qualified person to sit behind the old man's desk and make the decisions that will keep bringing in profits for all of us."

Standing, Reece smiled at his sister, then motioned for her to sit in the chair he had just vacated. Chris, neatly attired in a dark green business suit, took the seat. Grasping the cushioned armrests, she gulped a deep breath of air, then glanced from Kenny's frowning face into Reece's twinkling topaz eyes. Pressing her toe to the floor, she boosted the swivel chair into action, whirling it around and around as she laughed.

"Are you happy, Landry?" Kenny asked, his hound-dog cheeks flushed pink. "You send my mother to a rest home, you persuade my wife to divorce me and now you hand over my company to my sister. You've taken your revenge on me, haven't you? Everything I've had, you've taken away from me."

"I haven't taken a damn thing away from you, big brother." Reece took a good look at Bradley Kenneth Stanton, Jr., and was amazed that he actually pitied the man whom he'd envied all his life. "Your mother had a nervous breakdown after Willard Moran confessed to killing B.K. I wasn't responsible for Alice's illness. If you're going to blame anyone, blame the man who loved her enough to kill for her."

Kenny glared at Reece. "Well, I can certainly blame you for taking Tracy away from me. You just couldn't leave her alone, could you? What did you do to persuade her to divorce me? Did you promise to marry her?"

"I didn't promise Tracy anything," Reece said. "She knows I'm not interested in her. All I did was drive her to the airport to catch a flight to Reno."

"Humph!" Kenny picked up his briefcase from the edge of B.K.'s desk. "I suppose if I had befriended you the way Chris did, you'd have handed the company over to me, but because I refused to accept you as my brother, you're willing to ruin the company our father spent his life building into a small empire."

Reece chuckled. God, why had he ever thought he wanted to be like Kenny? Why had he ever envied the man his life? Reece realized that he'd been blinded by the glitter of a world forbidden to him. Now that that world lay at his feet, he discovered he didn't want it as much as he'd thought he did.

"If you and I were like this—" Reece wrapped his index and middle fingers together "—I would still want Chris in charge of Stanton Industries. I didn't vote in her favor as an act of revenge against you. I did it because she's the best person for the job."

"I suppose you two think I'll just tuck my tail between my legs and crawl out of here," Kenny said.

"No one would ever think that." Chris whirled around one last time in her chair, then stuck out her foot under the desk to stop her spin. "There's a place at Stanton Industries for you, but it isn't in administration. It's in sales. You're the best salesman I know, Kenny. You inherited that from Mother. My goodness, we both know how persuasive she always was collecting thousands of dollars for her charities. You have that same special way with people."

"What position are you offering me?" Standing in front of his sister's desk, Kenny laid down his briefcase.

"You two work out an agreement suitable to both of you," Reece said. "If you need me for anything, you know where I'll be, Chris. And if you don't need me, then I'll see y'all at the next board meeting."

When he walked out the door, he heard Kenny ask Christina where Reece was going.

"He's going to find happiness," Chris said.

Elizabeth delved her glove-covered hands into the warm clumps of earth, crushing the small clods and sprinkling the soft dirt back to the ground. April showers were long overdue, forecast for tomorrow. She wanted to get the new plants set out so that they could soak up the rainwater that would nourish them.

Margaret McPhearson stood at the edge of the porch, shaking her head as she watched her niece. "Just look at you, Elizabeth Sequana. You're getting dirty, and after I persuaded you to fancy up a bit."

Elizabeth packed the earth around the last plant, then got up and removed her gloves, tossing them onto the steps. "I didn't get dirty. See." She held up her hands, then glanced down at the denim skirt and red silk blouse she wore. "But I can't just sit still waiting for Reece to arrive."

"I don't see why you can't sit down and take it easy. Just because you've been blessed with a total lack of morning sickness doesn't mean you shouldn't take good care of yourself." Margaret walked down the steps and out into the front yard.

"I almost wish you hadn't told me that Reece is coming here today. I've been waiting nearly six weeks. I'd begun to doubt he'd ever—"

"Nonsense. You knew, deep down here—" Margaret thumped her fist over her heart "—that he'd find his way back to you."

"I have to admit that I did try to contact him mentally a couple of times, to let him know that I loved him and I was waiting."

"Maybe you should have used the telephone instead of trying to break through that shield he keeps in place in his mind." Margaret put her arm around Elizabeth's shoulders. "It wasn't easy for me to break through, not at first, but in the last week or so...well, I'd say that, in time, you'll be able to read Reece Landry like a book."

"I wish I had the courage to let you tell me what sort of future you see for Reece and me." Elizabeth turned into her aunt's arms, hugging her.

Margaret patted her niece on the back, then stepped away from her, looking her squarely in the eye. "I wouldn't tell you, even if you asked. You've got the power. If you want to know, look for yourself."

When the front door of the cabin opened, MacDatho bounded outside, O'Grady following at a slower pace. "You 'bout ready to head for home, Margaret?" O'Grady asked.

"Not yet. I want to stay and meet this Landry fellow."

"Are you sure he's coming today?" O'Grady sat down in one of the large wooden rockers that Elizabeth had stationed across her front and back porches. "Seems he'd have called and let Elizabeth know he was coming."

"I'd say he assumes she already knows, which she does because I told her so." Holding on to the side railing, Margaret walked up the steps and sat in a rocker beside O'Grady. "She could've picked up on it herself if she wasn't so all-fired afraid that if she reads his mind, she'll discover he doesn't love her."

"Why don't you two go on home to Dover's Mill?" Elizabeth gazed up at them, the overhead noonday sun almost blinding her. "It may be April and a fairly warm day today, but that wind's chilly and I wouldn't want either of you catching cold."

"We're both healthy as horses," Margaret said. "Besides, we're not going anywhere till we meet your young man."

Elizabeth groaned, knowing when to admit defeat. She wasn't sure she would have gotten through the past six weeks without Aunt Margaret. Leaving Reece had been the most difficult thing she'd ever done, but it had been the right thing to do. If she had made things too easy for Reece, he might never have realized what was important in this life. He might have gone on wrapped up in the past and unable to give or accept love.

"He's coming up the road." Margaret stood, motioning for O'Grady to do the same. "You introduce us, Elizabeth, and then we'll be on our way. Now, you remember what I told you. You take him down to Mama's honeymoon cottage. I've got a surprise waiting there for y'all."

"All right," Elizabeth said. "If he stays, I'll take him to the cottage."

Elizabeth heard the approaching car, then turned to see a new, sleek, dark green Jeep Cherokee pull up and stop in front of the cabin. Reece Landry emerged, big and tall and incredibly handsome in his navy blue cotton slacks and his cream-colored pullover sweater.

"Lizzie." Reece stood at the side of the Jeep, taking in every inch of the woman who'd never been far from his mind these past six weeks. Everything he'd done to put his life together had been for her. And now, free at last from the emotions that had bound him to his past, he had come to her, hat in hand, so to speak, hoping she wouldn't send him away.

"Reece." Elizabeth had to restrain herself from running to him, but she would wait for him to come to her. Only a few feet separated them, but they were his distance to cross, not hers.

"So this is the infamous Reece Landry." Margaret McPhearson, her dimpled chin held high, the sun gleaming through the strands of her white hair, took hold of the railing and began walking down the steps.

"You must be Aunt Margaret." Reece looked at the old woman making her way slowly down the steps. An elderly man followed closely behind her.

MacDatho raced around the corner of the house, pouncing on Reece. Reece scratched his ears. "Hey, Mac, how are you, boy? Have you decided to be friends?"

Elizabeth didn't take her eyes off Reece. She felt her aunt's presence when Margaret walked over and stood beside her, O'Grady taking his place on her other side. "Aunt Margaret, O'Grady, this is Reece Landry."

"We already know that." Margaret waved her hand in dismissal. "What I want to know is why it took you six weeks to get here?"

"I had a lot to settle back in Newell," Reece said.

"Have you got it all settled now?" Margaret asked.

"Yes, ma'am, I do."

"Thought so, but I wanted to make sure." Margaret held out her hand in front of Elizabeth, motioning for O'Grady. The old man stepped forward, took Margaret's hand and led her to the delivery van.

Elizabeth waved goodbye to her aunt and O'Grady as they drove off down the road, then she turned back to Reece. They stood staring at each other, neither moving an inch.

"I've missed you, Lizzie."

"I've missed you, too."

MacDatho sat down beside Elizabeth, always her faithful companion. Why doesn't Reece say something else? she wondered when the silence between them dragged on for endless moments.

"It's a bit chilly out here. Would you like to come in?" She wanted to scream at him, to demand that he tell her why he'd come. Was he here to stay or just for a visit? Had he come to her or had he come for her? Or was he here to say goodbye?

"Elizabeth?" Reece took a tentative step in her direction.

"Yes?"

"Am I too late?"

"Are you... What are you saying, Reece?"

"I'm saying that I know what I want. I know what will make me happy, and it isn't running Stanton Industries or living in Newell in a mansion or lording it over Kenny that our father left me an equal share of everything he owned."

"What will make you happy?" Elizabeth's heartbeat roared in her ears. This was the moment she'd been waiting for, the moment Reece would come to her, his past behind him.

"Spending the rest of my life with you, Lizzie, that's what would make me happy." He took several giant steps, lifted her off her feet and whirled her around in the air.

She squealed with delight, drowning in the joy of being in Reece's arms. He slid her down his body, depositing her feet on the ground. She lifted her arms around his neck, gazing up at him with all the love in her heart glowing in her blue eyes.

Lowering his head, Reece took her lips in a kiss that took her breath away. She clung to him, responding with equal fervor as he deepened the kiss. He ran his hands over her back, her arms, her waist, her hips. She grasped his shoulder with one hand while she threaded her fingers through his hair at his neckline.

When they had kissed until they were spent, Reece lifted her in his arms and started up the steps, taking two at a time. MacDatho followed them inside the cabin, but stopped outside Elizabeth's bedroom and lay down in the hall.

With Elizabeth still in his arms, Reece eased his knees down onto her bed, the two of them clinging to each other. When she lay beneath him, he started kissing her again as he unbuttoned her blouse. With eager hands they undressed each other. Clothes flew into the air, landing here and there in the room. A shirt on the dresser, a blouse on a rocking chair, slacks on the floor, socks at the foot of the bed, briefs on the nightstand.

"I want you to marry me, Lizzie. I want to spend the rest of my life here in Sequana Falls with you." He kissed the hollow in her throat, his hands inching their way down from her waist to lift her hips. "I'll draw an income from my stocks in Stanton Industries, but I have no desire to be involved in running the company. You can teach me about the nursery business. We'll see if I have a green thumb."

Elizabeth reached up, grasping his shoulders. "You won't be bored living so far away from civilization?"

"I'll never be bored as long as I'm with you, don't you know that?"

"I love you, Reece. I love you so much." She gave herself to him, completely, wholly—her body, her heart and her soul. She was his now and forever.

Reece accepted her offer, thrusting into her with fierce possession, taking her completely, wholly, and giving himself in the same way. At long last he had found a home, a place to truly belong—in the arms of the woman who had been destined to save him from his past and give him a future he'd never dreamed possible.

Their mating was fast and intense, their passion having built to an almost unbearable point by six weeks of abstinence. Their bodies moved in unison, hot and raw and wild, their hands and mouths seeking and finding, giving and taking until fulfillment flung them over the precipice and into total satiation. They clung to each other, their hearts united, their souls forever one.

Elizabeth lay in Reece's arms. He petted her hip. He nuzzled her neck with his nose. She sighed with happiness.

"Elizabeth." Cupping her chin in his hand, he lifted her face. She smiled at him. "I love you. I love everything about you. Your blue eyes, your sweet lips." He kissed her quickly. "I love your body. I love the way it feels when I make love to you. Like nothing I've ever known. And I love your good heart, the way you care about everyone and everything."

A teardrop fell from Elizabeth's eye, ran down her cheek and onto her jaw. One by one other tears followed. "We're going to be so happy."

"Are you looking into our future?" He kissed her on the shoulder.

"No, I... Aunt Margaret did, but she wouldn't tell me what she saw." Elizabeth remembered her aunt telling her to take Reece down to her great-grandmother's cottage today, that she'd planned a surprise for them.

"Well, she'd better have seen a wedding and children and a long, long life for the two of us together." Reece lifted Elizabeth up and over to lie on top of him. He traced a slow, seductive line down her spine.

"Before dark I want to take you to my great-grandmother's honeymoon cottage. I want us to spend our wedding night there."

"We'll go. Before dark." Reece rubbed himself up and down against Elizabeth. "That leaves us all afternoon to make love."

"Let's not waste a minute," Elizabeth said, situating herself to take him into her body.

Elizabeth led Reece through the woods to the small Victorian A-frame cottage standing in the middle of a tiny clearing. A picket fence enclosed the yard where tulips and jonquils bloomed in profusion.

"My great-grandfather built this little cottage as a wedding present for my great-grandmother. They spent their wedding night here and every anniversary for the rest of their lives together."

"I can see why you want us to start our married life here," Reece said, lifting Elizabeth into his arms.

He carried her up the walk, up the steps and onto the porch, MacDatho following. The front door opened to Reece's touch. He carried her inside, then set her on her feet. Mac stretched out across the floor, guarding the door.

Elizabeth glanced around the living room, but saw nothing out of place, nothing unusual. What had Aunt Margaret meant about a surprise for Reece and her?

"What are you looking for?" he asked.

"Aunt Margaret told me to bring you down here today, that she'd prepared a surprise for us." Elizabeth tugged on his hand. "Come on, let's look in the bedrooms."

She led him into the front bedroom, the one that opened out onto the porch. She gasped when she looked at the bed. There lying on the antique, wrought-iron bed was a wedding dress—her great-grandmother's wedding dress, yellowed with age to a golden cream.

Reece watched Elizabeth as she touched the silk folds of the skirt, as she fingered the lace bodice. He came up behind her, wrapping his arms around her.

"I'd say Aunt Margaret sees a wedding in our future," Reece said.

Elizabeth turned in his arms, burying her face against his chest, breathing in the heady aroma of masculinity that surrounded Reece.

She felt a sudden intrusion into her mind. Smiling, she returned a message to her great-aunt, who had wished her happiness, then told her to take Reece into the back bedroom.

"Come on, I think there's more to our surprise." Elizabeth led him to the small bedroom at the back of the cottage. The last time she'd been in the room it had contained a cot, a cane-bottomed chair and a rickety table that sat by the window.

She opened the door, but stopped dead still when she realized what her aunt had done. The room was now a nursery. The baby bed that had belonged to both Aunt Margaret and her grandmother was the focal point of the room. A crocheted baby shawl lay in a cradle beneath the window. A padded rocking chair rested in the corner, and an open steamer trunk filled with antique toys had been placed against the right wall.

"It looks like a nursery." Reece followed Elizabeth into the room. "I'd say your aunt is trying to tell us that we're going to have children one of these days." He whirled Elizabeth around in his arms. "Would you like that, Lizzie? Would you like a houseful of children?"

"Would you, Reece?"

"Nothing would make me happier than for us to have a child. A little girl who looks just like you."

"Would a little boy do the first time? He won't look just like me, but he'll have my blue eyes."

"Are you saying you've looked into the future and seen our first child?"

"I didn't try to look into the future. It just happened."

Reece lifted Elizabeth off her feet. She wrapped her arms around him when he sat in the rocking chair with her in his lap.

"Wouldn't it be wonderful if our son was conceived on our wedding night here in this cottage." Reece slid his hand up and under Elizabeth's skirt to caress her thigh.

"I'm afraid he couldn't wait," Elizabeth said.

"What do you mean, he couldn't wait?"

"I'm already pregnant, Reece. Six weeks pregnant."

"You're what?" He sat up straight in the rocking chair, almost toppling Elizabeth to the floor. He grabbed her just as she began to slide off his lap.

Tightening her hold around his neck, she looked into Reece's amber eyes—warm, glowing eyes, filled with love. "Come November, I'm going to give you a son."

"When did you find out?" Reece laid his hand across her stomach.

"I've known since the night he was conceived, our last night together. I knew before we made love."

"You wanted my child, even though I had nothing to offer you, even though I couldn't make a commitment?" He hugged her close, his lips covering hers in a tender kiss. "How did I get so lucky?" he whispered against her mouth. "Why me, out of all the men in the world?"

"Because we were meant for each other," Elizabeth said. "You came to me in my dreams, a stranger who entered my heart and never left it."

Reece held her in his arms as they sat in her great-grandmother's rocking chair. Late afternoon turned to evening while they sat in the honeymoon cottage and talked about their future. Mac-Datho found his way to the bedroom, curling his big body into a ball of black fur beside the rocking chair, occasionally glancing up at his mistress and the alpha male in her life.

Love knows no boundaries and cannot be confined. It transcends time and space. Love is the greatest power on earth and in heaven. Elizabeth and Reece did not question destiny's hand in their happiness; rather, they accepted fate's assistance as a blessing.

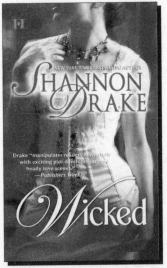

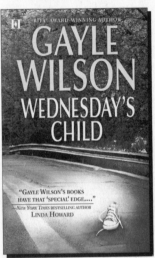

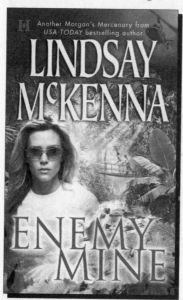